Addict

Other Books by Lexi Blake

Masters and Mercenaries: The Forgotten
Lost Hearts (Memento Mori)
Lost and Found
Lost in You
Long Lost
No Love Lost

Masters and Mercenaries: Reloaded
Submission Impossible
The Dom Identity, Coming September 14, 2021

Butterfly Bayou
Butterfly Bayou
Bayou Baby
Bayou Dreaming
Bayou Beauty, Coming July 27, 2021

Lawless
Ruthless
Satisfaction
Revenge

Courting Justice
Order of Protection
Evidence of Desire

Masters Of Ménage (by Shayla Black and Lexi Blake)
Their Virgin Captive
Their Virgin's Secret
Their Virgin Concubine
Their Virgin Princess
Their Virgin Hostage
Their Virgin Secretary
Their Virgin Mistress

The Perfect Gentlemen (by Shayla Black and Lexi Blake)
Scandal Never Sleeps
Seduction in Session
Big Easy Temptation
Smoke and Sin
At the Pleasure of the President

URBAN FANTASY

Thieves
Steal the Light
Steal the Day
Steal the Moon
Steal the Sun
Steal the Night
Ripper
Addict
Sleeper
Outcast
Stealing Summer
The Rebel Queen

LEXI BLAKE WRITING AS SOPHIE OAK

Texas Sirens
Small Town Siren
Siren in the City
Siren Enslaved
Siren Beloved
Siren in Waiting
Siren in Bloom
Siren Unleashed
Siren Reborn

Nights in Bliss, Colorado
Three to Ride
Two to Love
One to Keep
Lost in Bliss
Found in Bliss
Pure Bliss
Chasing Bliss
Once Upon a Time in Bliss
Back in Bliss
Sirens in Bliss
Happily Ever After in Bliss
Far From Bliss, Coming 2021

A Faery Story
Bound
Beast
Beauty

Standalone
Away From Me
Snowed In

Addict

Hunter: A Thieves Novel, Book 2

Lexi Blake

Addict
Hunter: A Thieves Novel, Book 2
Lexi Blake

Published by DLZ Entertainment LLC
Copyright 2015 DLZ Entertainment LLC
Edited by Chloe Vale
ISBN: 978-1-937608-46-0

This is a work of fiction. Names, places, characters and incidents are the product of the author's imagination and are fictitious. Any resemblance to actual persons, living or dead, events or establishments is solely coincidental.

Sign up for Lexi Blake's newsletter
and be entered to win a $25 gift certificate
to the bookseller of your choice.

Join us for news, fun, and exclusive content.

There's a new contest every month!

Go to www.lexiblake.net to subscribe.

A Note From Lexi

Some of you might notice a big change from the first version of this book. If you're going back and re-rereading Addict, you might wonder why a key character's name has been changed. In the originally published version the tech guru is named Brandon Bellamy and his company is called Bellacorp. Well, that wasn't his real name. His real name was and has always been Dante Dellacourt and his company Dellacorp. If you haven't read my Faery Story trilogy this information means nothing to you and the name change is completely insignificant. If you have read Bound, Beast and Beauty hopefully you just went, oh, yeah, I get it and now know what the human version of Dante did with that tech he stole from Meg in Bound. The name change—as most crappy things in my publishing life—was contractual. The Faery Story books had a different publisher. Now I'm publishing them myself and human Dante can find his place in the Lexiverse.

Chapter One

"You look really good, Kelsey," Zack Owens said with a small smile of satisfaction.

My uncle sat across from me in the limo that drove us toward the downtown Dallas building that housed the Council. It was a massive, modern building and it was going to be my new home.

"Thank you. I think it's the bangs." I sat back in the plush seat. The stylist at the salon in Venice had assured me that the bangs softened my face. I was getting used to seeing the world through a fringe of brown hair. Bangs notwithstanding, I was sure I did look better than the last time Zack had seen me. It wouldn't take much. It had been three months before and I'd been pretty messed up. The last time I'd seen my uncle, I'd been covered in blood, and a whole lot of it had been mine.

It had been the night I'd discovered I wasn't what I thought I'd been. I'd spent the first twenty-six years of my life in the false belief that I was human. That night three months before had taught me I was something different and given me an entirely new family. Some of them, like Zack and little Lee Donovan-Quinn, were awesome, and some, like the King of all Vampire, were a major pain in my ass.

Zack Owens had been on my doorstep a full thirty minutes before I'd been told to expect him. Luckily, I'd gotten up early. I was still on Italian time. It would be days before my body rearranged my internal clock, or so my boyfriend told me. We'd taken an overnight flight from Venice two days before I was supposed to report to the king. I'd taken the time to pack up my small house and get things ready for life in the Council's compound.

"Italy agreed with you." My uncle was an attractive man who looked to be in his mid-twenties. He was dressed casually, but for him that meant a pair of tailored slacks and a cashmere sweater. He was eight years older than me, but he looked my age or younger. Zachary Owens is a werewolf and the servant of the king of the supernatural world. His master is a vampire named Daniel Donovan, and serving him is apparently the family business. I'm the king's death machine.

My proper title is *Nex Apparatus*. It's the title held traditionally by a vampire, but I'm not a vampire. I'm something even rarer. I'm a Hunter, the love child of a lone wolf and a human. I was born with the spirit of a wolf in my body, but without the wolf's aversion to silver, nor am I tied to the cycles of the moon. According to the King of all Vampire, I was born to track and kill demons on the Earth plane. The king wanted to change the title of the office I held to something a bit more innocuous. He, himself, had been the *Nex Apparatus* at one time and I was sure he would prefer to pretend he wasn't forcing another person into the role he'd hated. He wanted me to refer to myself as sheriff.

It had been months since I last saw the king, and I was a bit nervous at the thought of our reunion. We hadn't parted on good terms. I'd shot him the bird and promptly run as fast as I could away from him. Despite the fact that I'd been ordered to wait in my well-appointed jail cell for the king's chosen trainee, I'd run off with Marcus Vorenus. My trainer was in a small feud with Donovan and his partner, Devinshea Quinn. Marcus and I had run all the way to Venice where we'd set up house and he'd begun my formal Hunter training. It might not have been wholly Council approved, but it had proven effective.

"You seem much more confident," Zack commented.

Training will do that for you. So will really amazing sex with a hot Italian. "I suppose I am. I'm much more in control."

Zack leaned forward, and for a second I thought he would reach out and touch me. Werewolves tend to be tactile creatures, especially with their families. I smelled like his long-lost brother. It would most likely be comforting to Zack to be able to touch me. My uncle hesitated and then moved on to more business. "Your rooms are ready. I think you'll like them. We set up everything according to Marcus's specifications, right down to the type of towels you prefer. Marcus seemed very thorough."

I wasn't particular. If a towel was fairly clean, it worked for me, but Marcus believed in having the best of everything. Apparently when you're a billionaire you don't settle for hand-me-down towels.

"Is this really necessary? I have a perfectly good house."

Zack had picked me up at my small suburban house. It wasn't anything special, and my hot Italian boyfriend had commented on the need for additional space and a maid. But it was mine and I was comfortable in it. The thought of being forced to live in the Council's compound made me anxious. It pointed out the fact that I was still basically on probation. A Hunter is considered a dangerous creature in the supernatural world. The training process can take years. I'd finished the initial three-month schooling in mental discipline and I felt perfectly in control in a way I never had before. Long hours of focused concentration and working on emotional honesty and balance had given me self-confidence. Yeah, I hadn't really had that before. I usually sought confidence in the bottom of a tequila bottle.

The werewolf shrugged. "I think you're stuck with us for a while, Kelsey. It won't be so bad. The building is actually really nice. I've lived there for years. Once you've convinced the king you have control, he'll let up." He cocked a curious eyebrow. "We were informed that you weren't coming back alone."

I smiled brilliantly, thinking of my gorgeous hunk of man. "I'm not. If the king is going to force me to live in the building, then he should be prepared to house my boyfriend, too."

Boyfriend wasn't exactly the term Marcus preferred, but I wasn't going to call him master anywhere but in the comfort of our bedroom, or when it was absolutely necessary in terms of vampire tradition.

"What's his name, Kelsey?" Uncle Zack asked with an indulgent smile. "You're having dinner with me and Lisa and Courtney tomorrow night, so I'd like to be able to give my wife a name. She's excited about meeting you finally and meeting your intriguing European boyfriend. I'd also like to be prepared for how horribly my daughter will mangle his name."

My face fell and Zack suddenly frowned my way.

"You don't know?"

It seemed like it should be obvious to everyone that Marcus and I had become lovers. It had been practically inevitable. Our mental connection had led to a close friendship that had finally become a physical desire I couldn't walk away from. In my understanding, it was a typical relationship between trainer and Hunter. It wasn't a grand love. It was more of an infinitely warm and comfortable friendship. I was thrilled daily to wake up next to him and have his strength at my call. I'd gotten so used to being physically near the vampire that it felt odd to kiss his sleeping form good-bye when I'd left with Zack. It felt strange to not have him close, but I was determined to prove how far I'd come not only for myself, but for Marcus as well. It was a testament to my progress that I was able to admit I wanted to make him proud.

Zack shook his head. "No one told me his name, Kelsey. Marcus's assistant mentioned we should be prepared for two people, but she didn't mention your boyfriend's name and you haven't mentioned him either. He must have high standards because the list of necessary household items Marcus faxed over made Dev's eyes widen, and Dev doesn't consider much expensive. He's had workers renovating your apartments for weeks."

Lucia must have thought it was obvious as well, or she likely would have mentioned it to Zack. Marcus's assistant had been in charge of our travel plans. The beautiful twenty-four-year-old Italian had traveled with us. She was coming to America as a mail-order girlfriend. Marcus had promised a vampire named Michael House a girl of his own, and Marcus always kept his promises. The lovely dark-haired woman and I had become friends. She was the first female friend I'd made entirely on my own. I tried not to think of Liv Carey, since I didn't consider her a friend any longer. She'd sold me out to Donovan. I was still finding it difficult to forgive both her and my brother, Nathan. Marcus thought I should, but it was the one thing I was proving to be stubborn about.

"I suppose it will have to be a surprise." I attempted a smile I didn't feel.

If Marcus didn't want them to know he was coming, then I wouldn't tell them. My loyalty was first and foremost to my lover, but I wasn't sure how Marcus intended to keep it a secret. The plan was for both of us to move into the building later in the day. We'd discussed our living arrangements on our plane trip back from Venice. Marcus was supposed to be waiting in our rooms after my training was finished for the day. I was counting on it. I panicked at the thought of Marcus lying to me. He'd only really promised me the three months of training. Maybe this was his way of easing out of the relationship. Maybe he would dump me on the Council and go back to his cushy life in Venice.

"I have all the paperwork finished," Zack told me. "All you have to do is fill in his name. Marcus explained to the king that it would be best if you had a lover. Something about having a physical outlet. I don't understand all this Hunter and trainer stuff, but I did get that Marcus thought you should be…close with someone."

I nodded. It was a slightly embarrassing conversation to have with one's uncle, but werewolf society isn't as inhibited as human society. They're more open about these things. "I've been told I should try to keep a lover with me most of the time. It's easy for me to slip back into emotional distance if I don't have an…anchor, I guess. It's the lone wolf part of me. Apparently the wolf half of me prefers to push away as many people as possible. Being really intimate with someone helps to ignore the impulse."

It was true. I was growing to accept the emotional part of myself. I tried to ignore it but that became impossible when someone else felt my emotions and forced me to acknowledge them. Marcus wouldn't allow me to pretend they didn't exist and he wouldn't let me shove them down.

"Your father fought that instinct, too, Kelsey." Zack's eyes were a warm chocolate brown. My eyes. I'd always hated them because they weren't like my brothers' green eyes. It was good to see the familiar in my uncle's face. And I was glad to hear him talk about my father. "He tried really hard to not be anything like your grandfather. It's good to see you're carrying on the family tradition. I thought I could show you some pictures tomorrow night, maybe some home movies, though I should warn you he mostly growls during those. I know this has been a shock for you, but I would like to be your uncle. I would really like to teach you about your father."

Three months of focused meditation had changed my mind about a lot of things. "I would love to see a picture of him and hear stories. I will admit it's hard to think of you as my uncle. You look younger than me."

"I'm thirty-four." Zack took his master's blood on a weekly basis. The queen, who also took the king's blood, had explained that Daniel Donovan's blood was better than Botox. "Oh, I get carded when I try to buy beer, but I am most definitely thirty-four years old. I suppose if Lee had known about you, we would have been more like brother and sister than uncle and niece. He didn't though, and I feel a definite paternal responsibility toward you. You should have caught me before I had a daughter of my own. I might have been the cool uncle then. Now I'm the uncle who really wants to know who you're sleeping with so I can run a background check on him." I stared at him and Zack's eyes narrowed. "Kelsey, you have to have Council approval for a long-term relationship."

"I thought that was just for humans." I wondered if this was why Marcus had decided to sleep in. He'd said it was because I should meet with the king on my own the first time, but what if he'd wanted to avoid a scene? All my carefully constructed, calm inner walls started to shake a bit. I was good right now. I was stable. If Marcus left me, I had to deal with a whole lot of shit I wasn't ready to deal with at this point.

The brown-haired man who looked so much like a male version of me sighed. "The king thinks you're too valuable to risk. Anyone sleeping with you on a more than casual basis needs to be approved. I've tried very hard to respect your privacy, but I can't now."

A flare of righteous anger flamed inside me. I was still smarting from my last meeting with the king. "You mean Donovan thinks I'm too dangerous to risk hurting someone."

"No, he thinks you're in a delicate state," Zack tried to explain patiently. "You're very important, and he doesn't want the wrong person to influence you. There are a lot of people who would love to see you out of the king's influence. I'm afraid the king doesn't particularly think you have good taste in men."

My heart hitched at the thought of Grayson Sloane. I could still see him in my mind, his big, beautiful body ingrained in my memory. Gray haunted my dreams. The truth was I should be glad I was going to live in the Council's complex. It would give me access to the library. I wanted to read up on contracts. My ex-honey was a "legacy" demon, meaning he'd been born under a contract. Gray's mother had agreed to give birth to him and signed a contract that gave Gray thirty-five years on the Earth plane. When that time was done, he would reside with his father on the Hell plane.

I meant to get his hot ass out of that contract.

"So you can see how anyone with as much influence on you as a boyfriend is going to be carefully vetted for a while," Zack concluded.

My cell phone trilled and I started at the sound. I slid my finger across the screen to answer it without thinking. "Hello?"

"What is wrong, *cara mia*?" Marcus's deep voice was soothing even over the phone. "I was pulled from a nice dream about you. You're agitated. Has the king already made you anxious?"

"No." I hadn't realized our connection worked over such a long distance. I hadn't done anything to shield my emotions. We were twenty miles from each other, but Marcus felt my anxiety. "I haven't even made it to the Council building yet. I was talking to Zack about our living arrangements. It occurred to me there could be trouble."

"Ah." I could see his face. He would be giving me that half smile I found devastatingly sexy. "You're worried about the apartments? *Bella*, if they don't suit you, I will simply have them redecorated. Devinshea is usually thorough. I doubt he refused us our list. I already received confirmation that our clothes and the furnishings from Venice arrived. Everything will be ready for you."

"That wasn't what I was afraid of." It was useless to lie to Marcus and I didn't even want to. "Zack wants me to fill out the paperwork to get our relationship approved by the Council."

There was a long pause. "Is he serious?"

"He seems serious to me." I glanced at my uncle. Yep, there was all kinds of seriousness there.

"But we are both known to the Council. Why should they have any say over our personal relationship?"

"They're worried about outside influences."

Marcus cursed. He did it often, but only in Italian. "I did not foresee this. It never once occurred to me that they would question our relationship. I should have known. None of the Council has ever met a Hunter, much less have a true understanding of how the training works. I'll get dressed and I'll join you as soon as I can. I'll call the king and demand a meeting."

"Hey. It's fine, baby." It was nice to be the calm one for once. Marcus sounded almost desperate. I was the one now getting the fine edge of his anxiety. Maybe it was reasonable that they didn't know. Marcus had explained everything to me, that our closeness was almost inevitable. I suppose Donovan and the rest of the crew might think Marcus and I were an odd couple. "I wasn't worried about them keeping us apart. I've been with you for months. I don't think you could influence me more if you tried. I was worried…"

"You were worried I was leaving?" Marcus sounded a bit incredulous. "That's ridiculous, *cara mia*. I have no desire to leave you. As I said before, only this morning I was dreaming of you. I adore you, *bella. Ti penso sempre.*"

I am always thinking of you. I'd learned some Italian. It mostly concerned dirty words and love phrases. I could also order a gelato.

"I'm crazy about you, too," I said with a smile in my voice, thinking about how he'd adored me last night. There was a reason he was still in bed. "Don't worry. I'll take care of it. I'll fill out their dumb paperwork. It's a stupid formality. I'll see you tonight."

"All right, if you're sure." I heard the yawn he tried to politely suppress. I could see him stretching his magnificently masculine body. The sheets would tangle around him and show off his lean strength. "I have many things to do before I head out to Dallas. *Cara*, if you do not mind…"

I laughed into the phone. This had become a daily ritual for us in Italy. I shouldn't have been surprised he would ask here. The man liked the flavor of coffee. "I'll see what I can do, but it won't be the same. You'll have to get used to the American version."

I disconnected the call, and Zack was looking at me, pen in hand.

"So Marcus Vorenus then," my uncle said as he filled in the name. "I've always liked Marcus, myself, but Dev is going to be upset. He thought he'd gotten rid of him. Maybe I'll just shuffle this paperwork through. Dev can find out all on his own."

That faery was going to have to get with the program or he would be dealing with me. Donovan's partner had issues with my lover, and I wasn't sure exactly what the problem was. Initially I'd thought it was because Marcus had an affair with the wife Dev Quinn shared with the king, but I'd come to believe Marcus had never actually touched Zoey Donovan-Quinn. Whatever his problem was, I wouldn't let it affect the only healthy relationship I'd ever had with a man. "He'll get used to it. We need to find a Starbucks. Marcus is a grump until he's had an espresso."

Zack's eyebrows arched curiously, but he gave the driver the instruction anyway. I knew he was waiting for an explanation, but none was forthcoming. I liked to maintain a little mystery.

Zack set aside the paperwork and leaned back in his seat, casually crossing his legs. "You have a long list of people requesting meetings. I have your training schedule, and we need to decide who's getting your consult time. Dev was serious about you being the Council's in-house investigator. You have potential clients piling up."

I sat up straighter. I was anxious to get back to work. I'd been worried that the king would force me to "train" ten hours a day and leave me with no way to make a living. I was the mistress of a billionaire, but I wanted to earn my way. I wasn't stupid. My relationship with Marcus wouldn't last forever. I needed something to fall back on. Besides I liked my work. "Anything interesting?"

"I think you'll be very interested in some of them." He pulled out a sheet of paper and passed it to me.

I studied my schedule, which seemed super extensive. Pretty much every minute of my day for the next three weeks was scheduled. There were no blank spaces on that piece of paper. "Tell me he's kidding."

"Dev never kids about a schedule."

"When am I supposed to work on a case?" That damn faery had me training on every weapon known to man. I was attending some form of therapy. He'd enrolled me in a class titled "Magical Creatures and How to Destroy Them." I had a personal trainer and daily hour and a half sessions with her. I looked up to my uncle with a bit of panic in my eyes. "When do I take a nap?"

He nodded sagely. Werewolves understood the need to work in a good nap. "I'll look into it. As for your caseload, you have an assistant and an hour blocked off from six to seven. We'll move it when daylight savings kicks in. You have to keep your office hours at night. Most of the supernatural world is nocturnal."

"I'll get so much done that way," I groused. An hour wasn't enough. Did Dev think I could simply listen to a problem and solve it? I wasn't psychic. Detecting took time.

The limo pulled into the parking lot of Starbucks. It wouldn't fit into the curved drive-through. That was fine with me. I hopped out of the car as Zack's cell rang.

"It's my master," he said, touching the *accept call* button. "Hey, get me a latte, will you? And maybe some of those cookies that look like tiny sliced breads? And see if they have scones. Hello, master…"

I shook my head and wondered if Starbucks was really prepared for a couple of wolves. I doubted it. A red Porsche pulled into the slot next to the front door as I breezed through, letting the smell of coffee wash over my newly opened senses. I held the door open for the man who had gotten out of the Porsche. He was tall and lanky with dark eyes.

"Thank you, love." And he had an upper-crust British accent. I was surrounded by Euros even back in the States.

I ordered two espressos since it seemed I'd need an enormous amount of energy to get through the day Quinn had planned for me. Along with Zack's venti latte, I bought up most of the baked goods and a chicken salad sandwich. My tummy was grumbling. The breakfast Lucia had fixed was gone now, and it seemed like it would be a while before Quinn scheduled in some food. We were going to have to talk about my snack schedule.

The wide-eyed barista promised to pack everything up, and I headed to the bathroom while my order was being prepared. I took care of business and then washed my hands, catching a glimpse of myself.

I stared at the girl in the mirror. She seemed slightly foreign to me. I sometimes didn't recognize the vibrant face that stared back at me. This girl looked well taken care of. She smiled readily and laughed often. She was a woman who joked with her lover and didn't hesitate to jump him when she felt the need. My dark-brown hair was thick and for the first time in my life cut into something fashionable. I had playfully pushed Lucia out of the way to apply my mascara this morning. She'd shoved right back because Marcus was right about the single, tiny bathroom in my house. I'd begun to actually give a crap about properly applied makeup. I still didn't wear much, just mascara and some lip-gloss, but it made a difference.

Things were going to change now that I was back in the States. I didn't get to simply be Marcus's protégée. For months he'd coddled and protected me even while we trained. For months I hadn't worried about anything but when dinner was or how my meditation sessions were going. I'd let the world slide away, and here I was back in it.

Sighing, I realized I was going to have to change again. I had to find a way to balance this happy, carefree woman with the *Nex Apparatus* I was going to become.

I had to find a way to live with the fact that I hadn't talked to my mother or Nate or Liv in months.

Or Gray Sloane. Yeah, I really tried not to think about him.

Pocketing my gloss, I headed back out to pick up my enormous bag of food and caffeine. I nearly ran into the dark-haired Brit.

"Excuse me," I said with a smile.

"Not a problem, love." He stepped back, gallantly giving me space. "I think you shocked the staff with your order. They're busy trying to replace the biscotti."

"Probably should have called ahead, but you never know when the urge for biscotti and scones is going to hit, do you?" I asked, flirting a little.

He was an attractive man with well-formed lips, and he obviously had a flair for fashion. Unfortunately, he was also setting off my gaydar. It was perfectly fine to flirt with a boy who liked boys.

"I'm happy to find a place that properly brews tea. If I don't order iced tea, I get a sad bag shoved in lukewarm water." He shuddered at the thought.

"We're not big on hot tea here," I admitted. "And that's a shame. I developed a taste for Earl Grey while I was in Italy."

The man smiled, but suddenly it didn't seem so friendly. "Yes, but then I'm sure Marcus Vorenus would only spring for the best for his mistress. Tell me something, Ms. Atwood. Does the king know you're fucking his former patron?"

In the dim light of the hall, his eyes seemed the slightest bit red. I was really going to have to work on the whole integration thing. At least depressed Kelsey wouldn't have spent time flirting with a freaking demon.

"It's Owens. My name is Kelsey Owens." If he thought I would run screaming from the coffee house, he was in for a surprise. I really wanted that chicken salad sandwich.

His lips quirked up in a semblance of a grin. "Ah, you've embraced your long-lost papa. That is sweet. He's practically a saint to the royal family, you know. Does it bother you that he thought of the queen as his daughter when his actual daughter was treated so poorly? The queen gets everything, doesn't she? She had your father's love. If she'd wanted it, she certainly could have had your lover. If the queen crooked her finger, he'd be in her bed in a heartbeat. He'd forget you the minute she glanced his way. Do you really think he'd be with you if he wasn't obliged to train you? Your own brother thought you should be in a cage. Marcus Vorenus is only doing his job, which is to keep you firmly in control. The minute the king is satisfied he has you in his grips, Marcus will fly right out of your life. No man stays with you."

It was like he stared into my soul and pulled out my deepest fears. He'd summed them up neatly—I was unlovable, unworthy. I was jealous of Zoey Donovan-Quinn. Marcus leaving scared me more than I wanted to admit. I took a deep breath and tried to let those feelings go. They weren't worthy of spending time and energy on. Another thing Marcus had taught me. "What do you want, demon?"

The demon crossed his arms over his well-made chest and glared down on me. "I want a woman with some constancy. Is that too much to ask? This is why I have no interest in the fairer sex. A good man falls madly in love with a woman. He offers her everything he has. He proposes marriage, a family. What does she do? Oh, she runs off with the first Italian billionaire to come along."

"You're Gray's brother," I said as the pieces fell into place. It made perfect sense. Gray mentioned his older brother was an empath, and no one unattached to Gray would care that I'd left him.

The demon's eyes flared briefly. "I'm rather surprised he mentioned me. He doesn't like to admit he has a family...until we're useful, of course. It doesn't matter. He is the only brother I have and I care for him."

My expression must have registered my extreme doubt.

"I'm perfectly capable of loving people," the demon said. "Demons are fully functional when it comes to emotions. Believe me, love is absolutely the most destructive force in the world for some people. All of the truly horrible acts I've committed I did because I loved someone."

"Did Gray send you?" I have to admit, there was a place deep in my heart that I'd locked away, and it flared to life at the thought of Gray reaching out to me.

"Not at all." The demon flicked lint off his tailored coat. "He would be perfectly upset with me if he knew I was anywhere close to his one true love. Unfortunately, his one true love turned out to be a whore."

I rolled my eyes. I wasn't going to be offended because a demon called me names. It was in their job description. "Are you going to continue to insult me or get to the point?"

Was my espresso ready? I was starting to lag.

"You're a tough one, aren't you," the demon purred, his lips curling upward. "You're going to be fun. I like a challenge." He pressed a piece of paper in my hand. "Here's the address for a rather exclusive club downtown. I've made sure your name is on the list. Be there at two a.m. My brother needs you."

The demon started to walk past me. I put out a hand to stop him.

"What's wrong with Gray?" Even I could hear the tension in my voice. I was sure the demon could feel it.

He knew he had me. It was right there in the way his lips curled up in victory. "If you want to find out, come to the club. I'll be waiting for you. And don't you dare bring that vampire with you."

The demon walked out the doors as the barista walked up with my food. I stood there holding it as the Porsche sped off. The door opened and my uncle walked in.

"Kelsey? What's up?" He snagged the bag I was carrying. "Nice, I could use a sandwich."

I gulped the espresso as I followed my uncle back to the limo. I watched as he wolfed down my sandwich. It didn't matter. I'd lost my appetite.

Chapter Two

My appetite had come back with a righteous vengeance two hours later as I sat in the elegantly appointed private dining room in Ether. I'd only been to Dev Quinn's notorious nightclub once before, but if he had his way I would be a permanent fixture. He probably saw me more as a member of the security team than a guest. I looked across the table and thought that Devinshea Quinn probably saw almost everyone as a potential employee.

"I hope your flight was good." The prince was all smiles and cordiality. He was third in line for the Seelie *sidhe* throne, but the Fae were much more interested in the man for his status as a fertility god. "I certainly wish Marcus had allowed me to send my private jet for you. It would have been infinitely more comfortable for you and your boyfriend."

"Marcus is an environmentalist, I'm afraid," I murmured as a perfectly cooked steak was placed in front of me. It was a lovely bacon-wrapped filet the size of my fist, and there were two of them. I wondered if there were a couple more somewhere.

"Marcus is stubborn. I'm sure turning down my generous offer was his last insult. From now on when you fly you can use the jet. You're Lee's daughter and Zack's niece. Like it or not, you're a member of our family, and I want you to feel like one. Anything you need, you only have to ask for it." Quinn was apparently playing good cop today. He was all charm, and when he wanted to pour it on he really could. When he focused on you, you felt like the only person in the world.

The steak melted in my mouth. Quinn was wrong about Marcus. He really was an environmentalist. He belonged to all sorts of green political groups and he always flew commercial. First class, of course, but commercial. He'd told me vampires should be concerned about the environment. They would have to live here for a really long time, but it didn't surprise me that Quinn thought it was an insult.

My boyfriend and my boss did not get along.

"Did Zack get the paperwork done on your friend?" Quinn asked as though it was an everyday, ordinary occurrence for one to have to get Council approval on whom one slept with.

"I filled everything out. You have your paperwork, Mr. Quinn."

He enjoyed his steak and the Chianti that paired with it. "I'm looking forward to getting to know this man. He must be special. Where did you meet?"

"A nightclub." It had been Ether. Quinn had introduced us himself. I had been a large part of his "push Marcus out of town" plan. I was kind of looking forward to the moment when he realized it hadn't worked. "He loves dancing." Marcus did, though not hip-hop or anything modern. He'd been teaching me to tango, but it always got me so hot we ended up going at it on the floor. I thought of something else. "He's also an excellent cook."

For a man who hadn't physically eaten food in millennia, he watched a lot of Food Network. When it became apparent our bonding was completely successful, he'd been thrilled. Marcus is a particular class of vampire called academics. They aren't the physically strongest of vampires, but their mental powers are unmatched. They can bond with certain females on such a profound level that they can taste the food she eats. He'd promptly banned protein bars.

Quinn sat back, taking a drink from his wine glass. His lips turned up in an arrogant grin. "I'm happy you found someone. I'm surprised Marcus allowed you to date, but I'm happy if you're happy. You're practically glowing, so he's doing something right. I think I was the one who told you this man was out there."

I felt my lips curl up. "If I remember correctly, you told me Marcus Vorenus would be a good lover."

Quinn's eyes changed suddenly, flooding with that emerald green that signaled the emergence of the ancient fertility god who shared the faery's body. I'd been told the god's name was Bris and he had a completely different personality from his host.

"I was the one who told you that, and it's still true," the fertility god said, looking me over carefully. "The vampire is a good match for you. I'm rather surprised the two of you managed to stay away from each other. The pull between a trainer and a Hunter is very strong. An academic is as likely to get obsessed with a Hunter as he is with a companion."

"He said it was up to me." Marcus had waited for me to make the first move.

The god receded, and Quinn made the transition almost imperceptible. "Well, it's for the best, I suppose. Know that your boyfriend is welcome. Anything he needs, let me know. I can find him a job if he wants one."

"As long as he passes your vetting process," I said with no small amount of bitterness.

The unbelievably gorgeous faery stared at me across the table with a concerned look on his face. "You don't like me much, do you?"

"You haven't given me a reason to like you, Mr. Quinn." I finished the first steak and went to work on the second. "Let's see, you've manipulated me. You've used me to further your own plots. You put me in a cage."

"That was Daniel's idea," Quinn interrupted. "I'm not afraid of you."

"Well, I'm not exactly afraid of her, Dev." A deep Texas drawl filled the room and I looked up to see the King of all Vampire striding across the dining room. Big and broad, with an impossibly muscular frame, sandy-blond hair, and all-American good looks, Daniel Donovan oozed authority. It was just my luck that the king was a daywalker. I'd been hoping to avoid him until later, much later. "I think I can handle her, but she could hurt you. She could hurt Z and she could hurt our children if she wanted to."

I flushed and set my fork down. The bad cop had definitely shown up. Donovan strode across the room in his jeans and black T-shirt. He was casual, but there was no denying his magnetism. The faery was gorgeous, but Donovan screamed power. His demeanor answered one of my questions. The king still considered me some form of dangerous animal.

"I couldn't hurt them if I was in Italy," I said flatly. "Perhaps you should have left me there, Your Highness. I can get back on a plane this afternoon if you like."

The king leaned against the edge of the table and glared down at me. Arms crossed over his powerful chest, I could tell he was still pissed off. "Do you have any idea the chaos that stunt of yours caused? Your uncle has been my faithful servant for over ten damn years. You walk in and now I have to question his loyalties. Did you really think I would let you get away with it?"

"Daniel, what are you doing?" Quinn stood up as four big, burly werewolves walked in. I recognized one of them as Trent, the queen's guard. He was carrying handcuffs and leg shackles. He approached me, a grim look on his face.

"You going to fight me, sweetheart?" Trent popped the cuffs open.

I put out my hands. "Nope."

His hands covered mine and he was far gentler with those cuffs than I would have expected.

It didn't matter that Trent was a thoughtful jailor. I felt the need to fight. The need to run as fast and far as I could flared inside me. Rage began to build. It started in my gut and threatened to spark like a wildfire. The wolf inside me started beating on her cage. She wanted out. She wanted to fight.

This had been Donovan's plan all along. I wondered why he hadn't come to Venice and arrested me there. Anywhere I ran he would find me. I had two choices. I could let my beast out and they would kill me, but not before I'd killed a bunch of them, or I could stay calm and let them take me to my cell. The cell at least offered tomorrow. I fiercely brought down my mental walls. The last thing I needed was to scare the hell out of Marcus. He would know what had happened to me soon enough.

"Did you hear me?" the king was asking.

"Yes," I replied, the world already receding at the periphery of my vision. In this place, I could think calmly. This was a place unavailable to the wolf. We shared a soul, but I was in charge, and I pushed her out of my calm oasis.

Trent was securing the shackles and he did the oddest thing. He leaned over and I heard him whispering in my ear. "You can do this, Kelsey. You can beat this."

I wasn't sure what he meant. I couldn't beat anything. I wasn't allowed to fight at all.

"I'm putting you in a cell," the king enunciated. "I'm going to chain you up and leave you there because you can't be trusted. You're an animal and you proved it by running away. Hell, you proved it in that arena."

"All right." I heard myself respond and I felt the chains snapping on, but my mind was already elsewhere. It was all a part of Marcus's training. He'd taught me I was stronger than my instincts and that sometimes the true fight wasn't about violence. I let myself relax and focus on something good. I could tune out negative forces in this moment by focusing on something positive from my past. I wasn't an animal no matter what Daniel Donovan claimed, and he couldn't turn me into one.

Vaguely, I heard Donovan continue to rage at me as I was hauled up, but I could feel the cool of the Italian night on my skin. It was six weeks earlier and I was back in Venice. It was the night I decided to become Marcus's lover.

* * * *

They fought over who got night number four in the rotation. I always knew which night it was because the girls fought over who got to feed the master. At first I thought it was funny that a group of grown women were fighting over who got bitten that night. Lately, it was irritating. Night four, it seemed, was about how long Marcus could hold out before he gave in to the urge and had sex with whoever happened to be his meal for the night.

Vampires like sex with their blood, but Marcus preferred having a mistress to random partners. Marcus was considered picky by the standards of the supernatural world. He was a vampire with enormous amounts of money and influence, yet he'd purchased only three companions over his nearly two thousand years. A companion is a special female with blood that makes a vampire stronger and faster than a vampire with no companion. Companions are rare and vampires have been known to fight wars over them. Helen of Troy had nothing on a truly bright companion. The fact that Marcus had the money to purchase one but chose not to said a lot about his standards.

I'm not a companion. I'm rare, but not in a glowy, feminine way. I'm a strange combination of wolf and human. My DNA gives me good instincts, makes me faster and stronger than a human. It also makes it necessary to shave my legs twice a day. Laser hair removal was definitely in my future. Why did I think Marcus wanted anything more from me than to train me and send me on my way? The only other man who'd really wanted me had needed the marriage to placate his father's interests. Gray claimed to love me, but his father had been interested in producing a child with someone from my gene pool.

I belted the robe around my body as I thought through the situation. I was looking for a way out. I was being cowardly, and cowards never got what they wanted. Besides, if I thought about it rationally, I could see Marcus's not so subtle attempts at seduction. He'd made no secret of his wish to take our relationship past friendship, and while he'd been perfectly gentleman-like, there were certain signs of his growing impatience.

I'd asked for books and Marcus had brought me a bag of them. He'd told me he'd bought all the English language books he could find in Venice. Apparently, all Americans read in Venice is erotica. It was all over the house. I would sit down for a minute and find a book marked with a passage Marcus thought I would find particularly stimulating. When I'd very nicely demanded a thriller with a mystery that didn't concern where to shove a butt plug, I was given a copy of a Steve Berry novel complete with chapters I was sure he hadn't written himself. The man wrote thrillers, but there was a scene with some of the dirtiest sex I'd ever read between two people trying to chase down an ancient society bent on destroying the world.

I had to admit, it made the book even better.

Pulling my courage around me, I walked down the corridor and straight to Marcus's door, where the women argued in Italian.

Lucia looked up and a slow smile spread across her face. "Can I send them away, Kelsey? Please, tell me I can send them away."

"We won't need them anymore." The words were confident, but

inside I was a whirl of nerves. I slept beside Marcus every night. At bedtime, I would start out at the edge of the mattress and by the time morning came, I would cuddle against him until his skin was my blanket and his arms wound around me. I would wake up and feel how much he wanted me, but I hadn't been ready. Tonight, I was ready. I couldn't stand the thought of these women fighting over what should be mine.

Lucia sent the women away in a flurry of Italian. There was moaning and complaining and tears from one, but finally the hall was quiet and Lucia gave me a reassuring hug.

"He's going to be so happy, Kelsey," she promised. "I believe he thought you would go back to the Council without him."

Without Marcus? My whole world seemed to be Marcus. I could barely imagine going back to Dallas, much less returning without him. "Do you really think he wants me?"

I knew he liked me, but I'm not a great beauty like Zoey Donovan-Quinn. I'm…just me. My body's fine, but I don't have large breasts. I'm more athletic than centerfold worthy.

"Stop panicking," Lucia said affectionately. She smoothed back my hair. "He wants you so bad he can't stand it. I knew you were ready when you let me take you to the spa today. Why do you think I had them wax you, silly?"

I grinned. I'd known why she did that. Marcus might be Italian, but he preferred certain body parts a little more Brazilian. "I thought you were torturing me."

I gave Lucia one last smile and walked through the door. We had connecting rooms. Marcus had owned this house in Venice since the 16th century, but like Marcus himself, the place looked damn good for its age. Everywhere I glanced I saw wealth and opulence, but there was nothing more beautiful than the man in front of me.

Marcus stood looking down at the fire. He was partially dressed for our evening out. He had on slacks and a dress shirt, but not his ever-present tie and suit coat yet. He seemed so lonely I wanted to rush to him and throw my arms around his lean body. He was often like this. It must be hard to be the oldest person in the world, to have no one who shared his stories, his experiences. All of his friends were gone. Though he helped the king overthrow the corrupt Council, I knew he missed them. They'd been his comrades for millennia.

He turned toward me and his face softened. "You're not dressed. I thought we were going out tonight. Go and get ready. I will join you as soon as I've dined. I know a restaurant in Cannaregio. It has the best wine selection. At least it did back in the thirties. I thought we would see if it's still good. I should be no more than ten minutes and then I'm all yours, *cara mia*."

"But Marcus, it's night number four," I pointed out quietly.

He shook his head and I saw his weariness. "I've decided to push my limits. I will not need extra time. I'll feed and we can go."

My heart ached because I could feel his loneliness. It was a part of our connection. I could sometimes feel what he was feeling like it was my own emotion. It had to be extremely strong to transfer to me. Marcus wanted a lover, not some random female body in his bed. He longed for it. He longed for me.

This was why I couldn't deny him a moment longer. I could feel his need.

"That's a shame, Marcus." I unbelted the robe and let it fall to my feet. I wasn't wearing anything under it but my own clean skin. It made me vulnerable, but I was betting everything on the fact that he wanted me. "I was hoping to catch you with your defenses down."

The vampire's fangs lengthened and, if I wasn't mistaken, that wasn't the only part of him that got bigger as he stared at me. "*Mia amore, sei un tesoro.*"

"That's good, right?" I wished he would touch me. Everything would be all right if he would touch me.

"You're sure?" His eyes never left my body. He gazed on it, looking up and down as though memorizing the hills and planes. It made me feel beautiful. He pushed his desire my way, a warm wave that rolled over my skin. I realized how much restraint Marcus had shown. If he'd let this loose on me before, I would have given in easily. He'd waited until I was ready, and now feeling his desire was a gift. I'd spent my whole life feeling solitary even when surrounded by people. I couldn't do that with Marcus.

"I want you, Marcus. I want to be your lover."

He moved faster than my eyes could track. One moment he was standing by the fire and the next he was in my space, his nose running along the line of my neck. His hands barely touched my shoulders. "I want a mistress, Kelsey. It means more than lover. I am not a modern man, *bella*. I don't understand modern relationships. I want you for my mistress. I want to take care of you, to be responsible for you."

I didn't see how he could possibly be more responsible for me than he already was. I lived in his home, slept in his bed, depended on him for my very sanity. His hands tightened on my shoulders, strengthening our connection. It hummed along my skin and reminded me of everything I stood to gain if I gave myself to this man.

"I am not calling you master in public," I vowed as my hands found his lean waist. Master was the traditional term for a vampire lover.

"But in private?"

A naughty smile swept over my face. "I'll probably do whatever you like, my master."

He took a small step back and held his arms slightly away from his side. "Then undress me, my mistress. I want to feel your hands on me. I've wanted it from the moment I saw you."

I stepped toward him and pressed my body against his, loving the places where his skin kissed mine. He went still, allowing me to explore. Now that we were here together, he seemed infinitely patient. Stretching up, I kissed the strong line of his jaw as my fingers worked the buttons on his dress shirt. My hands lovingly smoothed the shirt off him. Marcus's chest was a thing of pure perfection. I let my palms run across smooth muscles. His skin was slightly cooler than a human's. "Did you look like this when you were human?"

I was fascinated by the stories he could tell. Some nights I listened to him talk for hours.

His lips curled up in a supersexy grin that let me know he liked how I was looking at him. "Not quite. When a vampire turns, he becomes an almost perfect version of himself. Nutrition wasn't the same in those days, especially for my people."

Marcus had been among the first Christians, and he'd also been among the first martyrs. He'd been thrown to the lions back in the day. By back in the day he means the early first century A.D., and he'd actually taken out the lions and promptly been thrown into the ring with slightly more intelligent competition. His body showed no signs of his gladiatorial past, though I know it's all in there. My honey knew how to fight, but I wanted the lover.

I worked off his slacks, pushing them past muscular hips. I quickly discovered that Marcus wasn't a great believer in underwear. His big cock pulsed against my fingers as they brushed it.

When he was gloriously naked, his hands pulled me roughly to him. He pressed our bodies together, pushing his pelvis against mine. My nipples were hard pebbles against the strength of his chest.

"You belong to me," he said as his fangs lengthened further and I was drawn into his magic.

I sighed as it ran along my every nerve and my pussy started to throb. I could feel myself getting wet and soft as he pulled me in. His fingers tangled in my hair, and he pulled my neck to the side.

When his fangs pierced, I came like I never had before.

* * * *

"What the hell is wrong with her, Hugo?"

Somewhere in the distance, I could hear the king speaking.

An unfamiliar voice with a crisp British accent responded. "There's nothing at all wrong with her. She's doing what she was trained to do. It's called focused meditation. You pushed her into a place where her two options were to allow her rage and fear to take over or go to a place where you can no longer touch her. She's one of Marcus's girls, isn't she? He always did a damn fine job with Hunters."

"Can she hear me?" the king asked. "Can you bring her out of it?"

"Marcus could," Hugo allowed, and I heard Donovan sigh. "She'll come out when she decides it's safe. Is this why you called me here, Your Highness? You want me to work with Ms. Owens? Why isn't Marcus continuing to work with her? I find it hard to believe he doesn't want to do it. It's been a long time since we had a Hunter to train. Academics tend to fight over them. Marcus always had a thing for these girls. He was damn good at training them and he genuinely cared about them."

I blinked a couple of times and took a deep breath as I let go of the vision.

"She's out," the man named Hugo said. He was a thickly muscled man with a broad smile. "Hello, Ms. Owens. It's a pleasure to make your acquaintance. I'm Hugo Wells. Your trainer is a good friend of mine."

My hands were shaking. I'd meditated before, but never under duress. It seemed I had some adrenaline pumping through my system.

Hugo Wells drew my hands into his large ones, rubbing them briskly. I felt his warmth. It was a little like when Marcus touched me, but not anywhere near as strong.

"You're an academic."

"I am," he replied surely. He was an attractive man who appeared to be roughly forty years old, but he was a vampire so he could be a thousand for all I knew. He had blue eyes and salt and pepper hair. "You'll stop shaking in a moment or two. It's an aftereffect of the intense meditation." His kind face smiled on me, and I could feel a wave of satisfaction being pushed my way. I might shield against that from another vampire, but I'd come to trust academics. Hugo was trying to give me what I needed. "You did a damn fine job, Ms. Owens. You were able to go passive when you needed to. Marcus would be proud of you. You scared His Highness, though. He sent the prince to fetch me. Lucky for him, we academics are daywalkers or he'd be sitting here with no knowledge of what was happening."

"Why would the king care?" I asked, still a bit unsettled.

It had been so real. I could still feel the warmth from the fire. Marcus had laid me down on the carpet in front of the hearth and made love to me over and over again that night. He'd been insatiable and I'd basked in his affection. I'd had sex before, and with one man I'd felt that elusive closeness and intimacy everyone looks for, but I could feel how Marcus wanted me, how he needed to touch me. It's unlike anything else. I didn't have to hope or have faith. I knew in that moment I was beautiful.

I wouldn't feel his hands on me again, I realized, and I felt tears well. I would miss him so much in this cell.

"Don't cry, sweetheart," Hugo Wells said, and I felt a calming wave rush over my senses. "It's going to be all right. Like I said, you did well."

The king knelt beside the chair I sat in. "I'm sorry, Kelsey. I had to make sure you had control of yourself. I couldn't have you walking around here like a ticking time bomb. You did well. Marcus did everything he promised."

I looked down and the cuffs had been taken off. I was still sitting in the chair I'd occupied before the king interrupted my lunch. I looked around and everything was the same. I had no idea how much time had passed, but I was still in the same room. I'd expected a cell of some kind. "This was some sort of test?"

Trent was at my side with a tissue. He tried to hand one to me, but I wasn't taking anything from the asswipes who had put me in cuffs. He managed to look a little hurt, but I really wasn't concerned with his feelings.

"Well, I'm as surprised as you, Kelsey." Quinn stood beside his partner, his dark head shaking. "Daniel didn't bother to mention it to me. I would have told Albert to hold off on the soufflé. It's very delicate and the timing on serving it has to be precise. It's likely ruined now."

Donovan rolled his blue eyes, and I might have laughed because sometimes Quinn sounded like a nagging wife. I might have laughed, but I could still see Trent standing in the background. He had a gun visible on his belt. I had no doubt whom he would use it on.

"I planned a perfect meal to get back in her good graces," Quinn complained. "Do you have any idea how long my goddess will rage at me if I don't get this girl to like me, Daniel?" Quinn's green eyes turned to me. "I've basically been on parole since you left. Zoey was extremely angry. She actually blamed me and Daniel for you fleeing the country."

I had to admit, as jealous as I could be of the queen, she was awfully likable sometimes.

"She cut me off for two weeks." Quinn sounded like a boy who'd had all his toys taken away.

"I got cut off for a month, Dev," Donovan shot back, looking irritated at how the conversation was going. It was obvious to me he wanted his partner to shut up.

Quinn didn't get the message. "Well, you're too stubborn, Dan. You have to grovel when she gets in that state. I've found that getting me on my knees puts me in the perfect position to…"

"Dev," the king barked through clenched teeth. "Guest."

The faery shrugged. "She's practically a wolf. You know they aren't prudes."

I wasn't. It didn't bother me at all that Quinn wanted to talk about screwing his wife. If he was a friend, I'd have a long conversation with him about how good Marcus was at oral sex, but he wasn't and he wouldn't care. I didn't really have anyone to talk to or giggle about my suddenly awesome sex life with. A vision of Liv Carey swept across my mind, but I shoved it ruthlessly down. I wasn't ready to deal with her or Nate or my mom. I'd talked to Jamie, my oldest brother, on the phone several times. That was about as close as I wanted to get to my family.

"She was raised human. Treat her like it." Donovan turned from his partner, focusing on me, and there was an apology on his face. "Would you like to finish your lunch with Dev?"

I saw an opportunity in that face. I sighed and let myself look down, like I'd been properly chastised. What I wanted to do was beat the shit out of both of them. I would settle for getting the hell away. "I'm not hungry anymore. What's the next thing on my schedule, Your Highness?"

Quinn's face fell. I suspected his wife had told him to make friends or else. "But I had a lovely meal planned and then I was going to show you your rooms. The apartments are beautiful. I connected two units and completely renovated the bathroom per your trainer's instructions. I understand you need a peaceful setting."

"I'd rather see my office, Mr. Quinn," I replied. "I'm jet-lagged and I just want to get through the day. I want to be able to go to my cell and be with my boyfriend."

"It's not a cell, Kelsey," Donovan insisted. "There are no bars on the doors."

"I can come and go as I please?" I found that hard to believe.

Donovan's face fell. "No. You can move around the complex all you like, but I need to know when you leave and where you're going."

"Then call it what it is, Your Highness. A cell," I said, knowing it would make him feel guilty and therefore more amenable to what I was about to suggest. "I would like to see my office and meet my assistant. If Mr. Wells wouldn't mind?"

The Brit smiled. He was a dapper gentleman and he held out his arm. "I would be delighted, dear. I suspect I'll be seeing much more of you. The king requested I spend some time here. Am I taking over her training?"

Donovan nodded shortly, his brows knitting together in a defeated expression. I was frustrating to him. I got the feeling the king preferred to be the good guy, and I constantly put him in a position to play the opposite role. "Yes, she needs an academic. I would love a shot at training her myself, but I doubt she would allow me to do it. You've trained Hunters before and you don't have a companion."

I put my arm through his and he placed his hand over mine. He sighed and I knew he felt the sensation, too. Marcus had explained it as something like being on the same frequency. An academic's brain worked differently than the other classes, and for some reason it harmonized with mine.

"I do have a mistress," Wells reminded the king.

Donovan shook his head, his jaw tightening. "Then don't sleep with her, Hugo. She has a boyfriend. Marcus managed to keep his hands off her. I don't understand this whole connection thing."

"Because you're not an academic, Your Highness," the British vampire replied.

The fertility god was back. "Daniel, it's a little like a drug, the connection between trainer and Hunter. I don't understand how it came about, but it serves an important purpose. Academics form close bonds with the females they take to their beds. Kelsey would be able to feel the emotion from her academic lover. It teaches the Hunter that she's desirable and lovable. It trains her to be able to accept love and affection from others. It's extremely important. She's dangerous if she doesn't have close connections to others. It's why I advised you to allow the Italian to train her. He wanted her the moment he saw her."

Daniel smiled sadly. "I think there have to be reasons Marcus chose to leave her alone. Your host has done an awful lot to push Marcus as far from our circle as he can."

"He will have to accept it one day, but for now, perhaps it is best Marcus doesn't watch Evangeline grow up. It could be…disconcerting later."

"Yeah, I know," Donovan said. "I'll miss the hell out of him though."

The faery wrested control of his body back from the fertility god with a deep frown, as though he hadn't appreciated the conversation. "We don't have to worry about it. Now Kelsey, feel free to look around. Hugo, her office is on the fifth floor. Justin Parker is going to be assisting her, but he won't be up until nightfall, which is almost thirty minutes away. I'll let Angelina know to send him up to the office. He has all the information you need on your hours and the generous salary you'll be provided."

I nodded as Hugo was finally able to lead me out of the dining room door and into the hallway.

"What was all that stuff about Evangeline?" My curiosity was growing about the feud between Quinn and Marcus. I wished the fertility god had kept talking because Marcus was mum on the situation. "That's their baby girl, right?"

Wells nodded. "She's the biological daughter of the faery prince and the queen. She's also an extremely bright companion. She's almost as bright as her mother, probably will be as she matures."

A lot of stuff finally made sense. "Quinn thinks Marcus will want to take her as a companion one day."

"I suspect so." There was a hint of chill in his voice. It wasn't rude, but he lowered my hand and walked beside me without touching me. His next question had a hint of disdain to it. "Is your lover a supernatural creature?"

He was upset with me about Marcus. I hid my smile as we walked toward the elevator. "Yes, he is."

"And how was Marcus when you left him?" It took everything I had not to giggle. He was worried I'd ripped Marcus's heart out. I had a vision of Marcus forlorn and heartbroken over little old me.

"Asleep." It had taken me several minutes to force myself to leave him. He'd looked beautiful sleeping peacefully in my too-small-for-both-of-us bed. We'd had to cuddle, and this morning I hadn't wanted to leave the comfort of his body behind.

Wells stopped in the middle of the hall. "You left your trainer without even a good-bye? How heartless are you, girl? Perhaps I should tell the king to train you himself. If you cannot form a bond then there's no purpose in bringing me into it at all. I would only find myself involved with a creature who cannot love."

"Would you?" I'd wondered about this for a while. Before Marcus and I had run off together, the king had talked about another academic training me. "If you trained me, is it inevitable that you would fall for me?"

I'd felt an instantaneous connection to Marcus the moment I saw him. While I felt the spark when Hugo Wells touched me, it was a small thing compared to what Marcus did to me.

Wells crossed his arms over his big chest and I felt the weight of his disappointment. "Perhaps not. I've trained three Hunters over the years. One of them was too old when we found her. She'd been through too much and I couldn't reach her. She was cold. There was no way to touch her or form a connection. It was one of the most heartbreaking relationships of my life. I have no desire to repeat the experience. As I told the king, I have a mistress who I care about. I will not ruin my relationship with her for a woman who couldn't even accept a man like Marcus Vorenus."

I got in the elevator and Wells reluctantly followed. I pushed the button for five and grinned up at the vampire. It was fun to tease him. "Well, he is a large man. He can be rather intimidating the first time you see him, but I promise you I accepted him just fine."

The vampire flushed slightly as he stared down at me. It reminded me that though Donovan might be a modern sort of man, most vampires were products of their times. Hugo Wells was slightly shocked I would speak that way, but he was like Marcus. Academics are extremely tolerant. "They didn't even ask you his name, did they? The king and the prince assumed they would get their way."

"Nobody but my uncle has asked me," I admitted. "I've only been gone for a few months and my training has been…intense. I spend every minute of the day with my trainer, and when I sleep he's with me, too. I'm not sure how they think I picked up a lover along the way."

Hugo Wells sighed, smiling with a relieved expression. "What is the name of this boyfriend you light up over, dear?"

"His name is Marcus," I said with a happy sigh. "And I doubt he'd ever let you close enough to train me. He does that personally. He's also the tiniest bit possessive."

"I can imagine. I'm pleased to hear it, dear. It will be good to have him back with us. Henri Jacobs is here, too. It's been a long time since we three old academics got together." The elevator door opened and Wells gallantly held out his arm again. I slipped my hand through it and we walked down the hall. "I hope Quinn doesn't give him too much trouble."

"He isn't on the Council anymore. He's only here as my boyfriend and trainer. Quinn will have to deal with it. I'm not giving him up."

"I hope it's that easy. Quinn is a funny fellow. He likes to get his way and he can play dirty to get it."

I saw the door to my office and told myself I could handle Quinn. I wouldn't let him come between me and Marcus. He'd already cost me Gray. I wasn't giving up another man I loved because Dev Quinn didn't like him. That faery would discover I could play as dirty as he could.

Chapter Three

My office was a lovely three-room space. It shared the floor with several other businesses serving the supernatural community that had sprung up in the Council's compound. As we walked toward my office, I noted I shared space with a therapist, a doctor, a dentist, and a lawyer. A stunningly handsome man with pale-blond hair and blue eyes was coming out of his office as Mr. Wells and I walked past.

"Good afternoon, Felix," Wells greeted the man who smiled openly.

He appeared to be approaching forty and wore a sport coat over his slacks and dress shirt. It was a testament to Marcus's flair that I considered the man walking out of the therapist's office to be somewhat casual.

"Hugo, good to see you," the man said. He studied me for a moment and then held out his hand. "I suspect you're Ms. Kelsey Owens. It's an honor to meet you. I held your father in the highest regard."

I shook his hand, wondering if I would ever get used to the fact that my biological father had been someone people valued. Apparently the simple fact that I was his daughter bought me some respect with a lot of people. It wasn't a feeling I was used to. The man I'd grown up believing was my dad was neither respected nor loved. "It's nice to meet you. I guess I should point out I'm not my father. I have an appointment with you next week. I'm sure my father wouldn't have needed a psychotherapist."

Wells and Doctor Felix Day both broke out in great wails of

43

laughter. The blond shrink finally wiped his eyes with a shake of his head. "I have known few people who could have used some time on my couch more than Lee Owens. Just because he was a loyal and brave man doesn't mean he wasn't completely insane. I look forward to discussing it all with you over the next few months. See you soon, Kelsey."

"It appears you already have a client, dear." Wells nodded toward my office at the end of the hall.

The vampire's grip tightened on my arm as I glanced down the hall and saw a woman in a pretty yellow skirt and white sweater standing outside my door. She looked lovely, but then Liv always did.

"Not a simple client then? I can feel your emotion. You're very angry with that woman. Take a deep breath. Acknowledge the emotion without letting it get the best of you. It's all right. I'm with you. You won't be forced to do anything you don't like." The vampire's hand gently pushed the sleeve of my sweater up and his thumb rubbed soothing circles across the skin on my wrist. He pushed a sense of calm toward me and I accepted it. It helped me think with a clear head.

Act. Don't react. My life had become a series of psychiatric homilies. *Acknowledge the emotion so it can't get the best of me.* I remembered a time when I acknowledged the emotion by drinking a bottle of tequila and pretending it didn't exist, like the rest of the human world. Of course, that was before I realized I had a violent, bloodthirsty she-wolf sharing my soul, and she loved to react. So I took a deep breath and promised I wasn't going to fight. I didn't need to. I won by simply staying calm.

Liv turned toward us and her eyes lit up. "Kelsey, they said you were coming back, but I didn't quite believe it."

She walked toward us, her heels clacking on the hardwood floors.

Everything about Olivia Carey was delicate and feminine. She was a witch of moderate power and I'd met her in high school. I'd been an outsider all my life, the weird kid no one really wanted to be around. Growing up, I'd only had my two brothers, Jamie and Nathan. Jamie was six years older, so he had taken the role of protector. Nathan had been my playmate. The man who raised us had been a hard, violent person who despised my existence for reasons I only so recently understood. It had been difficult to make friends under those circumstances. Liv had been the first person outside of my brothers to take that chance.

44

Of course, she'd also been the person who offered me up to the king on a silver platter. Rather than giving me a heads-up on the whole "you're a freak and the king wants to put you in a cage" front, she kept her mouth shut and encouraged me to walk into the cage on my own.

"You look great," Liv said with a wary smile.

She looked fragile, like she hadn't slept much lately. It struck me that Liv was the type of woman the king would likely sit down with and discuss her troubles and find out how he could help her. He would treat a woman like Olivia with respect and kindness. He wouldn't scream at her and slap leg shackles on her to see if she'd turn from Jekyll to Hyde for him. I wasn't the girl men opened doors for or sought to take care of. I suppose that was why I'd immediately fallen for the two who'd done those things for me.

I turned my chin up to look at my escort. I focused on keeping my emotions buried under a nice protective wall. The last thing I wanted to do was upset Marcus. I'd managed to shield when the king had tested me. I wasn't going to upset him over this. "Could you take me to my rooms instead, Hugo? It's been a long day. I think I'd like to take a nap and wait for Marcus."

Liv's lips turned down as she turned from me to the vampire. "Kelsey, please. I need to talk to you."

As for Hugo, his eyes narrowed as he glanced from Liv to me. "I read your file, Kelsey, dear. This is the friend who betrayed you?"

"Yes," I replied. "I would prefer to avoid her."

"You can't avoid me forever," Liv said stubbornly.

"I can sure as hell try," I grumbled.

Wells took a step toward Liv, his eyes not unkindly. "It would be best if you waited to confront her when her trainer is around. She has strong emotions concerning you and while she's doing an excellent job of controlling them, it would be easier if Marcus was the one with her. I'm merely a stand-in."

"Why does she need someone with her?" Liv's questions became rapid-fire bullets, pelting the vampire. "What are you doing to her hand? Are you trying to control her? I want to know what's going on. I tried to call her for months, but someone named Lucia kept putting me off."

"Ms. Owens is in training," Hugo began.

The door to the elevator dinged suddenly. It startled me for a moment, a sure sign I was emotional. I turned, looking for a threat, but I smiled as my world was filled with glorious, grubby little boys. My mood went from dour to shiny in an instant.

"Kelsey!" Lee Donovan-Quinn plowed off the elevator and powered down the hall. He was nine years old and so heartbreakingly handsome I feared for women everywhere when he came of age. Now he was a boy in a T-shirt and jeans, with sneakers that needed to be tied.

I knelt down and braced myself for impact. I had a ton of reasons I didn't want to come back to the Council HQ. Lee was the one reason I did. Somehow I'd formed a connection with this kid, and I didn't even try to deny it.

"Hi, Lee," I said as he threw his arms around me.

He'd written me while I was in Italy, his warm e-mails full of questions about how my training was going. We'd talked a few times over the computer, his little face a welcome sight as he told me all about how school was and which Xbox game he was currently playing. I'd written him back or told him about all the places Marcus took me to. Holding Lee in my arms made me understand how much I had come to care for the boy. I couldn't help myself. I kissed the top of his thick dark hair. It felt right to be with him.

It had occurred to me that he was Donovan's way of keeping track of me, but I didn't care.

"Papa told me you were back, but he said I shouldn't bother you while you were working," Lee explained.

"But Lee said he was going to help you," another voice said. I smiled over at Rhys, Lee's twin brother. They were perfectly identical except for the eyes. Lee's were a warm chocolate brown while Rhys had his father's emerald eyes. Rhys also had Dev Quinn's fertility powers. He was a cute kid, but he made me want to shield my womb.

"Lee says you're a detective and that you need people to help you on your cases," a third boy explained. He was Sean Quinn and he could certainly have been the twins' brother. His father was the future king of Faery. Declan Quinn held the Faery seat on the Council. Sean Quinn looked me up and down. "She is pretty." He nodded as he turned to Rhys. "I think she would do well. My father talked about her before she fled. I believe he was definitely interested."

Rhys smiled up at me, looking like he'd come up with the best plan ever. My every instinct went on high alert. His plans usually involved kissing. "It's a great idea. I think you'll really like my Uncle Declan. He's looking for another wife, and you would be perfect."

"Except that she's with Uncle Marcus," Lee said with a huff. "Duh. I don't think Uncle Marcus is into sharing."

Lee Donovan-Quinn. The only freaking one of the bunch who knew me and he was nine years old. "He isn't. Sorry. You'll have to look elsewhere for your dad's new honey."

Sean Quinn shrugged. "Maybe it's just as well. Father told Uncle Dev he also thought you would be a beast in the sack. I don't know why he wants to put you in a sack, especially if it forces some violent change in you."

"Yes." I tried valiantly to suppress the wealth of laughter threatening to burst out of me. "I will avoid any sack your father tries to put me in."

Rhys's brilliant green eyes narrowed, all thoughts of matchmaking obviously forgotten as he moved on to more important matters. "If Uncle Marcus is here then he brought us candy."

Lee high-fived his brother. "Yes!" He looked back at me in explanation. "Mama thinks my anger issues can be solved by keeping me away from sugar and soda. It's not working, Kelsey. I just get angry about not having candy and soda."

I smoothed back his hair. "Well, I happen to know your Uncle Marcus made a stop at a nice candy shop before we left Venice. You'll have to go see him about it though. I would be quick. Your Uncle Marcus has quite the sweet tooth himself, and he might eat them all up before you have a chance to get any."

Lee's eyes got big at the thought of missing out, but Sean Quinn shook his head. He greatly resembled his superarrogant father in that moment. "Uncle Marcus is a vampire, Kelsey. He doesn't eat candy."

Hugo laughed behind me. "Oh, I assure you he can now. Your Uncle Daniel might be a king, but Marcus is an academic, like me."

"One of Uncle Marcus's superpowers is that he can taste the food I eat," I explained. "He can only do this with very close female friends, but once the bond is formed, he can taste food through me."

I heard Liv react to that. Of course, she was probably shocked a man like Marcus would form a bond with someone like me. I hadn't been a hot commodity while we were friends. I ignored her, preferring to explain to the boys. "It's been a really long time since Marcus had a girlfriend like me. He hadn't even tasted Reese's."

"No way," Lee said, dumbfounded. He tried to live off them. Peanut butter cups and Dr. Pepper were Lee's dietary staples before his mother had outlawed sugar.

"It's true. I bought a whole bunch of them because they're the best stuff in the world and he didn't believe me. He told me,"—I went into my best Marcus impersonation, complete with a bad Italian accent—"I have tasted chocolate and I have tasted peanut butter. I do not see how putting the two together makes them better, *bella*."

"Did he like them?" Rhys asked, an expectant smile on his face.

"He made me eat the whole bag," I assured them. "There's an awful lot he hasn't tried yet. I think we should make an afternoon of it."

"He should try root beer," Rhys said.

"And Skittles," Sean offered.

I stood up and smiled at Hugo. "I'm so glad I have a werewolf metabolism."

Liv was still there. "Kelsey, I need to talk to you."

The boys were busy planning a menu that would kill a diabetic. As I looked down on them affectionately, I realized I was in perfect control. Hugo patted me on the back, and I knew he could feel my satisfaction in my own progress. I kept my voice down, and there was little anger in it as I spoke to the woman I used to love dearly. "I don't have anything to say to you, Olivia."

"Fine," she replied dully. "You don't have any interest in hearing me out. I get that. I make one mistake in ten years of friendship and the great Kelsey Atwood has no more use for me. Fine. I'm not here as your friend. You obviously don't need me now that you're in good with the vamps. But I am here as a client and you can't turn me away. I'm still a member of this community and I need your services."

I sighed, seeing straight through her. "Liv, I don't have time to waste on some wild-goose chase you and Nathan cooked up to manipulate your way back into my life."

Liv's voice was low so the boys couldn't hear her. "You bitch," she breathed righteously. "I loved you like a sister for years. I did what I did to protect you and you don't even ask me for an explanation. You're just judge, jury, and executioner. I might have been wrong, but I also loved you. You know what, Kelsey? Maybe I was wrong. Trust me, sister. I don't particularly want to waste my time getting back into your life when I know I'm not perfect enough for you. I would spend the rest of the time waiting for you to turn on me. I need your professional services."

Hugo's hand slid over my shoulder. It was a good thing, too, because Liv was getting to me. I didn't like seeing myself through her eyes. All the years of friendship played through my head, including the fact that once she'd saved my life. I'd spent months stewing in happy, comfortable anger. Was there something to what Liv was saying? I settled on dealing with the problem I could handle. "What's this case you need my help on?"

Tears sprang to Liv's gorgeous eyes, and that did nothing to alleviate the guilt that gnawed at my gut. There were dark circles under her eyes. I wondered exactly what had been happening here while I was happily ensconced in Italy. It didn't look like the time had been kind to my ex-friend.

"It's Scott," she said. "He's missing."

I felt a warm hand push itself into mine.

"Do we have a case?" Lee asked, his face so serious I had to school mine.

"Looks like it, buddy," I replied. "Let's take the rest of this meeting in the office."

* * * *

Sean and Rhys split at the first sign that the day had taken a distinctly work-like tone, but Lee sat in the chair beside mine, his brown eyes looking Liv over. His small hands were steepled in front of him and a distinctly somber air surrounded him.

"And this Scott is your boyfriend?" Lee asked seriously.

Liv stared at me, her lips a flat line. "He's nine, you know. He's not exactly assistant material."

"My actual assistant can't be here until he wakes from his undead stupor. Lee's the best I got. Besides, he's very astute. He knows pretty much everything that goes on in this club, which means he knows more about the supernatural world than most people. He's also an awesome little thief." I glanced at the boy who carried my father's name. "You know she's a teacher at your school, right?"

It would intimidate a lesser child, but Lee was having none of that. "She teaches high school. She hasn't had the chance to suspend me yet. Did you have a fight with him?"

"No, not exactly." Liv sat back in the comfortable chair I was sure Quinn had decided looked like something out of a film noir.

My office had a distinctly art deco look to it. I kept expecting a femme fatale to walk in at any moment, but I just had Liv and her gentle, accusatory eyes. I was feeling the sting of her earlier indictments.

Was I being too harsh on her? On everyone? Marcus thought so. I knew that. I felt his disappointment every time I wouldn't take a call from my mother. But I was truly stubborn and pushed through, unwilling to deal with unpleasant emotions.

"Scott is too lazy to ever get involved in an actual fight." It was so much easier to focus on the case. "Has he been working lately?"

Scott's employment history was spotty to say the least. He preferred to mooch off his perpetual fiancée. They'd been engaged for four years. Most people would have been married in an elaborate ceremony, popped out a couple of kids, and gone through a righteous divorce by now, but Liv and Scott hadn't even set a date yet. Scott was content to mooch off her not very profitable career in mentoring tomorrow's supernatural creatures.

"He got a job at a club downtown," Liv offered.

"Is this his usual work?" Lee asked. It was a good question. If I hadn't known the man we were discussing, it would have been my next line of inquiry.

"He's worked in restaurants mostly." Liv sighed when she realized I really was letting him help me.

Hugo sat in the background, studying one of the many volumes lining the walls of my office. I noted it was a book on forensics. I wasn't certain when I would need that unless Quinn intended for me to become a medical examiner as well. Unlike Lee, Hugo didn't seem terribly interested in playing detective.

"Scott managed some restaurants, mostly fast food and delis," I explained to Lee. "It's different than running a nightclub, as your papa could tell you. The last time I talked to Scott, he was managing a burger joint in Addison."

"That's when he met this guy named Julius," Liv said with a grim expression. "I knew he was bad news. He was starting a club downtown. Brimstone is the name I heard it called. It's underground. Ether has become too mainstream for some folks. Dev doesn't allow drugs and he's serious about the whole 'place of peace' thing. Some folks want a more…liberal establishment."

"So this is where the criminals go," Lee observed astutely.

"Probably," Liv admitted. "Scott turned him down the first time, but this Julius guy came back with an offer for a lot of money."

That didn't seem right to me. Scott was a dipshit. He rarely held a job for more than six months. It wasn't that he was dumb. He was intensely lazy. He started out well, all full of enthusiasm and vigor, but then work would mess up his football-watching schedule or conflict with bowling night. Inevitably, his good intentions failed and he either walked out or got fired. Why would some guy with money want Scott on the team? "What exactly did this Julius want Scott to do?"

Liv's hands fidgeted with the strap of her leather purse. "He wanted Scott to be in charge of the bar. He was supposed to do all the ordering, deal with vendors, liaise with the kitchen staff, and hire the bar staff. He's done it before."

I nodded, thinking about the problem. Scott had run bars in restaurants before, but I wouldn't call him an expert. "Why Scott?"

Hugo glanced up over the book he was reading. "What sort of being is your fiancé, Ms. Carey?"

Liv bit her lip as she turned to the vampire. Nervous. She was actually nervous about being close to the academic. I could have told her Hugo was harmless unless he decided to have an intellectual discussion with her, and then all bets were off. Academics will fight if they have to, but they prefer intellectual pursuits to anything else. Well, almost anything else. Marcus was pretty fond of sex, I'd discovered.

"Scott's a shapeshifter." I answered for my reluctant client. "He's not what I would call powerful though. He doesn't practice often. He mostly does dogs. It's easiest for him."

Hugo's intelligent eyes narrowed as he considered the problem. "He's a true shifter, then. That's rare and fairly innocuous. He wouldn't have a pack, per se, so he wouldn't have loyalties to outside forces. In addition, he would be managing people who more than likely do have packs or families. Often shifters and were creatures have prejudices against each other. Your fiancé is an excellent choice if his employer wishes to make all creatures welcome."

Liv nodded and I could see her start to relax. "That makes sense. The club was supposed to open a month ago. I was going to attend the launch, but the night before Scott told me I wouldn't be allowed in and I shouldn't ask questions. He kept going in to work at night but he stopped talking about it. Then last week, he stopped coming home. I tried his cell but I get voice mail every time I call. I went to the address I had but they wouldn't let me in. They told me to go away if I knew what was good for me."

Despite my anger with her, I certainly didn't like the idea of Liv in danger. I wanted her safely miserable. "Liv, you should never have gone there."

"What was I supposed to do?"

"Talk to your coven leader. Or you could have called Jamie." Anything but walking in there herself without any backup. Again, I felt the guilt of avoiding her. Anything could have happened if she'd walked into that club.

"I did call Jamie," Liv admitted. "He put me in touch with someone else."

The hair on the back of my neck stood straight up. Dots I didn't want connected were on a collision course. There was only one person Jamie would have sent Liv to with me out of the country. "I need that address, Liv."

She pulled a piece of paper out of her purse and slid it across the desk. My heart sank. It was the same address the demon had passed me.

Grayson Sloane was in serious trouble and I had a new client.

Chapter Four

By the time I met my assistant, I had a ton of work for him to do. After Liv left, two more clients had popped up, but their cases seemed fairly inconsequential. One needed me to track down a spouse who'd run out on his child support and the other wanted to know if her boyfriend was cheating on her. The first was solved by a simple skip trace and the other answer was probably yes. She was obnoxious. I would have been cheating on her.

"Hi." Justin Parker greeted me with a somewhat uncomfortable smile. His eyes looked pretty much everywhere but where I was standing.

"You didn't want this job." It didn't take a lot of detective work to see the kid was anxious and a little intimidated.

"But it's a cool job," Lee argued, frowning at the vampire.

"I just got here. How can I already be in trouble?" Justin was a new type of vampire. I like to call them veeks. Geek turned vamp. They like blood and MMORPGs. They can't dress for shit and are socially awkward. I couldn't blame them much for the last two parts. Marcus tended to lay out my clothes, and he was forever telling me which fork to use.

Justin Parker was prime veek. He was all arms and legs and big sad eyes. He wore a Halo T-shirt and sweatpants and carried a thermos in his hand.

"Tell me your mom didn't send you a snack." I wouldn't put

anything past a veek. The millennial vamps aren't known for their raging independence.

Justin shook his head. "It was my girlfriend. I get hungry. Do we have a fridge?"

"There's a kitchen next to the bathroom," I offered. "Look, I'm sure Quinn pressured you into this. I assure you I can work without an assistant. I did for years."

Lee looked up at me. "I can help you. You don't need another assistant."

"You have to go do homework, buddy." I'd talked to his mom not five minutes before. She'd known exactly where to find him and, unlike her husband, she hadn't sent the cavalry in to save him. She'd called and politely requested I send him home for dinner. "Your mom wants you home. If you want to be allowed to come back tomorrow, you need to get your butt upstairs."

Even Lee could see the sense in that. "Okay. Tell Uncle Marcus I'll see him tomorrow and to save me some candy." He stopped at the door and came back to me. He motioned me to kneel down before whispering his question in my ear. "How are you going to get to that club?"

I smiled at the sweet, smart boy. "Don't worry about it. I won't be able to leave until one thirty in the morning. You'll be asleep by then. I'll find a way out and I'll tell you all about it after school tomorrow."

Lee nodded and hugged me before running out the door.

"The king's son seems taken by you," Hugo noted as he glanced around the office.

"I like him, too," I said, smiling. My smile disappeared as I took in my veek assistant. It was best to put our relationship on a realistic footing. He was really a spy for Donovan. I wasn't an idiot. I handed him the list of things I had for him to do. "As long as you're here, I could use some help. I need you to run a skip trace on Greg Houston. I want to know where he is and how much money he has. Second, find out if Lance Belton is screwing someone other than his girlfriend. We have a file on him. Call his friends and lean on them for info. Call a man named Alan Kent. He's a shifter so we probably have his number on file. I need to talk to him tonight. Tell him to meet me at Ether at ten or so. If he gives you trouble about it, remind him who I am now. You're a vamp, use that persuasion thing."

Justin's eyes had gone wide. "I'm actually not very good at that."

"Consider it practice then," I offered as Hugo and I edged closer to the door. "Also, this place needs snacks. There isn't any food in that fridge. Get me snacks and some beer. No one has beer around here. And peanut butter cups." Another thought struck me. "And find me a comfy couch. That thing Quinn bought is pretty, but I can't nap on it. Think big pillows. If you need anything, don't call me. I'll be screwing my boyfriend, eating, or sleeping. All of those are serious things for me, Justin. Do we understand each other?"

The veek shook his head, clutching his thermos. "What's a skip trace?"

"Look it up on the Internet, Justin," I said, swinging the door open. "I bet you're damn good with computers."

Hugo was laughing as he walked beside me down the hallway. "I feel sorry for Mr. Parker. I believe he will find you a difficult employer."

"I'll give him more of a chance tomorrow." The elevator started toward the seventh floor and some small amount of freedom. My heart was starting to race as the doors opened and I got out. Marcus was here. I could feel him. Warmth spread through me.

Hugo stayed in the elevator. "Tell your master I will call upon him later this evening, after he's had suitable time to welcome you home, of course. Kelsey, it was a pleasure to meet you. I look forward to seeing more of you."

I waved to the vampire as the door closed and then raced down the hall. I hadn't seen my apartment yet, but I didn't care what was in the place. I cared who was in it. I pulled out the key Quinn had given me and threw open the door. Marcus was standing there waiting like he'd known I was coming, and he had. He'd known I was there the same way I had known he was. He'd felt my presence deep in his soul.

"Good evening, *bella*," Marcus said warmly, his eyes already heating up.

I stood and for a moment I couldn't move. I simply stood there, taking him in. He was heartbreakingly beautiful. He had pitch-black hair that he slicked back, but I loved it when it got loose and fell over his eyes. His face could have been carved by Michelangelo. Marcus always reminded me of a gorgeous bird of prey, with dark eyes and a lean body.

"I missed you," I breathed as I went to stand in front of him.

His hands pulled me into the firm strength of his body. "Not as much as I missed you," he said, tilting my head back.

His mouth covered mine, and I thrilled as his fangs popped out. I loved the feel of them. I loved to work my tongue around them while we kissed. If I accidently nicked myself on those sharp teeth, Marcus would groan as he tasted the blood. He would go a little wild. I nicked myself as often as possible.

His tongue played with mine and I felt his hands drop below my waist, cupping the cheeks of my ass. Marcus would play the gentleman much of the time, but when we were alone, he let all of that go. There was no gentleman in our bed. He tugged on my hair, and I let my head fall back. He growled as he ran his nose along the side of my neck.

"Mine."

"Yours," I agreed. My whole body softened in response to his dominance. Marcus could be incredibly indulgent, but he liked to rule in the bedroom.

A vision of Gray Sloane, his massive, muscular body working over mine, assaulted me. I shoved it aside. Even when I was with Marcus, Gray was somehow with us. Sometimes I wished I'd never met that half demon because it seemed nothing I did could loosen his hold on me.

"Bed?" I asked, coming up for air.

"Later." Marcus pulled my shirt over my head. It was tossed to the floor. He flicked the front clasp of my bra, and I was naked from the waist up. His hands covered my breasts. "Have I told you how beautiful you are?"

He was good at that. Sometimes I thought Marcus's goal in life was to make me feel good about myself. "Not today."

The tips of his fingers brushed my nipples, making them hard and ready for more. "Then allow me to correct the oversight. You are stunning, *bella*. I dream about your breasts."

My breasts aren't the biggest in the world, but when Marcus's voice went low and he couldn't take his eyes off my chest, I couldn't help but feel sexy. I let my hand slide down his hard body to find his cock. Marcus might like to be in charge, but he also liked it when I misbehaved. I cupped him. "I dream about your cock."

"*Voglio fare l'amore con te.*" His hands found my hips and he pulled me against that magnificent erection. My hips rolled against it of their own accord.

I want to make love with you, he'd said. I smiled as I kissed him and gave him my own wording. "*Ti voglio scopare.*"

Marcus growled, and suddenly I was straddling his hips as he carried me toward the couch. His hands cupped my ass as he pressed my core against his. His big cock pushed against me, and my clitoris was ready for action. "I want to fuck, too. I love it when you talk dirty to me."

My back hit the soft velvet of the couch. Marcus had it shipped from our home in Venice. He seemed to think it was the perfect size to throw down on. We'd screwed numerous times on that bad boy. He tossed me on the couch and efficiently pulled my jeans off, dragging the silky panties with it. He stood over me, still fully dressed as he looked down on my naked body. I knew what he would want, but he liked to ask for it.

"Touch yourself, my mistress," he commanded, his eyes dark.

This was where I'd needed to be all day. I let go of all my worries and concentrated on pleasure. All that mattered was being with Marcus. Nothing else could invade my brain at this point. I let my hand wander down my belly to my plump and already ripe pussy. I spread my legs so he got a good view, letting my feet go wide. There was no room for self-consciousness between us. His need rolled off him and into me, making my blood pulse through my system in a rhythmic fashion. He wanted me more than he wanted his next breath and I responded. Arousal flooded my system.

Marcus liked to watch. He liked to know I would play just for him. My clitoris was already throbbing when I stroked my finger over it. Pure pleasure rushed through me. Something about that wave from Marcus made foreplay unnecessary. I could feel how much he wanted me, and my system replied with pulsing arousal. I was ready for him from the moment he turned his eyes my way, but he liked to play. Marcus never went directly to the point when he could draw out the sex.

"Like this?" I asked, delicately rubbing until I was breathless.

"Yes. Make yourself creamy and ripe for me."

Not a problem. I was already there, but I made a big show for him. My finger slid over my clit and down my labia. It wasn't like I needed more arousal. It poured out of me, and I couldn't help pushing a finger into my pussy. It wasn't anywhere close to what I needed. I needed his thick cock pressing in, but I would take it for now.

I fucked myself with my finger, adding another when it wasn't quite enough. I knew how good it felt to have Marcus's thick cock delving deep and I pulled on the memories. I remembered that first night when he'd loomed over me, his big dick piercing me. He'd thrust in and out, in and out. His hips had hammered and I'd screamed in pure pleasure.

I thought about that night as I fucked myself with those fingers. That first night had already saved me once today. I'd gone to that place in my mind when Donovan had tested me. I went there again because it had been one of the best moments of my life. I let it run along my mind, pulling me into my perfect memories.

That night, I'd spread my legs and welcomed him in. He'd moved inside me and for a moment I'd forgotten about Grayson Sloane. I'd lost myself and it had felt so good.

"Let me taste." His commands had grown guttural. He was on the edge now. It wouldn't take long before I had him.

I held my hand out. He drew the saturated fingers into his mouth. He sucked off the evidence of my arousal, his tongue circling the fingers and making me sigh.

Marcus groaned and his hands worked the belt at his waist. He shoved his slacks down and was on me without bothering to take off the rest of his clothes. He spread my legs. His big dick unerringly found my slit and pushed in to the hilt.

"You feel right, *cara mia*," he whispered. His satisfaction slid across my skin.

He was so hard I had to shift to adjust to his size. It was odd but the pain did nothing to deter me. I liked a bite of pain. His cock was too big, but he shoved in anyway and I adjusted to accept my lover. He felt so good as he started to thrust into me. I heard a deep groan come from the back of my throat. He thrust in and pulled out savagely, as though the day we'd spent apart had been too much and he needed to mark me again.

I wound my legs around his lean waist and pushed back against him. He angled up, finding that place deep inside me that made me want to howl. The she-wolf who lived within me needed this. Somehow, I could feel her moving inside me, animating me. She lived for violence and sex. I could get a two-shot with Marcus—a mighty orgasm and enough of an edge to satisfy my wolf. I let my head fall back so he could see the long line of my throat. I knew he could hear the pulse of my heart and the throb of blood pumping through my system. He held my head still, forcing me to look into his eyes. Heat flashed through me as his eyes darkened, going to a pure black and crowding out the white as he let me see the vampire living deep in his soul. He ground himself against me as his eyes pulled me in.

This was the best place in the world. I surrendered to his magic and let it take me along. There was no danger here, no harsh realities. There was no betrayal in this place. In this world, I was his, and he was mine. We were all we could ever need. I felt the great force of Marcus's will and clutched his silky hair as he struck. I sobbed as he pulled on the vein in my neck and I came forcefully.

Marcus was still feeding when his orgasm hit. His body tensed, but he kept his fangs securely in my neck as he pumped into me. His pelvis thrust and thrust until he had nothing left. Finally, he drew one last time on my vein. I shuddered as he released his hold then fell on top of me. He didn't try to keep his weight off me. He knew I found comfort in it. I loved to be surrounded by him. Everywhere our skin touched I felt a sense of connection. It had been a long day without his skin next to mine. My arms wound around him, and I hated his shirt in that moment. It kept me from him.

He rested against me, letting softness replace the quick and hard fucking he'd given me. I needed this. I needed long, luxurious moments when he stroked me and our intimacy seemed to be the only thing of importance in the world. Time stretched out as I let his satisfaction sink into my soul. Every time we made love, I believed a little more that I was worthy of his affection.

After a long moment, he kissed me softly and moved his weight to the side.

"Come with me, *bella*. I've drawn a bath for us. I wanted to spend time with you before the rush of visitors come calling on our door." He stood and gracefully discarded the rest of his clothes. I watched him, loving every inch of skin he exposed. I sighed as he cradled me to his chest and carried me into the master bathroom. I always felt delicate and feminine when he carried me around.

This was where I'd wanted to be all day. I sank back against my lover in the hot water, his arms wrapping around me. He kissed my hair lovingly. I'd wanted to be skin to skin with him. I craved it like an addict. Marcus had told me that one day I wouldn't need this. He'd explained that in a few years, I would be the one who likely walked away, but I couldn't see it happening.

"I ordered dinner for you. Tomorrow, I'll prepare it myself, but tonight I wanted the time with you. I needed to be with you. Tell me about your day, *cara mia*," Marcus demanded softly.

I glanced around the magnificent bathroom. It was a gorgeous monstrosity of marble and mirrors. The tub we were in was built for two and jetted. The water swirled around us. Despite Marcus's wealth, our home in Venice was quite sedate and European. It's gorgeous and tasteful, but trust me, no one does decadence like a faery prince. I could practically swim in that tub. I didn't know what a steam shower was, but it seemed like fun.

Marcus reached over to grab something from the tray he'd placed at the head of the tub. He passed me a glass of white wine and I sipped it. This part of our day was more about him than me, but I was getting used to fine wine.

He sighed. "Such a good year. That Pinot Grigio is like heaven. I'm going to have fun raiding Devinshea's cellar. Now tell me, did the king treat you kindly?"

I frowned. "No. The king was an asshole."

Marcus chuckled as he nuzzled my neck. It was always like that. He was obsessed with my neck. He liked to feed from my neck or sometimes from the vein that ran through my thigh right next to my pussy. Usually though, he preferred the neck. He liked to feed and then kiss me senseless, so I could still taste the faintest hint of blood on his tongue. It was a sweet feeling to know my body fed and sustained his. "You think many people are assholes, Kelsey. What did he do to you today?"

Oh, so many things. This was my time to complain, and Donovan had made it super easy for me to do so. "He put me in chains and threatened to chuck me in a cell. Let's see. I'm an animal who can't control myself. I ruined his relationship with my uncle. I'm pretty sure he blamed me for the situation in the Middle East, economic recession, and Miley Cyrus."

Marcus went dangerously still behind me, and that was when I realized I'd made a huge mistake. His hands cupped my shoulders, and I knew if I turned, his face would be a polite mask. He rarely showed his anger. I knew to be afraid if he got ruthlessly still.

"What did the king do, *cara*?"

"He was testing me." I shrugged negligently to try to defuse the situation. His irritation brushed at my consciousness, so I knew it was super bad. He wasn't able to contain his anger. "It was no big deal. He wanted to see if I could handle myself emotionally, and I did. You didn't even feel it."

"Which only proves you are good at shielding your emotions, Kelsey. You're still at a delicate stage. He could have ruined three months of work in a single, oafish instant."

I smiled and rubbed my back against his chest. "Well, you should tell him that."

"Believe me, I will." He sighed and settled back down.

I would totally let Marcus handle the king. Donovan regarded my mentor as a father figure. He regarded me as a lethal moron, so Marcus was my go-to guy when dealing with that particular vampire.

"I met your friend Hugo." I said it almost shyly because if he hadn't liked that first part, then he was really going to be pissed at the next part. I thought about not mentioning it to him, but he was going to find out.

"Hugo is here?" He sounded pleased at the prospect. "Excellent. I will arrange to spend some time with him. Did he mention why he was here? I understood he wanted to stay in London."

This was the bad part. I winced as I spoke. "Uhm, I'm sure it's a mistake and we can get it all cleared up, but he thinks he's supposed to be my new trainer."

And just like that my tub time was over. Marcus was out in a shot. I pouted and stared at him from the warmth of the tub while he dried his perfectly cut body with short, angry strokes of the fluffy white towel.

"If it helps, Donovan thinks you're still in Italy."

Marcus nearly growled. "It does not help, *bella*, that the king believes I would allow you to leave me behind. Not only did I allow you to leave me behind, but apparently I allowed you to take a lover while you lived under my roof. This may be Daniel's way. Daniel may allow his wife to sleep with whomever she would like and bring them home to their bed, but that is not the way it will be between us."

Then he was off in a litany of Italian. When Marcus got going, he could speak at a hundred miles an hour. It was kind of one of his superpowers. I simply nodded and agreed with everything he said and wished I hadn't opened my damn mouth. Marcus was a possessive man. He'd never tried to hide that from me. He was calm, almost annoyingly calm, ninety-nine percent of the time. That one percent was a doozy, though. As he continued to rage, he got dressed. I felt bad for Donovan. Then I remembered what an asshole he was and I smiled to myself. After what he'd put me through, he kind of deserved a pissed-off Italian coming for him.

A nice-sounding chime played through the house. Even our doorbell sounded elegant and rich. It was a definite step up from the rented duplexes and single-wide trailers I'd grown up in.

"Naturally, the crowd shows up now." Marcus finished buttoning his dress shirt and stared down at me. "Get dressed. I am sure this is about you since no one even believes I am here."

He turned and stalked out of the room.

I sighed and got out of the tub. My stomach grumbled. With the exception of that truly excellent orgasm I'd had, it had been a crappy day. I barely had any breakfast, then my lunch was interrupted. No one had offered me a snack. Now dinner was in distinct jeopardy as well. To top it all off, I had to deal with a pissy vampire. Having never been in a real relationship before—I can't count Gray as our relationship had been short and apparently under the influence of drugs—I never realized how much another person could affect me. My days could often be decided as good or bad strictly on the influence of Marcus's mood.

The good news was, most of the time, Marcus was lovingly indulgent. The bad news? When Marcus was in a crappy mood, he had two thousand years of shit he could throw around.

I wrapped a towel around my middle and wondered what I should wear tonight. Jeans and a T-shirt would be comfy, but I had no idea if Brimstone had a dress code. If it was anything at all like Ether, people would dress to the nines. I didn't give a shit if I stood out at Ether, however, I was trying to blend in at this new place. I had the added complication of hiding the fact that I would be seeing Gray tonight from Marcus. I had been planning to be open and honest with him, but now, as he yelled at whoever had shown up at our door, that seemed like a bad plan.

"Slow down, Vorenus," a familiar voice said. "I don't speak Italian."

I rolled my eyes. The last thing I needed was a visit from Trent Wilcox. He never showed up unless I was in trouble. Being a "face the music now rather than later" type girl, I strode out into the living room ready to know what fresh hell the Boston native was bringing me.

Trent Wilcox was in his late thirties. I suppose if you go for the meathead type, he was an exceptionally attractive man. Like super hot and muscular. His dark-brown hair was cut military style, and his T-shirt could barely contain his ginormous biceps. He looked like a guy who spent way too much time at a gym, but he was a werewolf, so his muscles were au naturel. His clear blue eyes found mine. I saw a look of surprise cross his face. He gave me a perfectly natural for a man once-over.

"Thank god. I don't know what's wrong with your boyfriend." Trent shook his head as he started walking toward me. "I can't get him to speak English."

"Then let me make it plain to you, Mr. Wilcox." Marcus's hand was suddenly around the big wolf's throat. He managed to dangle Trent a couple of inches off the ground, which was a feat because Trent was several inches taller than Marcus. "Take your eyes off my mistress. Now."

"Damn it, Marcus," Trent gasped. His eyes widened and his feet kicked, trying to reach the floor. I was surprised to say the least. Marcus was typically a very nonviolent-type vampire. He tended to leave that sort of thing to me. "I'm sorry. What am I supposed to do? She's..."

"Half naked." Marcus growled as he turned his unnaturally dark eyes to me. I have rarely seen that pure vampire part of Marcus. Sometimes it came out when we made love, but he was always in control. Tonight seemed different. Tonight those pitch-black eyes bore into me and his will rolled across my skin. Persuasion pushed at me. That was all vampire, with none of my indulgent trainer. "I told you to get dressed."

I knew he was right. I should go and do as he asked, as he'd asked me to in the first place. Still, I stood there. It's a perversity of my nature that I have a strong aversion to any sort of authority. He was pushing persuasion my way. Oh, he wasn't attacking me with it, but the threat was there. My wolf didn't like that much. "Since when do I follow your orders, Marcus?"

"Since you decided to become my mistress, Kelsey. You agreed to belong to me. I do not allow my mistress to expose herself to other men. Your body belongs to me. It is not for his eyes." He kept Trent dangling.

I wondered if the wolf would start turning blue soon. His neck was muscular and thick. It didn't look like Marcus could get his whole hand around it so I thought he was pretty safe. Marcus might be pissed at the king, but I couldn't let him kill the queen's guard.

His anger fed my own. I shoved back at his will. Despite the sex, my she-wolf was prowling in my gut again. "You possessive freak, I am not going to meekly obey you."

I'm pretty sure my she-wolf is also an alpha bitch.

"I wish you would, Kelsey." Trent's muscles strained. "This really fucking hurts."

Marcus ignored his prisoner. His arm showed no signs that he couldn't hold him there all night long. His fangs were out, and he enunciated clearly around them. Nothing in his face told me he wasn't completely serious about what he said next. "You will obey me in this or we will be done, my mistress."

I took a tight rein on my anger, but couldn't help flipping him the bird as I turned away. He wanted to play that way? Oh, I would show him. I could walk out on anyone. I could burn my own fucking house down without a thought. I was not the girl who took ultimatums well. I would get dressed and walk right away from him.

I stalked into the bedroom and was assaulted by lilies. I stopped, staring at this room we were supposed to share. Marcus had filled it with gorgeous flowers. My favorite flowers.

They were tasteful, as was everything Marcus did. There were Asian lilies on the dresser and on the small table beside the bookshelf where he'd stocked my favorite books. Sitting in the middle of the bed was a wrapped bouquet of gorgeous orange and black lilies. They were the kind my mother used to grow in the tiny bed in front of our crappy duplex. Sometimes those lilies were the only beautiful things in my life. I'd told Marcus about them one night while we lay together in front of the fire.

I touched the lilies and felt all of my anger flee. Even the she-wolf kind of yawned and gave up. How could I stay mad at a man who remembered almost everything I ever told him? I was used to walking away the minute something went wrong, but my life had changed three months before. I couldn't walk out. I needed Marcus more than I needed my pride.

I walked to the closet and liked the fact that my clothes were on the right side of the huge walk-in while his suits and sweaters hung neatly on the left side. I selected a pair of well-made black slacks and a ruby red sweater.

Marcus was a man of his time. Trying to treat him like the dudes I dated in college wasn't fair to him. He made no secret of it. He enjoyed the modern world and gave me an enormous amount of latitude. He never minded when I took the lead or cussed or got into a fight. He merely asked that I be faithful to him, and part of that for Marcus was a certain amount of modesty. If I'd thought about it for two seconds, I would have seen it from his point of view. I was half naked in front of another man. It was bound to bother Marcus. I was going to have to apologize.

I don't like to apologize.

I slipped on black boots with a small heel and went to brush out my hair. Marcus had slowly gotten rid of every ponytail holder I owned, so I was forced to leave it long. I selected one item of jewelry. It was the only piece I possessed. It was a small red and gold heart made from Venetian glass. I fell in love with it while at a jeweler's in Venice. Marcus bought it for me. Normally I didn't wear jewelry of any kind, but I was conceding this argument, and he liked to see me wear it.

When I was certain I looked every inch the lady, I walked back out.

Marcus had let Trent down and was pacing the floor. Trent was sitting on the couch massaging his neck.

"Better?" I asked Marcus in an even tone that let him know I wasn't willing to fight anymore. We'd only had a few fights. They tended to end with Marcus and I throwing down with some raucous sex. We didn't have time for that tonight, so I didn't want to fight.

Marcus didn't look even slightly guilty as he studied me from well-groomed head to properly accessorized toe. In his mind, he'd been completely in the right. "You look lovely." He approached me and gently touched the heart I was wearing. "But then, you always do." He kissed me. I got the feeling it made our wolf guest uncomfortable. "Thank you, *cara mia*. I'll leave you alone to work now. I must go and have a discussion with our king. Mr. Wilcox says he has come on some business. You will be fine without me, no?"

I wrapped my arms around his lean waist and went on tiptoes to kiss him again. I sighed as he deepened the kiss and wound his hands in my hair. It wasn't something he would normally do. He wasn't a big fan of the PDA. In public he would hold my hand and he would give me a light kiss. Tonight, he seemed to have something to prove.

When he let me up, I answered him. "I'll be fine. I'll be late, though. I have some stuff to do on a case."

"See me before you leave, Kelsey," Marcus said, walking to the door. "I would not have you go out without making sure you are protected."

I nodded, trying hard not to get too excited by what that meant. He would share his blood with me. It would blow my mind. I wasn't a companion. I wasn't his wife. By all vampire traditions, he shouldn't share his blood with me unless he needed to save my life. He couldn't seem to help himself though. He came up with some flimsy excuses, and I always took them. The truth was, I wanted that blood. No drug ever made me feel the way Marcus's blood did.

The door closed behind him. I was left alone with Trent Wilcox, asshole werewolf and the king's official lackey. He also had shoulders about a mile wide. Not that I noticed or anything.

"Sorry," I said, not sounding sorry at all. "He can be a little possessive at times."

"He's fucking insane is what he is, Kelsey." Trent growled, the sound way more animal than man. It was odd but I found that growl slightly comforting. "Do you have any idea the things he threatened to do to me if I so much as look at you the wrong way again?"

"I can only imagine." It was nice to see Trent on the ropes for once. "You'll have to forgive him. He cares for me. He doesn't understand that other men don't have any interest in me at all."

"I wouldn't say that," Trent muttered. His eyes softened marginally. "Are you okay? You know, after what happened today?"

"You mean after you and the big boss threatened to lock me up again? Somehow I'll survive. I don't think it's the last time you'll try to kick me in the gnads."

The big guy managed to look offended. "We didn't do that. It was only a test. You know how dangerous you are."

"Terrifically dangerous to a vampire king." Donovan was kind of the most powerful supernatural creature on the planet. I was supposed to believe he was afraid of little old me?

He stared at me for a moment. "Marcus hasn't told you, has he? You haven't read the histories."

Yeah, when I read it's usually a nice juicy thriller or a romance. "Nope. Not my style."

"I'm talking about the histories written by academics concerning Hunters. Your boyfriend wrote several of them. It seems academics like to keep records, and god knows the Council does. Donovan found them when he had the libraries moved from Paris to here."

"Records about other Hunters?" I was interested in that. As far as I knew I was the only Hunter in the world.

"Yeah, I can get them for you. Maybe then you'll understand why Donovan's been so hard on you and why he's going to let up from now on. You did great today. He was impressed."

"Donovan is hard on me because he's an asshole."

Trent shook his head. "He's hard on you because the last Hunter who was found and trained past the age of twenty killed over three hundred people before they were able to put her down. She killed her entire family and moved on to slaughtering whole villages in South America."

"What are you talking about?" Marcus hadn't said a thing to me about that. Actually, now that I thought about it, he hadn't talked much about other Hunters. I knew he'd trained a couple, but he never talked about them. I thought maybe it was a little like ex-girlfriends. It's not in trainer etiquette to talk about your ex-Hunters or something.

What if he had different reasons? Even earlier today, Hugo had mentioned something about a girl he'd tried to train being too old when they'd reached her. He'd said it was heartbreaking.

Had that woman been the one who tore apart villages?

Trent leaned against the wall, sighing. "I was worried you didn't know. You seem so level-headed that when you pulled all that guilt trip shit, I was worried. The king's a good guy. Now that he knows the training will take, he'll back off."

"So I was too old." There was still so much I didn't know. If there was one good thing about being forced to live in the Council headquarters, it was the fact that I might have a chance to learn more about myself, about this thing I was becoming.

Trent stood back and shrugged. "There's a reason the Council tried to find them young. I think having a family helped you. I think who your dad was made a difference, too. Your real dad, that is."

"I didn't know him." Lee Owens. I thought about him a lot. I think I dream about him.

"He's a legend in my community. I've only met two loners, and Owens was so different from the other one. Lone wolves, well, they have that name for a reason. They drift and keep drifting. Your dad stayed. Your dad was different, and I think that's why you're different. He had a strong heart. You do, too."

Thinking about my real dad made me emotional. I'd grown up with a complete asshole for a father figure, but maybe my real dad had left me something important. Maybe he'd managed to leave me a piece of his soul. If I didn't watch it, Trent was going to see me cry like a baby.

"I want to read those histories." There was a whole book out there describing other women like me? Yeah, I wanted to read it.

Trent nodded. "I'll get them to you. Maybe then you can find it in your vengeful she-wolf heart to think about not hating the king. He was only trying to protect the world. He reads a lot of comic books so he thinks he can do that."

"I'm not vengeful. Well, maybe a little." Something about the way Trent called me a she-wolf made me want to smile. But I was still pissed at him so I didn't. "So everyone knows about the whole elderly Hunter goes cray cray and kills everyone thing?"

"Not everyone. Donovan studied it carefully after he found out about you. You were supposed to be brought in a decade ago."

I'd been told this part of my history back when I first met the king and his Council. The king's coup a decade before had saved me from being kidnapped and brought to the old Council for training. I often wondered about what would have happened if I'd been brought to Paris.

I wonder what my life would have been like had I met Marcus at the age of sixteen. "Did the queen know? Why would she encourage her son to talk to me if she thought I might go bat shit?"

Trent's lips curled up in a smile. "Yeah, she knew all about it. I think the king gave her a hearty lecture on the subject, but Zoey Donovan-Quinn doesn't play by anyone's book but her own. She's an 'innocent until proven to be a stone-cold killer' kind of girl."

"You like her." Somehow it made me feel better that one person hadn't thought me capable of destroying whole towns.

"She's incredibly likable, but don't tell her I said that. I have to admit, I kind of like a hard-headed woman." He seemed to remember he had something to do here. "Now, let's talk about your job. I hear you've already started meeting with clients. I'm supposed to help you."

"Great." I knew exactly what strings Trent's "help" would come with. "I get a bodyguard. Well, I get a jailer. How long is Donovan going to keep you on top of me?"

"It's not like that," Trent tried to explain. I didn't care to listen. I was already walking out the door. He hurried behind me as I made my way to the elevator that would take me down to Ether. "Come on, Kelsey. Please give me a chance. This doesn't have to be hard."

"How about I make it easy by staying home like a good girl and not getting into any trouble."

He smiled at the thought. "You couldn't stay out of trouble if you tried. The boss wants you to have backup. That's all. Now calm down. We'll go downstairs, and I'll buy you a burger. I saw the menu the vampire planned for you. It's very…nutritionally balanced."

I frowned at the thought. Sometimes Marcus got weird ideas about eating vegetables and shit. I could really use a burger.

"So I told them to chuck the kale salad and ordered us bacon cheeseburgers, fries, and some beer." Trent dangled the proposition tantalizingly in front of me.

My stomach responded in the affirmative. I gave in. I needed that burger. I didn't even know what kale was. "Fine. But this doesn't make us friends."

"I wouldn't dream of it," Trent promised.

Chapter Five

I might not have liked Trent at that point, but I did like being around a wolf. I feel comfortable around werewolves. They're kind of like my people even when they're assholes. So I tipped back my beer and settled in beside him as we watched the show currently playing in Ether.

"Donovan's saying something about how much he respects Marcus and how happy he is to have him back." Trent gestured to the two men pretty much everyone in the club was watching.

Marcus had apparently tracked the king down to the club level of Ether. Donovan had been talking to a couple of shifters when Marcus had approached him. It had quickly dissolved into some seriously angry dinner theater.

"Yeah, well, Marcus isn't having it," I pointed out as Marcus began speaking rapidly. His hand jabbed at the air. He had the general look of a man who wasn't going to take it anymore.

For the most part, Marcus is a private man. It was only after I became his lover that he allowed me to see the range of his emotions. He tended to play things close to the vest. Every once in a while, though, his Italian temper flared, and the man could rage. At those times he didn't care that he had an audience. This particular audience was out of luck since the entire argument was being conducted in rapid-fire Italian. Turns out the king has an ear for languages. So Trent and I were making a game out of figuring out what the men were saying.

"Obviously." Trent laughed as the king put his hands up in

submission. "That would be his 'Sorry, I fucked up' face. I think he conceded that Marcus can stay your trainer."

"Like he has a real choice in the matter." I snorted. We'd already bonded. It wouldn't work so well with anyone else.

"Well, Donovan might have conceded, but it doesn't look like your guy is done. That dude is pissed." Marcus leaned over the table that separated him and the king, his eyes narrowed. Trent took a long swig from his third beer. It was kind of nice to eat with someone who could keep up with me. It made me feel less like a freak. "I'm surprised His Highness is putting up with this. Anyone else and his ass would be on the ground unconscious."

"Not just anyone else," an amused voice said from behind us.

I turned and saw Dev Quinn watching the byplay between his partner and Marcus. He held three bottles of beer in his hands. He passed them out, keeping the last one for himself.

The fertility god hopped onto the barstool beside me like he owned the place, which he did. "I think you'll find there are four people in the world who can get away with embarrassing the hell out of Dan. Zoey does it on a regular basis. I save it up for those times he's truly pissed me off. Then there's Marcus. Dan loves Marcus. Marcus saved him after his turn. He can get away with almost anything."

"Who's the fourth?" Trent asked curiously.

"Our father-in-law." Quinn had a rueful smile on his face. "Of course, Harry would never yell at Daniel. Daniel is perfect."

"I bet he yells at you." From what I understood, the queen's father was human. I wondered how he took his baby girl being claimed by a fertility god.

"Less and less as the years go by, but in the beginning, I was his whipping boy," Quinn explained. He winced as he watched his partner. "Shit, what did Marcus say?"

The king had left placating mode and was now getting in his mentor's face. Marcus didn't look inclined to back down. It wasn't hard to figure out which buttons Marcus would push. He'd already pushed them once.

"I think Marcus just pointed out that the king might let his wife play around with other men, but he doesn't do that." I hoped I wasn't about to have to get between them.

Quinn sighed and called over a waitress. "I'm going to need something stronger than this." She went off to do his bidding. "I wish he hadn't gone there."

Something was off in this situation. Quinn was entirely too calm. I should have ignored it. I should have let it go. I couldn't. "Shouldn't you be all pissed off that Marcus is back?"

It was harshing my buzz. Quinn was supposed to get his panties in a wad, and I was going to laugh.

The fertility god smiled brilliantly. He might be an asshole, but he was also a hottie. "I'm perfectly thrilled to have Marcus home and happily settled down with a mistress." He pushed the neck of my sweater aside. "I see he's already fed tonight. That's healing quickly, Kelsey. Either you're more wolf than any of us suspects or Marcus is feeding you, too."

I felt Trent stiffen at the words, and he took a sudden interest in his beer. Wolves and vamps don't always get along. Wolves tended to get pissed when vampires took she-wolves as lovers. I wondered if Trent truly viewed me as a she-wolf. I am, of course, but wolves tend to recognize my scent. None of that explained why Quinn would be so smugly self-satisfied at the thought of my relationship with Marcus. I wasn't an idiot, though. I could take a logical leap. "You think if he's involved with me, he'll leave your daughter alone."

"Oh, Kelsey, I know Marcus," Quinn admitted. "He's intensely loyal once he's involved with a woman. He won't ever leave you, not even for his so-called destiny. And I knew exactly who was coming back with you. I never let those things get by me. I simply wondered if you would tell me. Now, Alan Kent is sitting at the bar. He said you were looking for him. Is there anything I should know?"

I turned to the gorgeous faery, with his perfect face and more arrogance than anyone should be allowed. He might technically be my boss, but he wasn't getting an inch from me. "I was under the impression there wasn't anything you didn't know. Excuse me."

Hopping off the barstool, I glanced at my boyfriend and the king, who seemed to be settling down. It didn't look like it would come to blows, so I was probably safe to deal with the next situation of the night.

Alan sat at the end of the bar, nursing a beer. He was dressed in jeans, boots, and a Western-cut shirt with pearl snaps. It was one of the better ensembles in his wardrobe. Alan was a few years older than me. If I remembered correctly, he'd recently turned twenty-nine. He looked older. He drank too much, even for a shifter. Like Scott, Alan was a pure shifter. Also like Scott, he wasn't strong. They lived on the periphery of the supernatural world. They would never be able to handle themselves against a wolf or a vampire, so they tended to keep their heads down. It's a sad truth of our world that if you aren't an alpha, it's best to try to not be noticed. I often thought that Scott and Alan would have been much happier in the normal world.

"Kelsey." He nodded sullenly. Like Liv, his eyes were baggy, as though he hadn't slept much lately. His thin lips turned down as I took the barstool beside him. I realized his frown wasn't for me. "Mr. Wilcox."

My eyebrow arched at that. Alan wasn't the polite type. He must be completely terrified of Trent. Fortunately, I wasn't. Trent was a little like a muscular tick. He'd dug in and I was going to have to burn him to get him off me.

I had to back up to be able to see him. The man loomed over me. "I don't need your help with this, Trent."

I heard the growl from the back of his throat. It made Alan go a nice shade of white. It made me roll my eyes. If I showed that wolf even a hint that he could intimidate me, I would never get rid of him. "You can watch me from another table, Wilcox. Go away."

He didn't try to hide the growl this time. He leaned over, deliberately getting in my space. Trent Wilcox was easily a foot taller and had at least a hundred pounds on me. I smiled slightly and held my ground. "Watch it, baby girl. One day you're going to push me too far and I won't care how much trouble I'll get in."

He stalked off and pointedly sat down at a table about ten feet away. He would still hear everything. I shrugged because he was probably right. I'd push him too far one day and we'd throw down. Part of me was looking forward to it. I hadn't killed anything in a couple of months and the wolfy part of me was getting bloodthirsty. Tonight, however, I was going to have to settle for having pushed him back.

Alan peered back at Trent, wariness plain in his eyes. There was a fine tremble to his hands when he picked up his beer and glanced back at me. His lips turned down in a sullen frown.

Now we could get down to business. "There, now that the hall monitor is gone, we can talk."

"Don't know what you want to talk to me about," Alan replied, staring forward.

So he was going to be stubborn. "I want to talk to you about Scott."

The trembling was a bit more than fine now. Alan had to force his hands to stop shaking. He set down the beer bottle. I could practically feel the frustration pouring off him in waves. "Since when do you give a shit about Scott?"

I didn't. I firmly believed the world would be a better place without him. He was a case I was getting paid to solve and nothing more. So why did I say what I said next? "I care about Liv, and she cares about Scott."

It really should be easier to hold a mean grudge. I consider myself a tough chick. Just three months past I killed an alpha and two beta wolves. Shouldn't that chick have a hard heart? Hell, apparently I came from a whole line of hardened killers who had to be caught early or put down hard.

But I was also my father's daughter and he hadn't been typical, either.

"You haven't acted like you care about Liv." Alan pointed his beer bottle at me. There was a lot of accusation in that half-finished malt liquor. "She says you won't talk to her. She's been crying about it and shit. I don't understand chicks."

"Obviously." I didn't like the thought of Liv crying. The truth was, Liv could easily have been convinced that what she did was best for me. Donovan and Quinn could have told her any number of things that could happen if she didn't get me to comply. I would rather she had told me what was going on, but there was a real possibility that she thought it was for the best. I shoved aside the thought. "Have you talked to Scott lately?"

He shrugged and I noticed the way his shirt hung off his thin frame. I hadn't seen Alan in a couple of months. We weren't close or anything, but I think I would have noticed if he'd joined a diet group. He used to have a nice beer belly going. Today, he was painfully thin. Like an emaciated supermodel without the pretty face.

"I see him from time to time." Alan's eyes shifted from the bar back to where Trent sat. They moved quickly, as though not wanting to miss anything. "He works a lot."

"Yes, I heard he got a job managing the bar at the new club downtown." I saw now that I had to treat Alan like any other reluctant witness. The trick with witnesses is to stay calm. You have to give them a nonjudgmental place to talk. Deep down, they all want to tell their story. They might give you a sob story about not wanting to get involved. Don't listen to it. It's crap. Everyone wants to be the center of attention, and that's what you have to make them. It also helps if you know something about their nature. "It sounds like a pretty good gig to me."

Alan liked to correct people. It gave him a sense of superiority. If I wanted him to talk, I had to give him a reason to. "What the fuck do you know, Atwood?" I didn't correct him on my new surname. "It's a piece of shit job exactly like the rest. He thinks he's hot shit now that he's working for Julius Winter? That dude's no better than Quinn, maybe worse. Scott doesn't go out anymore. He's always working, and for what? He's not making good money, and he has to put up with all the..."

Alan clammed up and fast. His face went white. That look on his face told me Scott was in serious trouble.

"I can help him." I kept my voice quiet. I didn't want to spook him further, but I needed to point a few truths out to him. "Do you know what I am now, Alan?"

"You're the *Nex Apparatus*." Alan whispered as though he didn't want to say it too loud.

"I am the king's death machine." It was what *Nex Apparatus* meant in Latin. "I'm a Hunter. Whatever is hurting Scott, I can kill it. I just need to know what I'm getting into. What kind of creature is this Julius Winter?"

Alan stood up and started to scratch at his chest as though he couldn't help himself. His hands moved in paranoid twitches. Sweat ran down his brow despite the fact that Ether was always kept at 70 degrees. "He's a rat fink bastard is what he is. You know what they do? They give you some and it's awesome. I mean, it is seriously amazing. Like nothing before."

I was still and schooled my face into a passive expression. I got the feeling that whatever they were giving away at Brimstone, it wasn't coupons for happy hour specials. Someone was dealing and Alan was high. If it was affecting a supe this way, it was some powerful shit. Supernatural creatures metabolize drugs differently. Faeries can handle their liquor, but not hard drugs. Give a werewolf or a shifter a shot of heroin and they'll just get pissed off you used a needle on them. Whatever this was, it wasn't a street drug. "Did they give you a little taste and then try to charge you through the roof?"

Alan's red-rimmed eyes filled with tears. "You have no idea. I needed it, you see. I had to do it. I didn't want to sign anything. And I don't want to do what I have to do. But, Kelsey, if I don't, they'll cut me off. Please tell me you understand."

He looked so lost standing there, scratching at his own flesh. He didn't even realize his claws had come out. He'd scratched through his shirt and thin lines of red dotted the ruined fabric. Someone had to talk him down.

I turned to look for Marcus because no one on the planet was better at persuasion than my lover. "Wait here for a minute, Alan. I know someone who can help you."

I was turning to cross the distance that separated us. Marcus's head came up, sensing I needed him. He stood with a curious expression on his face. Donovan glanced up as well, his eyes following Marcus's line of sight.

"No one can help me, bitch." Alan snarled as his claws sank into my arm. Pain shot through me as he turned me around with a twist. "But killing you might buy me some time."

His free claw swung in an arc that was meant for my throat. That claw was coming for me and it would split my jugular and then no amount of Marcus would likely stop me from bleeding out. I pulled away with all my might, something that should have sent weak-ass Alan across the room. He held me tight. I barely managed to avoid getting my throat slit. Alan's claw did damn near take out my eye, though. He dragged his sharp nails across my cheek, gouging deep. I felt every inch of that tear.

I kicked out to get him off me and landed on my ass because Alan was already being assaulted on two fronts. Trent had his clawed hands around Alan's neck. Somehow, Alan seemed to be pulling away from the big alpha. He couldn't get away from Marcus, though. Marcus didn't need to lay a hand on him. Alan stopped trying to pull away from Trent. His eyes went blank and glassy and his hands suddenly sank into his own belly. Blood began to flow from the wounds.

"Marcus, stop," I yelled. Well, I tried. My face was totally fucked up and apparently having working muscles aids in the yelling experience.

All around me the club was coming to a standstill as the blood started to flow. Quinn was on some sort of walkie-talkie and security had been called. Donovan was suddenly standing next to Alan, and I hadn't even seen him move. He had his hands on Alan's, trying to pull them away from his bleeding belly.

"Trent, take his left hand," Donovan ordered.

Trent joined the effort, pulling at Alan's claws.

Marcus's eyes had gone pitch black, his face a mask of pure rage. He stalked toward me. I could see his mind was still inside Alan's.

"Marcus, let him go." The king was yelling now. He appeared to be having trouble holding Alan's hands away from his body. You have to understand. I'm talking about the King of all Vampire. The dude's kind of super strong, and he wasn't able to break Marcus's hold.

My vampire lover said nothing, merely tightened his fist, and Donovan was swearing again as Alan renewed his attempts to gut himself.

"Marcus, please." I put my hands on either side of his face. I needed him to focus on me. While the idea that his brain could trump Donovan and Trent's brawn did something for my girl parts, I had other problems to consider. First, getting clawed by a hopped-up-on-freaky-drugs shifter hurt like shit and second, I still had a job to do. "I need him. You can't kill him. He has information I need."

"He cut you." Marcus's fangs gleamed in the low light of the club. "He would have killed you."

"And you can fix me," I promised. "But if you kill him, I can't get what I need out of him. Please. This is important to me, Marcus."

The vampire flashed his fangs and waved his right hand in an almost dismissive manner. Alan went limp, like a marionette who'd had its strings cut. Donovan and Trent had to catch him before he hit the floor.

Marcus gently pushed my head to one side, studying what Alan had done to my face. It hurt like a motherfucker, and I was pretty sure my face was a mask of nastiness. Blood flowed freely down my neck and on to my chest. My lover's face turned savage. Not killing Alan had been an indulgent act on his behalf, and one it looked like he regretted.

"Does it hurt?" Marcus asked with a frown. I knew he was deciding how much blood I would need and if he should do it here.

"Not bad," I lied, trying to smile. The muscles on one side of my face didn't work anymore, but I knew he would prefer privacy. I would, too. For some reason, I didn't want Trent to watch me sucking on Marcus's chest. It's weird, but knowing he would watch made me pause.

Marcus shook his head and took my hand in his. "Liar. Come along. It isn't serious. We'll fix it upstairs. I believe you will find the king now desires a word." The king was, indeed, towering over me. Marcus waved him off. "Upstairs, Daniel. I need to take care of her, then she can answer your questions."

Donovan nodded. He obviously didn't like it, but he let it go. I seriously doubt he would allow his wife to answer questions while she was bleeding and half her face was slowly sliding off her body. "Fine. I'll be up at your place in fifteen. I've called Henri and Alex. They're the best doctors we have."

Marcus started to lead me away. I turned back, trying to speak to the king. "He's on something. I need a toxicology report. Also, check his clothes and shoes to see if we can tell where he's been in the last twenty-four hours." Something was seriously wrong with Alan and his body was my best evidence. "Maybe I should stay here until Henri gets here."

Henri Jacobs was a doctor and an academic. He was also Marcus's friend. I didn't mention the other doctor. I'd been hoping to avoid Alexander Sharpe entirely.

"It's fine, Miss Owens," a softly accented voice said. Henri pushed his way through the crowd. His beautiful wife was behind him. Kimberly Jacobs had an ice pack in her hand. Henri looked at me and frowned. He nodded to Marcus. "Make sure she gets enough. I would not want that to scar."

"Here." Kim handed me the ice pack. "It'll take the sting out until Marcus can fix it."

I thanked her, putting the cooling pack to my face. Henri assured me he would get everything I needed. Marcus had enough of my stalling and simply lifted me up and started for the elevators.

As we passed Dev Quinn, it was hard not to notice the look of utter satisfaction on his face. I made a mental note to ask Marcus what he'd meant with that crack about "so-called destiny."

Ten minutes later, I sighed as I pressed my mouth to Marcus's chest and the rich velvet of his blood flooded my body. It was almost like a dark, deep chocolate, and I couldn't get enough of it. At the heart, of course, it isn't the taste that keeps you coming back. It's what it does to your body. That blood gives you a hint of the vampire's strength. You feel happier, safer, more alive than you could ever feel without it. It was the best drug I'd ever tried, and in my fucked up youth, I'd tried them all.

"Keep drinking, *cara mia*," Marcus said.

I knew if I could see him, his fangs would be large and his eyes big and dark. It's pleasurable for a vampire to share blood. If we had time, I was sure we'd make love again, but I could already hear the living room filling up with people.

Marcus's hands loosened around my hair, his signal that I'd taken enough. He wasn't telling me I had to stop, merely that I could when I wished to. I took one long last mouthful and licked the hole on his chest. The minute I stopped sucking, it closed as though it had never been there.

"Better," he proclaimed after carefully studying my face.

He kissed my forehead, and I glanced at myself in the mirror. If it hadn't been for the blood on my skin and clothes, you wouldn't know I'd been in a fight at all. I regretfully pulled the sweater off and turned on the water in the sink. I had blood from my cheek to my neck and across my shoulders. Marcus's eyes darkened, bleeding out until there was no white left.

"Baby, we have a whole roomful of people waiting," I tried pointing out.

The king and Quinn were both out there. Trent and a security team had followed them. As soon as Henri Jacobs knew anything, he would be on his way up.

It didn't matter, though, because I was now half naked with a vampire attached to my neck. Marcus sat on the marble counter of the bathroom and wrapped himself around me. He licked the blood from my skin with long, luxurious strokes of his tongue.

There was a short knock on the bathroom door.

"Kelsey, are you okay?" Liv's voice was thin and reedy.

"Go in and see for yourself," another feminine voice insisted. "Is Marcus decent?"

"He's clothed," I replied as he tightened his legs around me. He fully enveloped me, and he wasn't letting go.

"Good." The Queen of all Vampire pushed her way into the bathroom. Her eyes widened at the sight that greeted her. "Well, I suppose that was inevitable."

Liv's mouth hung open for a moment. "Oh, my god." She held up her dainty handbag. "Do you want me to...I don't know...detach him from you?" She turned to the queen for support. "Can I do that?"

I didn't think going after one of the most powerful vampires in the world armed only with a Coach bag and righteous indignation was a good idea.

Zoey Donovan-Quinn smiled and shook her auburn hair. "I wouldn't advise it."

"Is this normal?" I asked as Marcus pulled my hair gently to get better access. There seemed to be a spot behind my ear he'd missed.

"Oh, yeah," the queen said with a negligent wave of her hand. "Daniel does it all the time. If I nick myself while shaving, he comes running." She took a seat in the upholstered chair attached to the vanity. "So, how was Venice? Lee said you had a good time."

Marcus licked my cheek with a sexy groan. I was sure he knew there were other people in the room, but he didn't seem to care. He scraped his fangs along my skin.

"It was really nice. I've never been out of the country before," I replied because I couldn't think of anything else to do. "Marcus took me all over the city. I saw the San Marco piazza, but I had to make Marcus go away before the pigeons would land on me. They didn't seem to like him. Is he going to stop any time soon?"

"When the blood's gone," Zoey explained as though she was talking about the weather. She got up. "And then he'll probably do that thing where he listens to your heart. Let him. It soothes them. I'll let Daniel know it's going to be a while. Liv was freaking out. We were having our monthly Bunco session and, of course, someone had to rush in and tell us you had been horribly mauled by a rabid shifter. And I was winning. I never win. I think Neil cheats somehow. One day I'll figure it out." Zoey opened the door. "Oh, and if Danny starts like yelling or something about how long it's taking, don't worry about it. Take your time. His bark is way worse than his bite." She smiled brilliantly. "His bite is actually quite nice."

Liv stood back, her cheeks pink with obvious embarrassment. "I'm sorry I interrupted. I was worried. Are you sure you're okay?"

I gave her a thumbs-up. "I'm good. He got in a good swipe with those claws. Damn near took out my eye. Marcus fixed it."

"I'm glad to hear that," Liv said awkwardly. "Oh, good, he's done with the blood part."

Marcus's head came up and he caught me with his pitch-black eyes and hopped down from the counter. Without a word, he took my hand and sat down in the chair previously occupied by the queen. He pulled me into his lap and immediately shoved his ear right over my heart. His arms wrapped around me and I could feel his heart start to beat in time with mine. Soothing. I was calming as he did.

"See, that's freaky," Liv said.

"He's a vampire," I pointed out. "And honestly, compared to Gray he's practically normal."

Marcus growled low in the back of his throat.

"And way better at making me happy," I said placatingly. I decided to not piss off the vampire, who had obviously had enough stimulation for one night. I decided to go with it. I stroked his hair and felt him relax against me. I turned my attention back to Liv. "How bad is it out there?"

Her mouth flattened. "They're all there, Kels. It's like a power player convention."

Marcus didn't look like he was moving any time soon. I threw my former BFF a pleading look. "You have to stall them."

"And how am I supposed to do that?" Liv asked. "They're vampires. I can't whip out some pigs in a blanket and call it a party. Though it would work with the wolves. You don't happen to have any of those mini sausages, do you?"

Marcus gave me one last squeeze and then released me suddenly. "I will handle the king, *bella*. You get dressed. You are feeling better?"

I studied that gorgeous face for a moment, my hands cupping his cheeks. I wanted to soothe him, but he seemed to be back to his calm self. If he'd done anything abnormal, he wasn't embarrassed by it. "I'm peachy now, babe."

"I'm feeling better myself." He set me on my feet. "Don't take too long. I have questions as well."

He nodded politely to Liv, slipped on his jacket, and left the bathroom.

Liv and I stared at each other for one long moment before we both dissolved into giggles. She walked over and threw her arms around me. After a second of hesitation, I hugged her back. The truth was I didn't have enough friends that I could give up on them so easily.

I had missed her.

"I love you, Kelsey," Liv whispered. "I'm so sorry about what happened. If I could take it back I would. I just…I miss you."

I nodded, surprised that I felt tears pricking the back of my eyes. I shrugged them off. "I missed you, too. I promise, I'll figure out what's going on with Scott."

"I know you will. I trust you."

I trust you—the three most burdensome words in the English language. They were certainly the three most likely to get me into trouble.

Chapter Six

"You know you could have avoided that scrape if I'd been where I should have been. I should have been sitting right beside you." Trent finally got his say in two hours later. I'd felt his eyes on me from the moment I walked out of the bathroom and into interrogation hell. Trent wanted to yell at me then, but he'd had to wait in line.

"And what would you have done?"

"Gotten in between the two of you and taken that freaking claw for you. He almost took out your damn eye." Trent's jaw was a tight line, and he studied my face as though checking for damage. "I supposed you used vamp blood to fix it."

"Well, I didn't want to let it heal on its own."

"If you'd let me take the attack, you wouldn't have had anything to heal," he insisted.

All of this served as a vicious reminder to never let my guard down. The last thing I needed was another lecture. The king was concerned I'd almost gotten my ass handed to me by a second-rate shifter who usually turned into a large Labrador retriever. It wasn't pretty because when Alan was drunk and he shifted, well, he's wasn't exactly housebroken. But that was neither here nor there. He shouldn't have been able to fight me at all. It should have been an easy one, two, and he's out. I'd received lectures on the subject from Donovan and Marcus.

For the first time I could remember, they were working in complete harmony. It was fucking up my life.

And every minute they lectured on, the clock ticked away. After a while, they settled into Marcus's office with Quinn, Henri Jacobs, Alexander Sharp, and Hugo Wells to discuss revising my training schedule. It was great that I hadn't even started but I'd managed to fail. Now I had exactly thirty minutes to get the hell out of here if I was going to make my meeting with the demon. I tried yawning.

"I'm not saying you're not good. You got him talking. I was impressed with that, but I should have been there. If I'd been where I was supposed to be, I would have handled him for you, Owens," Trent was saying.

My eyes narrowed. "Who the fuck do you think you're dealing with, Wilcox? Do you think you need to come in and save the little girl from the big bad shifter?"

"Obviously," he shot back, leaning forward. He didn't have issues with getting into my personal space. "I don't buy that crap about you being a real *Nex Apparatus*. That's all political. You shouldn't be put in those situations. You could get hurt."

"Welcome to the twenty-first century, meathead. I can take you down any time I want." Trent was an alpha, but he didn't want the responsibility of his own pack. I could still handle him. I had no doubt about that. I just didn't have time to tonight.

He laughed at the thought. He sat back and crossed one leg over the other. "Keep believing that, sister. You couldn't handle a weak-ass shifter tonight much less me. I suppose you could always call your boyfriend in. When you're two thousand freaking years old, I guess you learn a few tricks."

"Asshole," I said, getting more pissed off than I probably should. He was irritating. "Do you think I didn't see the way the king came to your aid? You didn't even have the strength to hold the shifter's hands still."

Trent frowned, his face going stubborn. "That was Vorenus. He might be an academic, but he's a badass when he wants to be."

"I don't think so. It wasn't all Marcus. Alan was stronger than he should have been. He was on something and it was strong. Maybe it was like PCP for supes."

"He smelled funny," Trent allowed.

He had my attention now. "Funny how?"

The wolf shrugged. "He was sweating a lot, even though it was cool in the club. His sweat smelled, I don't know, sweet. It was his scent, but also something else."

I processed that information. I was sure it was a drug. I needed to ask Gray's brother if he knew anything when I talked to him tonight. If I talked to him tonight…

The door to Marcus's office opened and the men filed out one by one. The king walked straight up to Trent and motioned that it was time to leave. "Let's go, Trent."

The big wolf turned from his boss and back to me again. "I think I'll stay, Your Highness. I'm going to back her up tonight."

"I thought he was the one who sent you in the first place," I pointed out, confused at why he had to tell his boss what he was doing.

Donovan shook his head. His eyebrows shot up. "She's the *Nex Apparatus*. Why does she need backup?"

Quinn moved in and whispered something directly in his partner's ear. Donovan didn't look like he believed whatever the faery had said. "Are you serious?"

Quinn smiled and shrugged. "To each his own."

"Okay, now I remember." Donovan seemed willing to go along with whatever Quinn had proposed. "I gave the order, but she'll be fine tonight. You can…back her up…some other night. Tonight, we're leaving her in the capable hands of the academics. They have full control of her training now."

Trent stood up. I noted he managed to respect the king's personal space. His big hand pointed toward me. "Your Highness, she's up to something."

The king stared at me for a moment. "You up to something?"

"Probably," I admitted with a shrug. He would never believe an innocently worded protestation. Not coming from me.

The king sighed. "If you have to kill someone, please do it quietly. Otherwise, sign in and out with the doorman. If you're going out tonight, I really would feel better if Trent went with you."

I gave yawning and stretching the old college try. "Your Highness, it's my first night back. I want to get some sleep."

No one actually looked like they were buying that line of bull. Marcus had excellent timing, though.

"I will make sure my charge behaves, Daniel," Marcus promised.

"She's in excellent hands. We'll keep you updated on her progress."

Trent started to protest. He was cut off by the king. "Come on, Trent. Let's go downstairs and I'll buy you a beer. We should talk."

Donovan said good night and left with his contingent. I was left alone with the academics and one Alexander Sharpe. I didn't like Alexander Sharpe. You could say I took exception to his former career. In his human life, he'd been Jack the Ripper.

"Miss Owens, such a pleasure to see you again," the vampire said with a creepy smile on his face. At least, I think that was supposed to be a smile. He reminded me of a hyena getting ready to pounce.

Marcus's hand reached for mine. Previously, Marcus had attempted to trick Alexander into believing I was his mistress in order to provide me with protection. Alex had seen right through it. Marcus wanted there to be no question of our relationship status now. "Alexander, you have your orders. Don't you have something to do?"

The vampire, who happened to also be a doctor, politely bowed. "Of course, Marcus. I shall check in on our insanely high patient at my earliest opportunity. It was my pleasure to strap him down in the containment facility earlier. Hospitals these days are like luxury hotels. We did it right in the old days, you know. One little lobotomy and the problem was solved."

"You will follow Henri's directions as to care for the patient," Marcus said, his voice going hard.

Hugo Wells and Henri Jacobs took seats across from us. There was talk of a nice long meeting, and I panicked a bit. Marcus had promised I would behave. I needed to misbehave.

"Let me know if you need me," Henri said, dismissing the younger vampire.

Sharpe didn't look like he wanted to be dismissed, but took it with a nod. His eyes were on me as he left.

I put him out of my mind and focused on the problem at hand. "So, the king is giving my training to the academics?"

I scooted over to be closer to Marcus. It was an unconscious action on my part. At this stage of my training, I wanted to be physically connected to my trainer at all times.

"Yes, *bella*," Marcus said with pleasure. "The king has conceded that your training should come under our purview and no other. It is as it should be. I am your trainer, and Henri and Hugo are at your service. I believe you will find that Henri has forgotten more about medicine than most doctors ever learn."

"Though I am more acquainted with supernatural creatures, I'm also quite capable of treating a human," Henri said. He always spoke softly and with a hint of a Dutch accent. "I believe you're right about the shifter. He was definitely given something that enhanced his strength. We'll know more in the morning."

"And Hugo is a lawyer," Marcus pointed out.

Academics tend to get obsessed with subjects. Marcus's subject was history. It made watching any film set in a past era with him a nightmare of nitpicking. I preferred watching futuristic Sci-Fi as he couldn't point out the historical inaccuracies of the future. I tried watching *The Tudors* with him. He nearly had an apoplectic fit.

"That's good," I said, smiling at the English vampire. "I can use a lawyer in house. I'll probably need a good defense for some of the crap I'll pull."

Hugo smiled broadly, obviously enjoying the drama of the evening. I was glad someone did. "As your counsel, I would say the first, best line of defense is to not get caught. I suppose tonight will be a field test in our charge not getting caught." Hugo sat forward and explained my situation succinctly. "She needs to go to a club called Brimstone. I had not heard of it. According to her client, it is brand new."

"And apparently very exclusive," I added, thinking about the demon earlier in the day. He'd said I would need him to get in. At least I wasn't going to have to lie to Marcus to do it. It looked like academics stuck together.

Marcus contemplated the situation. "Do you know where the club is?"

I gave him the address and knew what was coming next. "I've been told I won't be allowed to bring you."

"Ms. Carey did not mention you wouldn't be allowed to bring a friend," Hugo said, puzzled.

Moment of truth. Either he trusted me or he didn't. I'd gone back and forth and finally decided I wasn't going to lie to Marcus. "Liv isn't the only reason I need to go."

I briefly related the story of my caffeine-loving demon and his claims that I needed to go help out a friend in trouble.

"Who is this friend?" Marcus's dark eyes narrowed. His voice was one big heaping dose of suspicion.

"Grayson Sloane." I reached for his hand. "Do you want to talk about this privately?"

"Should I be worried?"

"No, I want you," I assured him. "But he was important to me once. Can you understand why I would want to make sure he's safe?"

"We're talking about the demon Kelsey was involved with before she began her training?" Hugo asked.

"Yes, though he is only a halfling," Henri replied, watching me with no small amount of sympathy. "He managed to get past her defenses. A spell was used by another demon. I've been told Mr. Sloane had no knowledge of the spell at the time, but I'm certain Kelsey was hurt all the same. He's under a contract, a legacy."

"Ah," Hugo breathed, understanding the predicament.

I'd been told that Gray had been bred in the hopes his father could pass on his psychic powers to a son. Gray had the power, but he refused to use it the way his father wanted him to. I doubted he would have that luxury when he lived in his father's world. Gray's dad wasn't satisfied with him, though. He'd offered Gray a deal. Gray could have forty more years on the Earth plane if he produced a child with a Hunter. As I was the only Hunter in the world as far as anyone knew, and Gray had started seeing me before the deal was struck, Gray accepted, thinking he could use the time to find a way out for all of us.

I had not taken the news well.

"Kelsey, tell me you do not wish to start an affair with this man," Marcus said, his voice quiet, and I could feel his vulnerability.

I hugged him. "I don't. I told you. I want you. If you say the word, I'll pack up now and go straight back to Italy with you. I'll forget everything about this place and I'll be happy just being your mistress."

Marcus's lips quirked up briefly. "I doubt that seriously, *cara*. Somehow, I think you would be bored. Now, if you are going to go, do you intend to inform the king?"

I was surprised he hadn't put up a fight. "You're going to let me go?"

Marcus's palm came up to cup my face. "If you feel it's important, then I'm willing to trust you. We'll consider it a field test. I, personally, do not believe the king needs to be involved."

"Not at all," Hugo agreed. "This is a matter for academics. We need only call the king in if things go terribly awry."

"I doubt that will happen," Henri said. "We have handled many dangerous situations without the aid of a king. It raises the question, however, of how our Hunter is going to get out of the complex. Regardless of what he said tonight, I believe the king will attempt to monitor her. If he finds out she's left, he'll sic that wolf on her." He said something in Dutch, his lips curling up.

Marcus frowned and replied in Italian.

"What?" I asked.

Hugo chuckled. "Don't mind them. Henri is simply teasing your trainer. You'll find after a few hundred years of friendship, it's easy to poke at each other. We know all our soft spots."

And that was all I was going to get. It was easy for them to tease each other privately since they seemed to know each other's languages. "I'll find a way out without informing the king."

Marcus stood up and helped me off the couch. He went to the front closet and pulled out a jacket. I let him wrap it around me. He reached back into the closet and came out with a Browning automatic and two extra magazines. It seemed we had our own mini armory. "Knives?"

"Just the small one." It was only surveillance after all. It might have been hard to get weapons into Ether, but I doubted this place had the same rules. Marcus knelt down and strapped the knife around my ankle then helped me into my boots. It was cold outside and the boots were warm and allowed fairly easy access to the weapons hidden there. I zipped up my jacket. Marcus stood back up and his hands went to my waist.

"Be careful, *cara mia*," he said, touching his lips to mine. "Come home to me."

"I promise." I would. Marcus was the first person to trust me and he proved it by understanding I needed to do this and I had to go alone. He would be waiting for me, and it gave me an enormous amount of strength.

Henri promised to meet with me the next afternoon to go over what his lab discovered. I opened the front door and was surprised to see a boy in footie pajamas sitting across from the door, as if he was waiting. He had a Nintendo DS in his hands.

"Lee Donovan-Quinn," I said in my most motherly voice. "You should be in bed."

He smiled up at me and got to his feet. "But you have to go to that club and that means you need a way out without Dad knowing you're gone."

The kid was hell on wheels. I wondered how his parents had survived his toddler years and feared for a world in which he could drive. "I suppose you know a way out. What am I saying? Of course you know a way out."

His arrogant grin said it all. "I do and I printed out this map for you."

"How did you get the address?"

"Stole it."

I sighed and checked my back pocket. Sure enough, it was empty. "All right. Lead on, buddy."

Lee's chocolate brown eyes lit up like it was Christmas. "Let's go. It's really cool. You're going to love it."

I did not, in fact, love it.

I muffled my shriek as I went headfirst down the compound's laundry chute. About halfway down, I realized my folly. Seriously, when falling into a large vat of unwashed underwear, many belonging to werewolves, always, always go in feet first. One would assume that with heightened senses, werewolves would be very clean. One would assume wrong. Wolves aren't at all judgmental when it comes to the nastier smells. To a wolf, it's all one big bouquet. They revel in strong odors, as evidenced by their undies.

"Don't forget the cameras when you come back in," Lee shouted down.

I stared up and saw his little face craning forward to look down the chute. I knew beyond a shadow of a doubt that he wanted to slide down and join me. It didn't make any sense to him that he couldn't come along. I'd resorted to threats of not allowing him in my office to get him to go to bed. They were empty threats because I knew I would never follow through, but it had worked.

"But they're off now?" I needed that clarified.

"Yeah," the boy replied. "I turned them off myself. The dude at security will figure it out sooner or later. If the cams are moving or have a green light shining in the back, then they're on. I told you about the blind spots. Stay in them and Dad won't be able to see you."

Guilt gnawed at me. I was helping the boy go behind his parents' backs and probably not being a great role model. I'd never thought about being a model anything until I had to deal with Lee. I'd never been around kids I had any responsibility for. No one ever depended on me before.

"Go to bed, Lee," I said in my best big sister voice. "I'll talk to you about it after school tomorrow."

"Tomorrow's Saturday. I have a basketball game, but then I can come find you. Marcus didn't eat all the candy, did he? I only ask because Mama is bringing the snacks tomorrow and it's apples and mineral water. It's so embarrassing. All the other kids bring Gatorade at least. Mama read the label and didn't like the sugar."

"I promise he still has a bunch of junk for you," I said, climbing out of the basket. "Go to bed."

He grinned down at me in the darkness and then his face was gone. I studied the quiet room. At this time of night it was completely empty, the only light coming from the streetlights outside streaming through the small windows. The camera was right where Lee had said it would be, and the fact that it was neither moving nor had the green light Lee had warned me about gave me confidence. I shook my head as I realized how lucky I was the kid was on my side. I would hate to be up against him. I followed the short path he'd given me and in minutes, I was crawling out a window and falling gracelessly on my ass on the street below. I growled, got up, and let the night air wash over me. It was a cool, crisp January night and I reveled in the freedom. It had been months since I had been allowed even a minute alone. I breathed deeply and realized how much I missed this.

My father, my biological father, had been what's known as a lone wolf. It's a rare genetic anomaly in a world of rare DNA. Lee Owens had been stronger, faster, and more ferocious than a normal werewolf. It also made him different. While normal wolves prefer pack life, the lone wolf wants solitude. According to my uncle, my father fought the urge all his life. I didn't feel a desperate need to wander the earth, but I did need alone time. I hadn't realized how much until tonight.

The club known as Brimstone was twenty blocks from Ether and in a completely different universe. Ether is in the middle of what Dallas natives call the West End. It's surrounded by swanky hotels and hotspots. As I ran through the night, I realized that Brimstone was surrounded by something entirely different. The buildings took on an air of neglect in this part of the city. I opened my newly found senses and let my legs take me where I needed to go. Marcus had done more than merely teach me how to meditate. I'd spent some time with Italian wolf packs learning how to use my heightened senses. I'd had to learn how to access that wolf part of me without allowing her to take over.

I'd also learned how to run. The freedom I'd felt those nights I let loose and ran through the countryside with the wolves had opened something inside of me I hadn't known existed. The queen had told me I would find I "belonged" in wolf culture, and it had been true while I was in Italy. Marcus had stayed with me for weeks while I immersed myself in their lifestyle. I wasn't so sure how I fit in with the American wolves though. The Italians had appreciated my rarity. The Americans seemed to be suspicious of it.

None of that mattered as I gave my legs leave to do their worst. At this time of night, in this part of town, I could run freely. A human would most likely ignore me, thinking I was a stiff wind breezing by. My instincts were strong, and I hadn't plowed into anyone yet. Pure joy suffused me as I opened all my senses and let loose.

I'd easily memorized the map Lee had drawn for me. I had a feeling he was going to turn out to be a much more effective assistant than Justin Parker. I made the final turn and halted suddenly in front of the address I'd been sent to.

I also managed to surprise the demon waiting on me.

He gasped. I couldn't blame him. One minute he was alone and getting pissed off that I wasn't there and the next I was two feet away. It wasn't easy to scare a demon, but that was kind of the point of me.

"Hello," I said, enjoying the fact that he made sure I wasn't holding a weapon.

"You're late." Gray's brother was dressed in an open-throated dress shirt and neatly pressed slacks. His dark-brown hair was perfectly cut to frame his face. I wondered what he looked like in his demon form. He had perfect hold of this guise. Without the red tinge to his eyes when the light caught them, I would swear I was standing next to a human. From what I understood, Gray's brother was a full demon with none of that pesky mortal DNA.

"I got held up," I explained. "Some asshole on freaky drugs tried to take me out. Do you know who Julius Winter is?"

The demon nodded with an approving smile. "Gray said you were quite good. Julius Winter is the owner of this club. I don't know exactly what he's up to, though I suspect he's also the one pushing drugs about the city."

"He's a demon, then?" I studied the warehouse we stood outside. It was perfectly nondescript, like any of a thousand bland warehouses that dotted the city. From what I could see, there were very few windows and only the one door on this side. They definitely didn't want prying eyes.

"A very old one." He was looking me over and he shook his head at my clothing. "This won't do."

I straightened my nice black cashmere sweater, wondering what the hell he was talking about. It paired nicely with the gray slacks and tailored leather jacket. The outfit was perfectly respectable. "What's wrong with it?"

"You look like someone's sweetheart," the demon pointed out. "Does the vampire dress you himself? Are you wearing a chastity belt? I wouldn't put it past him."

I rolled my eyes. "I dressed myself, asshole, and Marcus trusts me. He knows exactly where I am and why I'm here."

"Does he now?" the demon said as though he was intrigued by that bit of information. "We'll see how he feels at the end of the night, won't we? Come along. I have your cover set up, but I need you to change clothes. The good news is, most of the girls change here anyway."

The demon turned and walked toward the warehouse. I stopped because I felt eyes on me. There was an abandoned building directly across the street, and I was sure someone was watching me from one of those windows. I didn't have time to figure out who it was though, since the demon wasn't big on waiting. I rushed to catch up and took my place at his side just as he held up his hand to knock. He caught himself and took me by the shoulders.

"You must remain quiet, Kelsey," he instructed. "Human women in this place are to be seen and not heard. Do you understand?"

"If I'm not allowed to ask questions, then why the fuck am I here?"

"I'm not saying you can't talk to staff if the occasion presents itself, but do not, under any circumstances, even look Julius Winter in the eyes. Once you get to the top level of this club, you must play your part or you'll get us all killed."

"Fine," I said shortly. Now I was really interested.

The demon knocked three times on the door in a sharp, staccato rhythm.

"What kind of club is this anyway?" I asked.

"A sex club, of course, dear," was the even reply.

Of course. What had I been thinking?

Chapter Seven

Matt straightened his tie as the elevator began its climb. I'd been told to refer to him as Matt. Obviously demons aren't normally named Matt. They get douche names like Hixelfrax and Beezle. Whoever names them is serious about the xs and zs. But Matt wasn't about to tell me his real name. On the Earth plane he would likely go by several aliases, but there was no way he was giving me the real deal. Demons jealously guard their real names. If you're dumb enough to try it, you can call a demon to your hand, but only if you know his or her real name.

His eyes slanted my way. "Stop fidgeting."

"You try having a piece of dental floss shoved up your ass and we'll see how you like it," I grumbled back.

I tried not to look at myself, but it was hard because the entire elevator was mirrored. Pretty sure I didn't want to know why they'd done that. I was just thinking about the fact that my ass was hanging out. We'd been allowed into the club after Matt had explained he'd procured me for his brother. I could tell the bouncer wasn't that impressed. He'd looked at me differently after I walked out of the dressing room. The demon had taken charge, briskly ordering me out of the nice clothes that covered me up and into lingerie. I don't even know if I could call it that. Marcus had bought me a ton of pretty, frilly things he liked to see me in, but they tended toward filmy nightgowns and beautifully made corsets.

I was dressed in a white lace demi-cup bra that pushed my boobs up and made them look a lot bigger than they were. There was the white thong currently stuck between my ass cheeks. Thigh-high white hose and four-inch stilettos completed the look. Gray's brother had brushed out my hair and placed a white mask over my face. I didn't know what I hated more, the shoes or the so-called underwear. I longed for my nice cotton bikinis and my comfy Uggs. Apparently both of those were a no-go in the house of sin Gray was currently residing in.

I was grateful for the mask as the elevator stopped on the fifth floor, and my heart started to race. I reminded myself that I was here on a case. I was going to make sure Gray was all right. That was all. I didn't have any interest in him beyond the fact that he was my brother's best friend and potentially had information I could use.

So why was my heart thumping as loud as the heavy rock beat that filled the space as Matt led me out onto the floor?

We stopped at an elegantly appointed desk. A tuxedoed man sat behind it, looking ever so competent. I was fairly certain he was a demon, but I couldn't tell if he was in his form or a borrowed one. Demons manifest on the Earth plane in two ways. Some can change their form, flowing from demon to human-looking in an effortless transition. Gray can do it, but I'd decided his brother was the other type. It's much more common for a demon to possess a human body. I hoped whoever Matt was inside had agreed to host him. There are humans out there who are crazy enough to do it.

"My Lord," our host said deferentially. His eyebrows arched as he looked me over. "Trying something different tonight, My Lord?"

Matt laughed as though the thought of hanging with me was the most ridiculous thing ever. "Not at all, Kevin. Let Tristan know I'll be requiring his services. This one is for my brother."

"Very good, sir. Lord Sloane does like slender brunettes," Kevin said, nodding us in.

We walked past the security desk and into some combination of a strip club and a place for swingers. All of the women were dressed in a similar fashion to me, though they seemed to favor leather and dark colors. I was the only one in the room wearing white. Naturally, every eye turned to me.

Behind my half mask, I studied the room. The space had been redone to resemble a grand ballroom. The floors polished hardwood and the room was lit with chandeliers. The walls had those white panels favored in European palaces. It had an old-world feel to it, if one ignored the stripper poles at the far end or the various women and men tied up and being spanked across the room. There was also a bar, naturally, and several intimate spaces with antique couches.

I turned and there he was. He was sitting on a couch, his big body lounging negligently. He was wearing tight black jeans and a dark shirt he'd left open as though he'd walked out of the bedroom without bothering to button his shirt. It left his perfectly cut chest on full, mouth-watering display. The tattoo that covered the left half of his torso looked sexy as hell in the low glow of the room, and I wondered if it still vibrated on his body after I left. His face was a tribute to masculine perfection. Marcus was the perfect European male, all fine lines and aesthetic grace. Gray was an all-American hunk of masculinity. He screamed dominant male and for good reason. He was and made no apologies for it. He was the kinkiest man I'd ever met. He preferred to tie up his sexual partners, and when I was that partner, I'd been happy to let him do it.

I was thinking about doing it right now.

His deep blue eyes glanced lazily around the room. He had a female at his feet, her head resting on his lap. He didn't seem terribly interested in her. He was talking to another man, whose face I couldn't see. He was smaller than Gray with almost white hair. Gray stopped midsentence when his eyes caught sight of me.

"You do seem able to catch my brother's attention, don't you?" Matt said, satisfaction oozing from his pores.

Gray sat up, and I noticed that his hair was longer than it had been when we were engaged. He used to wear it in a strict, military-style cut. It was a little shaggy now, reaching to the tops of his ears. It was thick and wavy. I'd always wanted to run my fingers through it. I flushed under his gaze, unsure if it was the outfit I was wearing or complete and abject shame that I had a man who cared about me and I couldn't help but think about someone else.

He was the ultimate bad boy. Grayson Sloane was a half demon who'd lied to me, used me, and had potentially tried to trick me into going to Hell with him. And I was shaking at the thought of his hands on me. I was also resolute. No matter how much I was attracted to the man, I was going to resist because I knew the score.

Marcus was good, and Gray was bad.

Gray was also observant. He stood up abruptly, his face going cold. He stalked across the room as another big man moved to intercept me. He was shorter than Gray, though he still towered over me. He didn't have great control over his form. His eyes gave him away. They flashed between red and brown.

"New girl, huh?" The demon's shirt was off and he had a girl on a leash trailing behind him. She didn't look terribly upset to be on a leash. I wondered how much she was getting paid. I hoped it was a lot.

"This one is for my brother." Matt attempted to dismiss him with an imperious wave of his hand.

"Oh, it's you," the man said, bowing at the waist. "I didn't recognize you, My Lord. His Lordship has enough pretty brunettes, don't you think? This one looks practically angelic. That's really not his style."

"I'll decide what my style is, Kall," Gray snarled at the smaller demon. "Go away and don't look at her again or we'll have a problem. Do you understand?"

Kall bowed from his waist again, his head down as he murmured, "Yes, My Lord."

Kall slunk away, pulling his girl behind him.

Gray turned to Matt, his face tight. "Explain yourself, brother. How dare you bring her here."

Matt's eyes had rounded as though shocked at our reception. "I thought you would be thrilled, brother. This is the woman who caused you such distress, is it not? Here she is. I didn't even have to threaten her. The moment she heard you were in trouble, she was scrambling to get here to you. There's no doubt she still cares for you. You know I can't stand to see lovers kept apart. I know the feeling too well myself."

"I'm not in trouble." Gray finally turned my way, his eyes starting past my knees and working their way up. I felt his gaze like a caress along my flesh.

The woman who had previously had her head in Gray's lap crawled across the room and attached herself to his leg.

"Don't leave, master," she begged prettily.

Gray shook his head, staring down like he'd already forgotten she existed and wasn't pleased to be reminded. "Go. Now."

He pointed to the elevators and she crawled off, her head hung low.

It was a disgusting display, and I wondered if that wouldn't have been me had I stayed with him. "Well, if you're not in trouble, then I'll feel free to get on with my life, Sloane. Matt, where are my clothes?"

The demon with the upper-crust British accent waved his hand. "Probably in the incinerator by now."

"What?"

He gave a negligent half shrug. "Well, they didn't suit you, dear. It looks like some old man picked them out, perhaps trying to de-tart his 'much too young for him' girlfriend."

Matt apparently didn't like my current lover. That was no reason for him to leave me without pants. "You asshole. How am I supposed to get home in this?"

"That's your problem, dear. I've done my level best to help. You can't expect me to solve all of your problems." Matt's mouth turned up in a slow smile. "And now my date for the evening is here."

A thin, young man with curly blond hair and blue eyes was walking toward us. He kept his eyes downcast and sank to his knees when he reached us. "My Lord, how may I serve you this evening?"

Matt studied the young man, his lips thinning as he reached out to touch his hair. "I'll think of something, Tristan. And tell the colorist your hair should be a bit lighter to get it perfect."

Tristan didn't look up, merely kept his head down. "Of course."

"Come along, now. I know public sex is all the rage here, but I prefer a bit of discretion. I'm going to take my sweet puppy somewhere private to play our games." Matt's face turned serious as he regarded Gray. "I'm making do tonight, brother, as I have every night for the last ten bloody years. The object of your affection is in your grasp. I suggest you don't let her go."

With that I was left alone with the man who had lied to me. I was left alone with the first man I ever loved. With the man I couldn't get out of my head.

"You're supposed to be in Italy." Gray made it sound like an accusation.

"I just got back yesterday." I really wished I had more clothes on. There was something super weird about standing around a foreign place wearing thigh highs, a bra, and a thong. It was a little like a nightmare I used to have. I noticed that the man Gray had been talking to was watching us now.

"So it only took you twenty-four hours to get into serious trouble," Gray complained.

It wasn't how I expected the reunion to go. I was the injured party. I was the one who had come to save him even though he'd treated me like crap. The least I expected was some gratitude. "I'm on a case."

"That's your excuse for everything, sweetheart," Gray said flatly.

Tears welled in my eyes and I fucking hated that. Only Gray ever made me lose control. That mask was coming in handy. I should have been happy. He was making it easy on me. I could go home to Marcus and cuddle up and know that I was in the right place with the right man. The time I spent with Gray had been a huge mistake. "Then it can be my excuse for leaving. I can see you have everything under control here, Sloane. I won't bother you again."

His hand wrapped around my upper arm and he drew me close to his body. Every inch of my skin came to life the second he touched me.

"You bother me every second of every day, Kelsey mine, and it's far too late for you to leave." He pulled me into the confines of his muscular arms. His mouth went straight to my ear and he whispered. "I'm undercover, sweetheart, and now you are, too. You know how to play this role. Keep your mouth closed and look submissive. Please don't fight me on this. I'm trying to keep you safe. You have no idea what you've gotten into. Play along with me and I'll explain everything in a while."

I nodded. I knew exactly what he wanted. I was capable of keeping my mouth shut when the occasion called for it. I'd been in the business long enough to know that listening was way more important than talking.

"You're a sight for sore eyes, gorgeous." His hands slid along the curve of my hip. "I missed you, Kelsey mine." He tensed, and I knew he was aware we were no longer alone. "Come along, sweetheart."

Gray turned with my hand in his. He acted surprised to see the tall, thin man standing behind him. I had a glimpse of what I could only call a walking cadaver. His cheeks were hollow, his arms bony. The dude could stand to eat a cheeseburger. Or four.

Gray pulled me to his side and bowed his head. "Your Grace, I apologize for the interruption. My brother brought me a gift. I was…excited at the prospect."

I felt my fingers tighten around Gray's and he responded with a reassuring squeeze. He knew exactly what had me freaked. There's a hierarchy in the demon world. Marcus had given me many lessons on how the demon world worked. Much like the feudal system, there were serfs and nobles. Gray's father was a bigwig in that world, so he and his brother were referred to as "My Lord" by lesser demons. The fact that Gray had called this demon "Your Grace" meant he was even higher than Gray's father. This demon was a duke. He probably got called into meetings with the big cheese himself. He was not someone I wanted to mess with at this stage of my career. I hadn't come up against even one baby demon, much less a duke.

The duke gave me an appraising look. I could practically feel his gaze crawling over me like a spider with icy cold limbs making his way across my flesh. "Well, Lord Sloane, I can certainly see where she would catch your interest. She's very pretty, but to me she looks a bit like all the rest. You must widen your repertoire. Some people are saying you've gone a bit soft. You were involved with someone last year?"

Gray tensed but his voice was slightly rueful. "Yes, I was. She was a werewolf."

So they didn't know who I was. That was a point in my favor and Gray's. It would probably look bad for him to have been involved with the king's *Nex Apparatus*. People are wary once they realize you have a nickname that translates to death machine. It doesn't have the same appeal as Cuddles or Snooki Bear.

The duke laughed lightly. "You do like a challenge. You'll have to tell me the story some time. I can see it has not had a happy ending or you wouldn't be in here with a different brunette every night." The duke reached out to touch me. Though it went against every instinct I possessed, I stood still and compliant. The touch of a single finger chilled me. I shivered despite the warmth of the room. "Perhaps you can help our Lord Sloane. He plays with the girls every night, but has yet to fuck a single one. I rather think he needs a good fuck."

"Don't we all, Your Grace." Gray gestured to the couch he had formerly occupied. "Could we continue our discussion? I find myself anxious to get business out of the way."

The duke smiled. It was creepy. It was one of those smiles people get right before they slit your throat. His hair was long and completely white. It wasn't so much a color in and of itself. It was more like the complete absence of color. It appeared soft, like if I touched it, it would dissolve. Those ethereal strands brushed the middle of his back. I'd only needed the briefest glance to see that his eyes were an icy blue. He held out his hand and I found myself following Gray back to the couch. I knew what I was supposed to do and began to sink down around his ankles.

"No," Gray said sternly. He indicated his lap and pulled me close when I hesitated. "When I give an order, you follow it, sweetheart. Unless you would prefer I redden that pretty ass of yours in front of the room."

I wanted to slap him silly. Only like one percent of me was curious about the spanking part…but in private, of course. I nodded my assent, not wanting the duke to even hear my voice. The less he remembered about me, the better. I was already thinking about how I would cover this whole thing up. I didn't like to think of the lecture I would get from Donovan if he found out I spent the evening in the presence of a duke of Hell while wearing a thong and thigh highs, being publicly petted by a man he'd warned me to stay away from. I was fairly certain it wasn't the image the king wanted his law enforcement head to portray. In the end, I decided it was best to do what I always tended to do with the king. I would lie through my teeth.

"You'll get used to the lieutenant. He's got a thing about discipline," the duke laughed. He took a long drink of what looked like Scotch or whiskey. "I have a feeling about this one, Sloane. She's different."

Gray shrugged. He was playing it cool, but his hands slid across my skin as though they couldn't help themselves. He pressed his nose against my throat, breathing in deeply. His senses weren't a wolf's, but they were at least as good as a vampire's. I had no doubt he'd caught a scent he didn't like. As Marcus had spent the better part of an hour wrapped around me not too long ago, I could bet what I smelled like to Gray. His hand tightened on my leg. "I don't know about that, Your Grace. In the end they're all the same—just little girls with daddy issues."

Yep. I was going to beat the shit out of him when I got out of this.

"Perhaps." The duke sighed as a half-naked servant pressed a cigar into his hand. He lit the stub and the demon breathed in the aroma deeply. "Now, let's dispense with all the boring courtesies. Please call me Julius, and I'll call you Sloane."

"As you wish, Julius," Gray replied cooly. "We were talking about distribution, if I recall."

"So you believe you can move my product more efficiently?" Julius asked.

My ears were now fully engaged. Alan had mentioned this Julius person earlier. I was sure the product he referred to was the same thing that turned lazy Alan into a crazy psycho killer. I would love to get my hands on some of that shit.

"You're doing a good job with the club downstairs," Gray allowed. "It's an excellent way to bring in the outliers, so to speak. There are plenty of supes out there who prefer to remain off the king's radar. The minute you step into Ether, you're on it. However, you're severely limiting your clientele if you only disperse Brimstone here."

Julius Winter smiled and leaned back, crossing one long leg over his knee. "Tell me something, Sloane, have you tried my product?"

Gray's face split in a humorless grin. "No. Would it even have an effect on me?"

"You might get some high off of it," Winter said. "Other than that, I doubt it. I try it from time to time to check the quality. I have a human company formulating the drug. I find it so much neater than operating in a trailer somewhere. If the human authorities ask, Dellacorp has all the paperwork to prove it's an experimental drug. Unfortunately, they cannot handle my distribution."

"Do you have any idea how many supes I deal with on a regular basis?" Gray asked, playing with my knee. "I handle the dregs, but I also deal with the power players."

"I've been told the so-called power players on this plane aren't fond of you, Lieutenant," Winter said with raised eyebrows. "I like the idea of having law enforcement on the team, but I worry about your effectiveness. Arresting the king's boy toy on a regular basis hasn't made you popular."

I bit my lip because the idea of Quinn being Donovan's plaything was super funny.

"I've left Quinn alone for the last couple of months," Gray replied. "I'm done trying to play good cop. It doesn't work with that crowd.

Look, we all know the king is going to cancel our contracts when they come up. It's time to figure out which side we're on."

"And you've decided to come back into the fold?" Winter sounded suspicious.

Gray leaned forward. His blue eyes were almost purple now. "Being good's gotten me nowhere. I'm done fighting my nature. When Donovan cancels the contracts between our people, fighting will break loose. When the war comes, I will be at my father's side."

Winter's long fingers tapped against the cushion. "I dined with your father a week ago. He's convinced. He says you've been practicing your talents. He's pleased with your progress. You saved him a lot of trouble by pointing out the men on his staff who were plotting to betray him."

"If we're going to take down the vampires, we can't continue to fight among ourselves," Gray said. "We have to band together if we're going to win."

Winter regarded Gray and seemed to come to a decision. "I agree with you, Sloane. We won't win the coming battles if we continue to war with each other. I think you and your brother can help me. You boys make a good team. Your rough masculinity along with his gentler hand could prove formidable. I'll think on this and meet with you again. I would like to introduce you to my human partner. Come to dinner the day after tomorrow. Bring your brother and perhaps your lovely submissive."

Gray nodded as the duke rose. He let Gray know he could remain seated with a graceful gesture of his hand. He completely ignored me. "And Sloane, I heard a rumor that Vorenus is back in town."

Gray frowned. "I can confirm that for you, sir. He's definitely here in Dallas."

Winter sighed. "I'd rather hoped the rift between the king and Vorenus could be made permanent."

"He's an academic," Gray said. "His mental powers don't work on our kind."

"Spoken like a child, Sloane. Don't underestimate the academics. They might not be as strong as the warrior classes, but no vampire has held power without their support. If you separate the king from the academics, his reign will be a short one. If we manage to dethrone Donovan, the vampires will be in utter chaos." Winter was quiet for a moment, his hands steepling as he thought. "The rift was because of the king's daughter, correct?"

"I believe so," Gray replied.

I went still because this might not be about the case I was on, but I was interested. I'd never had the reasons for the fight between Marcus and the king fully explained to me.

"Yes," Winter said. "The girl is a companion. I seem to recall some prophecy about Marcus and a girl of the queen's line. Try to discover what you can about this. If we can use the child to get Vorenus out of the coming fight, it would be to our betterment. Perhaps if the girl went missing, the king would blame the academic. It wouldn't be the first time a vampire stole the companion he wanted. We will discuss it further. I'll see you on Sunday evening."

Gray nodded his assent and the duke walked off. The minute the elevator closed behind him, Gray stood and set me on my wobbly feet. I felt sick at the thought of…all of it. There really was a war coming, and the demons weren't planning on playing fair. I was staggered at the thought of what an all-out demon war would mean to the plane. Humans would be caught in the middle, and once they realized what was happening, no place would ever be safe again. Supernatural creatures might be stronger than humans by far. Even weak supes can take out a human without much trouble. Single humans, even a group, were easy to deal with. But if we were exposed, we would be dealing with roughly three billion people who weren't known for welcoming new ideas with open arms. They tended to use bullets, and our strength wouldn't save us.

I wasn't going to be able to lie to the king this time. I stared up at the man I'd been engaged to and wondered if we would be on opposite sides in the coming war.

"Don't look at me like that," he said under his breath. A servant approached. "I'm going to need a privacy room. Which one is available?"

The servant pulled out a set of keys and handed one to the lieutenant. Gray dismissed him and pulled me along. I supposed this was the part of the evening when he yelled at me. It was a recurring theme with the men in my life. I seriously needed some more girlfriends.

Gray slammed the door shut and immediately put a finger to his mouth. He let his eyes move around the room to let me know we were being listened to and potentially watched. "Get undressed, sweetheart."

I stared at him, my eyes wide. I wasn't willing to fuck him to cover up my presence here. I might be stupid, but I wasn't throwing away everything I had with Marcus so Gray could look good on camera.

Gray's mouth firmed stubbornly. He never did like to have his authority questioned. "We'll take a shower before we start."

He wanted to talk where we couldn't be heard. I frowned and gave him a no-funny-business look as I unhooked my bra. Gray's eyes were dark as he shrugged out of his shirt. The tattoo on his chest had been added to. The dragon seemed longer than it had a couple of months ago.

I happily got out of the shoes and was immediately reminded of how big Gray was. He towered over me. Marcus was a comfortable four or five inches taller than me. We were evenly matched when I wore heels. Gray had a foot on me and at least a hundred pounds. I always felt delicate and feminine around him. I averted my eyes as he got out of his pants and tossed them on the bed.

"Get out of the clothes, Kelsey," Gray whispered directly into my ear. "They're watching. They have eyes and ears everywhere, but they won't be able to hear us in the shower. I promise it's nothing I haven't seen before."

Gray walked into the bathroom, leaving me with a view of his spectacular backside. I reluctantly pushed the thong off. It hadn't been all that good at covering me up, anyway. I rolled the thigh highs down and followed Gray into the bathroom.

Nudity doesn't bother me. Not at all. Marcus would say it's the wolf part of me. If Gray Sloane had been anyone else, I wouldn't have the insane urge to cover up. My body was what it was—a tool to be used. Except it had been a way to express something with Sloane. For the first time in my life, I'd made love with a man and it had been beautiful and meaningful. We'd learned each other through kisses and touches, long nights spent wrapped in each other's arms. He'd played my body like a finely tuned instrument.

Gray was already in the huge shower when I walked in. I watched his big body as he stood under the spray. Every inch of the man was muscled, from his broad shoulders to his strong legs. His back was to me, but that didn't mean he wouldn't know I was there. His hand moved to his side, to the tattoo that now covered most of the left half of his torso. His head was down, as though he dreaded the coming conversation as much as I did.

"Does it still bug you? That dragon, I mean?" I opened the stall door and walked inside. He turned those nearly purple eyes on me, and I saw the wealth of pain there.

He frowned and his voice was way quieter than mine had been. "I haven't felt it since the last time I saw you. It hasn't moved. It hasn't heated my skin. It's been dead on me until the minute you walked into the door tonight. Now, it's practically vibrating."

I lowered my voice, following his lead. "It's grown."

"It does that sometimes. I don't know exactly why. It grew, but I didn't feel it. Well, not moving. I did feel something from it. It was overwhelming at times."

"What does a tattoo feel, Gray?"

His stare nearly bore through me. "Loneliness. It was lonely without you, and now it's trying to peel off my skin to get to you. Why did you come back?"

"My training in Italy was done." I shivered because he was taking up all the hot water. I couldn't help but stare at him. Grayson Sloane was a thing of beauty. "The king agreed to three months alone with Marcus, and then we had to come back."

"Is it true?"

"Which part?" I had to ask because there were a lot of things about my new life that Gray wouldn't like.

"Are you the *Nex Apparatus*?" The question ground out of his mouth like it was hard for him to even say the words.

I nodded slightly. He grimaced before slapping his hand against the marbled wall. I waited to see if he was going to put a fist through it. Things had a way of getting destroyed when Gray got angry.

"I should have taken you," Gray swore. "I should have picked you up and shot my way out."

"I wouldn't have gone with you." I wasn't sure that I was telling him the truth. I had been pretty desperate that day. Even knowing how he'd lied to me, I might have followed him.

"Of course not. I'm so sorry, Kelsey. I wish you weren't mixed up in all this. I thought Vorenus would protect you. I thought he would keep you out of this. It's the only reason I was able to walk away. It seems to me he simply took what he wanted without considering what was best for you."

"He didn't have a choice." I defended my lover. "Donovan wasn't going to let me lounge around Europe. Marcus cares about me. He's doing his best with what he's got."

Gray looked a little savage. His hand went to my throat, his thumb sliding down to my collarbone. And yes, I should have smacked that hand away, but it felt so good to connect with him. "Yeah, I bet he is. Tell me something, Kelsey. How long did he wait? How long were you out of my bed before he pulled you into his? Don't try to lie. I can smell the fucker all over you. He's been feeding off you."

"He's my lover," I returned just as savagely. "He's a vampire. Do you believe I would allow him to feed from anyone else? And Gray, I was in his bed the night I left you."

I was feeling mean. He'd been pushing me all night. It was time to get a little of my own back. I didn't mention I hadn't had sex with Marcus that first night. He'd held me while I cried over Grayson Sloane.

"Do you know what they've done to you?" Gray asked, his voice a low growl. "They've made you completely disappear. Any trace of you as a human being has been erased. You no longer show up on any computer system. You're a ghost, Kelsey. According to official records, Kelsey Atwood was never born."

"They don't want anyone to be able to trace me." Marcus had explained that the king would be taking me off the grid, so to speak. I had a fake license and passport under the name Kelsey Owens, but even she could disappear at the drop of a hat.

"There's a wedding planner in your old office. They closed your bank accounts, and now your house is under a holding company's name," Gray explained.

"I have a new account. It has plenty of money in it."

"And it's at Quinn's bank," Gray pointed out. "Quinn giveth, and Quinn can take it all away. Face it, Kelsey. They own you. You have a Council appointed lover and a Council approved life. If you deviate from the script they will take it all away, and you'll be left with nothing. I sit up at night and worry about it. I worry that one day you'll simply disappear because you won't be convenient anymore. You've gotten involved with people who can get rid of you in a heartbeat."

I didn't like the sound of that. I hadn't considered the fact that Quinn had control of my money, my property, my everything. I didn't even exist anymore. I wasn't about to let Sloane know that scared me so I did what I do best, I shoved right back at him. "And you're getting chummy with your father. I'm sure you know what you're doing. You're not in over your head or anything. Maybe you're happy in the family business. Tell me something. You planning on dragging some other idiot female to Hell with you now?"

Sloane gripped my arm and pulled me close. I could see his fangs gleaming in the low light of the room. They only came out when he was emotional or horny, and they definitely made an appearance when he was both.

"No, sweetheart, the only woman I intend to drag with me is you." He slapped at the marble again and growled as he rested his head against the shower wall. "How do you do this to me? I am not fucking like this. I know you'll never believe me but I've never been a possessive asshole with anyone except you." He turned to look at me, weariness stamped on his face. How many sleepless nights had he suffered since we'd parted? "Kelsey, I'm sorry. I had no right to make decisions like the ones I made. I thought I was doing what was best for us. I never intended to take you with me. I would never have allowed that to happen. Things got…crazy. I know you were under some powerful magic, but I wasn't. I've had to deal with the fact that I lost you every day."

He stared pointedly at me, and I knew he couldn't say it. He loved me, but he'd given up the right to say it. He'd given up the right to have me say it back.

He shook his head as if to clear it. "You're like a fucking drug, Kelsey mine. I can't work with you."

I pulled the towel off the rack because I was cold and sat on the bench. "Too bad. I told you before I'm on a case. Liv's boyfriend is missing, and this is the last place anyone saw him. He works here. I have to talk to him."

"No." Gray ran a hand through his wet hair to get it out of his eyes. "If you go into the bar, I doubt you'll walk out again. Someone will recognize you in there. Tell Liv I'll handle Scott. I have no idea how, but I'll handle him. Can't you see we have much bigger problems than that idiot getting addicted to Brimstone?"

"He's on the drug, too?" A pit opened in my stomach. I'd seen what it did to Alan. Scott wasn't my favorite person, but Liv would be devastated.

"They're all on the drug," Gray said sadly. "Julius's been testing it on his staff."

"What's in it?"

"I don't know," he said, frustrated. "Why do you think I've been trying to set myself up as a supplier? He'll let me use it, but I haven't gotten close to being able to take a testable amount off site. I would go ahead and use…"

"Don't you dare." I was shocked he would even offer to try. I didn't want him using something like that. We had no idea how it would affect him.

He smiled slightly. "It would likely have no effect on me at all, sweetheart. I'm a demon. My blood is strong enough that something like this won't harm me. Winter is trying to get supes hooked. I'll know more once I can get my CTU techs to test it."

"Henri Jacobs is testing a user's blood." I quickly told him what had happened.

"Jacobs is an academic. Dutch, I believe, turned sometime in the seventeenth century." Gray was an encyclopedia of knowledge when it came to the vampires he considered close to the king.

"He's also a doctor. He's certain he can isolate the drug. I'll let you know what I find out. If you can bring yourself to work with me…" I held a hand up because I heard the door open. It was the outer door. Someone was walking into the room we were in. "Someone's coming."

Gray picked me up, and suddenly my back was against the wall and he was arranging my legs around his waist.

"Moan," he commanded as he gripped my ass and started to simulate sex.

I played my part. I buried my face in his chest and held on for dear life. I could feel his erection rubbing against my stomach. His breathing picked up and I couldn't help but think about how good this had been between us. Gray had been the best sex I'd ever had. He'd been the first man to give a damn about me in bed.

I closed my eyes and thought about Marcus. Marcus was good for me, and I was good for him. Marcus and I worked. Gray and I would tear each other apart.

My hand went to his torso, running across his skin, feeling muscled flesh under my palm, and then an electric heat flashed through me.

Gray hissed and his head fell forward, and I could feel that dragon vibrating, begging for my touch.

"Please," Gray said.

I couldn't help it. I ran my hand along his tat, fascinated by how it responded to me.

Gray moved against me, his cock against my pelvis now, and I could feel the hard grind on my clit.

I heard the bathroom door open, and through slitted eyes I saw the servant from earlier sneak a peek in. When he realized what was going on, he gently closed the door and hightailed it out of there, most likely to report to Winter that the lieutenant was, indeed, breaking his celibacy.

After a moment, Gray let my legs slide down. I kind of wanted to punch him because I'd been close. A few more thrusts against my clit and I likely would have gone up in flames. I stood unsteadily as his hands shook. His forehead fell against mine, his hands finding my hips.

"They're watching me, Kelsey," Gray said. "If they think for a second that I'm lying to them, they will kill me. I don't think I have a choice about working with you. Winter pretty much ordered me to bring you to dinner Sunday night. Tell Marcus I need to meet with him."

"He'll love that." I didn't even want to contemplate how that conversation would go.

"I don't need the kind of trouble he can give me. He's your boyfriend, your lover, whatever. You're in a relationship with him. It's not fair to him to lie about it."

"He's my trainer. He knows I'm here and he knows I came to look for you," I said stubbornly. I wasn't some loose woman lying to my boyfriend. I was a professional on a job. Sure the job ended up with me simulating sex and wearing a thong, but I was a professional all the same. "He trusts me. I'll have him call you tomorrow."

Gray shook his head. "No, all of my phones are tapped. I'll contact him. And Kelsey, I'll go down and talk to Scott. I promise. I'll make sure he calls Liv. Okay?"

I nodded because it was all I was going to get tonight.

"Now, go get dressed," Gray said. "I need to get you out of here."

"What are you going to do?" I asked because he wasn't following me.

He smiled, but there was no humor in it. "I'm going to do what I have to do, Kelsey mine. I'll do what I've done since you left me. Walking around here with a hard-on the size of a Mack truck would probably raise suspicions. I'm supposed to be a satisfied man."

I nodded and closed the door behind me.

Chapter Eight

I had on Gray's coat as he escorted me through to the elevator. I'd cleaned up, but still had been forced back into the "clothes" Matt had given me. Only Gray's big coat covered up my near naked state. It swallowed me, and I was grateful for the warmth. It was January, and I shivered at the chill. It was extremely cold considering it was Texas. As Gray walked me through the lobby, I noted a light snow had begun outside. I looked up at the chilly night sky in wonder as it fell all around me. I grew up here in Texas so I've rarely seen it snow.

"Keep the mask on until you're sure no one's followed you." Gray surveyed the area around us, his whole body tight with anxiety.

I hesitated. I felt like I hadn't done what I'd come to do. Scott was right there. "Are you sure there's no way…"

"I am not taking you into that part of the club." Gray pulled me along as he crossed the street. I could see his pickup in the distance. "It's full of outliers—all the criminals who don't want to deal with Donovan are regulars in that club. Most of them are now addicted to Brimstone. You probably haven't met them, but I can't take the chance that one of them will know your scent or have seen your face. I don't trust Scott anymore, either. He's in too deep."

"I can't leave him there." I had no idea how I could go back to Liv without doing everything I could to save that asshole she loved. She couldn't help the fact that she had terrible taste in men. She also had wretched taste in girlfriends, and I would hope that wouldn't stop someone from saving me.

"I told you I would handle it, sweetheart," Gray insisted.

"And stop calling me that." It was hard to be around him. "Marcus won't like it."

Gray laughed for the first time that whole evening with genuine mirth. "He would prefer *cara mia*, I suppose." He grinned and it softened the hard lines of his face. "I might have a little fun with this, Kelsey. Vorenus can dish it out all day. It'll be fun to see if he can take it. The man isn't famous for keeping his hands off other men's women. Your boyfriend is quite the player. Ask the king."

"I'll take a pass, thanks." I didn't need to hear stories of how Marcus chased after Zoey Donovan-Quinn.

We were comfortably out of sight of the club. I slipped the mask off my face. Gray clicked a button on his keys, and the security alarm chirped on his truck. Something to his left caught Gray's attention and his head turned. He smiled, and I followed his eyes. My brother Jamie walked out of the abandoned building across from the club. He had a camera around his neck, and I had no doubt there was a gun in a holster under his coat. I smiled broadly and rushed to hug him.

"Kelsey Jean Atwood." Jamie picked me up and whirled me around. I hugged him tight. Most of my life, any positive male influence I'd enjoyed had come from this man. My brother. I loved him unconditionally. He might be my half brother, but Jamie Atwood had my whole heart. "I thought we'd never get you back in the States."

I smiled up at my big brother, who was six years older than me. "They had to drag me back kicking and screaming. I'm so international now."

"And you've stopped wearing pants," Jamie pointed out, looking at my bare legs with a fierce frown.

Gray sighed and reached out to shake my brother's hand. "That was not my idea in any way. I'm just as surprised as you to see her. Can you get her home?"

"Of course," Jamie replied, slapping his friend on the back. "I'll e-mail the pictures to you tonight. I got a lot of good shots, but I'll need someone to ID all those faces. I'm doing surveillance on Winter's place tomorrow."

"We're going in Sunday night, so get me everything you can," Gray requested.

"We?" Jamie asked, looking between the two of us.

Gray nodded, not looking pleased at the situation. "Yes, she's on his radar. He requested I bring her along to our business meeting. I have no doubt he's told my brother to come with Tristan. You know Julius. He wants his business partners to have wives or lovers. It gives him someone to threaten when he needs to keep us in line."

Jamie snorted. It was a family trait. "He's going to threaten my sister? He has no idea."

Jamie had seen me fight. He was a true believer now.

"The fact that he has no idea who she is, is the only reason we're still alive. Take him seriously, Jamie. He's a duke. His human form might be non-threatening, but he could kill her. Don't underestimate him. And I'll figure out what's happening with Scott. I don't want you going into that bar." Gray backed up toward his truck. "Take care of her, Jamie. And Kelsey, tell Vorenus I'll call him in the morning."

Gray got in his truck and with a final nod my way, turned the engine over and took off into the night.

Jamie stared at the truck as it sped away. "He's making a man-date with your boyfriend?"

I rolled my eyes. "No, it's about work. Why didn't you tell him I was with Marcus?"

He shook his head. "I'm not going there with him. Look, Kels, I did what you asked. I didn't leave him alone. We've managed to get back to being friends. He lost his damn head over a girl. I wish it hadn't been my sister, but we're good, Gray and me, as long as we avoid the subject of you. Nate, on the other hand…"

I brushed a hand through the air. The snow was starting to come down now, falling on my skin. "I don't want to hear about Nate."

Jamie's eyes narrowed, a sure sign he was irritated with me. "He's completely alone, Kels. He won't talk to Dan anymore, or Justin or Blake or Mike. He's been with those guys since he was seventeen freaking years old."

Too bad. I was the injured party. Everyone kept forgetting that. "I don't see how it's my fault."

Jamie took my arm. "If you would just talk to him. Tell him you forgive him. Kelsey, he thought he was doing the right thing for you.

Tell him it's okay to be friends with the same guys he's been friends with for years. I'm worried about him. He's skipping classes."

"Hey, he has a guilty conscience. It's not my fault he decided to betray me to his gaming group." I didn't mention that, at one point in time, they'd been my gaming group, too. I'd never met them in person. I played with them over the computer and they'd gotten me through many, many a lonely night. I knew the names they used when we played online games. Now I wondered which one Justin was. I would have to think about maybe not being so mean to him tomorrow.

Jamie frowned as he started clicking off talking points. "Yeah, you got a real bad deal out of it, Kels. Your life is rough, little sister. Let's see, Marcus sees to your every need. You work because you want to, not because you have to. You have an entire team working to train you to be some sort of superhero. Tell me, deep down, you don't like this. I remember your childhood. You and Nate spent all your time reading comic books and pretending to be X-Men. Did you ever think about how hard it was for him to realize his sister was the one with all the power?"

"If I could give this shit to him, I would." I was lying. Jamie was right on one count. I was getting comfortable with the strength and power at my fingertips. I kinda liked playing the superhero. And if Jamie had watched out for me while we were growing up, Nate had been my playmate. Nate was only a year older than me. We'd been each other's companions.

"So let's add up the score," Jamie continued. "Kelsey lives in a big, rent-free condo with her rich, powerful boyfriend, and Nate doesn't even have his gaming group anymore. How much does he have to pay?"

"Don't make it sound like I'm some sort of princess," I complained, surprised at his attitude.

"Marcus treats you like one," Jamie shot back. "Tell me something, Kels, when was the last time you cooked your own food or did a load of laundry? Does Marcus make you do the dishes?"

"No, we have staff." I frowned and knew I was probably pouting. "I also have to answer to the freaking king for everything. I'm basically his prisoner."

Jamie glanced down at my feet. "You seem to have forgotten your ankle monitor."

"I snuck out, okay."

His eyes were dark and judgmental as he stared down at me. "Like I said, you have a hard life. You haven't talked to Mom, either."

I wanted to talk to my mom even less than I wanted to talk to Nate. "She lied to me, Jamie. All of my life, she's lied to me. She lied to all of us."

"And she raised you," Jamie replied, his mouth firming with indignation. "She sacrificed for you. She took it every time Dad used her as a punching bag. Do you know how easy it would have been for her to have 'taken care' of the situation?" Jamie sighed and rubbed between his eyes. "I'll drop it, Kels, but I wish you would think about it for a while. I know what Nate did was wrong, but he loves you. He did it because he loves you. Mom loves you."

I thought about all the times Nate and my mother protected me. I pulled Gray's coat around my torso, trying to shove aside the fact that I really did miss them. Forgiving Liv earlier had settled something inside me. "It's not like she doesn't know I'm safe and stuff. I talked to you. I assumed you talked to her."

Jamie leaned against the light pole. "Marcus kept her updated."

"She's talked to Marcus?" He hadn't mentioned that small fact to me.

"Yeah, Kels. She called because she was freaked out and you wouldn't talk to her. You're her daughter. You can't go missing and not have her get scared. Marcus calmed her down. They've been talking once a week. He tells her you're okay and gives her the occasional story about the stuff you've been doing. I hope I'm not getting the guy in hot water, but he talks to Nate, too."

I had to think about that for a moment. Marcus hadn't tried to push my family at me. He mentioned them. He told me he thought I should reconcile and when I threw a temper tantrum at the mention of Nate's name, he let the subject drop. I hadn't asked him to ignore my family. "I'm okay with it."

Jamie nodded, relief on his face. "I'm glad because Marcus is a good guy."

I slid my brother a sly grin. "I'm surprised to hear you say that. I would have thought a vampire would be the last guy you would want me dating, much less living with."

He let loose a long sigh. "My standards have come way down.

Marcus can't get you pregnant in an attempt to please his father. He can't marry you, thereby obliging you to go to the Hell plane with him. He's practically the fucking boy next door in my book."

I chuckled at the thought, lacing my arm through my brother's and leaning against him. "But you and Gray seem fine."

Jamie sobered quickly. "He's my best friend. I've started to think of him as having a terminal illness. I kind of wish he could find a woman who would make these last years happy. I just don't want it to be my sister." Jamie straightened up. "Now, the way I figure it, I can do one of two things. I can haul your butt home or I could tell you that I've been casing this place every night for two weeks and I happen to know that Scott takes the trash out and has a smoke at three-thirty every night. I heard Gray mention you were looking to talk to him. This way you don't have to go into the bar."

I grinned up at my brother. "You're kind of awesome, James. Has anyone ever told you that?"

"All the time, sister," he replied. "And we won't mention this to Gray. Now tell me all about Italy."

Fifteen minutes later, I watched as the back door to the warehouse opened and Scott came out right on time. He'd been athletic in high school, and the vestiges still clung to him. Had he been a normal human, he would have gone to fat a long time before given his love of beer and lack of any kind of exercise. He and Liv had started dating in college, and he'd never left her couch until a couple of weeks ago. I thought he was a complete loser, but then it took one to know one. I wasn't sure how he would take me coming to save him.

He stared up at the air for a minute. He didn't seem as surprised by the snow as I'd been. He shrugged it off as though it was a nuisance. He pulled a pack of cigarettes out of his front pocket and was lighting it as he slung the big garbage bag over his shoulder. He started to make his way to the dumpster.

I stepped out from behind Jamie's truck. I was surprised he hadn't smelled me. It took him a moment to even register that I was standing in front of him.

"Kelsey?" he asked hesitantly.

"Hey, Scott, what's up?" Jamie was waiting inside the cab of his truck. I didn't want Scott to feel like I was ganging up on him.

Scott's brown eyes went all kinds of suspicious. "I thought you were gone."

We weren't big on conversation, Scott and I. "I came back."

Scott stilled. "Are you here to kill me?"

I sighed. I should get used to it. In the past, the *Nex Apparatus* had pretty much been an executioner. If I wanted people to not start crying every time I showed up, I better start rehabbing my image. "Scott, if I was going to kill you, you'd already be dead."

I probably wouldn't try very hard.

"You should get out of here." Scott nervously took a drag off his cigarette.

As much as I wanted to get home to my cozy bed and cuddle up with my vampire, I had a job to do. "Come with me. Liv wants you to come home."

"So she sent you after me?" Scott frowned, his face hardening. "Tell her to move on, okay? I'm done with her."

I didn't buy that for a moment. Scott wasn't energetic enough to find another girlfriend. He was completely dedicated to making Liv's life miserable 'til death parted them. "Tell her yourself. I'm under strict orders to bring you home. Do you know how much Liv will bitch at me if I come back empty-handed?"

Scott's eyes closed, and I could have sworn he was in pain for a moment. When he spoke, the words were ground out of his mouth. "I can't leave. Tell her I don't love her anymore, damn it. Tell her I have another girl."

He was lying, and that pissed me off. I decided to throw him off his game. I knew he only gave a shit about two people in the world. Liv wasn't doing it for him at the moment, so I tried door number two. "Alan Kent tried to kill me tonight."

The garbage bag dropped and the cigarette hung precariously off his slack lips. "He did what?"

I shot him a fairly sympathetic look. "Alan's in trouble. He's on something called Brimstone. It caused him to attack me tonight. Lucky for me, my boyfriend is better than a first aid kit. Alan's in the vampire version of a hospital. I don't think it's a pleasant place to be. Why don't you come with me so you can visit him?"

Scott stood in the concrete lot as the snow drifted down. After a long while he shook his head. "I can't leave, Kelsey. You have to go. There's nothing you can do. Just watch out for Liv."

I was going to argue when the door from the back came open again. The man Gray had called Kall stalked out, his face set in stark lines. Anger seemed to radiate from him. At least he wasn't dragging his girl by the collar anymore. He was alone and dressed to leave from the looks of it. His thick body and large arms were encased in a well-tailored suit that had likely been chosen to fit into the high society he was moving through. He had some issues with the whole blend-in portion of his costume since he was rapidly losing control of his form. I couldn't tell if he was a halfling, like Gray, or simply a young demon. I rather thought the latter. I also bet he wasn't high up on the royalty scale. Gray never lost control of his form. His fangs came out when he was mad or horny, but that happened with all demons. This guy's horns were peeking through his dark hair.

"You." He pointed a clawed finger at Scott. "Explain why the incredibly expensive bottle of Scotch I left with your staff is now half empty." He had the bottle in his hand.

I read the label, but it didn't matter. I wouldn't know the difference between it and a bottle of rotgut. I drank what the bartender put in front of me. I wasn't a connoisseur.

Scott sighed. "Sir, I run the bar in the club downstairs. You want Martin, who runs the VIP floor."

I got the feeling Scott didn't like dealing with the VIP guests. Knowing him the way I did, he would definitely be more comfortable with the shifters and weres in the regular bar. It made me seriously wonder what they promised him to get him to take this gig. He always wanted to run his own bar, but it would have nothing in common with the elegant club at the top of this building.

"Don't you fucking tell me what I want, you piece of shit slave," Kall said, throwing the bottle at Scott. It hit him squarely across the jaw and made his head swing back.

I'd been hoping I could get through this whole evening without a fight. Okay, another fight. When Kall walked up to Scott and slapped him, I knew that wasn't happening. Asshole needed to learn a lesson about how to treat staff. I might not love Scott, but I wasn't going to let him get his ass kicked over something like this.

"Don't touch him again," I said quietly.

"Stay out of this." Scott was looking down at the ground, his head held in a submissive position. His voice was low, almost pleading.

Kall was anything but submissive. He leered at me and smiled, his fangs on display. "Now why would we want the lovely lady to stay out of this? She's the only thing that's gone right all evening long." Kall lost interest in beating up the help and walked up to me. "What happened, honey? Sloane can't get it up, can he?"

"I don't want trouble," I said calmly. "Why don't you go find this Martin person and yell at him about your pilfered hooch?"

Kall shrugged. "Screw the booze, honey. I'd rather spend a little time with you."

"I don't think Master Sloane would like that," I said, remembering proper Dom/sub formality.

Kall laughed. "Nice. I wouldn't worry about Sloane, though. He won't be back for seconds. He's on a mission to play with every athletic brunette in the Metroplex. Just between you and me, he's pathetic." He put his hands on the coat Sloane had wrapped around me. "I can take care of you, honey. I promise I won't treat you like Sloane. I won't tie you up and leave you unsatisfied. I'll make sure you remember who your Master is."

"Take your hands off her." Jamie walked up from behind us, his feet sounding on the concrete. I knew he would have his semiautomatic in his hand, and it would likely be aimed at the demon's head.

Kall frowned as he regarded my brother. "Who the hell is that? Do you have a pimp? Winter said we wouldn't have to deal with pimps. We're supposed to be able to buy the girls outright."

Charming. I could add human…whatever trafficking to Julius Winter's many sins.

My brother moved beside me. "She's not for sale."

"You can't shoot him, James," I pointed out with a sigh.

I wished that jerk Matt hadn't taken my gun and knives. I wouldn't be able to use the gun any more than Jamie could, but the knives might have come in handy. The gun would be too loud. Someone would come to see what was going on and then the fight would really be on. The knives, on the other hand, would have been nice and quiet. I hoped Marcus didn't make me write a thousand-word essay on why a Hunter should never allow someone to take her weapons.

Kall was staring at my brother like he wouldn't mind getting to know him, too. "Yes, James, let's not be hasty. Why don't the three of us go inside and have a chat. I think we can come to an agreement that suits all three of us." He smacked Scott. "Get in there, slave. We'll need a privacy room."

Scott actually started to walk toward the door.

"Scott, you stay where you are," I said in my best alpha voice.

Scott stopped on a dime.

Kall didn't look pleased. "You have a problem with my orders, slave?"

"No, sir," Scott said, avoiding his eyes.

"Then why are you standing here?"

"Because she scares me more than you do," Scott admitted.

Kall threw back his head and laughed. He smacked Scott's face. "Watch this, son. This is how you handle a whore."

He reached out to grab me by the wrist.

"Do you have this, sis?" Jamie asked.

"I got it," I said surely as the demon pulled me toward him. I heard Jamie click the safety back on the gun. Kall pulled me into the circle of his arms.

"This is more like it," he said. I could smell the liquor on his breath. One hand held me by the wrist while the other started to make its way toward my ass. "You be sweet to me, honey, and I won't hurt you. Well, too much."

I made him no such promise as I brought my four-inch stiletto down as hard as I could on the bridge of his foot. It sank in about a quarter of an inch or so. I had to forcibly pull it out of his flesh. He started to howl, but that went counter to my game plan, which included a quiet and dignified exit. Also, I didn't want security on my ass. I punched up and caught him in the jaw, effectively silencing that first shout.

"Heads-up. I found a two-by-four." Jamie tossed it my way.

"Nice." I caught the board. It was good to have backup. Jamie was kind of the perfect guy for the job because he simply let me work. I smacked dumbass Kall across the face with my handy two-by-four, and he hit the deck. Several body blows followed. Kall managed to get exactly one punch in. He managed to hit my shoulder with all the force of a thirteen-year-old girl slapping at someone who took her boyfriend. I kicked him in the balls. Demons totally have balls and they like them dangling and not shoved up into their body cavities just as much as the rest of the male population.

The whole time Jamie yawned and stretched and generally let me know that when I was done playing, he was ready to go. I took the hint and pulled Kall's head into my hands. Marcus had taught me a neat way to internally decapitate an enemy. The loud crunch Kall's neck made as it twisted and broke proved I was a quick study.

I took a nice deep breath of cold air and tried to find Scott again. I'd lost track of him during the fight.

"He ran." My brother pointed toward the club.

Scott stood in the doorway. He stared out as though trying to make the decision to stay or risk running with me. His face was taut and his eyes downcast as he slowly shut the door.

Jamie shook his head and reached for my hand. "We need to go. You did your duty. You talked to him."

"Yeah, you should go," Kall said, looking up at me because he really couldn't do anything else.

"You're still alive?" That was disappointing to say the least. It goes to show you, if something seems too easy, it probably is. I kicked at him, trying to figure out if he was going to pop up and start chasing me. "Jamie, he's still alive. What am I supposed to do?"

My brother snorted and gave me a "what the hell" look. "I'm not some hotshot demon hunter. Don't look at me."

"Well, I'm still in training," I huffed in explanation. "Should I maybe cut his head off?"

"Do you have any idea how long it takes to grow another body, you bitch?" Kall growled. He was slurring his words. I wasn't sure if that was from the alcohol he'd consumed earlier or the fact that his neck bone was sticking out.

Jamie's eyes didn't leave the back door of the club. "Decide fast, Kels. Someone could be out here any minute. We don't know Scott won't turn us in."

There was only one thing to do. I couldn't leave him lying there. "Fine. We take him with us. Get his feet." I picked up his hands and his head hung precariously.

"Nice," the demon said. "I can see your hootchie."

Jamie neatly stepped on his balls as he went to pick up the demon's feet.

"Thanks, bro." Gosh, I'd missed Jamie.

"That's what I'm here for," Jamie said with a grin as we loaded our should-have-been-dead body into his truck.

Kall, who turned out to be a complete wuss, complained the entire time. He didn't like being stuffed into the trunk of an SUV. I thought it was extremely roomy myself, but there's no pleasing some people. If Gray had been driving me and my victim home, Kall would have been exposed to the elements. The snow fell fast and hard, coating everything. It made cool patterns on the windshield as Jamie quietly pulled out of the alley and began to make his way back to the West End.

Ten minutes later, Jamie pulled into the alley behind Ether. It was almost four-thirty in the morning and I still needed to figure out what to do with Kall. It was times like these I wished there was a Hunter loop. I could see the post in my mind.

This is Kels101 and I'm new to the group. Has anyone had to deal with a demon who won't die? He also won't stop talking. I doubt I'll be able to get him up the laundry chute, so I need options. Please help.

Yeah, there's no loop for Hunters since as far as anyone knows, I'm the only one. There was only one place for me to turn. I got out Jamie's phone to put a call into Marcus. He'd told me the academics were there for consultation. I'd had my first little hiccup. It was time to turn it over to smarter people.

"Um, Kels." Jamie's face had scrunched in that way it used to when we were about to get into serious trouble, and he pointed to my side window.

I turned and saw Donovan standing there, arms crossed and lips turned down. Trent stood next to him, shaking his head as though his disappointment was too much to contain.

"I told you she was up to something," the tattletale werewolf said.

Chapter Nine

I gotta admit, my first instinct was to tell Jamie to hit the gas, but the truth is Donovan would have just flown after us. Sometimes it's better to go ahead and rip that bandage right off no matter how much the sucker's going to hurt. I rolled down the window. "I can explain everything."

Donovan's lips rose slightly as though he was trying to contain his amusement, and my chances of survival went up tenfold. An amused Donovan was a Donovan who likely wasn't going to throw me in a prison cell. "I look forward to the explanation, Owens." He nodded to my brother. "She drag you into this, James?"

Jamie shrugged and turned off the car. "I was already involved, Your Highness. I've been working the case for a month or so."

Donovan took that news with his usual stoicism. Trent, however, was sniffing the air around him.

"Kelsey, come on. Get out of the car. What the hell did you get yourself into?" Trent pulled the door open, and I found myself outside fast.

The big were lifted me up like I weighed nothing and sat me down. My feet sank in the snow covering the alley. The stilettos were open toed and the chill immediately got to me. The minute I was on my feet, Trent was all over me. He sniffed my hair. His hands started to push the coat off my shoulders. He started to run his nose along my skin. I did what I would have done to any man who got handsy.

I punched him straight in the face.

"Fuck," Trent cursed as he held his nose and took that all-important step back. Blood dripped from the offended appendage. "I think she broke my nose."

I contained my gleeful giggle because he sounded like he had a horrible cold. I totally broke his nose.

Jamie was out of the car and pushing at Trent. He was in full-on big brother mode for the second time that evening. "I'll break more than your nose if you touch my sister like that again, you prick."

Trent's eyes widened and he looked as innocent as he could ever look. "I wasn't trying to hit on her. I was trying to get her scent. Damn it, Owens, that hurt."

Donovan chuckled as he watched the scene with an air of amused fascination. "I hope the CC cameras caught that. It would warm Z's heart to see that exchange. Your dad used to do this thing where he sniffed every inch of her at least once a day."

"He was her dedicated guard." My father had been the queen's personal bodyguard. It made sense that he would need her scent around him. "Trent's a pervert."

"I am not." He tried to push his nose back into the proper position. "I'm trying to do my job. I'm a wolf. I live by my nose. Your uncle would have done the same thing."

"My uncle would have asked," I shot back. The coat I was wearing came open as I railed at Trent, and his blue eyes got wide.

"Yo, Owens, what the hell happened to your pants?" Donovan asked in that tone he used for the dumbasses in his life. I didn't take it too personally. He used it on Quinn and the boys, too.

I rebuttoned the coat and tried not to feel like I was explaining a compromising situation to my father. The man I'd grown up with wouldn't have given a shit. I'd been told my real dad would have cared very much. Though Donovan appeared to be twenty-one or so, it was hard to forget he was actually pushing forty with a wife, a whatever Quinn was, three kids, and an entire kingdom dependent on him. He was kind of the ultimate authority figure in my world, and usually that made me pissy with him. Tonight, it felt different. It made me realize how much I'd missed not having a dad to yell at me for sneaking out and showing back up at four-thirty in the morning with no pants on. He didn't even know about the body in back yet.

Gray was right. I have daddy issues.

I sorta stared at my feet and tried to come up with something he could understand. I was betting that in the entire time he was the *Nex Apparatus*, Donovan never found himself in a thong. "I was undercover."

"On a street corner?" Donovan asked in a low voice. His arms were crossed over that big chest of his as he studied me carefully. "Did Marcus know you were planning on running around the city in a bra and panties?" The king sniffed the air. He sighed and frowned down at me. The dude really had a disappointed dad stare going. "Damn it, Owens. Is that Sloane I smell on you? Tell me you didn't."

I felt Marcus walk into the alley. How to describe it? It was like a wave of calm suddenly washed over me, and I knew he was coming my way. When I turned, he was coming out of the building, still dressed in his suit and tie and still looking gorgeously masculine. Henri and Hugo were with him as well.

"You've already broken rule number one, Kelsey," Hugo pointed out. Rule number one was to not get caught.

It had been a hell of a night, and Marcus was safety and comfort all wrapped up in a really attractive man package. I ran and threw myself in his arms. He caught me. I heard him chuckle.

"I knew perfectly well she was meeting with the lieutenant, Your Highness. I would, however, like a report on how she came to lose her respectable clothes." Marcus took a peek under Sloane's coat. His dark eyebrows rose at the sight.

Henri slapped Marcus on the back. "Don't think too much on it, old friend. Remember Vivienne? Hugo's poor Hunter couldn't keep her pants on, either."

Hugo smiled broadly with the memory. I got the feeling the academics were looking forward to my antics. "Such a lovely girl. Terribly brutal, but lovely all the same."

"I couldn't get into the club dressed like I was," I explained.

"What kind of club was this, *bella*?"

"It was a sex club," I mumbled.

I could mumble all I liked. Almost everyone had superhearing. Trent huffed. Marcus frowned, and Donovan groaned.

"Jesus, Kelsey, don't mention it to Dev," Donovan practically pleaded. "I'll never hear the end of it. He's been bugging me to open a sex club since that Sanctum place turned him down. I'd never get him out."

"Only the top level is a sex club," Jamie explained. "The rest is a bar. It's seedier than Ether, but along the same lines. It's an outlier place. It opened up a month back. There were rumors about drug running, so Sloane went in undercover."

Donovan nodded, accepting the explanation. "And I suppose it's run by demons. I can smell them everywhere."

Marcus kept his hands on my shoulders as I turned back to the king. "It's run by some bigwig demon. Sloane is trying to nail him for running drugs."

"So the shifter was on something," the king concluded. "It has to be strong because I was having trouble holding him. Did you get some?"

I shook my head. "Sloane is trying to set himself up as a distributor. I'm going to this guy's house for dinner on Sunday as Sloane's date. He's hoping this Winter guy will give him the go-ahead, and he can get some real insight into the operation. He wants to meet with Marcus tomorrow."

"Yes, I would like a word with him," Marcus remarked calmly.

"You'll liaise with the lieutenant?" Donovan seemed eager to get a yes out of Marcus. When Marcus had been on the Council, one of his jobs had been to deal with Gray. He was Gray's contact. His relationship with me might make things uncomfortable, but Marcus didn't seem to mind.

"We will handle it," Hugo assured the king. "We have protocols in place for dealing with local law enforcement. We've not used them in many years. We haven't had a Hunter to train since…"

"April 30, 1945," Henri said sadly. "Stupid Soviet Army. Our girl had done her job. She had infiltrated the bunker in Berlin and taken the bastard out. It was all covered up. I believe they said the man committed suicide."

"Yes, yes," Hugo agreed. "Ridiculous, of course. She got shot in the back by the Soviets. Marcus couldn't get to her fast enough."

Marcus's arms tightened around me. "Which is why we take our charge's safety seriously. We won't be working with the government any time soon. We need to keep her existence secret. If the US Army finds out, they'll try to ship her off to assassinate whoever is the latest enemy of the state."

Donovan's mouth was hanging slightly open. "Are trying to tell me a Hunter took out Hitler?"

"Oh, yes, Your Highness," Henri said with a negligent wave of his hand. "We're responsible for many such helpful acts. Hugo was responsible for the Marat assassination."

"Yes," Hugo said, patting me on the back. "Not that the bloody frogs deserved it. I was also responsible for pinning it on the Corday girl. That particular Hunter was one of my favorites. Married the girl. She was lovely, too. Now, I recall she was also wearing no pants when she killed Marat. Assassinations are a messy business, dear. Your instinct to shed your clothing proves you're right for the job."

I grimaced. It was time to reveal the less successful part of my evening. "You might think differently when Jamie opens the trunk." I turned back to Marcus. "The assassination part of my night didn't go so well."

"Damn it, Owens," Donovan cursed. "I told you not to kill anyone."

"No. You told me to do it quietly. I did. No guns whatsoever. Now he won't shut up, so I had to bring him with me." I walked around with Jamie, who opened the trunk. "Though he's been quiet since we pulled up here. Do you think he finally died?"

"No, but he peed himself," Trent said, whiffing the air.

Donovan peered down into the trunk. "Damn. His head's on backward."

"Nicely done, Kelsey." Henri gave me a fatherly pat on the back as he looked down at my handiwork. "That is a perfect example of atlanto-occipital dislocation."

"If you mean the bitch tried to my pull my head off, then yes, it's fucking perfect," Kall said bitterly. He stared up at the king and tried to cast his eyes away. It didn't look like Kall was happy about this impromptu meeting with royalty. "I would like to point out that our contracts are still in effect, King Daniel. That bitch had no right to kill me."

Donovan's fangs gleamed in the low light. "Might I take the time to point out that those contracts are between Vampire and demonkind. I believe you will find that my *Nex Apparatus* is not a vampire."

Kall's eyes flew to me. "She's the *Nex Apparatus*? But that's not fair."

Donovan laughed, and I heard Trent chuckling beside his boss. "Trent, it's a good fucking night. Do you know how long it's been since I got to torture someone to get much needed information out of them?"

"Been a while, boss," the werewolf allowed. His nose was already perfect again.

Donovan shook his head. "See, it's the little things you miss when you get to the top. No one ever lets me torture demons anymore. They consider it beneath me without ever thinking about how much I enjoy it." The king turned to me. "Good job, Owens."

I gave him a jaunty salute and breathed a silent sigh of relief because it looked like Trent had been right. Now that Donovan was fairly certain I wasn't going to massacre his friends and family, he was using a much lighter touch with me. "Nice to know I could help."

Donovan nodded at his wolf, and Trent picked up Kall with one brawny arm. The demon's head hung limply to the side.

"You can't torture me," Kall yelled. "It's in our contracts."

Donovan thought about it for half a second. "I can't torture a living demon. Henri, isn't this whole head hanging on by a thread thing usually fatal?"

Henri nodded vigorously. "This body is very much dead. I would expect it to begin to rot within a day or two. I'm surprised he's still in there."

"I don't know how to leave. This is the only body I've ever been in, damn it," Kal explained.

"I can totally torture a corpse. There's nothing in our contracts to stop me from doing that." The king poked at him. "He can't feel anything, can he?"

Henri considered the problem for a moment. "Do we still have some holy water? I assure you, if we submerge the head in a vat of holy water, we'll get a response."

Donovan snapped his fingers and a big grin lit his face. He was like a kid on Christmas morning. "I like the way you think, Henri. Owens, I expect a full report tomorrow night. We're all having dinner at your uncle's. We can meet in his office, and you can update me on your progress."

Donovan and Trent walked back into the building carrying their new plaything. Kall was crying openly and begging the king to let him die.

Dude should have paid more attention in demon school.

Marcus slipped his hand into mine and used his free hand to shake my brother's. "Thank you for bringing her home, James."

Jamie grinned. "It's always an adventure with my sis. Good night, Marcus. Go easy on Gray tomorrow."

"I will be a gentleman, of course," Marcus promised. "Come along, *bella*. It's long past time to get to bed. Good night Henri, Hugo. We'll meet again in the afternoon to discuss what Henri has learned about our patient."

I quietly followed Marcus back into the building and toward the elevator that went to our floor. I was anticipating a pretty hearty fight. Marcus had been upset when I confronted Trent wearing a bath towel that had covered way more of me than my current ensemble.

"Marcus," I began as I followed him on the elevator. He pushed the button to our floor and the car began to climb.

"Hush," Marcus said. After we passed the second floor, he reached over and pushed the emergency stop button. He turned to me with hooded eyes. "Show me."

I hesitated. "You're going to be mad."

He leaned back against the wall. "Am I? Were you working, *cara mia*? Did you intend to end up in a sex club with your ex-fiancé?"

"Of course not," I assured him.

He stared at me intently, and I wasn't feeling a wave of calm from him at that point. Nope. Things were heating up and Marcus didn't mind sharing that with me. Lust. He was sending out a lusty vibe. Marcus had his own kinks. He tended to get horny when I did violent things to people who richly deserved it. Marcus liked bad girls, and I fit the bill.

"Did you willingly put yourself in a compromising position with the lieutenant?" His fangs were out, his dark eyes large. His voice was like thick honey. I knew there was a bit of persuasion being pushed at me. I could push back, but it felt good.

"I didn't do anything with Sloane that wasn't important to our cover," I promised him.

"Then show me," Marcus commanded.

I let the coat drop to the floor.

He sighed, letting me know he appreciated the sight. "Very nice. It makes me feel sorry for Sloane. He was only able to look while I am free to touch." He motioned me to come to him and then turn so he didn't miss an inch. His hand came out to caress the bare cheeks of my ass. He gently snapped the thong against my skin. "This is quite lovely."

I let down my mental walls so he could feel how much I wanted him. I needed this. It had been a craptastic day, and there was nothing that would make me feel better than being in his arms. He squeezed my cheeks before he pulled me against his body, his front to my back. His erection nudged insistently against my ass. Being mostly naked meant I could feel his hands on my skin, the silk of his shirt against my spine.

Marcus let his hands run up along my torso until he cupped my breasts through the soft material of the bra. His tongue licked along my neck, up to my ear where he playfully bit down, causing me to shiver with arousal.

"I missed you every moment you were gone, my *bella*," the vampire whispered in my ear. "We need to make some things plain between us."

His clever hand made its way down my body. He slid his palm over the flat of my belly and teased his way past the band of the thong. With firm pressure, he began rubbing circles all around my clitoris. I let my head fall back against his shoulder as he continued to lecture me in the nicest way.

"I'm speaking to you as your trainer and your lover, Kelsey." He kept his thumb on my little nub while his long fingers gently thrust up into my pussy. He filled me with his fingers. My breaths were ragged as I approached that sweet spot he was steering me toward. "Are you listening?"

"Yes." I was pretty much going to agree with everything the man giving me the orgasm said. I've found it's a logical course to take. I would have agreed with almost anything the man said because he was amazingly good at finding my G-spot.

"Excellent," he murmured, curving his fingers up. "This is important. I'm an old-fashioned man, my mistress, but even in my human life I thought the entire idea of death before dishonor was ridiculous. You do what you have to. You survive by any means necessary. If that includes fucking your way out of a situation, then I expect you to spread your legs and when you're done, you come home to me."

I bit my lip and thrust my hand back into his silky hair. The pleasure burst over me. I twisted to the right and was able to get my mouth over his. He quickly took charge of the kiss, thrusting his tongue into my mouth.

He dislodged his hand and turned me fully into the cradle of his body. "Do you understand me, Kelsey?"

"I do, baby," I replied. "Always come home to you."

Marcus worked the belt of his slacks, and I realized he wasn't patient enough to wait until we got home tonight. He shoved aside the string of my thong. Then my back was against the plush wall of the elevator. Marcus pushed his way inside me. He sighed as he seated himself and began to thrust deeply. His pelvis was grinding sweetly against me, and I started to come all over again. I held on, locking my legs around his waist while he rode me.

Marcus's body stiffened when he rammed into me one last time. He kissed me as he emptied himself and murmured love phrases in Italian. When he was finished, he set me down on my feet and straightened his clothes. Gently, he took off his own coat and wrapped it around my shoulders. I should have known he wouldn't want me wearing Sloane's clothes. When he was sure we were presentable, he hit the button to continue our journey. He picked up Sloane's coat and laid it over his hand.

"I'll return it to him tomorrow," he promised. "I will be sure to express my gratitude for his care of you."

"You won't start a fight or anything, will you?" I was worried at the thought of my boyfriend and my ex having a sit-down.

Marcus smiled. "*Bella*, have you ever known me to be less than a gentleman?"

I let him lead me out of the elevator, where he'd proven he could play the bad boy. "Please remember he's bigger than you. If you get in a fight with him, don't let him hit your face."

The vampire opened the door, and I was surprised at the fact that this place already felt like home. "I will endeavor to retain my beauty for you."

I yawned and after a long shower, finally went to bed. Outside the snow fell, and the world was wrapped in winter.

Chapter Ten

"Kelsey, wake up, you totally have to see this." An excited voice broke through my peaceful slumber, dragging me out of sleep. Lucky for him, I recognized his voice or baby boy might have found himself on the floor with my hands around his throat.

We really needed to work on our security.

"Go away, Lee," I muttered and tried to turn over. I reached for Marcus and was met with only an empty pillow where he should have been. I pulled the comforter over my head and prayed my little friend would take the hint.

"I think she went back to sleep," an unfamiliar voice said.

I brought the comforter down only as far as my chin. I was kind of naked here and Lee had brought a friend. "Who are you, and why are you in my bedroom?"

The small blonde girl with big blue eyes smiled brightly.

"Hi, I'm Mia," she said as though that should explain everything. She was the same size as Lee and they looked like they weighed roughly the same. I noticed this because I thought briefly about how much effort it would take to toss them both bodily from my rooms. Then the door opened, and I thought about how poor Gulliver must have felt when all those irritating Lilliputians interrupted his sleep.

"My father has counseled me on many occasions that it's better to flee from a sleeping woman than to wake one," Sean Quinn said as he and Rhys joined the crew. I noticed that both the boys had chocolate bars in their hands. Marcus was somewhere, and he'd sicced this bunch on me. "Father believes that when a woman is asleep, this is the best time to take one's leave."

I heard Mia sigh and saw the slight roll of her angelic eyes. Smart girl. She was wearing a thick coat and had a hat on her head. She greatly resembled the shrink I'd met the day before. She had his eyes and the set of his mouth. I was betting her last name was Day.

Rhys took a bite of his Snickers and shrugged off his uncle's advice. "My papa says that if I ever want to have a goddess of my own, I should never, ever listen to your father."

"What time is it?" I was not going to lie here listening to dating advice from nine-year-olds. Though from what I'd seen and heard of Declan Quinn, Rhys was probably right on.

"Nine o'clock," Mia supplied helpfully.

"Shit," I growled. I shook my head when I realized I had an audience with tender ears. "Sorry."

"It's all right," Lee said. "My mama says stuff like that all the time. I'm allowed to curse, too."

"Only if a shark bites off your arm or you're getting chased by dinosaurs," Rhys clarified.

Lee nodded as though he looked forward to both incidents. "Yeah, but then I'm allowed to say the F word."

"I can't believe Marcus let me sleep all freaking day," I muttered, sitting up. I pulled the covers around me and tried to figure out how to get rid of the gang of children in my room.

"It's nine o'clock in the morning," Mia corrected.

I hadn't been aware that morning had one of those, too. I snuggled back down under the covers. "Then go away. Come back after noon." I thought of something. "Aren't you supposed to be playing basketball or something?"

"It got canceled because of the snow," Lee explained. "See."

He shoved a mittened hand at my face. The small snowball slipped out of his palm and went straight under my covers. I screamed and used that word Lee is only supposed to use in the event of a dinosaur attack.

"Guys," Liv said from the doorway in her best teacher voice. "I told you to wake her up, not put her in a killing mood."

"Make them go away," I begged. If my boyfriend hadn't been completely incapable of fathering children, I would have checked to make sure my birth control was up to date.

"Sorry," Lee mumbled.

"Breakfast is ready," Liv announced. "If you want French toast and bacon, I would eat it before the bottomless pit there gets her hands on it. Go."

The Lilliputian crew ran out of my bedroom in search of food. I rubbed my eyes, still sleepy. I do not do well on short sleep. Liv walked over, carrying a mug of coffee. The aroma was heavenly and my will to live was on the rise. She was dressed in jeans and a thick sweater, her hair pulled back in a ponytail.

"Well, good morning, sunshine." She grinned as she passed me the coffee. "Did you have a rough night last night?"

I took the coffee and thought about Italy. No one ever invaded my bedroom in Italy. No one sent small children in to torture me with snowballs. "I did, in fact, which is why I should be sleeping now."

"Ain't happening, Kels." Liv sat down on the bed. She giggled as she peeked under the covers. Like I said, the supernatural world doesn't have the hang-ups about nudity the human world has. "And look, you're all naked again. Seriously, this is a habit with you."

I groaned. "I was wearing underwear last night, Liv. It wasn't like I was running around the city nude. Wait, oh shit, is this already a story that's going around?"

The supernatural world *was* big on gossip, however.

I didn't like the amusement on Liv's face. "Well, let's just say that there's a reason people fight over the security jobs in this building. It's a cushy job where they take turns monitoring the numerous security cameras that cover almost all of the public places in the building."

It took a moment to grasp what she was saying. I laid back and curled into a fetal position, carefully avoiding the already melted gift Lee had left behind. "Oh, god, I made a sex tape."

Liv giggled viciously. "I can't believe he stopped the elevator and fucked you. It was hot, Kelsey. I have to admit I've always thought Marcus was kind of scary, but I see the appeal now."

"Tell me this isn't happening." Visions of my ass on the Internet flooded my brain. I would be a weird meme somewhere, a cautionary tale to all other Hunters.

"It's all right, Kels," Liv assured me. "I only got a copy because

Scott is drinking buddies with the security guy, who got his ass kicked by your uncle when he realized what he'd done. Zack has spent the majority of the morning erasing everything and threatening to kill anyone who forwards it. He's making Quinn do a system search to make sure all the copies are gone. That's how I got stuck with kid-sitting duty. Quinn's running around making sure your dignity is maintained, and the queen is nursing a sick friend. So, I get the kids. I tried to explain that I teach high school, but they didn't listen. They were too busy talking about candy and how cool you are."

"I'm never leaving this room again." I could totally live right there. It was a nice room, and I never had to face anyone again.

"If it makes you feel any better, Quinn didn't see the problem. He said he and the queen have been caught doing it on tape all over the building."

Yep, this never happened back in Italy. I sat up because it was obvious I wasn't going back to sleep. "Tell me something, Liv."

She knew exactly what I was going to ask. That's what happens when you're friends with someone for a long time. "Your butt looked great."

I sighed. I would have to be happy with that. I put aside all the fun stuff because Liv and I needed to talk. It wasn't something I was looking forward to. I hadn't been successful the night before, and Scott was in more trouble than I could have imagined. "I talked to him last night."

Liv's face fell. She braced herself. "He wouldn't come home, would he?"

I reached for her hand. "I don't think he has a choice, Liv. He's in deep. Whatever is going on in that club, it's bad. I think he's hooked on the same drug Alan was on."

Big fat tears sprang from her eyes. "Alan died last night. Henri Jacobs wants you in his lab in an hour. That's why I woke you up."

"Shit," I cursed. "Liv, I'm so sorry. Just because Alan…"

She held out her hand to stop me. "I know. I know. Kelsey, you tried. Promise me that if you can save him, you will."

"I promise," I said solemnly.

Liv got up and walked to the window. I could see it was still snowing, big flakes turning the world into an icy wonderland. "I don't love him anymore, you know."

I wasn't sure about that, but I kept my mouth shut. She needed to talk.

"I haven't loved him for a long time. I know he's a shit, but he wasn't always like that. He was…so sweet when we first met. He got comfortable and decided he didn't need to woo me anymore. I let it happen. I was comfortable, too. I hate dating. When he asked me to marry him, I said yes." Liv laughed hollowly. "He didn't actually ask me, you know. He said we should probably do it, and then when I would try to set a date, he'd come up with excuses. I haven't tried to pin him down in eighteen months. I knew it wouldn't work. I know I shouldn't have watched that tape of you and Marcus."

"It's fine, Liv." I meant it. I'm honest with myself, at least. If someone had sent me a tape with Marcus fucking, I would have watched it.

She turned back and brushed away her tears. "I should have respected your privacy, but I sat there and watched it and realized I want that for me, Kelsey. I want someone who can't wait to have me. I want someone who needs me the way Marcus needs you. He's passionate about you. I was so envious of you."

"Liv," I started.

She shook her head. "I don't love Scott anymore, but I can't leave him to fate. Let me help you, Kelsey. I need this so I can move on."

"Of course," I said immediately. "You can come with me to see what Henri found out."

Liv nodded and gave me a watery smile. "I'll be good, I promise. I remember how to play Watson. Now, you better grab a shower. I'll go make another round of breakfast. I'm sure the kids ate everything. They're like locust. Marcus gave them a big bag of candy and they inhaled it."

I got up and started to make my way to the bathroom. "Where did Marcus go? Is he helping Zack erase the tape?"

"No, he told me he had a morning appointment to make," Liv explained. "He also told me to keep you out of trouble."

"He's meeting with Sloane." Sneaky bastard had left me sleeping because he knew damn well I wanted to mediate.

"Okay," Liv said, her eyes wide. "I'd love to be a fly on that wall."

I shook my head and went off to take a long shower.

* * * *

Kim Jacobs waved us into her apartment. She was a beautiful brunette who always dressed like she'd stepped off a runway in Milan. I found her intimidating because I couldn't put together an outfit to save my life. Lucia put pants and the proper tops close to each other in my closet so I couldn't screw up. In the past, I would have simply picked out whichever black T-shirt smelled like it was the cleanest and called it a day. Today I was fairly presentable in straight-legged jeans, a cashmere sweater, and fashionable boots that I could kick a little ass in.

"The mad professor's in his lab," Kim cracked as she pointed the way through the apartments. This particular unit was two apartments connected through a short hallway. There was a living area for Henri and Kim attached to the small hospital the complex maintained. "Hugo's in there, too. They've been chatting all morning about how fabulous you are. It's like you're a rock star."

"More like a..." Liv began.

I knew where that was going and elbowed her. Liv managed to shut her mouth.

"I'll try not to sing," I promised Henri Jacobs' companion.

"Kelsey." Henri walked out of his lab dressed in his customary slacks and dress shirt, but minus the coat and tie. He'd exchanged them for a heavy apron and surgical gloves. He was far more animated than I'd ever seen him. His face was lit up with what I would have called glee. "You're just in time. I was about to begin my autopsy."

I was so glad that I didn't have Lee with me. It had been a close thing. Mia's mom, Sarah, had shown up to take the kids to her apartment with the promise of movies and hot chocolate. Lee had tried to explain that he had work to do. Before I could set him straight, the blonde girl had given him a pointed stare. Needless to say, Lee was watching movies and I wasn't having to argue about taking a nine-year-old to an autopsy. It was good to know there was one person in the world who could control Lee Donovan-Quinn. While Lee would have wanted to join me, I had no such problem with Liv.

"Um, Kels. Maybe I should sit this one out." She turned a rather sick shade of green.

"Why don't you sit with Mrs. Jacobs?" I offered. "Did you talk to Alan at all last night?"

The companion nodded sadly. "I stayed with him for a few hours. I've been with Henri long enough to have picked up some nursing skills. He was pretty out of it, but I'll tell you what I remember."

"Excellent." Henri practically shooed them off in his excitement. Dude really liked autopsies. "Come, come, we are waiting on you."

I gave Liv a wave and followed the vampire through the short corridor that led to the hospital.

"We?" I asked curiously. Marcus was out and Sharpe wasn't an academic, so he should be safely in a dead stupor by now.

"I would like to introduce you to the newest member of our team," Henri said as we passed through stainless steel swinging doors. The smell of formaldehyde assaulted my senses.

"Wow, that's a ridiculously strong odor," I complained as I entered the small room that was currently serving as a morgue. I couldn't miss the dead body on the table. Hugo was asleep at the desk, his head laid across his arms. He muttered some very British things in his sleep.

Academics are different. On almost every level, they prove a bit strange in the vampire world. There are different classes of vampires, but mostly this describes the vampire in terms of strength and power. The majority of the vampire ranks can be placed in a category called the warrior class. In the warrior class, there are subclasses with the power to call wolves or some other wereanimal. There are warriors who can fly and some who can shift their shapes. There are other classes. Just a few months before, I'd met a magician. He could form illusions so real you would swear you can touch and taste and smell them. I had, up to this point, avoided the class known as the primals. These were vampires whose DNA got screwed up and when they turned, they regressed into something ancient and terrifying.

For the most part, all of these classes follow certain rules. During the day they're in a dead stupor, unable to walk, move, or communicate. It's when they're vulnerable. If you were in the room with one, you would swear you were viewing a corpse. Not so with the academic. For some reason the academic needed no such rest. When they slept, it was in a normal human fashion. Marcus often woke up looking for his share of the blankets because I was a cover hog. For Hugo Wells, it meant talking in his sleep and snoring lightly.

"Ignore him," Henri said with obvious affection for his friend. "He's always required his beauty sleep. Me, I can go for days when focused on a problem."

That was when I noticed the new guy. He was tall and lanky, with dark-blond hair that reached to his shoulders. His back was to us, his head moving to some music only he could hear. Henri slapped him upside the head, and the man turned around.

"Hey," he complained, pulling out his earbuds. He had a phone in his hand. I could hear the music from across the room. It sounded a lot like complaint rock. You know the type. It's a lot of whiny boys talking about how girls don't love them. It made me want to claw my ears off.

"Casey, you must pay attention," Henri said with a frown. "We have a guest."

Casey turned to me, and I knew beyond a shadow of a doubt that I was looking at a brand spanking new vampire. That dude had likely turned in the last year or so. I would have pegged his age at around twenty, but unlike Donovan, who exuded power, this one was full of the raw idiocy of youth. He also dressed like an emo disciple. He had on a black and purple striped hoodie and jeans that really needed to be pulled up. I appreciated the Converse, but everything else about him was way too Hot Topic for me.

"Now we're talking, Henri." Casey turned on the charm, which for him included what I think was supposed to be a seductive smile. "Hello. It's so nice to get a girl in here. It's a complete sausage fest, if you know what I mean."

"I don't," I replied flatly.

The baby vamp eased up to me, and I caught the edge of his persuasion. It wasn't the first time some idiot vamp had hit on me. Acceptable females were few and far between in our world. "I'll explain it all to you, sweetheart."

Henri rolled his eyes. "You'll have to excuse Casey, dear. He only turned last year. I'm afraid his vampire life has not been what he expected."

Casey frowned. "It kind of sucks, forgive the pun. I got killed in a professional accident."

"You were skateboarding," Henri corrected.

"It was going to be a profession. I was getting good. I should have worn a helmet…and maybe watched for oncoming eighteen-wheelers. So anyway, I wake up and there's this big, scary dude standing over me."

"We tend to refer to him as Your Highness," Henri pointed out.

Casey ignored him. "He tells me I'm a vampire and…that's like totally awesome because I thought I was dead and shit. I'm thinking, yeah, vampire. They get all the chicks, and they are so hot in Hollywood right now. They have to drink blood and at first, that's like whoa, yuck, but then…wow. Awesome stuff. Only then I find out I'm some sort of egghead vampire."

"I prefer the term academic." Henri turned to me with an all-suffering expression on his face. "He required a patron. Marcus, Hugo, and I drew straws."

I knew who'd drawn the short one. I patted his back sympathetically. "Sorry. It's for the best. Marcus would have killed him by now."

Henri shrugged as he pulled out a tray covered in sharp instruments. "Casey is excellent with technology. He can fix almost anything, and I don't even understand half of what he can do with a computer. He's actually valuable when he's not talking. I try to tell myself that I most likely made my own patron want to throw himself on a stake in the beginning."

"So who's the chick?" Casey waggled his slightly bushy eyebrows at me invitingly. His persuasion purred across my skin. It tried to tease and tantalize. I was used to Marcus's power, and this boy moved me not an inch. "Please say she's for me."

Henri moved into position over the draped body on the autopsy table. "She's Marcus's mistress. Feel free to hit on her. I'm sure Marcus will be amused."

Casey went completely white. "Shit. Look, Henri, I'm sorry. I didn't know. We don't have to tell him, right? He's busy and stuff." Casey turned back to me and now his persuasion was a little stronger. It was good to know his survival instinct was stronger than his libido. He didn't want me to talk to Marcus. "I didn't really hit on you. I mean, I hit on everyone. It's not a big deal."

"She's also our Hunter," Henri continued. "Kelsey, please show him."

I did so. I gently shoved him out of my brain. Casey's eyes got wide, and his hands flew to his head.

"Owww." He groaned and his hands massaged his temples. "That hurt. What the hell?"

Hugo's head came up off the desk, his sleepy eyes amused. "Did the obnoxious bugger try to hit on our Hunter?"

"He did, indeed," Henri confirmed. "He'll have a headache for hours."

"Nice one," Hugo mumbled as he stretched his big frame. "Good morning, dear. I hope you had a lovely, albeit truncated, sleep. Have we gotten to the autopsy already?"

Hugo came to stand at my side, his clothes slightly rumpled. He reminded me of a college professor. He tugged on a pair of gloves from the box on the table.

Henri threw back the drape that covered the corpse, and I tried to view the body in an intellectual fashion. Whatever had animated Alan Kent was gone. His spirit, soul—whatever you want to call it—had fled this life. Now his body was my best evidence.

"How did he die, Henri?" Just hours after death, he was already past full rigor and well on his way to decomposition. Supernatural creatures decompose very quickly. It was why Henri couldn't wait to perform the autopsy. Within a day or so, we would likely be left with nothing but soup.

"His wounds would not heal," Henri explained. He handed me a pair of latex gloves, and I slid them on.

Alan's belly showed deep puncture wounds. He'd caused them with his own claws, though Marcus had been behind the injury. I doubted he would feel guilty about it. It brought up a few questions, though. "I know Alan's not exactly the strongest shifter in the world, but he should have been able to heal that, right?"

"Absolutely." Henri had a scalpel in his hand. "Something else is wrong. I can't be completely sure until I open him up. From the wounds, I would guess that he didn't sever anything important. The king and his guard were able to keep the claws from sinking too deep. He, perhaps, perforated the large intestine. This should have healed quickly. I've known weak shifters to survive much greater wounds."

"Gross."

I glanced over to find Casey standing beside me. His mouth was pulled back slightly, giving him a general look of distaste.

I ignored the baby vamp, who better get used to gross stuff. "So why didn't he heal? Did anyone try giving him blood?"

By blood, I didn't mean a transfusion, per se. In our world, vampire blood is the ultimate medicine.

"Alexander and I both tried," Henri confirmed. "We attempted both an oral and a topical application of blood. Neither worked. Forcing the patient to actually ingest the blood made things significantly worse."

"I've never heard of a shifter being allergic to vampire blood." I'd never heard of anyone being allergic to vamp blood. It was a universal curative. "Maybe it's because Alex's blood is evil."

Hugo laughed sharply. "She has a point. I've been trying to figure out a legal way to execute that bloke for years. I didn't like the way he was studying our Hunter last night, Henri. He never took his eyes off her."

"Bah," Henri said as he put the scalpel to a point under the corpse's left shoulder blade. "Kelsey can take him." He cocked a brow as he pointedly stared over at Casey. "Are you sure you can handle this?"

He did not ask the same question of me. I'd actually been the one doing the gutting before, so the aftereffects didn't bug me.

Casey snorted and waved off the question. "Do you have any idea how many episodes of CSI I've seen? This doesn't bother me at all. I'm a vampire. Dead bodies are my stock-in-trade."

Henri shook his head and began his Y incision. He started across the chest, clean cutting to the sternum and then back up the right side of the torso. He made the leg of the Y down to the pubic bone. Gently, he opened the cavity to expose the sternum. "Casey, pass me the bone saw, please."

But Casey was on the floor at my feet.

"He's out," I announced, picking up the small circular saw and handing it to the doc. "Never saw a vamp pass out before."

"Such a pain in my ass. Shove him out of the way," Henri yelled over the whine of the saw.

I leaned toward Hugo. "Have you ever heard of any substance that causes an allergic reaction in a shifter?"

"Silver, of course," Hugo said as Henri pulled open the sternum.

"Wolfsbane in a werewolf."

"This wasn't silver." Henri gently cut the heart out. He held the organ in his hand. It looked perfectly normal for a disgusting body part. "The heart is perfect. Silver would have caused it to enlarge at the very least. The rest of the organs look fine, except for the bowels, of course. Marcus did a number on those."

Hugo and Henri worked together as though they had done this a hundred times before. Henri pulled the organs out. Hugo weighed and measured them. I was handed a clipboard and dutifully wrote down the numbers that made up the end of Alan Kent's life. Everything was perfectly normal, I was assured. Until we got to his brain…

Henri peeled his scalp back and we went through another round of whirring saw sounds before he was able to lift a portion of the skull out.

"*Schijt*," Henri breathed as he got his first look at Alan's brain.

"Shit is right, Henri." Hugo's face was a mask of perfectly genteel horror. "That's the entire prefrontal cortex."

I peered over. Even as a layman, I knew something was terribly wrong. There was a huge dark spot on the front of the brain. It appeared black against the gray of the rest of the brain matter. "That's bad, right?"

"Yes, Kelsey." Henri gently touched the brain. A black puss oozed out. "This drug has completely ruined the impulse center of his brain. He had no control over his own actions. If there are others out there like this, we're in deep trouble."

I sighed because it was going to be another long day. Casey came out of his stupor.

"Is it over?" Casey asked, his eyes wide. He managed to get to his feet.

"Not by a long shot, buddy," I promised. The day was only starting. "Henri, I'm going to need a sandwich."

Casey groaned as he caught sight of the exposed skull. He slithered back to the floor.

Yep, a really long day.

Chapter Eleven

I managed to down two turkey sandwiches, three teeny tiny chocolate chip cookies, and a Dr. Pepper before the next crisis required my attention. Apparently, with only Kim and a small human staff, they weren't prepared for my appetite. I could have made my way back to my own apartment, but I was feeling lazy. Casey skulked into the small kitchen and slumped down in the seat across from me.

"Are you done fainting?" I asked. He was still pretty pale, even for a vamp.

"I didn't faint," Casey complained. "I…I…shit, I fainted. I totally lost it. What the hell kind of vampire am I if I can't handle one tiny autopsy?"

I poked around the kitchen to see if I could spy anything else even vaguely appetizing. Kim Jacobs was big on salads. There was lots of green stuff in her fridge and not one single slab of meat. "You'll get used to it."

"How many have you seen?"

"That one," I replied. "But I've probably killed way more people than you have."

Casey looked innocent and naïve all of the sudden. "I haven't killed anyone. All the girls I feed off of get paid by Henri. You don't think I'd have to kill someone if Henri, you know, got sick of dealing with my shit?"

"I think they'd probably make arrangements." I remembered what it felt like to find out life wasn't what I thought it would be. "And I suspect Henri will show you a whole lot of patience."

Casey smiled slightly. "I would never say this to him, but he's actually a good guy. I was terrified when I thought that Italian guy was going to be my vampire dad. He scares the crap out of me."

I shook my head because I didn't get what was so scary about my guy. "He's a sweetheart."

"Maybe if you're doing him, he is, but otherwise, he's spooky." He sat back in his chair and regarded me seriously. "So you're some kind of superwolf?"

"I'm not a wolf, exactly. I'm also not human. I'm kind of a freaky combo. I'm really good at killing stuff, so here I am."

Casey's mouth split into a chagrined expression. "And I'm a vampire who doesn't want to kill anything."

The door from the living area opened and Liv walked in, bringing along her unique feminine energy. "I learned some things you might find interesting."

"Like where Kim Jacobs hides the beer?"

"I don't think she drinks beer, sweetie," Liv said with a sympathetic pat on my back.

"I miss beer." Casey sounded a little morose.

Liv gave him a long stare. "He doesn't look like he's old enough to drink."

Casey sat up straighter as he tossed Liv his best come-hither look. I had to give it to him. He was an optimist. I'd tossed him out of my head not two hours before, but here he was hitting on the first woman to walk in. "I'm a vampire, honey. You can't judge a vampire by his rugged good looks."

"He's a newbie, isn't he?" Liv shook her head as she gave him a once-over.

"Oh, yeah, he's like a year old and get this. He's a pacifist." I pushed a chair out for my friend. It was good to be back together with Liv. It felt right.

It made me wonder what Nate was doing.

"Oh, that's so cute," Liv cooed, much to Casey's obvious dismay.

She dismissed him entirely and turned to me. "So, Alan was sort of in and out of consciousness last night. Kim told me he talked a lot about some clinic. He'd been visiting this clinic, and it sounded strange. Kim thought he might be selling blood or buying blood. She wasn't sure because he wasn't terribly coherent."

Casey had a superior look on his face as he pulled a card out of his back pocket. "Could you be talking about the East Side Clinic on Greenville? I found it in his wallet last night." He held the card in between his middle and forefinger. When I reached for it, he snatched it away. "Not so fast, sister."

I growled at the newbie who obviously didn't understand the order of things. "Casey, I haven't killed a vampire yet. Would you like to be the first?"

He passed me the card. "Fine. You're no fun."

"Liv, what do you say we head over to Greenville?" I asked, eager to get somewhere, anywhere.

"I don't think that's such a great idea," Casey said, standing up. There was a stubborn look in his eyes. "Henri and Hugo went to get some sleep, and your trainer isn't here. I don't think you should go out without one of the team."

"Good news for me then that you happen to be free."

Casey's eyes went wide. "Oh, that's an even worse idea."

I grabbed my coat. It was time for a field trip.

Twenty minutes later, Casey nudged me awake when the train stopped a couple of blocks from our destination. I yawned as the train doors hissed open and followed Casey and Liv out into the too-bright daylight. The snow on everything made it extremely light outside. Though Marcus was a daywalker, we still were fairly nocturnal. Being awake the last couple of days was making me tired and grumpy. My boots crunched in the snow as we moved down the stairs to the street below.

We started the walk up Mockingbird toward Greenville.

"Does she always fall asleep wherever she's sitting?" Casey asked Liv.

"It's her special gift." Liv shivered as a cold wind whipped through the buildings. She brushed the snow off her gloves, but it kept coming down. We'd taken the train because it seemed easier than trying to drive in this stuff. Texans aren't the safest drivers during icy conditions. "Have you ever seen anything like this?"

Casey held his gloved hands up. "Don't look at me. I'm from Austin. This kind of freaks me out."

"Apparently everything freaks you out." I gave the vamp a friendly slap on the back.

I actually kind of liked the little wimp. Maybe it was because he was an academic and I was a Hunter, so we kind of naturally fit together. I felt like taking the vamp under my wing, so to speak. However, when we'd gotten ready to go, I hadn't given him a gun. I thought that was a bad idea. Liv, on the other hand, had a nice semiautomatic with silver ordnance in her coat pocket. I hoped she could hold it since she was wearing thick gloves. This snow crap wreaked havoc on my defense protocols.

"That's it." Liv pointed to a building halfway down the block.

The clinic was small and looked neat and antiseptic in that way all medical buildings should look. I want any clinic or hospital I end up in to look like twelve OCD freaks spent the day scrubbing the floors with bleach and a toothbrush.

"It looks closed." Casey was studying the building carefully. It gave me hope that maybe he would be effective in the field.

Sure enough, the lights were off. It didn't surprise me. Most of the buildings were closed down for the day. The minute it started snowing, all of the news channels had begun their apocalyptic countdown. There was five inches of snow on the ground. It was a winter Armageddon in Texas. Everything shut down. It was Saturday, and this wasn't a residential district. There was an apartment building at the end of the block, the only place where I could see people out and about. There were some kids out on the sidewalk yelling and throwing snowballs at each other. At this end of the block it was quiet, the streets relatively empty, and that was helpful because I was about to commit a big old crime.

"I guess we'll have to come back when they open up." Casey didn't sound terribly disappointed. I got the feeling he would prefer to be back in his cushy room watching TV.

Liv and I shook our heads and crossed the street. I'd been hoping the place would be closed. I didn't want to run into anyone who could ID me later. I studied the clinic as we approached it, noting the security camera attached to the outside of the building. I had learned from my young thief friend. It wasn't moving, but I could see the light on.

Silently I pointed up, and Liv nodded, making sure she stayed out of range. I had to pull Casey back though. He was going to walk straight into the shot and perhaps preen for a close-up.

"Camera," I said shortly.

His mouth made a silent O, and he nodded. He gave me a thumbs-up. I remembered what Henri had told me about him. He was a technohead. That could work to my advantage.

"Can you take it out?"

"Where would I put it?" Casey asked.

I had to hope he was better with technology than he was at listening. "I meant can you render it useless without shooting it or causing a whole bunch of noise?"

A look of recognition passed across his cute boy face. "Oh, yeah. I can do that. It looks like there's an electronic lock on the door. I can probably break in. That's a bad idea though, right?"

I gave him a pointed stare.

"All righty then." Casey laced his fingers together and his knuckles cracked. "Let my criminal life begin."

He went still for a moment, breathing deeply and seeming to go inside himself.

"Hey." Liv looked around. "Where did he go?"

Casey moved past the cameras carefully. He studied the range of the camera and twisted his body to stay out of it. He was shielding. Most people wouldn't be able to see him. The camera wouldn't be deceived, of course, but we had other considerations. No one would think it strange that a couple of women were standing, talking on the street. A guy fiddling with a security camera might raise some questions.

"He's handling it, Liv." I watched him work. He couldn't shield from me. Liv's eyes would slide over a vampire when he was in that state. My senses were a bit more finely tuned.

"You can still see me?" Casey jumped gracefully onto the window ledge under the camera.

"Clear as day, buddy," I replied.

His fingers worked quickly to pull off the back of the camera. He started to study the wiring system.

"Cool." He gently pulled and tugged on the inside of the gadget. "Henri said you were a badass. Actually, he said something about you being an incredibly rare and powerful creature, but mostly, I just heard badass."

It might be nice to have someone on the team who actually spoke my language. "You'll have to help me translate when it comes to Henri and Hugo. I'm pretty good with Marcus. It's all in the eyebrows with Marcus. He can say the same thing in the same way, and it means something completely different because he arches that one aristocratic brow."

"I can help out with the professors. I'm starting to get what they're saying," Casey promised. He pulled a wire and then nodded back my way. "Camera's out. I'll have the door open in a sec." He pulled out the phone he'd been using in the autopsy room and connected some computery looking wires to it.

Liv stared at the place where Casey had disappeared. "It's freaky. He's invisible and you can see him. What am I here for?"

"You're pure muscle, Livvie."

She shook her head. "Obviously. I don't feel any wards on the building. That doesn't mean there aren't any on the inside."

The door clicked open and Casey smiled as he showed us the way in.

I patted him on the head as I walked through. He was a good boy. "I didn't realize cell phones could be so useful."

He put it back in his pocket and dropped his shielding. "I might have modified it in a way the manufacturer would not approve of."

"Well, I approve."

The clinic inside was cool and quiet. It smelled of antiseptic. The East Side Clinic was a model of clean efficiency. It had a small waiting room with functional seating and a desk for reception and triage. I glanced around and saw two more cameras. Casey nodded and quickly dispatched them.

"Liv, check those files, and see if you can find Alan's," I said quietly as I turned the blinds to a closed position. Now it would look like the clinic was merely closed, not being burgled. I tossed Casey a thumb drive. "You know what to do."

He did. It was the good thing about having a supergeek around. Marcus would have stared at me and asked what this strange thing did. Marcus appreciated many of the things technology had to offer, but he was useless when it came to electronics. I had to teach him how to use the remotes on our entertainment system, and half the time, he still erased my shows.

I took a leisurely look around. Walking into the back of the clinic, I noted three exam rooms and a locked door reading *Pharmacy*. I was interested in that pharmacy.

I slammed my foot against the door, but it didn't budge. "Casey."

He was at my side in a second. "Wow, that's some tight security." He pointed to the high-tech looking device attached to the doorknob. "Thumb scan. You need the right print to get in." He pushed against the door. "Considering how advanced the lock is, I bet this is reinforced with some strong stuff. I don't think we can bust it open."

"Use your thingee." I pointed to the phone.

"Nope." He shook his head. "That worked on the door because it used a sequential number code. This is way more sophisticated. I'd need my laptop and even then, it's iffy. Someone doesn't want you back there."

I huffed but accepted the inevitable. We didn't have all day. I had to consider the fact that someone would notice the security cameras were no longer giving them a live feed. We had ten minutes tops. I pointed to a door with a *Doctor Linford* name plaque on the door. "How about that one?"

Casey walked over and turned the handle. It opened easily. "I got this one, boss."

"Smart ass," I said as I walked past him.

The desk that dominated the room was neat and perfectly clean, with the single exception of a stack of files. I brushed through them. One was a financial analysis of the clinic for the accountants at a company called Dellacorp. Winter had mentioned that this was the company doing the clinical trials on his drug.

"Dellacorp? As in Dante Dellacourt?" Casey asked, looking over my shoulder.

"I have no idea who that is."

Casey looked at me like I'd said I didn't know who Jesus was. "Seriously? He's revolutionizing the entire way we look at technology. The new computer system Dellacorp Electronics is rolling out in a couple of months will move us forward light years. The processor is insane. He's a genius. He came out of nowhere seven years ago, and now he's one of the preeminent technological minds of our time. He started out in a small shop in Fort Worth where he developed his first generation processor. It doubled capacity."

"Good for him," I muttered, looking through the rest of the files. "It looks like he's expanding into the medical industry."

"Oh, Dellacorp is into almost everything." He had a serious case of hero worship.

I was going to have to point out a few truths to my new buddy.

"Including demon contracts." I shoved the files into my bag. I decided to take everything.

We needed to get going. Maybe I would get lucky. I tried to open a file cabinet. It was locked. I pulled hard and presto, no more locks.

"What do you mean demon contracts?" Casey's blue eyes were wide and innocent. I hated to be the one to crack that naïveté.

And there it was. A nice fat file marked *Brimstone Clinical Trial*. I pulled it out and shoved it in the bag before turning to the newbie. "No corporation takes over the world in seven years. No dude who used to have a shop somewhere goes from small business owner to king of the world in seven years, not without some help."

Casey's forehead wrinkled. "You don't think he sold his soul or something?"

"I don't think, Case, I know." I patted his arm in what I hoped was a soothing fashion. "I'm having dinner with the man tomorrow night at the duke's house. When I say duke, I don't mean some English dude. He's a duke of Hell. You don't do business with him without an ironclad contract." Casey's face fell and I felt for him. I never had anyone I looked up to that way, but if I had, they would have disappointed me, too. It was the way the world worked. "Let's go. We need to get home and let Henri make sense of all this medical jargon."

Casey nodded and followed me out into the lobby. I noted that his shoulders slumped forward a bit. I wondered if he had a family who still mourned him. It must be weird to know that they were out there somewhere, and he couldn't see them again. A picture of Nathan flashed through my mind for the second time that day.

"I found a file on Alan and one on Scott," Liv said, her pretty face tight with tension. "There's more, Kels. I know a bunch of these guys. They're weres and shifters. They had a couple of witches in there, but from what I can tell, those experiments didn't work. They had a stamp on them stating they terminated the tests. Do you think they're dead?"

"Were you close to any of them?"

Liv shook her head. "No, I only know the names."

Good. I could be honest. "Then yes, they're totally dead. That's what terminated usually means. Let's get going before we find ourselves in the same boat."

"This is serious." Casey stopped in the middle of the lobby. There was a panicked look in his eyes.

"Yes," I replied, agreeing with him and pointing toward the door. I didn't have time to play the shrink.

"They really are killing people," Casey said more to himself than either me or Liv. "This isn't some joke."

"No, it's not." I could practically feel the vamp's distress. He was like a mouse who thought there was cheese at the end of his fun maze only to discover a big fat cat waiting for him with its mouth open. Welcome to my world, buddy. "Let's go, and you can get back to your Xbox."

It wasn't said unkindly. I meant it as reassurance. He wasn't cut out for this, and Henri was going to have my head. I would give it to him on a silver platter, too. I hadn't been thinking. I shouldn't have even brought Liv with me, and she knew what she was getting into. If I needed backup, I should have taken up Trent on his offer. He knew the score and had experience in sticky situations. My only saving grace was the fact that this situation had turned out to be a breeze. We waltzed in, and we were about to waltz right back out.

The door at the front of the clinic opened. My day went straight to shit.

"I don't know how many there are," I heard a voice saying. "It's probably asshole kids trying to score some drugs."

I waved my hand for Liv and Casey to get behind me. We had some cover. The reception desk was in front of a wall of those pretty glass cubes a lot of offices use to separate spaces. Whoever was in the front didn't see us yet. I pulled my Browning automatic. Casey and Liv knelt down behind a desk. I noted that Liv had the semi in her hand.

"I'm going to die," Casey said quietly. "It hurt bad the first time. Do you think it'll be even worse this time?"

"Buck up," I ground out, trying some tough love. Now wasn't the time to coddle the baby vamp. "You're a fucking vampire. You might not like killing, but I assure you, you're damn good at it. If you can't help, then keep your head down and try to survive."

I gave both of them my most ferocious "keep your mouth shut" look and opened my senses.

"They were smart enough to take out the security cameras," one of them said. "Maybe we should call the police."

There were three of them, and they were armed. I could see through the blocks of glass. They were obscure figures walking through the lobby. I breathed in deeply. I thought two of them were human. The third made my skin crawl. Demon. I would have bet my life he was a halfling, like Gray. He would be tough, but mortal.

I turned my attention to Liv. I held up two fingers and pointed at her chest. She nodded that she understood. I then held up one finger and made a little horn over my head. Her face fell. I knew she got the picture. Casey seemed to be concentrating. I thought he might be trying to shield. I could have told him that it wouldn't work with the demon any more than it did with me. He'd gone to someplace inside himself, and I prayed I didn't get him killed.

I took a deep breath that had nothing to do with oxygen and everything to do with that piece of me that contains my wolf. My adrenaline started pumping. Part of me was thrilled at the prospect of a good fight. Instead of twitching, my body got righteously still, preserving my power and energy for the moment of attack. It was times like this that I could almost feel the change. I would never shift forms, though I'd been told tales about Hunters who managed to change their hands.

Still, I could feel the need. I could practically feel my teeth lengthen, my limbs loosen.

"Stop," the one who seemed to be the leader said. "Shit. What's a fucking vampire doing here?"

Demons have pretty good sniffers, too. He dropped his voice. "I'm getting one witch, a vampire, and something else. I don't like that something else. I…it feels wrong."

He had good instincts.

"I didn't sign up to fight vampires," one of the humans said.

"It can't be vampires. I have to be wrong. It's daylight. It must be something left over from the testing. You know they have all kinds of supes in here. Just calm down."

"We should get out of here." There was panic in the human's voice.

"If you run, my master will kill you, slave," the demon shot back. "I'll make sure of it."

I walked out from behind the glass partition because it was obvious they weren't leaving anytime soon. It was time to fight my way out. "And if you don't run, I'll be the one who kills you."

"It's only a girl." The second human appeared to be roughly twenty-five, and the dude worked out. He was a big, muscular guy. He slapped his partner on the back with a sigh of relief. "It's some dumb-shit druggie."

The demon was in human form. He was much more slender than his human counterparts, but looks were deceiving in his case. Demons didn't need massive muscles to be strong. His eyes went red and he took a step back, now obviously more wary than the humans. He knew I was something different, and different in our world could be deadly. "I don't know what you are, but you better not mess with me. Do you have any idea who I work for, bitch? I have a piece of his power."

"I don't care." I couldn't. I had to get Liv and Casey out of here. I couldn't give a crap who this dude's master was. "We can work this one of two ways. I can kill you quickly and walk out of here or…I can't think of another way, sorry."

I had no choice. If they reported back to Winter or the Dante guy, my cover was going to be blown. I needed to get into Winter's place. I couldn't risk it. I quickly raised the Browning and all hell broke loose.

I went for the humans first. Do I feel bad about killing a couple of guys in league with demons? Nah. I was doing them a favor because at some point that shit was going to get real for them. The first guy went down without a shout, falling backward. I started moving, rolling to take cover behind the desk because now the other guy was firing.

"I need backup at the clinic," the demon shouted into a cell phone. I tried to shoot it out of his hand, but he was quick.

The desk thudded at my back, thumping as they shot into it. I kind of hoped they would run out of the damn things.

There was a brief lull in the firing, and I felt something rush past me in a great gust of speed. The door to the clinic opened and then shut again. The demon cursed and seemed to try to take out his frustrations on the desk again. I was ready to take out some frustrations of my own.

Casey. The bastard had run and left Liv behind. He'd been quick, but I caught sight of the shirt he'd been wearing as he ran past the window. I swore if I survived this, that brat and I were going to have a long conversation.

Casey running left me with no choice but to get this done now. I no longer could pray that Casey was smart enough to take Liv out the back. I had to get her out of here and fast. Someone was going to hear the shooting. Someone would walk down the street, hear the obvious sounds of gunfire, and the cops would be called. I didn't know who I was looking forward to dealing with less—the Dallas PD or whatever the clinic considered backup.

Either way, Liv would lose, so I had to fix this situation now.

"Hold her down," the demon shouted. "The cavalry is on its way."

I wasn't waiting on the cavalry.

"Liv, you run when I give you the go!" I shouted, not waiting for a response.

I needed to get some distance between us and the clinic. Then I would have to swallow my pride and call my uncle or Trent to pick us up. Without pausing to consider the idiotic move I was about to make, I leapt on the desk.

"Go!"

I put a quick two rounds into the nearest guard. The last human shouted and went down, but not before he got off a shot of his own. I felt a massive force shove me to the side. I went tumbling onto the carpet as the bullet whizzed by.

The residual magic in the air gave the demon a momentary pause. Liv stood in the open, her palms up. She'd saved me by shoving me out of the way. Now she shook with the force of the power she'd used. The demon saw his opening. His hand was out and reaching for her.

I jumped up and put myself between the demon and my best friend. He grabbed my arm, and I felt the power in him.

"Bitch, this is from my master," the demon hissed. "Jack Frost says hello."

I gasped as cold entered my skin and the world around me seemed to freeze.

Chapter Twelve

The pain was horrible. I've taken a lot of damage, but this was something different. Pain is usually hot, like a flash fire through my system. There was nothing warm about this. It was foreign, as though ice had suddenly replaced the blood in my veins, and the chill went straight to my soul. My arm felt like it was swelling, and for a moment I actually wanted the damn thing to burst. It would relieve the horrible ache.

Then something even worse happened.

It completely went away. I couldn't feel anything from the elbow down on my right arm. It was like my forearm ceased to exist. The Browning dropped uselessly to the floor. Instinctively, I punched out with my left hand, hitting the demon squarely in the face, and he let go of my now useless arm.

I would have kicked out and continued my assault, but I dropped to my knees. Panic threatened. I could feel it welling up inside me because that chill was still in me. Alien. Foreign. It curled around in my body, and I worried that whatever had happened to my right arm was going to happen to the rest of my body. I looked down at my hand. It was sort of waxy looking, the skin going an odd opaque. Thick blisters were coming up as though I'd shoved it into a pot of boiling water.

And I felt nothing.

"Oh, shit." I was in trouble because the demon was back on his feet.

He walked toward me. His eyes had bled to red, and his hands were out. Those hands were coming for me. They contained Julius Winter's power. Somehow this shitty halfling—who I should be able to kill without breaking a nail—had the power to freeze off my body parts.

A smirk hit his mouth and his hands were squarely aimed for my throat. I scrambled, trying to move the gun to my left hand. I wasn't great with my left hand. Marcus made me practice with it, and I was grateful to him. It didn't look like it would matter. I couldn't get a grip on it fast enough. I fumbled and fell back on my ass. Just as the demon was about to wrap those cold hands around my neck, gunfire exploded, and his red eyes widened. His hands fell, shocked as a neat hole opened in his forehead. He slammed backward.

"Are you all right?" Liv stood over me. She still held the gun she'd used to save my throat from becoming Elsa's playground.

I wasn't. Not even close, but I was alive for the moment. That was all she needed to know. Nausea rolled in my stomach, but I managed to nod. "Nice shot." I forced myself to my feet, protecting my damaged hand. "Thanks, Liv."

"I have no idea how I did that." Her whole body was shaking. The gun she'd used to save me twitched in her hand. "What did he do to your arm?" She looked a little sick as she caught sight of my useless limb. "Oh god, Kelsey…"

There wasn't time for sympathy. I managed to get the Browning into my jacket pocket. "We have to go. They called for backup and the cops will be here any minute. I don't think we can use the train. They'll look for us there. We have to run and hide and hope my uncle can get to us before the bad guys do."

Liv helped me, putting her shoulder under my good arm. I shoved the bad one into my jacket, Napoleon style. I was worried if I let it dangle, it might fall off. We started to make our way to the door.

Suddenly Casey was standing in front of us, his blue eyes wide with pure anxiety. He went a little white as he noticed the bodies on the floor. He took a long breath and I saw his fangs lengthen. Blood. There was blood everywhere. Casey was a baby vamp so he had impulse issues. Yet another thing I probably should have thought about before taking him into the field. Luckily, he was also an academic, and control was their stock-in-trade.

Casey shook off the blood lust and got to the point. "Come on. I hot-wired a car. Dude, what happened to your arm?"

"Talk in the car." Liv pushed past him, dragging me along, and sure enough there was a nice SUV sitting on the snow-covered street.

Liv shoved me in the front seat then hopped in the back. Casey jammed the car into gear, and I held on for dear life. It was harder than usual since I only had the one hand to hold on with.

"I'm sorry it took so long. I had to find one with four-wheel drive," he explained. "It'll handle the ice better. I also called in. Henri is beyond pissed. Marcus is on his way. I don't know how he knows where we are, but he'd already called Henri."

I knew what had happened. Marcus had felt my terror and potentially my pain. The fact that he was out there, trying to get to me gave me great strength. Casey moved down the street as I heard someone pull on to the road behind us. I managed to turn in my seat. The van behind us was dark. I prayed it would stop and whoever was inside would go into the clinic and waste precious moments investigating.

Unfortunately, the van barely slowed down. When we turned, it turned, and I saw an arm come out of the passenger side window and a glint of steel reflecting our way.

"We have company." I pulled the Browning with my left hand, trying to keep the right hand as still as possible. "Keep your head down."

Liv lay down in the backseat, getting her head out of the way in case they decided to fire into the car. "Are they following us?"

"Yes. They're coming after us." I reached up and hit the button that opened the sunroof with the back of my hand.

Casey glanced my way. "Uhm, Kelsey, I don't think we need fresh air. If you haven't noticed, it's snowing. Let's keep the cold air out."

I groaned as I turned in the seat and got up on my knees. "You just drive, pretty boy."

Cold air blasted in from the sunroof. Casey was booking it and the wind whipped in. The last thing I wanted was to get more of my body frostbitten, but I had a better chance with a clear view of the car behind me. I got to my feet and popped the top of my torso through the sunroof.

Pure cold bit into my skin, chaffing every inch of me that was exposed. My lips cracked, but I concentrated on the van racing behind us. I held the Browning tightly in one hand, preparing myself for the recoil. I lined up my shot and pulled the trigger as I released the breath I'd been holding.

Just as I shot, Casey slid across a patch of ice, throwing me into the side of the car. My feet slipped on the leather seats and I slammed my head as I went down. My peripheral vision started to fade, but I managed to keep it together.

"Sorry." Casey wrestled with the steering wheel to get control over the vehicle.

He turned into the slide and the van behind us took advantage. There was a loud crack as the passenger shot at me through his window. He hit the mirror on my side of the car. I forced myself back up and managed to get a shot off while Casey straightened out the SUV and started toward the freeway.

Blood dripped down from my forehead, clouding my vision. Naturally, I didn't have a free hand to wipe it away with. I was going to miss my right hand if Henri had to amputate. I hoped Marcus's blood could heal it, but it felt really dead. I took a deep breath. I wouldn't have time to miss my arm if the rest of me got shot up.

Casey cursed as the wheels spun out again.

"Hey, could you keep it steady for more than two seconds?" I have to admit that I was the tiniest bit irritable.

"Don't bitch at me." Everything about Casey seemed tense. "I've never driven in this shit before."

The van behind us wasn't having the same trouble. Perhaps their security detail had been brought in from someplace cold. I struggled back into a position to fire from. Again, this is where Trent would have come in handy. I bet that Boston boy knew how to handle some snow. "Try to keep us on the road."

"Maybe we should wait until Marcus gets here." Liv hunkered down in the floorboard of the backseat.

"Not an option," I replied.

The back windshield cracked as it took a bullet.

"Owww!" Casey yelled. His right arm was bleeding freely, staining his shirt. "I think I got shot."

"Stay calm," I ordered. "Keep moving. Whatever you do, keep moving."

Casey tried. He really did. It became impossible when the van slammed into us and our SUV hit the side of a building. The impact jarred through my body and seared my senses. The sound of metal tearing hurt my ears. The airbags deployed, leaving an acrid smell hanging in the air. I wasn't wearing a seat belt, so I slammed against the side. Pain flared and then the sound of gunfire seemed more distant than before. I could hear someone shouting, but the world seemed hazy and then dark.

When I came to, it was to the sound of gunfire. I couldn't figure out what was going on. I was in a car. It was the car Casey had stolen, but it wasn't moving. The window had shattered and I could feel blood on my cheek. There was glass everywhere, though it was in tiny bits. I tried to sit up.

Casey had my Browning in his hand. He was firing out the sunroof, trying his damnedest to keep the bastards off of us. There was blood on his coat. Lots of it. He'd been hit more than once.

I groaned as I pushed myself up, which wasn't easy because only one arm worked. I looked into the back, desperate to make sure I hadn't managed to kill my best friend. Liv was still huddled in the seat, but she had one hand out of the ruined back window. She fired randomly. Her head was down, so she couldn't see a thing. I guess she had to try something.

That's the thing about being desperate. You're willing to do anything.

"Can you get us moving?" I had to yell to be heard over the loud pop of guns firing.

Casey grunted as his body took another bullet, slamming him against the back edge of the sunroof. If he hadn't been a vampire, that impact would have likely damaged his spine.

As he was, he groaned and took another shot. "No way. Car's dead."

"We have to run." I couldn't see any other way out. We were sitting ducks. Sitting, bleeding, one-armed ducks. At least I was.

"I don't think that's a good idea," Casey shot back. "They're closing in."

And then I knew he was here. I felt him like a calm wave pushing against the adrenaline and panic. Marcus brushed his mind across mine and he was calm, sure. He was certain he was going to save me.

Outside the car, the gunfire picked up. Someone was shooting, but this wasn't a handgun. This was bigger. I heard the lovely sound of a Remington twelve gauge being primed. I know my guns like most women know shoes or lip-gloss.

Casey slumped down into the cab, and I could see where all that blood had come from. His chest was riddled with bullets. Luckily, it looked like the day shift didn't use silver bullets.

"Someone else is here." His voice shook. I noticed a fine tremble in his hands as well. "There's some big dude with a shotgun. He's walking down the street shooting them down. When did we land in the middle of a Western?"

I forced my body to move. I managed to turn and look out the ruined window. Grayson Sloane. I couldn't help but smile because Gray was doing exactly what Casey said. He was walking down the snowy street, his big chest covered in body armor. He wore a Stetson on his head and his favorite boots. He looked like he'd walked straight out of a John Ford film. I couldn't take my eyes off him as he tore through the security force the clinic had sent after us. They weren't so tough without a huge vehicle behind them.

Definitely not as tough as my Texas Ranger.

Already, the white snow around us was turning a stark, brutal red. A scream sounded through the air, and I saw two of the men walk out of the van and draw their weapons. They aimed and shot each other in the head. Their bodies slumped to the ground. Marcus would never get his hands dirty when he could persuade his enemies to kill themselves.

"We're good now." I slumped over, quietly waiting.

I wasn't worried about the backup squad taking out my men. They were dead the moment Marcus and Gray caught up to them.

"I can't get the door open." Casey pushed against the driver's side door, but it was lodged shut. He turned his blue eyes to me, his face a stark white. He was as white as the snow falling through the sunroof. "I need to feed, Kelsey. I hurt real bad."

Luckily, the bullets he'd taken didn't look to be silver. They were already coming out of his body. He winced as one fell from his shoulder. It was probably the first time he'd been shot. I doubted combat had been in his training schedule. I reached out and took his hand.

"It's all right. You did good, Casey." I held out my left hand, showing him my wrist. He'd kept us alive, and I knew that had cost him. I owed him blood.

His eyes widened and his fangs were out, but he backed away from the offered appendage. He moved as far as he could before his back hit the door. "Not on your life, sister. I want to heal, not have Marcus take me apart."

Liv sat up, her disheveled hair all around her face. "He's right. That's not such a great idea. I can't imagine Marcus is going to be in a great mood after this."

There was the horrible sound of the door being pulled off the car. One minute it was there and the next it was being tossed aside like a toy.

"You alive in there, Kelsey?" Sloane asked, his voice tight.

I let his deep Texas accent wash over me before nodding. Now that we were safe, my body shook as I came down from the high of trying to survive. Now I was faced with the consequences. I was bleeding from several places, my head hurt, and I probably had a concussion. I couldn't feel my arm. I couldn't feel it at all. I was covered in blood, much of it mine.

Gray pulled the vampire out of the car, and suddenly Marcus was there. He reached in and gathered me into his arms, lifting me free from the wreckage.

"Oh, *bella*, what have they done to you?" he asked as he held me close. His beautiful face was stoically calm as he ran a hand over my face, my hair.

In the distance, I heard the whir of a siren.

"We need to move, Vorenus." Gray helped Liv out. "The police are coming."

"I can handle them," my boyfriend promised.

Up ahead, Casey stumbled toward Gray's massive truck. Gray carried Liv while Marcus held me securely in his arms.

"Let's make sure we don't have to," Gray said, hustling toward the still running vehicle. "I don't want all this caught on someone's phone and posted on YouTube. I'm supposed to be undercover."

"I apologize if saving Kelsey blows your cover." Marcus got into the cab of the truck. He pulled me up into his lap, arranging me into a semi-comfortable position.

Casey and Liv climbed into the back.

Gray's mouth was a stubborn line as he put the truck in drive. "That wasn't what I meant. I would give my life for her and you know it. I got us here as fast as I could."

"Stop fighting." My words were slurring slightly. Light-headed was a soft term for what I felt. The world was threatening to spin out of control.

"She hit her head." Casey leaned forward to look into the front of the cab. "She hit it a couple of times, and when we crashed, she wasn't wearing a seat belt."

"You mean when you crashed, Mr. Lane," Marcus accused the young vampire. "You were driving the vehicle. You crashed and my mistress paid the price."

"Don't." I was too tired to listen to recriminations. "Don't blame Casey. He did a good job. He didn't fuck up. I did. It was my fault."

I was so tired. I let my head rest against Marcus's shoulder. There was a fuzziness to everything. My head seemed as snowy as the world outside.

"Don't you fall asleep, Kelsey!" Gray barked the order, bringing me out of my twilight. "Vorenus, are you going to yell at the newbie or save your precious mistress? Cause from where I'm sitting, she's in a bad way."

Marcus forced my head up. "Kelsey, look at me."

My eyes weren't capable of obeying the command. They wanted to close and rest. I sighed and let them shut. If only all the people would stop talking, I could sleep. Sleep seemed like such a nice thing to do. I could rest my eyes for a few moments…

"Darling, wake up." Marcus shook me gently. "*Bella*, you must stay awake." He seemed far away. Sleep beckoned much more urgently.

The world began to go dark, but even that seemed nice after the ultra-bright of the snowy day.

"You open your eyes, Kelsey Jean Atwood!"

I couldn't ignore that sharp bark. My head came off Marcus's shoulder, and I was caught by seriously blue eyes. Gray had one hand on the steering wheel and one locked in my hair.

"You fight, Kelsey," Gray ordered. "You take that blood and you live, you understand me?"

He knew how to get my attention.

"Fuck you, Sloane." I said it out of habit and because I didn't like having my naps interrupted. He was right. Something was seriously wrong with me.

"Spit all the shit at me you want, but you take that blood and you take it now," he ordered.

I forced my head to move, to shift toward my boyfriend. Marcus popped sharp claws in his right hand and tore open a hole close to his neck. I needed that blood. My head kind of fell forward and I managed to get my mouth where it needed to go. I felt Marcus's arms tighten around me, holding me in place.

"That's right, *cara mia*. Drink." His breath was warm against my ear. I felt his anxiety as though he couldn't quite contain it, and I caught the edge of it. I must look pretty bad if Marcus was so worried I could feel it.

Rich, velvety blood filled my mouth. My head started to clear.

"Keep drinking." Marcus held my head to his flesh when I tried to pull away.

I gamely continued, but after another minute I couldn't take any more. I pulled away and sat up, so much better than I was before. My vision was clear, my thoughts lucid.

"Oh, my god." Liv moaned from the backseat.

I glanced over Marcus's shoulder and saw that my best friend was taking one for the team. She had her arms wrapped around Casey's shoulders. His fangs were firmly in her neck. Casey's hands were around her back, and Liv's head was thrown back in what looked like complete ecstasy. Her whole body stiffened and then she relaxed. I knew that feeling. Heaven. After a moment, Casey released the vein. Liv slumped against him, completely exhausted.

I couldn't help but stare, shocked at the sight of my proper BFF looking languid and sexy in the arms of a vampire. Her head rested against his chest, her whole body relaxed as he held her.

Casey shrugged. "If I didn't pull her in, it would hurt."

"Be ready for her to kick your ass later." Liv was going to be completely embarrassed that she'd had an orgasm in front of Marcus and Gray.

"I get the feeling she'll have to stand in line," Casey muttered.

I noticed he didn't shove Liv off his lap. He cuddled her close. Vampires are especially affectionate creatures after a feed. Casey wasn't attempting to fight that part of his nature. Liv's face pressed into his neck and he rubbed his cheek against hers thoughtfully.

"Is she better?" Gray ignored what was going on in the backseat. His attention was divided between me and the road. He didn't seem to have any trouble driving in the awful conditions.

Marcus looked into my eyes, studying them carefully. "I believe the concussion is gone."

My head was perfectly clear. I was able to think straight and reason. The vampire blood had done its job. It healed everything it could.

Unfortunately, it didn't bring back the dead things of this world.

"*Bella*, why are you crying?" Marcus's hand cupped my cheek. His dark eyes were filled with concern. "It's all right now. Everyone is well. I want a report on what happened, but otherwise it's fine."

I shook my head. There was nothing to do at this point except to show him. I pulled my dead right hand out of my jacket where I'd kept it cradled to my chest. I didn't need to look at it to know it was completely fucked, but the sight of it made me nauseous anyway. It was black and withered, as though it had been dead and gone for weeks, not mere minutes.

Marcus gasped as he caught sight of the withered thing that used to be my dominant arm. He never gasped. His breathing was almost always steady as a rock. "What did this to you?"

"Kelsey…" Gray's eyes were wide with horror. He blanched. He turned to the vampire as though he couldn't look at me anymore. "Give her more blood. It didn't work."

Marcus gently touched my dead hand. Not that I could tell by touch. I was watching him so I knew. His voice was laced with guilt and sadness. "It won't work. The flesh is dead." His eyes slid past me to the lieutenant. Now they were coldly furious. "You did not mention you were dealing with a duke of Hell, Lieutenant Sloane. There is only one I know of with the power to freeze objects with a mere touch of his hand."

"It was one of his servants." I explained what had happened. The whole time I had stupid freaking tears that wouldn't stop running down my face. My voice was still shaky as I finished. "He said he had his master's power. He said something about Jack Frost. Isn't that some old faery tale?"

The vampire squeezed my good hand in his. "No. That is merely one of the demon's names. Long ago, he took on the powers of the elements. He specialized in winter. This particular demon is extremely old and powerful. I would never have allowed you in the same city with him had I known he was here."

"Isn't killing demons my job?" I asked stubbornly. I didn't like being told I couldn't do something even when the effects of the bad idea being discussed were right in front of my face. It was a perverse part of my nature.

"I would never have let him touch her." Gray's hands tightened on the wheel.

"You are both children, idiotic children, to believe you can take on one such as him." His voice was low and controlled, which told me he was truly angry. "I can forgive Kelsey. She's young. It's in her nature to be arrogant. She could not have known this could happen. I blame myself. I've given her too much latitude. I preferred to be her lover rather than her trainer."

"It isn't your fault." I tried to soothe him. I used my good hand to rub across his neck.

"And I blame you, Lieutenant," Marcus continued, obviously unwilling to be comforted. "You knew who he was."

"I can handle him." Gray slapped at the dashboard. He wasn't as good at controlling his anger as Marcus. When he turned our way, his eyes were turning violet. "My brother and I can handle Winter and I can protect Kelsey."

"How can I possibly know this is true? Would you like to give me your brother's name so I might be familiar with his strengths and abilities? He is a full blood?"

"He is." Sloane turned onto the road that would take us home. "And you know I can't give you his name. He's going by Matthew on this plane for now."

Marcus huffed, an aristocratic dismissal. "Yet you expect me to trust my Hunter with you? It will not happen. The deal we made previously is done, Sloane. I will be taking my Hunter back to Italy in the morning."

"Marcus!" I couldn't leave. Twenty-four hours before I would have given anything to be back in Italy. Now it sounded like the worst idea ever. I couldn't leave things the way they were. I have a real thing about starting something. I had to finish it.

Something dangerous was going on, and I was the one to deal with it. It was kind of the point of me.

"No," he said firmly. "I'm your trainer. This is a job I would be hesitant to send a seasoned Hunter into, much less a green girl."

"Vorenus, I need her." Sloane sounded almost savage. "Winter is expecting that I'll bring Kelsey to his house. I can't walk in there tomorrow without her."

"You'll have to handle it yourself." Marcus's arm tightened possessively around my waist. "She won't be here."

"Do you understand what's at stake?" Sloane asked in a tight voice.

Marcus shook his head, and he was all arrogance himself. "Lieutenant, you make a mistake if you believe that I care. Do you have any idea the horrors I've seen? This world is filled with them. There will always be wars whether it's humans killing each other or demons slaughtering vampires. I'm finished with all of it. I protect what is mine. What happens to the rest is none of my concern."

Sloane turned into the parking garage. "You can't mean that. You can't mean to take away the best weapon we have to fight him. Do you understand what's going on? That drug can hurt the entire supernatural world. It might start here, but don't think it won't get to you eventually. She has to live in this world, too. It's her fight."

"Not any longer."

The truck stopped, and I was outside in one of those blindingly fast vampire moves. My good arm was wrapped around Marcus's shoulder. From the wall of elevators that led to the compound, I saw a group waiting. Henri and Hugo began jogging toward us.

Marcus turned back to Sloane. "If you ask me to choose the world or my lover, I will always choose her. When you live as long as I have, you come to see the world means very little." I felt terribly numb as he carried me toward the entrance. "Henri, you will prep the operating room. Our Hunter is going to lose her arm."

"What!" Hugo's voice rang through the garage.

Henri turned and began to run back up to the hospital unit.

Casey stood with Liv still unconscious in his arms. He cradled her carefully against his chest as though she was infinitely fragile. He looked super young and slightly scared standing there. Marcus's next words didn't give him any comfort.

"Mr. Lane, you will take care of Miss Carey, and then you'll come to the hospital. I require a word with you."

"Yes, sir," Casey managed. He was obviously not looking forward to the next hour or so. Then again, neither was I. I was about to get acquainted with the word amputation.

"Kelsey." Sloane's shout echoed through the garage. I glanced back over to where he stood alone now. His face was a mask of grief. "I'm so sorry, baby."

Marcus kept walking.

Chapter Thirteen

"How is this possible?" Henri examined my arm with a frown on his face. "This should have taken much more time. She was fine when I saw her earlier today. This damage should have taken many hours of raw exposure to the elements."

"It was Abbas Hiberna." Marcus's entire countenance was grim as he sat next to the gurney I'd been lain on.

Henri had spent the better part of an hour examining me. He'd taken x-rays and shoved me into his MRI. He'd spent what felt like an eternity studying those reports when I was sure they'd all told him the same thing. I knew what he was really trying to do. He was putting off the time when he had to call for the bone saw and relieve me of my arm.

Hugo cursed under his breath. "What's that bugger doing here? Doesn't he have a realm on the Hell plane to rule?"

"He's expanding," I said bitterly. The waiting was starting to get to me. The outcome was inevitable. There was a part of me that wanted to get it all over with. "Henri, is there any point in drawing this out? Cut the damn thing off."

I'd figure out what would happen later. I could guess. The king wouldn't consider me an effective *Nex Apparatus* without my dominant arm. Marcus could talk about taking me back to Italy, but I doubted that would last. I gave him a month tops before he started wondering what he was doing with someone like me. I had no illusions about my relationship with Marcus. He was attracted to me because I was a

Hunter. I was a dangerous, unpredictable creature and that got Marcus off. Without that, I had to wonder what we would find to do together. There was a big old piece of me that already accepted that I would be alone again.

I would have to learn how to do shots with my left hand.

Henri's face fell. "No, there's no reason to wait if you're ready, dear."

"I'm not going to get any readier."

The doors to the small operating room burst open and Gray strode in. I noticed the king wasn't far behind him.

"Kelsey, don't let him touch you," Gray commanded.

Marcus was on his feet immediately. "What are you doing in here?"

"I couldn't keep him out, Marcus." Donovan stared down at my arm and took a deep breath. His eyes came back up. "He called and demanded a meeting."

"Well, Your Highness, there's a word you can use," Marcus spat with more sarcasm than I thought him capable of. "It is no."

"I don't think he was going to accept a no." Donovan's eyes tightened as he examined my injured arm. "Right now, there are five Texas Rangers waiting outside the building for a search warrant that the lieutenant swears he can get to raid Ether in search of illegal firearms. I would tell him to go to hell, but we all know why I don't do that."

He didn't do that because Gray would find a whole bunch of illegal firearms if he raided Ether. I was sure Quinn was hauling some serious ass to hide the P-90s. The Rangers were the only law enforcement the king couldn't persuade to leave. They would be ready. Sloane's commanding officer might not like what he did or how he had to do it, but he wouldn't let his men go anywhere unprepared. They would be armed with anti-persuasion charms and talismans. Donovan might be the king of the supernatural world, but he was a Texan, and we were raised to respect those badass cops.

Gray wasn't listening to the king argue with his oldest ally. His eyes were on me. "Kelsey, sweetheart, you don't have to lose your arm. I talked to the king. We worked out a deal. I'm calling my father in…"

Chaos broke loose. Marcus got in Gray's way, trying to shove the big half demon away from me. Gray's fangs came out, and he pushed back at the smaller vampire.

"Stop!" Donovan placed himself between the vampire and the demon. "Both of you get to your fucking corners."

Marcus's fangs had come out and his fingers had sprung claws, but he took a step back. "He needs to stay away from my Hunter."

"You need to listen to me," Gray growled back, his eyes that shade of violet that let me know he was getting close to the edge.

Donovan shook his head. "Everyone calm down. I read over the files Owens managed to smuggle out of that clinic. I don't understand all the medical jargon, but I get the gist. Some asshole demon is playing around with drugs. This drug, called Brimstone, damages the impulse center of the brain leaving some intensely powerful creatures without any impulse control. That's so bad for us I can't begin to describe it. Now, I could go to the demons and yell and scream and try to enforce our contracts…"

"It won't work, Your Highness," Hugo interrupted. "Unless His Grace has been forcing the drug on vampires, there is nothing we can do. The contracts we have in force at the present time are only between vampires and demonkind. You've used that to your own advantage by designating a non-vampire *Nex Apparatus*."

Donovan sighed and ran a hand over his hair in a deeply weary gesture. "I know that, Hugo. Look, we can discuss the ins and outs of my decision making later. Right now, I'm going to let the lieutenant call his father to see if there is any way we can save her arm."

Marcus stepped back up. "No. If you think for one second I will allow my charge to sign a contract, you're out of your mind. I'll take her from this place, and you won't see us again."

Then he was off, yelling in rapid-fire Italian. The room was a powder keg again.

"Hey!" I was sick of the fighting and upset that no one had even bothered to ask my opinion. It was my arm and my soul after all. "Shouldn't it be my choice?"

The men turned to me. Donovan didn't look like his answer to my question was going to be yes. For that matter, Marcus didn't seem super interested in my opinion either.

Henri was the voice of reason. "Yes, dear. What do you want to do? I'll clear out the room if you like. This is my hospital, and I'm king here."

I closed my eyes and laid back. "Get rid of them, Henri, so we can get this done. I'm not signing a contract."

Marcus's hand reached out and squeezed mine.

"Kelsey, baby, I wouldn't ask you to do that." When I opened my eyes, Gray was kneeling beside me.

"The lieutenant is the only one putting anything on the line, Owens," Donovan said bluntly. "I would never allow you to sign a demon contract. Sloane believes he can bargain with his father."

Gray's violet eyes beseeched me. "I can convince him. It won't cost you a thing. Please, let me do this for you."

I was overwhelmed with his suggestion because I knew the truth. It might not cost me, but it would absolutely cost someone. Demons don't heal a person because they're looking to fill their karma banks. I had to believe if Gray could work a deal, he would owe his father something awful.

"If the lieutenant believes he can broker such a deal at no cost to my charge, then I agree. Hugo can go with him to ensure that there is no possibility Kelsey could be held accountable." Marcus stared down the lieutenant.

"No. No one is signing anything." I couldn't sign my soul away. I wasn't about to let someone else do it. I certainly couldn't allow Gray to do it.

An aristocratic sigh hit my ears, and I realized there was someone standing at the door. Alexander Sharpe stood in the doorway with a superior smile on his face. "Oh, so much drama over one little limb."

"We don't need your input, Alex," the king said sharply. "Henri can handle this on his own."

Sharpe was dressed in his usual dark suit, the tie perfectly knotted. "Oh, I apologize for interrupting. I was under the false assumption that the doctor was going to hack that arm off our lovely *Nex Apparatus's* body. If he knows how to save the limb, then I'll leave you in his capable hands."

"Stop." No one could mistake the king's reluctance. I got the feeling he'd almost rather I signed a contract than have to deal with the former serial killer. I was kind of with him on that one. Still…

"You can save the limb?" Marcus didn't mind dealing with Sharpe.

Sharpe walked in, and his eyes flared at the sight of my arm. He didn't flinch the way the others did. He seemed almost fascinated by the black, shriveled thing. He paid careful attention to the place where the dead flesh met the living. I sat quietly under his stare, though it made me uncomfortable.

After a long, silent exam, he sighed and nodded to the king. "Yes, Your Highness. I can save the limb without involving the lieutenant's father, though I will need the lieutenant himself."

"Whatever you need." Gray was on his feet, offering himself up.

"The Hell plane is going to eat you up," Sharpe said with a shake of his head. He turned back to the king. "I'm going to need counsel before I go any further. Mr. Wells, if you don't mind?"

Hugo sighed and followed the vampire outside to conference with him.

"Kelsey, I'd still rather bring in my father." Sloane was quiet but resolved. He ignored Marcus's low growl. "I know it will work. I don't trust that vampire. We can't know he isn't plotting something."

Marcus huffed. "Of course, don't trust the vampire. We should place more faith in the Hell lord."

Gray regarded Marcus sullenly. "At least we know why he's doing it. He'll do it because he wants an even bigger hold on me. I have a lot to offer him."

Marcus's smile was ruthless. "And Alexander will do it because I'll pull his heart out if he does not."

"He's a warrior," Gray shot back. "I doubt you could best him in battle, and your mental tricks won't work on him."

"Ah, but he sleeps, Lieutenant," Henri Jacobs pointed out. "And we do not."

The doors swung open again. Hugo strode back in, his face set in serious lines. I like to think of it as his lawyer face. "Your Highness, my client wishes to be assured of complete immunity from prosecution if he is to proceed."

Donovan's eyebrows climbed up his forehead. "Why?"

I didn't need a magic eight ball to answer that question. Alexander Sharpe was a doctor. An evil doctor. "You've been experimenting, haven't you, Sharpe?"

The vampire shrugged and flicked at his fingernails. "I am a curious lad."

"Dr. Sharpe will not answer any questions concerning the nature of his medical experimentation without the aforementioned immunity," Hugo stated. "Not that I'm affirming or denying that the doctor has actually been involved in any form of experimentations."

"Right." Donovan shook his head as though he wished he didn't have to do what he was about to do. "This had better work, Hugo. He has immunity."

Sharpe clapped his hand together. "Excellent. I'm going to need a couple of donors. I need a bit of the lieutenant's blood and the king's as well."

"Naturally," Donovan said, taking off his jacket nonetheless.

Gray sat down in the chair closest to my bed. He had his muscular arm out, allowing Henri to start a line. Henri's movements were quick and efficient, as though he'd done this a thousand times before, and he very likely had. In no time at all, Gray's blood was flowing into the plastic donation bag. The king stood to the side, waiting his turn.

"You want to explain what you're planning to do to me?" I watched Sharpe neatly fold his jacket and roll up his sleeves. There was an almost gleeful light in his eyes.

"I would love to explain everything now that I know I won't be executed for it." Sharpe was back at my side, holding my dead arm up for inspection. "I had a theory, you see. The king there is a miraculous thing. Back when he was a young lad thinking about taking over the Council, King Daniel made the intelligent decision to bring me on board."

"It was that or kill you." Donovan stood back, watching the small crowd. His blue eyes slowly patrolled the room. I got the feeling very little got past the king. "I didn't think I could get away with the better option."

Sharpe completely ignored his monarch. His face was more animated than I remembered. He enjoyed being the center of attention. "When the king brought a vampire on board in those days, he turned us again. He required a blood oath. I made it. I've had a lot of blood in my life, Hunter, and none of it could touch that bit the king gave me. My own special talents were greatly enhanced by taking the king's blood. It made me think."

"So the king's blood didn't give you his powers." I was grateful for that fact. I didn't like to think about a supercharged Alexander Sharpe.

"God, no," Donovan interjected. "If that was true, I'd never share it with other vampires at all."

"The king's blood strengthens whoever takes it." Marcus was the only one in the room who had ever met a king other than Donovan. I'd heard stories of how he dethroned the first vampire to rise with a king's power. Apparently, he hadn't been as sane as Donovan. "It doesn't change the power of the one who takes it. It intensifies the power. Even among non-vampire's, it has this effect."

Gray got out of the chair after finishing his donation. "What do you mean?"

Donovan took his place and Henri began working on him.

"Take Devinshea," my boyfriend said. He held my good hand in both of his, as though trying to give me his strength. "I remember when he couldn't control his magic. After he began regularly taking the king's blood, his fertility powers exploded. Even the queen's glow became stronger with her husband's blood."

"Yes." Sharpe sighed with longing. "She's almost too bright to look at sometimes."

"How is this going to help save my *Nex Apparatus's* arm?" Donovan asked impatiently as his blood began to flow.

Sharpe went over and opened up the large leather bag he'd carried in with him. It was a doctor's bag, but nothing modern. I would bet he'd brought it with him when he journeyed to the new world. "Well, Your Highness, your blood is going to act as an accelerant for the demon's healing powers. I could use one of the wolves' blood, but I think the demon blood is stronger. Your uncle can heal, but in the case of a serious injury, the lieutenant is naturally better able to not only heal, but actually regrow body parts."

"What the hell is that?" I asked as he pulled out an outrageously large needle. "Tell me you use that on horses."

Sharpe held up the needle, showing it off. "I think it's important that a doctor use the instruments he's most comfortable with."

I turned quickly to Marcus. "I'd rather have Henri cut it off."

Henri stared at Sharpe, a disapproving look in his eyes as he finished with the king. "You will use modern instruments or you won't work in my operating room."

"Fine." Sharpe began putting up his instruments of torture. "I can leave."

"Alex, don't try my patience." The king stood. "I've given you immunity. Now tell me how you know this is going to work."

Henri pulled out a tray of more properly sized needles for Sharpe's perusal.

"I know it will work because I've done it before." Sharpe *tsk tsked* over the small, modern needles, but prepped them anyway. "I haven't used a human being, but it certainly works on animals. I started with mice, as is customary. I punctured the specimen's heart with a needle and was able to heal the injury with a combination of the king's blood and a werewolf's."

Donovan's lips curled up in a snarl. "You want to explain where you got my blood? I know I didn't give it to you."

Sharpe looked as innocent as a serial killer could. "I only borrowed a bit."

"*Verdomme*," Henri cursed. I don't understand Dutch, but I've been around enough Euros to catch a curse when I hear it. "You stole some of the backup supply."

Henri kept a supply of the king's blood for emergency situations.

Sharpe shrugged as though pleased with his own crimes. "Yes, I did. Now might be a good time to point out what the words 'complete immunity' mean."

"Continue." Donovan bit off his words in an attempt to control his rage.

Sharpe practically purred. "My first experiment was an unqualified success. I continued on, giving each subject longer and longer periods of 'rest time,' so to speak."

"You mean you let them lie dead before you brought them back." Henri glared at the younger vampire, and a deep crease split his brow.

Sharpe's eyes narrowed as he took in the Dutch doctor. He continued to prepare his cocktail while he spoke. "Do you forget so easily, Henri?"

The Dutch doctor crossed his arms over his chest defensively.

Hugo sighed. "Don't bring that up, Sharpe. You know we never bring that up."

But Henri was off and running. "Do not even claim your perverse experiments have anything in common with my creature. He was a thing of beauty. He was a beacon of light. My creature was a kind and gentle soul." Henri's eyes got misty. "They couldn't understand him. Stupid villagers with their torches and pitchforks."

I couldn't help it. I laughed. His creature? Seriously? "Henri was Dr. Frankenstein?"

Marcus winced, and I knew I'd made a mistake.

"Don't mention that horrible woman's book," Henri said, sniffling. "She tricked me into telling her my story."

"You slept with her, Henri," Hugo pointed out. "You get extremely talkative with your lovers. I believe I warned you at the time that it's best to not talk to writers. They tend to tell all, if you know what I mean."

"I cannot help it that I'm attracted to creative females," the doctor sulked. "When she said she wanted to write my story, I believed she would make me the hero."

"Yes, scientists bringing corpses back to life are the stuff of heroes." I turned back to Sharpe, who had the needles ready to go. "So we have a bunch of zombie mice running around the complex? I ask because if they start eating people, the king is probably going to send me after them."

The vampire pulled a stool toward my bed. He waved Gray aside with a dismissive hand gesture. "I destroyed the specimens, of course. Unlike Henri, I don't get attached to my experiments. I don't cry when villagers poke pitchforks through their torsos and then set fire to my lodgings."

Henri sighed sadly. "Yes, Hugo and I had to run very quickly."

"Now, when I moved on to larger specimens, I did run into a bit of trouble." Sharpe examined my arm. He ran his fingers up and down, tracing the blue lines showing against the pale of my skin. I tried to pull back, finding the touch far too intimate from him, but he insisted. "I need to find a good vein, dear."

"What kind of trouble did you have with the larger specimens? And how large are we talking?" Donovan was all business now.

Though he didn't touch me, I could feel Gray at the top of my gurney. Marcus held my good hand and watched everything the vampire doctor did, but I felt Gray's eyes on me. Sharpe continued his happy horror tale.

"The larger animals proved difficult to control." Sharpe's fingers brushed along my skin, making me shiver with dread. I knew what he was looking for. He was looking for the best vein to push the blood through. He would start where the vein was alive and push it through the dead parts, making a river of life-giving blood. It made sense, and I hated the fact that he was the one doing it. "I would be on the lookout for a slightly deranged poodle. All right, dear, here we go."

I hissed slightly as he pushed the needle into my vein. He was a vampire. He didn't need a second chance. He got it right the first time. I didn't like his smile as he stood over me. "No problem."

"Sorry, dear, this is probably going to be intensely painful." Sharpe gave me a mischievous grin.

Marcus swore as the doctor pushed the plunger down, and I screamed. The pain came fast and hard, my body shaking and fighting. Donovan was suddenly in Marcus's place. He held my shoulders down, forcing me to remain still as fire coursed through my veins. I can handle a great deal of pain, but my entire forearm restructuring itself was a bit much.

Sharpe pulled the needle out of my arm and called for another.

I shook my head. I couldn't take any more. Tears streamed down my face and I begged, pleaded with them to cut the fucking thing off. Donovan looked grim above me as Sharpe found another vein and went to work.

I was about to pass out from the pain when I suddenly found myself walking on a familiar path. I stopped and studied my surroundings. My body felt perfect, my arm free of agony and whole again. I flexed my hand and smiled before looking around me.

I was in a park from my childhood. Green trees and grass, blue and green playground equipment. Chisholm Park. Up ahead in the distance, I could see the duck pond. I would walk home from Bell High School with Nate, and we would stop and watch the ducks swim. We would stay there for long periods of time, dreading the moment we would go home and face the man who'd raised us. Nate and I would sit and talk, and sometimes he would read to me to pass the time.

There was a comforting weight in my hand. I didn't need to look to the side to know who was holding my hand. He was the man who had taken me here with his mind. My lover.

"I miss my brother." The longing for my childhood companion was sharp.

"I know you do, *bella*." Marcus squeezed my hand gently. "When you're ready, you'll call him."

I nodded and sat down to look out over one of the peaceful places of my childhood. "Is it working?"

"Yes, it's working. I'm sorry for the pain. I should have pulled you in before he even began. I didn't believe it was something so horrible. I shall have a talk with the doctor after this is done."

There was a warm breeze, and I leaned into my lover's body. He was everything comforting to me. I loved the way his arms felt around me and how my head tucked under his when I rested on his shoulder. I loved his scent. He smelled of sandalwood and soap. We sat quietly for a moment. This was so much better than anesthesia, which would have made me throw up.

I hated the fact that I kind of wished Marcus was Gray.

"*Bella*, I believe it's finished now," Marcus said quietly, as though he was reluctant to break our peaceful moment.

I turned my face up toward him. I wasn't ready to leave. I wasn't ready to face everyone. The day had gone so poorly. There were ramifications I didn't want to deal with yet. Marcus and I were going to fight because he wouldn't like what I needed to do. I wanted some sweetness first.

"Just because they're done doesn't mean we are, right?"

A slow smile crossed his handsome face. "No, my mistress." He gently lowered me on to my back. The grass was soft against my suddenly naked skin. "We're not finished yet."

Chapter Fourteen

I flexed my hand, opening and closing it. I was doing it almost unconsciously now. It felt good to use my hand again. It was hours later and I was sitting in my uncle's living room waiting for dinner. I discovered that nearly losing my arm made me hungry. And thirsty. I was working on my second beer.

"It works like a regular arm, right?" Lee stared at it. I thought he might be waiting to see if it could launch rockets or do something cool and bionic now.

It was perfect, with the singular exception of the skin being lighter than the rest of the arm. It was like I'd tanned lightly, but only on one side of my body. Sharpe swore the two arms would eventually match.

"Yeah." I grasped my beer bottle with it. "It works like normal."

"I wish I could have seen it," Lee groused. "I bet it was cool."

Rhys smiled and nodded. "I bet it was cool, too. You should have taken pictures."

"I think it would be gwoss," a small voice said. My cousin, Courtney Owens, stared up at me. She was a tiny thing with huge brown eyes and thick hair. I bet her hair weighed more than her body did. She was four years old and couldn't pronounce an L to save her life. "I'm gwad Aunt Kewsey didn't wose her awm."

She wasn't great with Rs either. She was a baby she-wolf, and I kind of wanted to cuddle her because she was so damn cute. I was never a cuddler before I'd started training.

She was my blood. It was odd to think I had family I hadn't known before a few months ago.

"Me, too, kiddo." I was unable to stop myself from ruffling her hair. I'd never been around kids before. I was rapidly discovering I preferred them to adults. At least they were honest.

Liv sat across from me at the big dining room table. She took a long swig of beer. The events of the day had taken their toll. She normally didn't touch the stuff, but when Zack's wife, Lisa, had offered her one, she quickly said yes. She also said yes to number two, and to the shots of whiskey she'd taken before we'd even gotten here. "I don't like to think about what you had to go through to get it back though."

"Let's not talk about that part," I replied. Liv had told me she could hear me screaming all the way down the hall. It was my screams that woke her up and sent her to the bottom of the whiskey bottle.

The heavenly scent of enchiladas wafted through the condo. I was looking forward to some dinner and then a nice long nap. My office was closed for the evening.

Of course, if my boyfriend had his way, I was closed permanently. I'd been totally right about how Marcus would react. After I'd woken from his version of anesthesia, he'd started the process of taking us back to Italy.

Unfortunately, I wasn't sure I could go.

The front door opened and Lisa greeted more of her guests. My aunt had planned a big party to welcome me to the family, and she wasn't letting a little thing like my complete and utter disaster of a job get in the way. Lisa Hernandez Owens was a beautiful brunette with caramel-colored skin and a ready smile. She looked like nothing fazed her. Given her husband's dangerous profession, that was a good thing.

The king walked through the living room with my uncle trailing after him. Marcus strode behind, looking cool and collected. He'd spent the afternoon on the phone with Lucia. When I left our apartment, he'd been talking to her about flight schedules and pickups. Donovan must have caught up with him and asked him to join the meeting they were planning. Zack walked straight to me, one finger pointing my way. It was a very judgmental, parental finger.

"Give her a break, Zack," Donovan warned.

Uncle Zack obviously wasn't in the mood to listen. "Do you want me to poke out my own eyes? I have to review those tapes every day, Kelsey. I get enough of that crap from Zoey and Dev. I do not need it from you."

"Sorry." I was suddenly super interested in my beer bottle. It was kind of funny that he was way more pissed at me for inadvertently making a sex tape than he was for almost losing my arm to a demon.

"And you." Zack turned on Marcus. I saw Donovan's eyes light up with mirth. "You should know better."

Marcus's brows practically knit together. I bet it had been a long time since he had to deal with an angry relative. "How was I to know there were cameras in the lifts?"

"I think they're talking about kissing." Rhys nodded sagely to his brother and Courtney.

Lee made his "ick" face. Lee had zero interest in kissing.

"You've known Dev for the better part of a decade," Zack shot back. "You should know how paranoid he is. You should only do things like that in the privacy of your own home. Better yet, you shouldn't do things like that at all. She's a very young, naïve girl."

"No, I'm not." I thought about all the times I'd hauled a piece of tail out of some bar. It never worked out well. I decided not to mention that to my suddenly prudish uncle.

Zack's expensive shoe tapped an impatient rhythm on the hardwood floor. "I'm her oldest male relative. I'm responsible for making sure she doesn't get taken advantage of. What are your intentions toward my niece?"

"I think he intends to kiss her again." Rhys was watching avidly. His head swung back and forth between Marcus and Zack.

"Stay out of it, buddy," Donovan ordered.

"He already kissed her, Rhys," Lee argued. "Uncle Zack wants to know when he's going to marry her."

Rhys shook his head. "I thought he was going to marry Evangeline."

Donovan's hand came over his younger son's mouth. "Don't mind him. Carry on."

"Well, Marcus, I would like an answer." Zack didn't look like he was going until he got one.

"You know what," Liv said suddenly, the alcohol making her so much braver than she would normally be. "I'd kind of like an answer to that question, too. I'm her best friend. I have to look out for her. She's not smart when it comes to men. At least her last boyfriend offered to marry her."

"Because it was the only way he could drag me to Hell with him." I was sure my cheeks were flaming red.

"It was good you said no, then." Lee patted my back.

Liv gave Marcus her most ferocious schoolteacher look. "Vampires have that persuasion thing, you know. Girls can get in serious trouble when they turn on the charm. How do we know he isn't using it on Kelsey?"

Why was this happening to me? "Seriously, everyone stay out of my love life. I'm sorry Marcus and I…kissed where a camera could see it. It won't happen again."

"My intentions toward your niece are entirely honorable," Marcus said suddenly. "I would be happy to discuss them with you at your earliest opportunity. I intend to take my time, though. Kelsey is wary and needs a while to adjust to a fully functional relationship."

"You're serious then?" Zack pinned Marcus with his stare.

"I am," Marcus assured him. "But you might find Kelsey a bit harder to sell on the idea than you might think."

"The idea of what?" I was so not following the conversation. I noticed that the king had gotten grim.

"Can we move this along?" Donovan asked. "We have some important matters we need to decide. We can sort out the *Nex Apparatus's* love life at a later date. Marcus, if you don't mind?"

The king patted his son's back and turned toward the back of the condo where Zack's large office was located. Marcus bowed slightly to my uncle. "I apologize for any embarrassment my actions might have cost your family. Know I only acted the way I did out of my extreme affection for your niece."

"It's all right, Marcus," Liv said, waving him off. "Your butt looked good, too."

Marcus stared at the schoolteacher. "That isn't helpful, Miss Carey."

Liv turned a lovely shade of pink, her eyes sliding away. "Sorry, sir."

Marcus leaned over and kissed my forehead. "Enjoy your dinner, *bella*. We'll be retiring early. We have a plane to catch in the morning."

With that, he and Zack walked off to join the king.

"What the heck just happened?" Liv asked, her mouth slightly open. "Did Marcus tell your uncle he's going to marry you?"

"I don't think that's a good idea." Rhys shook his head.

"No one asked you," his brother replied.

"Stop, everyone." I had to catch my breath. "Marcus did what countless other men in the same position would do. He told my irrational uncle exactly what he wanted to hear. Now we can go home to Italy, and Zack won't bug Marcus anymore." There was no way someone like Marcus would marry a woman like me. It was ridiculous. Vampires married companions. Except Hugo had mentioned he once married one of his Hunters.

I found the whole conversation completely unsettling and was happy we could move on to other accusations.

"You're going home?" Lee's voice rose. He shoved a hand through his thick black hair. "You just got here. This is your home."

"Why are you weaving, Aunt Kewsey?" Courtney asked. "Don't you wike it hewe?"

No one can make you feel guiltier than a kid. They don't take into account little things like obligations. They only know that you promised them something, and now you're a ratfink bastard for not delivering. "Marcus thinks we should leave."

"What do you think?" Lee asked.

"No one asks me what I think." This was the way my life had gone since the king had decided to press me into service. I sat outside waiting while a bunch of men decided my fate.

"And they never will," Zoey Donovan-Quinn said as she stood looking at me. There was a baby girl on her hip and something in her free hand. The tiny girl was Evangeline, her daughter with Dev Quinn, though I knew the king claimed her as his own. He called the girl Evan. She was a mini me of her mama. She had dark red curls and pretty hazel eyes. She clung to her mother's sweater like a monkey, but grinned down at her brothers.

"Rhys! Lee!" she shouted and attempted to scramble down.

The Queen of all Vampire set her daughter down and the girl, who looked to be roughly three, ran into her brother's arms. Lee picked her up and twirled her around then passed her off to Rhys. Rhys and Courtney wandered off to play with the newcomer, but Lee stayed behind.

The queen greeted Liv. She sent me a questioning look when she noticed the near-empty beer bottle sitting near my best friend.

"She got bitten by a vampire for the first time." I sighed and took another swig of my own beer. My uncle had good taste. "She liked it. Now she feels guilty."

"I do not," Liv piped up. "I don't have anything to feel guilty about. I was only helping him out. He'd been shot several times. I was the only blood available. I didn't enjoy it."

I was supposed to believe that? "Yes, you did. Those moans weren't about pain, my friend."

"I have a boyfriend." Her lips turned down sullenly.

She was forgetting so many truths. "You have a boyfriend who's addicted to drugs and possibly aiding a demon in planning to take over our world."

"Oh, you can totally cheat on him." The queen sat down across from me.

"I didn't cheat." Liv stood suddenly. "I'm going to get another beer."

Liv stalked away in search of more alcoholic solace. The queen slid a framed picture across the table to me. I found myself looking at a man with curly brown hair. He was dressed in an army green T-shirt and jeans. He needed a shave, but he smiled gamely. My heart seized a little because I'd never seen one picture of this man, but I knew who he was.

"I had to promise him a case of beer to get him to stand still long enough to snap this one." Zoey looked down at the picture, her lips curling up with fondness.

This was my father. Lee Owens.

"I like that picture." Lee stared at the man he was named after. "He looks happy."

There was a fine sheen of tears in the queen's eyes as she put an arm around her son. "I know you do, buddy. He was happy." The queen winked at her son. "Baby boy, why don't you go do what you do best? Report back when you hear something particularly interesting."

Lee grinned that adorable grin and was off like a shot. For a human, he was fast and quiet. It was good to know I wasn't the only one who encouraged the kid's more criminally inclined talents.

"This was taken a few weeks before we left for England."

I knew the story. It was a few weeks before he died. My father had guarded the queen and when the old Council caught them, he'd been executed. The royal family blamed a demon for betraying them to the Council.

Yeah, I wanted to meet that demon someday.

"Your father was the best guard I've ever met, and believe me, I've run through some." The queen smiled down at the photo. When she looked up at me, she was super serious. "He was the only one who understood."

"Understood what?"

"That he didn't have to manhandle every moment of my day. Lee believed in me. He followed my lead until such time as he knew I was going to be horribly murdered. That actually happened more often than you would think. Trent and I get on all right. Mostly, we get along because I had kids by the time he became my guard. I settled down. I still don't tell him everything. I still sneak away from time to time. It makes him crazy."

I liked the idea of Trent freaking out because his charge gave him the slip.

"The point is, I told your father everything. I left nothing out. In exchange, he made damn sure I fought for my place." She said the last with emphasis and then sat back, waiting for my reply.

"I don't know what the hell my place is." I wasn't quite sure what she wanted.

She shook her head ruefully. "It's hard to remember sometimes, but I've sat where you're sitting, and I was even a bit older than you. I know you think we don't have much in common, but you're wrong. You got a raw deal in the childhood department. I think you can get past that. I had a crappy mother, too."

"Did she try to kill you?" I could win this particular war. The man who raised me had actually attempted to murder me. That story usually won me first prize in the awful parent contest.

The queen frowned. "No, but she ran off with an accountant. My point is, we're both women in a man's world. These aren't fuzzy, huggy men. These are domineering, take-charge, protect-the-women kind of guys. You have to fight or you're just something soft for their beds."

"I doubt Marcus thinks I'm soft." He couldn't possibly view me in that fashion. He knew how dangerous I could be. No one would ever think of me as sweet and feminine and in need of protection.

"Then why is he trying to haul you off the continent?"

I was honest with the queen where I wouldn't be with Liv. I didn't want Liv to think less of me or feel sorry for me, but I knew why he was doing it. "He doesn't think I'm smart enough to handle someone like Winter."

"Felix is going to have to work on your self-esteem issues." The queen shook her head. "Answer me this, is Marcus sleeping with you?"

"Yes." I was pretty sure she knew the answer to that question.

"I know Marcus. He wouldn't be involved in a serious way with you if he didn't respect your intelligence. He's a hard man. He doesn't care about much anymore. He cares about you, Kelsey. He'll run your whole life if you let him and perversely, that will make him care less about you."

"Marcus wants us to go back to Italy. He's not asking for my opinion." It rankled.

She pointed to the picture of my dad. "He would have pushed you, Kelsey. He would have pushed you to make your own way and demand your rights."

"Why are you doing this?" I didn't trust people to look out for me. She had to have an agenda. "Did the king tell you to get me to stay or to go?"

Zoey laughed. "Oh, Danny would be perfectly upset with me for having this discussion. He would love for you to turn out to be a good soldier, exactly like your uncle and Trent. I'm talking to you because it's what your father would want. He would want you to stand up and tell them what you'll do and what you won't."

The queen stood, leaving the photo with me. "Keep that. I have one of his hats, too. I want you to have it. It isn't much of a legacy, but it's yours. The real legacy he left you is in your power. Your father was a champion of what was right, not what was expedient or easy for himself. He would have laughed at the thought, but he was an idealist in a way Danny and Dev aren't. Daniel needs you to be more than a weapon. He needs you to be you."

With that, the queen walked away. I heard her greet her husband and saw Quinn picking up his daughter. He tossed her in the air and caught her again. She laughed and enjoyed it because never in her baby brain did she think he would let her fall. I never had that. My mother had loved me, but I never had that big strong man to count on. I stared back down at the picture of my biological father. The image in front of me grew watery. He wasn't a particularly handsome man, yet everything about him called to me. I wished so much in that moment that I could know him, any part of him.

"Don't cry." Lee put his hand over mine. "It's going to be okay, Kelsey."

He was nine, and he was trying to comfort me. He patted my back as he had seen others do before. I gave him a slight smile. "I'm all right. I'm just sad that I didn't get to meet my dad."

He smiled at me. "I have three. You could have one of mine."

"Three?" I knew about Daniel and Dev.

"Yeah," he said with a shrug. "Bris counts, too."

"Ah." I hadn't thought about the fertility god who had residence in Dev Quinn's body.

"He totally counts. He orders me around and gives me all kinds of advice when he takes over Papa's body. He's more comfortable with Rhys, though. I'm only a human."

I hugged him tightly. This child should never once feel that he was less than anyone. "Oh, Lee, you go so far beyond mere human I can't express it. Now, tell me what the word is."

His brown eyes lit up. Lee was a kid who loved subterfuge. "So, Uncle Marcus and Uncle Zack think you should go back to Italy. Uncle Zack was totally like 'no' until he heard Marcus say that Jack Frost was coming for you, and then he got on board with Uncle Marcus. Dad thinks you can totally take out Jack Frost. I think so, too. He doesn't sound that tough to me. He's like snow, and that's not so bad."

Lee hadn't had his arm frozen off, so I would make my own decisions.

"And Uncle Marcus says that the lieutenant guy is just trying to get in your pants," Lee added.

So much for Marcus's belief in my abilities. "Good to know."

I stood up. My decision was made. It was final. It would probably cost me the only man to treat me like a princess, but I wasn't cut out for the role anyway. I looked down the hallway at the door where the men making the decisions about my life were meeting. The door was closed to me. It might be time to kick it open.

Lee's hand found mine. He was looking at the same closed door. "You want me to go with you?"

I smiled down at him, surprised at the confidence he gave me. But this was my fight. "No, buddy. I think I have to do this on my own. How about we play some Xbox after dinner?"

"Cool." I expected him to run off and find his brother, but as I walked down the long hall, I felt his eyes on me. He watched with a slight smile on his face as I walked into the office. I winked back his way. This stand I was taking went beyond just me. It was for us—for those of us who didn't have a voice right now. We were either too young or considered too naïve or inexperienced. We had the right to speak and we needed someone who could stand for us.

It looked like that would be me.

I opened the door and was assaulted by chaos.

"You can't take her off the playing field," Donovan argued.

"I can and I will," Marcus snarled back.

My uncle was standing between the two men. "I think we need to talk about this."

"I'm staying." I had to practically yell to be heard over the argument the men in my life were having. Marcus and Zack were standing close to Donovan, trying to get the king to see their point.

"Kelsey, you will wait outside," Marcus said in that authoritative tone he tended to use on everyone but me. I had to admit, I kind of hated it being used on me. "I will be with you in a moment."

"No." I stood my ground. "I'm the *Nex Apparatus*. I'm the one whose butt is on the line. I make the decision. I'm staying."

Marcus sighed, and I saw his jaw tighten. "Kelsey, you will do as your trainer tells you to do."

"She'll do as her king commands her," Donovan said firmly.

"I'll do what I want." It was time to put my foot down. Kings and trainers were important, but this was my job. My life. The queen was right. I had to make a place for myself or be forever dismissed. Knowing my father would have stood behind me, with his game smile and his taciturn outlook on life, gave me a strength and confidence I didn't have before. He would have given me a big old thumbs-up, and that helped me stand tall. "Look here, Donovan, you might hold most of the cards when it comes to me, but I got the only one that counts. I can say no, and

I can mean it. I won't be doing your dirty work mindlessly. I won't assassinate someone because they disagree with you or you think it's a fun idea. If you want me to put my ass on the line, you better convince me. Start now."

I got the impression no one talked that way to Daniel Donovan. He stopped and the room went quiet. I wondered if he was going to call Trent in. Even Marcus seemed surprised I'd spoken to the king that way. I hadn't been raised to kiss his ass.

After a long, uncomfortable moment, Donovan smiled briefly before he began his pitch. "All right, then. Those files you stole tell the tale, Owens. The drug known as Brimstone is both highly addictive and fast acting. It works on the impulse center of the brain in shifters and weres. It doesn't work at all on witches. The witches they gave the drug to died."

"So Winter wants a bunch of psychopathic shifters wandering around? Is he trying to give you hell? It'll be hard to keep this out of the papers." Secrecy was important in our world.

"Henri is worried that there's more to this," Donovan explained. "Demons can have certain powers over the weak minded. This drug gives Winter a whole bunch of powerful, weak-minded soldiers."

"So he takes away their impulse control and then potentially influences them." It was a lethal one-two punch. Our own people would be the ones coming after us. "They could come after you."

"Or anyone Winter wanted gone." Donovan stood up from his chair. His blue eyes narrowed. "So, *Nex Apparatus*, are you in or are you going back to Italy?"

There was no question about what I needed to do. "I'm in."

Marcus cursed behind me. "You're not ready for this. You must listen to me, Kelsey. I know what I'm talking about."

I clenched my fists, willing him to understand. "It doesn't matter that I'm not ready. I don't get to choose this, Marcus. Can't you see that? This isn't some game where it doesn't matter if I play this round. I don't have two thousand years. I got today and maybe tomorrow, and if I sit on my ass while people around me suffer when I could help, then what the fuck does any of this mean?"

He slumped down in his chair, and his hand reached up to massage his brow. "That is a child's question. Only a child seeks meaning in that which is meaningless."

"Maybe it is." I was resolute. I was the one who had to sleep at night, and I couldn't do that if I was on a plane to Italy while the world was in turmoil. "But I gotta find out on my own. All I know is if I walk and people I care about suffer, I won't be able to forgive myself."

He nodded and stood suddenly. There was a distance between us, a remoteness to his stance that I hated. I reached out with my mind, but his was closed to me. "Then I am no longer needed. You have made your choice, and it seems my counsel cannot change your mind. Good night, Kelsey, Your Highness."

I had known he would probably walk. People do that when you don't live up to their expectations. I'd known that eventually he would leave me, but his walking out that door was like a kick to the gut. My heart felt like it was about to burst. It took everything I had to stand my ground. What I wanted to do was run after him, beg him not to leave me. Instead, I forced myself to sit. I had a job to do.

Sometimes, having a job to do is the only thing that keeps me sane.

"Kelsey." My uncle got my attention. I took a deep breath to banish the tears that were threatening. I could cry later, when I was alone in the bed I should have shared with Marcus. My uncle pulled me up and didn't even try to contain himself. He hugged me tightly. I felt him breathe in my scent. "I'm really proud of you."

I nodded because he was managing to do what Marcus hadn't. I pulled a tissue out of the box on his desk and wiped my eyes as he let me go, and I took my seat again. It was time to move forward. That was what I did best. "So what's the plan?"

"You'll go to the lieutenant's tomorrow." Donovan sat back down in his chair, a grim look on his face. Though he had gotten his way, it was easy to tell that he hadn't liked the cost. "This party at Winter's is at seven o'clock. I talked to Sloane extensively about it earlier today. He seems to know what he's doing. All you have to do is keep your eyes and ears open. Try not to bring too much attention to yourself."

"How much do the demons know about the new *Nex Apparatus*?" Zack asked. "If they know who she is, I think this is too dangerous. It could be a trap."

Donovan drummed his fingers along the heavy wood of the table. "I can't be completely sure, but I think she's safe. I haven't made a big announcement for obvious reasons. A lot of people saw her in the arena a few months back. They might question why I championed her…"

"They know," I said confidently. "Scott knew. It's a small world. They might not know exactly who I am, but they know there's a new death machine in town. What am I supposed to do? Am I supposed to hide because someone might know who I am? I won't be effective that way. I've already met Winter and if he knows who I am, I couldn't tell. I think he sees what he expects to see. I know he hasn't asked for my name. Gray wouldn't give it to him."

"I agree. Sloane is trustworthy when it comes to your safety," Donovan said. "I still wish I could send you in with backup."

I shook my head. There was no way we were getting Trent into that party. Despite the fact that the king, the queen, and Quinn had made threesomes fashionable, no one would believe Gray was involved in one. Though the idea was kind of hot. "Gray and I will be fine. I'm assuming Jamie will be monitoring the situation."

"Yes," the king acknowledged. "The lieutenant mentioned he was working with your brother. I think you're in good hands. Sloane and I might have had our trouble in the past, but I don't doubt he thinks he's doing the right thing. I have a very specific order for you, Owens, and I expect you to follow it."

"What's that?" I'd decide if I would follow it after I heard what it was.

"Don't die."

I gave him a jaunty salute. "I'll do my best."

The door to the office came open and Lisa Owens popped her head in. "Dinner's ready. I'm serving it even if you continue your business meeting. That might not mean anything to the king there, but once it's gone, the two of you are on your own."

"She means that." Zack stood and smoothed down his shirt after his wife had quietly closed the door. "She's serious about dinnertime. If we don't get out there, she'll leave us with a bowl of carrots or something."

I shuddered. After a really shitty day, I couldn't handle a vegetarian dinner. Zack walked out and I stood to follow him. I wasn't letting all that cheese and beef get away from me.

Donovan reached out and grabbed my hand. "Don't give up on Marcus."

I shrugged, unwilling to show him my true feelings. "I don't think there's anything to give up on. He was my trainer. That's the way these things go. If you feel like I still need a trainer, I'll take Hugo. I promise to keep my hands firmly to myself."

I was supposed to keep a lover around so I wouldn't feel alone. I was supposed to form attachments. I wondered if the king would consider a vibrator a proper physical outlet. I could get attached to one, and my vibe wouldn't dump me when I acted out.

The king stared at me for a moment, and I could practically see him trying to figure out how to handle me. He was silent for a moment before speaking. "You know what I've had to put up with every day for the past ten years? I've had to hear Marcus call my wife *cara*. That means dear in Italian. Never *cara mia*, which is my dear, just dear. He's done it since the day he met her. Z's always been a favorite of his. If I hadn't been around, he'd have been all over her."

"Are you trying to make me feel better?" If he was, he was doing a shitty job. Marcus probably would have stuck around to fight it out with the queen.

"I'm trying to make a point." Donovan leaned forward. "Every day for the last ten years, he's greeted her with a 'good morning, *cara*.' Until one day, a little over three months ago. He saw her and said, 'good morning, Zoey.' I didn't think much of it until I realized he never called her anything but Zoey or Your Highness after the night he met you. Marcus is a charming playboy until he decides to settle down, and then he's loyal to the bone."

"He walked out on me." I felt a hollow space open inside me. He was leaving me. I wondered if he would even say good-bye.

"I doubt he walked far." The king's blue eyes regarded me with something like sympathy. "I have some selfish reasons why it would be better if you and Marcus weren't together."

"You want him to marry your daughter one day." It was the only thing that made sense.

"She's a companion. You have no idea how much that tiny bundle of light scares the crap out of me," the king admitted. "The boys are easier. Evan…well, she makes me almost wish we'd only had boys. I love that baby girl. From the moment the midwife put her in my arms, I knew I would die for my daughter. I want her safe. Every vampire in the world is going to want her. I trust Marcus. It's the one thing Dev and I have fought over since we formed our triad. Still, I can see you need him, and he needs you. I have to believe things will work out as they were meant to."

"I wouldn't have taken you for a philosopher." The king was awfully hard to dislike when he was simply being a guy. It made me remember that we'd been friends once. We'd played together online before I'd turned into some weirdo, half-wolf, demon-slaying thing. It hadn't been much, but for a while that group of guys was all I had. Nathan had given that to me. I remembered something I should have told the king yesterday. "They're worried about the conference that's coming up in the next couple of years. They think you're going to cancel the contracts."

Donovan's face became completely enigmatic. He said nothing, just waited for me to continue.

"They want to fracture the vampires." I took a deep breath and told him the news no parent could possibly want to hear. "They're willing to use your children, Donovan. They talked specifically about using Evan to cause a rift between you and Marcus."

Donovan already knew. I read it on his face. The thought caused his fangs to lengthen though. When he spoke, they were large in his mouth. "Yes, the lieutenant mentioned it. I've already upped Evan's security. Trent is hiring some extra guards for the boys and Z, too. Bris has strict orders to take over the body if Dev does something stupid. I'm on it, Kelsey. If anything happens…"

My response was instantaneous. "The kids are my highest priority. I'll do what it takes."

Donovan nodded slowly, and I watched him calm down. "I appreciate that, Kelsey. Know that Dev and I will sacrifice anything for our wife and children. Now, we should get to the dining room table. Think about what I said. Don't give up on Marcus. You just fought for yourself, and you won. Now fight for him. He needs it. And try to keep your pants on this time."

"I make no promises." I would be seeing Sloane. My pants tended to dissolve around him.

The king followed me out the door, and we joined my new family for dinner.

Chapter Fifteen

Dinner was delicious, but my heart wasn't in it. All around me this new family I found myself in laughed and joked. The king sat at one end of the table. There was no plate piled high in front of him, but he sat there, Evangeline on his lap. He was content to cut her food into tiny squares. The little girl leaned back against her father and chewed happily. Lee and Rhys argued about which video games were best. Quinn had a long discussion with my uncle on the new high-definition television he'd bought. The women talked about new clothes and their kids. Liv joined in, telling stories about her job and what teaching high school supernaturals was like.

I was quiet.

I wondered if I would ever feel like I belonged somewhere. I'd felt like I belonged with Gray, but that was a lie. I'd felt like I belonged with Marcus, but I'd screwed that up as well. I found my eyes moving over to the side table where I'd stashed the picture of my dad inside my purse. He was a lone wolf. How much of that instinct to be alone was written into my DNA? Would I always push away the people who cared about me?

Lisa placed a piece of chocolate cake in front of me. The icing looked rich and dark. If Marcus had been beside me, his eyes would have filled with anticipation. He loved chocolate. His sweet tooth would have caused me to get overweight if I didn't have that trusty werewolf metabolism. His hand would already be on the fork. He would hold it to my mouth and tease my lips with it until I took a bite. We would enjoy the flavor, the taste so much sweeter because I knew he shared it with me.

How long would it take before the bond between us was broken? Would mere distance mean he couldn't feel my moods or taste what I tasted? Would I feel the same way about Hugo that I felt about Marcus? I doubted it. I hoped Hugo's mistress didn't hate me.

"Kelsey?" I was pulled out of my morbid thoughts by Liv calling to me. "Are you all right? Where did Marcus go?"

"He needed to pack." My answer was short and I couldn't look her in the eye. It was the same talk we always had. I fucked up and someone who could have been good for me was gone. "He's going back to Italy in the morning."

The table went quiet. I hated the way they stared at me. So much flipping sympathy. I couldn't stand it. I smiled. It was totally fake. I wanted the attention off me. I brazenly used my four-year-old cousin to deflect attention. "So Court, what did Santa bring you this year?"

Christmas had been about four weeks before. I'd enjoyed an Italian Christmas with Marcus. Christmas dinner had been nine courses.

Courtney's brown eyes were huge, and there was no mistaking her terror. "I don't wike Santa Cwaus. I don't wike his wong bweawd." She shook her head vigorously.

"It's all right, cupcake." Zack patted his daughter on the back. "Santa is never coming again. Remember Uncle Daniel killed Santa Claus."

My mouth dropped open. "You killed Santa? Dude, that's rude."

Donovan shook his head. "Turns out he was a demon. The old folklore on the guy was right. He was some bad shit. He liked to catch kids in his beard and pull them in and…"

He let me figure out the last part for myself.

"That was when Dan decided to seriously start looking for a sheriff," Quinn offered. "If you'd been around, you could have sent Saint Nick to his eternal damnation. Dan had to do it. The boys sulked for a month."

"Then fake Santa brought us new bikes," Rhys piped up with his eternal smile.

"Fake Santa was better." Lee finished off his cake. "But, hey, the

Easter Bunny is still out there somewhere. Kelsey can kill that."

"Good to know." I wasn't looking forward to that job. "Do I want to know what the Easter Bunny does to small children?"

Donovan shook his head firmly. "No, you do not. Ever seen Monty Python? 'Cause someone on that show has met the little fucker, let me tell you."

Courtney gave me a rundown of all the things that scared her. It was an impressive list. Ice cream trucks, trains, hairless cats, clowns, the color orange, string beans…the list went on. After a while she got tired of talking to adults and wandered off to play with Evan.

I was listening intently to stories about my father when there was a knock at the door. Lisa got up to answer it. I glanced at my uncle, who sniffed the air and then completely ignored whoever it was. It seemed a good hint that whoever was at the door wasn't a threat.

"Are you really going to kill the Easter Bunny?" Liv leaned forward. She had a hand on my arm and I could tell she was happily plastered. I was going to have so much fun with her tomorrow. Of course, there was still tonight. I wondered where Casey was.

"Yeah." I was much more cheerful. No one was looking at me like the lovelorn idiot. "And probably the tooth faery, too. Tell me something, Livvie. Do you think Casey is somewhere strumming his sad guitar, making up songs about how much he loves you?"

She flushed. It made me giggle.

"I was helping out." She frowned. I knew my BFF. She was thinking about him. She was thinking about the egghead, wannabe-skater-turned-pacifist vampire.

"Seriously?" I didn't have to say anything more. We had a shorthand, Liv and I.

She rolled her eyes like I was talking crazy. "No."

That no sounded an awful lot like a maybe to me.

"Dev," Lisa said, walking into the dining room. "Two of your bouncers are here. They said there's some trouble in the club."

The faery pushed back his chair with a sigh. "A club owner's work is never done." He leaned over and kissed his wife. "I'll be back." The king started to push back his chair, and Dev sent him a questioning look. "Stay here, Dan. I can handle the club."

I was watching Lisa. I didn't like the tight look in her eyes. Her jaw was rigid. She didn't look like a woman who'd greeted some welcome guests. Then there was the fact that she followed Dev out of the dining room rather than sitting back down. Something didn't feel right, and I've learned to follow my instincts.

I didn't have all the resources I needed on my own, but then I had a whole family around me. I turned to my uncle. "Do you smell anything odd?"

Zack breathed the air deeply. The king stared at Zack while the queen immediately stood and started counting children. The minute I asked the question, she went into protection mode. I kind of took it as a compliment. The queen knew when it was time to circle the wagons. Lee was still at the table, but Rhys had wandered off. Evangeline had toddled back into the dining room, but I couldn't see Courtney.

Zack didn't look terribly concerned. "It's Ray and Walter. They're bouncers. Huh. That's weird. Are they wearing perfume? I smell something sweet."

Something was wrong. Trent had mentioned a sweet smell on Alan. It couldn't be a coincidence. I figured the scent came out in the sweat. I stood calmly, pushing my chair back. Donovan stood as well.

I shook my head his way, an indication for him to stay put. "I'll handle it. You take care of the people in here."

"What's going on?" Zack stood up beside me. "My wife is out there."

My uncle is a badass, but he's not an alpha.

"Follow me." I made my voice deep and commanding. There was no doubt in my tone. I walked and he followed. The king nodded to me. Zoey clutched Evangeline as I strode toward the door. Rhys walked in and was surprised to find himself quickly in his mother's hold. Lee stood.

"Don't you even think about it." Lee's eyes widened at his vampire father's stern tone, but he quickly sat back down.

I felt confident that I didn't have a bunch of hangers-on. I didn't insist on my uncle staying behind. His wife was out there. A thought occurred to me. Lisa hadn't even tried to warn anyone, though now I could see she knew something was wrong. Only one thing could have bought her compliance. "Zack, is Courtney out there?"

His nose was in the air. He went stark white. "Oh god, Kelsey. She is out there and she's scared. So is Lisa."

I put my hand on the door. It made sense. Courtney and Lisa made good hostages. Devinshea Quinn was out of his element. I thought about the entryway, going over it in my mind. There were no plants in that part of the apartment. Even as I had the thought, I nearly tripped over a thin green vine snaking its way toward the dining room door. It was an ivy coming from one of the back rooms, I supposed. I picked up the pace. I wasn't sure what Quinn was planning, but I had to get my little cousin and my uncle's wife out of there before he did it.

"You stay calm." I put my mouth up to my uncle's ear. Whatever those bouncers were, they had good hearing. "When I open the door, take care of Courtney and then Lisa. I'll handle the crazed drug addicts. What are they, anyway?"

He pointed to his own chest. Werewolves. They would be strong and fast. They could change forms quickly, and then they would be even stronger and faster. I felt my uncle press something in my hand. A small, semiautomatic pistol shone in the dim light. I flicked the safety off. Zack pulled another gun from an ankle holster. I wondered briefly how many weapons my uncle usually wore to family dinners. His face was tense, his eyes dark. He was ready to change if he needed to.

The thin green vine slithered past me like a snake seeking prey. It easily fit under the door. I decided it was time to give Quinn a helpful distraction. I kicked the door open. I was pleased when it came off its hinges instead of merely swinging. I'm much stronger when the adrenaline is flowing.

It was definitely flowing then, and it mixed with rage when I saw the fucker had my niece in midair, with his claws around her throat. She dangled there. Her sneakers with Dora the Explorer kicked, trying desperately to find balance. Tears streamed from her brown eyes. I was betting Courtney had some new things she was afraid of.

Zack growled behind me.

"Please, Zack." Lisa shook as she watched the big wolf dangle her baby.

The entryway was large for a condo. The upper floors of the building were for the royal family and close friends. Like the rooms I'd been given, this one was more mansion than tight apartment. The entryway was grand. It gave Ray and Walter breathing space. The werewolf who held my niece was short and stocky. His claws were out, but they hadn't penetrated her skin. Yet.

"Drop that fucking gun right now, girl." The other wolf seemed to be in charge. He had a gun pointed at Dev Quinn's head. He was tall and thickly built. His claws were out as well. He wasn't being careful with Quinn. The minute the door opened, he'd wrapped his claws around the faery's throat, and there was blood dripping down Quinn's skin, staining the perfect white of his dress shirt.

"I think I'd rather keep it." I aimed at the big guy's head.

"You'll drop the gun, bitch, or I'll tear his throat out."

To Quinn's credit, he barely showed the strain of having someone's claws buried in his throat and a gun at his head.

I shrugged. Behind me, Zack had already dropped his gun. He was at his wife's side. Both watched their daughter. I realized that this was my show for now. I hoped they trusted me to run it. I caught sight of the glossy vine. It crept close to the floorboard. Quinn stayed calm. His concentration was obviously on getting that vine where it needed to go.

"I don't like him, so feel free." I gave the bastard my most arrogant smile.

"Thanks, Kelsey." Quinn sounded sullen. He winked though, letting me know he was on to my game.

He needed some time and a lot of chaos. I was willing to provide both.

"What the hell is it the two of you want?" I figured it would be nice to know if they were simply buckets of crazy or had an actual mission planned.

"We want the king," Big Were said.

Quinn rolled his eyes. "These idiots think that if they can kill Daniel, they'll get all the free drugs they can handle. They used Courtney to force Lisa to get me. Now they want to use me to get to Daniel."

"They're going to kill the king?" That was the dumbest plan I'd heard. Donovan could handle them with one hand tied behind his back. The only reason he'd struggled with Alan was he was trying to keep the shifter alive.

The drugs were warping their brains. I'd have to ask Henri if reasoning skills were being impacted as well as impulses. Part of me wanted to go get the king. The king could kill these idiots in no time flat, but this was my job. I was the *Nex Apparatus*, and I didn't pawn off my work.

"The king's death should satisfy Winter." The smaller were shook his head like he was agreeing with himself.

"Why don't you let the girl go?" I remembered how Alan couldn't control his hands at the end. If this asshole lost motor control, he could kill my niece.

"We're not letting anyone go, bitch!"

The wolf howled. He was losing the fight to maintain any semblance of control. The smaller wolf tossed Courtney aside like a rag doll and leapt for me. He changed in midair, his clothes tearing around him. He became a dark, snarling wolf. My instincts took over and I dropped into a defensive position, softening my knees and shifting my center of gravity.

Suddenly the gun popped out of my hand, like it no longer fit. I scrambled to try to get it back, but the wolf knocked me over. I kicked up. I noted that Quinn was struggling now. Lisa had her daughter in her arms and was hunkered down in a corner, protecting Courtney with her own body.

The wolf's claws tore through my sweater to get to the flesh of my shoulder. Pain flared, but I moved quickly, rolling to the side to avoid the worst of the blow. There was something wrong with my hand. It felt funny, but I didn't have time to look at it. I only briefly saw that it had taken on a reddish tone to the skin before I flipped the wolf over me. I heard him hit the wall behind us.

"Get down, Kelsey." My uncle was on his feet.

He hadn't had the same trouble picking up his gun. He fired twice. I knew the rounds were silver. It was standard issue for guards. The shot echoed. Zack pulled the trigger three times. The wolf should have gone down, but even with three silver bullets poisoning his system, he jumped right back up. He snarled and moved toward me.

It happened faster than Zack could get another shot off. I only had time to bring my arm up to try to stop his canines from latching on to my throat. I reached up and instinct led me. I caught the wolf by the throat and squeezed. The wolf's lower body slumped. I was surprised that I lifted the heavy wolf with no problem at all. I tightened my hold and blood poured from the wolf's throat.

"Shit, Kelsey, when did you learn to do that?" Quinn was suddenly beside me.

The wolf I held twitched, his feet kicking out, but I lifted him easily. I watched as the light that animated him died and he went still. I dropped the wolf, shocked at what I had done. The body hit the floor with a thud. That's when I noticed my right arm, and I was the one going still at the sight.

My arm wasn't my arm. It was scaly, the skin a deep red. Long, creepy nails jutted from the tips. Talons. I had flipping talons. Like the kind that could easily tear out a throat. Killing talons.

It was ugly and kind of a little baby bit cool.

"Well, Henri is going to want to see that, Owens." The king stood lounging in the doorway. His blue eyes took in the entryway. I wondered how long he'd been watching.

Quinn touched my creepy arm, pushing up my sweater so he could get a better look. I was too shocked to protest, couldn't take my eyes off the thick muscles and tough flesh. The king moved to my side, running his hand along the arm.

"Demon skin." Donovan turned my arm over and inspected the long talons on my fingers. "Nice. Can you change it back?"

A thought suddenly occurred to me. I'd only dealt with one of the drug-crazed employees. I pulled my arm out of the king's hand and looked for the second wolf.

"Whoa!" Quinn ducked as my claws barely missed scratching his face.

"Sorry." I pulled my freaky arm close to my chest because I definitely wasn't used to having talons.

Zack had his daughter and wife wrapped up in his arms. Courtney cried and clutched her father. Lisa was calm, but I could see the tension in her eyes.

Sitting across from them was a weird-shaped ball of green. There was no question of what it was. The vine had wrapped around the man so tightly, I could almost make out his face.

"He alive?" The king was smiling slightly at Dev.

The huge plant thing wiggled, and I would have sworn I heard a muffled scream.

"Of course." Dev put a foot on the werewolf who was neatly

wrapped in ivy. "He can't answer our questions if he's dead. I assumed you would want to talk to him. If not, then I can change his current status easily."

Lisa touched my shoulder. Her eyes widened at the sight of my demon arm, but she merely said, "Thank you. I'm taking Courtney out of here."

As she walked by, I noticed everyone was watching from the doorway. They crowded together. Lee pushed his way through.

"Cool!" Lee held his hand out to touch it.

Donovan pulled his son away. "She's not used to it yet so no playing. Lee, go with your mother. Z, I think you should take the kids home. Call Trent and have him come down to escort you."

The queen nodded. "I'll take Lisa and Courtney with us. Zack, they'll be in the guest room when you're done."

Lee started to argue, but his mother pulled him back into the dining room. I supposed they would wait there until Trent came down to get them. I stared at the body of the wolf whose throat I'd split open. There was still blood on my claw.

I'd used that claw and could still feel it sinking into flesh. I'd done that. Me. And now I had demon skin. I wasn't like the world's most frequent visitor to a nail shop, but I did like the occasional manicure, and I was never going to be able to have another one. I wasn't even sure my talons were paintable.

"Calm down, Owens." The king put an arm around my shoulder. He was in a distinctly paternal mode. "It isn't the first time you've had to kill someone and it won't be the last. He was going to kill you. I'm going to back Lisa on this one and say thank you. Now, let me take a look at that hand and we'll see what we can do."

If he could do anything about getting back my perfectly normal, not talon-tipped hand, I was going to let him do whatever he needed to.

"Look at that." Donovan traced the lines where human flesh met what he'd called demon skin. "This is where the frostbite was. You can see the line where Sharpe pushed that combo blood through."

We were alone, only my uncle and Dev staying behind.

"Your blood and Gray Sloane's, right?" Dev asked.

"What does it matter?" I couldn't keep the panic out of my voice. My arm was covered in rough scales. How was I supposed to walk around with a demon arm?

"Do you want me to call Marcus?" The king let go of the arm.

I'd been shielding fiercely. My trainer had taught me well. I could do it on a subconscious level. I definitely didn't want Marcus to see me like this. At least if he left he would remember my arm all human-like.

"No, she doesn't need him," my uncle interjected. "She'll be fine." He took my hands in both of his. He didn't even blink at my claws. "Kelsey, this is normal."

I felt my eyebrows lift.

"You're a Hunter," Zack explained. "Surely Marcus told you that strong Hunters can change their hands."

Marcus had told me that I might be able to do that one day, if I trained hard. I'd done it instinctively, and there was obviously something wrong with that scenario. "But I was supposed to get a wolf claw. I got a demon hand."

"Actually, that makes sense," Zack said. "You have Sloane's blood running through your body. You won't have that forever. The next time you change, it should be the wolf in you that comes out. But this is amazing. No one expected this to happen for years. You're extraordinarily strong, but now I need you to relax and think about changing your hand back."

"Let me help." The king's persuasion brushed on the edge of my consciousness. I opened my mind, allowing him in. His voice whispered in my head, convincing me that there wasn't anything wrong. My muscles relaxed and I felt my eyes close. The world took on a fuzzy, soft glow.

"Kelsey." My uncle snapped his fingers in front of me. I was startled back to reality.

I flexed my hand. It was perfectly human again—or perfectly whatever I was. God, it was nice to have that arm back. We'd had a shitty day, my right arm and I. A shitty, shitty day.

The king slapped my back, a gesture of affection from him. "Good work, Owens. Go get some sleep. You have a job tomorrow. I'm going to see if Henri can get anything out of these two." He lifted the cocooned werewolf, who wriggled, trying to break free. "Dev, get the corpse."

The faery sighed. "He always leaves the corpses to me."

Zack gave me a hug before walking into the dining room to find his wife and child. Donovan and Quinn left to take Henri his new subjects to study, and I found myself alone.

"Kelsey?"

"Lee." He was a sneaky thing.

"Not just Lee." Liv looked sober now. "He snuck me out, too. He's a hard-core kid. Are you okay?"

I held up my hand. "Totally normal."

"Awww." Lee was terribly disappointed. "The other way was cool."

I put one arm around Lee and the other around my BFF. Even if Marcus left, I wasn't without people who loved me.

Chapter Sixteen

I cleaned up and Lisa offered me a new sweater to replace the ruined one. My job was hell on a wardrobe. I waited until Trent came to escort the queen to her home. My uncle had walked Liv back to her place before joining the king and Dev. I walked up with Trent, the queen, my aunt and the children, Lee's small hand in mine. It was the first time I'd been up to the royal residence. The penthouse was stunning, and I didn't care. I couldn't see much past my own misery. Somewhere Marcus was waiting on a plane that would take him far away from me. I was about to be alone again.

I thought about that the whole way down. As we approached my apartment, I was still thinking about the fact that I had to do this all by myself.

"Owens, you want to grab a beer?" Trent asked as we walked out into Ether.

There was a convoluted path to get to the penthouse and back down. It proved beyond a shadow of a doubt that Quinn was completely paranoid. We exited Quinn's office elevator straight into the nightclub. I wasn't in the mood to party. All I could remember was that I met Marcus in Quinn's office. It was the first place we had sat together and talked.

"No." The last thing I needed to do was get drunk off my ass. I would end up hitting on the big were, and I was pretty sure it would embarrass the hell out of him. Alcohol and depression tended to get me in trouble. I look for affection in the strangest places, and he was actually quite attractive. Big and broad, Trent was solid. He was the kind of guy a woman could count on. I mean, if he cared about her. Trent was the kind of man who wouldn't walk away if he was invested. Not that he was invested in me. "I'm tired. I need to get home."

I needed to watch Marcus pack. I needed to get ready to be alone again.

Trent wouldn't leave me alone. He followed me out of Ether as I made my way into the residence wing of the building. The dude took his job too seriously. I tried to explain to him that I'd managed to take out the crazy drug addict all on my own, but he wasn't having it. He walked with me up to my room. He kept trying to get me to talk, but I answered every question he put to me as succinctly as possible. I wasn't in a "get to know you" kind of mood.

"Owens." He stopped me before I put my key in the lock to my apartment. When I turned to face him, he was in my space. He was an awfully big guy. He was only slightly smaller than Gray. "You sure you're okay?"

I practically growled at him.

His hands came up. "Hey, I'm just asking. You had a rough night. I know how these things go. Is the vampire really leaving?"

"You already know?" I hadn't told him and he hadn't been at the party.

The big were shrugged. He leaned against the wall. "It's a small world. You'll have to get used to it. Everyone knows everyone else's business. Marcus pulled aside Michael House's new girl down in Ether. He asked her to make his flight plans. You going with him?"

I shook my head.

I swear that werewolf smiled. "It's for the best, you know. You shouldn't be with some dead dude. You're a wolf. You belong with other wolves."

"I don't know a lot of other wolves."

He was kind of super cute when he grinned. He had one dimple. Not two, only one creased the right side of his face. "You know me. You know your uncle. We're not without connections. The full moon is a week away. You wanna run with us?"

I couldn't help it. A little smile tugged at my lips. "Yeah, I'd like that."

I loved to run with the wolves. It filled something inside me. I wasn't tied to the cycles of the moon, but I felt their pull. When the moon was full, I had a need deep inside to run and loved being part of a pack, if only for a night or three. I missed it. If Trent could get me in with the Dallas wolves, I'd think about being nicer to him. I'd killed their alpha and two betas a couple of months before. If he could smooth the way, I'd be happy.

He smiled back, leaning against the wall. "Good. You'll like the pack. They've been asking about you. I know you think you're going to have a hard time with them, but the majority was happy to see Castle go. And anyone who wasn't will have to deal with me. I'll drive you out. We have to go up to Denton, but it's worth it. Maybe we can grab some dinner first since I doubt you'll hunt the way we do."

I shook my head. I would run with the wolves, but I wouldn't be hunting down Bambi for supper.

He winked at me. "See you tomorrow, Owens."

He walked off and I was left with a choice. Open the door and deal with Marcus, or run like the coward I was. I gave serious thought to starting my monthly run early.

In the end, I slid the key in. I wanted to see him one last time before he went.

The condo was dark and quiet. I let myself in, sadness pulling at the core of my being. This wasn't how I thought this day would end. I expected to be wrapped around him, his head on my chest. He loved to listen to my heartbeat. I didn't expect to be mourning him.

He stood by the window. The condo was dim, but the snow outside illuminated the room. He'd drawn back all the blinds and stared down on the world below. Snow was still falling outside, an ethereal sight. He leaned into the large window, his forehead touching the pane. His hair fell forward, covering his brow. He looked gorgeous and disheveled, his normal perfection marred with concern. His skin was pale alabaster, nearly glowing in the moonlight. He was slightly alien and wholly untouchable—a lonely, unapproachable god.

His suitcase sat by the doorway. I glanced to the entryway table and saw Marcus's passport and wallet. My hand went to the Venetian glass heart around my neck. I hadn't taken it off. I supposed in time I would. I couldn't bring myself to toss it at him now.

"You can take the bed, Kelsey." His voice echoed through the apartment, but he didn't move at all. "I'll sleep on the plane tomorrow."

"Sure." He obviously didn't want to talk. I turned to start for the bedroom, but stopped because I couldn't let him go without saying a few things. It was his fault. He'd made me feel halfway lovable. It gave me a little pride. It also fed my anger. "You know, you're just like the rest. I thought you were different, but you're not."

"I'm like all the other men in your life, am I?" He laughed, but it was a hollow sound. "You wish to compare me to the lieutenant because I refuse to watch you die, Kelsey?"

"Bullshit." I didn't believe that at all. "You're splitting because I didn't do what you told me to do. You know, Marcus, it would have been easier if you'd listened to me in the first place. I told you it wouldn't work. I told you you wouldn't want me in the end."

He went back to watching the snow. "If that is what you wish to believe, Kelsey, then I cannot stop you."

Three Kelseys. He wasn't going to slip up and give me what I wanted. He wasn't going to call me *cara mia* or *bella*. I was Kelsey. I should be happy he wasn't calling me Miss Owens. He got rigidly polite when he no longer cared. I heard the king telling me to fight for him, but at that moment, I wanted to fight *with* him. I wanted him to feel as shitty as I did. It wasn't fair. He was the one leaving me over a professional decision. He was the jerk.

I crossed my arms over my chest. A nasty feeling had taken root in my gut. What can I say? Put me in a corner like that and I tend to turn bitchy. "The king is giving my training over to Hugo. Any thoughts on how to handle him?"

He sighed, the sound heavy to my ears. "Listen to him, Kelsey. Hugo doesn't have as much experience training Hunters as I do, but he's quite good at it. Do what he advises you to do."

Oh, that wasn't what I'd meant at all. "I meant sexually, Marcus. I know you like it rough. I was wondering if Hugo does, too. Or should I play the sweet innocent? Some guys like that. Is he as possessive as you are? I hope not. I thought I'd give Casey a try, too. Liv seemed to like his bite. He's a baby. I could train him."

That got him moving. Super fast, actually. One minute he was at the window, the next he was right in front of me. His eyes were obsidian and his fangs long. I had to hold my ground because I wanted to take a step back.

"Casey? Really, my dear, that is sad. I rather thought you would go after that wolf who keeps sniffing around what belongs to me." His accent was thicker. I appreciated him keeping it in English though. Sometimes when he gets upset, he forgets that I don't speak Italian.

I knew who he was talking about. It was ridiculous, but I would use it. "I don't belong to you anymore. I'm free to do what I want, who I want. You know, he did ask me out. It didn't take him long. Trent heard you dumped me, and now we're going out next Saturday. I've never fucked a werewolf before. Do you think Trent will want to do me doggy-style?"

Marcus growled. His hand tangled in my hair, pulling my head back so I was forced to look up at him. That bite of pain sizzled through my body. Marcus ran his nose along my neck. He was more vampire than man now. He was on the edge of losing control. And I kept pushing.

"I've heard the wolf packs can get crazy on a full moon." I gasped as his teeth dragged against my skin. I wondered if he was planning on getting one last feed in. I would fight him on that. He pulled me flush against his body. One hand held my head to the side while the other traced the line of my spine. "Do you think they'll invite me to join in on their orgy?"

"Not if they wish to live, *bella*."

I laughed. I also moved against his body. I loved the way he felt. I wanted more than anything to throw down with him one last time. "It's going to be hard to defend my honor from across the Atlantic."

He stopped, seeming to come back to his senses. His head came up and that awful blank look was back on his face. "Go to bed. I can't promise you I'll stay in control. I seem to have lost it tonight, in every way possible."

"You're really going to leave me." I knew I sounded pathetic, but I already missed the feel of him against my skin. My vision blurred, tears nearly blinding me.

Marcus stared at me as though trying to make up his mind. He reached out and brushed a tear off my cheek. "Yes, Kelsey. I'm going to do what I should have done long ago. I'm going to shut myself up in my villa on Poveglia. I'm going to be alone. I should have done it ten years ago. I was an idiot not to do it four years ago."

"Why? What happened four years ago?" I knew what happened ten years past. Marcus had aided the king in taking down the old Council. There was a piece of Marcus that thought he should have died with them.

Marcus slumped onto the couch. It was the first time I'd seen him move in an inelegant fashion. "Four years ago, the queen gave birth to her daughter."

God, my rival was a toddler. The thought made my heart clench. "Well, Vorenus, if it's any consolation, Donovan is ready to marry her off to you as soon as she's legal. I hope to hell you're both happy. I'm sure you'll find some other idiot to fill in the time between now and then."

"You don't understand. I don't want her. I will never be able to want her. She'll always be a child to me."

"You're right. I don't understand." I sank down across from him. I felt tired, but I wanted to hear this story.

"She was promised to me."

"By Donovan?"

He shook his head. "No. By a prophet named Jacob, though you would know him as Apollo."

I felt my eyes widen because I hadn't gotten that memo. There should be an *Idiot's Guide to Supernatural Creatures* given to me with my *Nex Apparatus* training binder. "Damn. Are you telling me the Greek gods still roam the Earth?"

He shook his head ruefully. "Many of the beings who pretended to be gods still roam this plane. Have you ever heard the term sympathetic transference? No? It's a condition in which a vampire bonds so fully with a companion that when she dies, she takes him with her. It's the only natural way a vampire can die."

I felt my heart break a little. "You want it."

"I want to love a woman so much that I die with her, yes. I stare eternity in the face and it seems so long. Do you know how many I have loved and watched grow old and perish? You grow selfish after a while because you truly understand how insignificant you are. I always believed that if I found that woman, I would enjoy a lifetime knowing that my time was almost over. It would lend it a sweetness, an urgency. It would make me feel alive."

He wanted to die. It was so much more complex than that, but at the heart of it was an end to Marcus's long life. "And this prophet told you that Evan would be the woman for you?"

"I was told that one of the queen's line would be the woman I would die with. I feel nothing for her beyond an almost fatherly affection. She's a sweet girl." His eyes caught mine. "I know you won't believe this, but I do love you, Kelsey. I have passion for you."

"Not enough." I wouldn't be the one Marcus died with.

"For it to work, the woman has to be a companion."

Of course. It was funny how hollow I felt in that moment. Months before a woman I'd met had told me not to get too involved with any vampire because he would always want a companion. It was written into their DNA. "I'm never going to be a companion. I guess you're smart to cut your losses."

"Kelsey, this is going to be hard for you to understand, but there will come a time when the bond between us will break, and you'll be the one to break it. You will wake up at some point and be strong enough on your own. You won't want me the way you do now. What you feel now is a biological impulse. I've done this several times and each time my Hunter has left me. Every single time. Do you know who they left me for? A wolf. In the end, you'll want a wolf. Trent knows it. It's why he's sniffing around you now."

"That's the most ridiculous thing I've ever heard."

"It's true. Hugo married one of his Hunters, but ask him about the two who left him. At the end of the relationship they felt some affection for their trainer, but their passion always turns to wolves. I'm caught between a woman who will leave me and a child I can never want."

I stood up. I'd heard enough. I couldn't compete with some grand destiny. The rest was bullshit. I wasn't about to give everything up for some random wolf. "Give it time, Vorenus. You're right. You should go to Italy. Don't come back until she's twenty-five or so. I'm sure it will be different then."

I walked to the bedroom to do what I should have done in the first place. I should have gone to bed. Falling onto the big bed I should have shared with my lover, I let myself cry. I tried to hold tight to my mental shields, but part of the training I'd so recently gone through was to let my emotion have its way. I wasn't wolf enough to find a mate there. I wasn't a companion, so no vampire would want me long term. As for the humans, I doubted I could keep one alive in my world. I was destined to be like my father—alone. The tears poured out and though I wanted to howl like my wolf brethren, I was silent. It didn't matter. Marcus didn't need to hear. He could feel my pain.

"*Bella*, don't cry. Please." He sat on the bed, his hand on my back. He tried to pull me up.

"Go away." I pushed at him, not wanting him to see me like this. "Leave me alone, Marcus."

He was insistent. He pulled me into his arms, his hand cradling my head to his chest. "I can't. I can't leave you. Nothing will ever happen with Evangeline. I won't allow it to. I want you. I want to be with you. I'm sorry for before. I simply can't stand the thought of losing someone so precious to me. Please forgive me."

His hands pushed at my sweater, trying to get to my skin. He pulled it off me and tore at his clothes. He pressed his naked flesh to mine and we both sighed at the comfort it brought us. He said nothing further, simply let me cry until I couldn't anymore. When I settled down, he stroked my hair.

"Can you forgive me, *bella*? I should not have threatened to leave. It was wrong of me."

"You didn't threaten, Marcus." I thought about the plane ticket he'd had Lucia purchase. "You were going to leave."

"I doubt it. I was already coming up with a thousand excuses to stay. If I wanted to leave, I could have left this evening. I was waiting for you, Kelsey. It was my own stubborn pride that kept me from returning to your uncle's. I thought that I could force you to see things my way. I do not want you to go on this mission."

"I have to." The events of this evening had proven it beyond a shadow of a doubt.

"I know how you feel, but I wish you would listen to me. Abbas Hiberna is incredibly dangerous. He's an elemental. There are only four elementals in all the world. Do you understand what that means? The stories say no one but another demon can kill an elemental. He won't fear you, even when he realizes what you are. I'm scared for you, *cara mia*."

"I'm scared for me, too. But I have to do this." I was resolute. Even if it meant losing him, I was meeting Gray tomorrow.

Marcus settled down beside me. His hands traced the lines of my body, but there was more comfort in the caress than intent. "I will stand beside you. I will help in any way I can, but you must promise me one thing."

I smiled in the darkness. "What's that?"

"You'll break your date with that werewolf."

He sounded so serious I laughed. "I promise, though it wasn't exactly a date. He offered to let me run with the pack."

Marcus's voice was tight and filled with cynicism. "Yes, I'm sure that was all he had planned. He can find his own mate. He should leave mine alone. Now, do you want to tell me why I smell blood on you?"

I did, actually. I snuggled close and told him about my night.

Chapter Seventeen

"You're alone?"

Gray's brother opened the door at six p.m. the following evening, but he stayed inside, well within the confines of the house.

I was a bit startled. I'd expected Gray, or perhaps his butler, Syl. I'd decided to be magnanimous on the way over and not punch the little shit demon butler in the nose. He'd fed me fertility drugs in an attempt to remake *Rosemary's Baby* Texas style. I decided to let it go because I didn't have time for retribution. Instead of Gray or Syl, I got Matthew.

"Was I supposed to bring a friend?"

Matthew sighed. "Oh, aren't you a sarcastic one? You know sarcasm really is a low form of humor." He finally stepped out on to the porch, his eyes searching the grounds. When he was satisfied I hadn't brought along an escort, he nodded. "I simply wanted to make sure the king hadn't sent along a spy. He's a damn tricky fellow."

I was actually starting to warm up to the king. I'd spent the early afternoon holed up with the king and the academics going over the game plan. I was to keep my mouth shut, gather as much intelligence as I could, and get back out of Jack Frost's house alive. Jamie was already set up. Frost was in a McMansion in North Dallas. The grounds were extensive, but Jamie had some good equipment. Even from the park across the street, he could cover parts of the place. I wouldn't be allowed to bring in weapons, but I was hopeful that if I needed it, my shiny new demon hand would make an appearance.

"Are you going to let me in or are we going to stand out here freezing all night?" My toes were already going numb because I'd been told I had to wear stupid sex shoes. Why couldn't men find Uggs more attractive?

The demon stared out as though not completely convinced we were alone. After a moment he seemed to remember his manners. "Of course, love. Come along. We have to do something about your appearance."

I followed Matt inside. I hadn't been in Gray's home for months, but I couldn't tell that he'd changed anything. "What's wrong with my appearance?"

I looked fine. I was sure of it because I totally hadn't dressed myself or done my own hair and makeup. I'd gone to the experts. It made me long for the days when my job consisted of hanging around outside of strip clubs and roach motels trying to catch cheating spouses. No one gave a shit what I wore there. I'd also been able to drink beer on the job.

Liv had picked out the black cocktail dress from the closet of clothes Marcus had ordered for me. The queen and her bestie, a werewolf named Neil, had come down to help prepare me for my evening out with a duke of Hell and a captain of industry. The wolf was insistent that my hair needed help. I'd sat patiently as he painstakingly straightened it. He and the queen had been perfectly pleasant companions, but it was easier for them to talk to Liv than me. I didn't know a lot about court gossip, and even less about kids. I stayed quiet and thought about the upcoming night. Though it hurt me to admit it, I thought about Gray.

Marcus was staying at my side, but I had to wonder for how long. He was looking for something I could never give him. Marcus might care deeply for me, but he would always long for that elusive woman who would complete his life. And yet, I couldn't bring myself to let him go. I would have to eventually, but I needed him so badly now.

Marcus and I had an expiration date. I didn't believe him about the whole "I would want a wolf one day" thing. I would be alone again.

"You look like you're going to an elegant restaurant." The demon eyed me critically. "You look quite the lady. I'm sure my brother will be thrilled. Unfortunately, you're not going as my brother's fiancée. You're going as his love slave. This won't do."

I leaned forward, frowning at him the whole time. "I am not parading around Dallas again in a thong."

"Of course not, darling. Little love slaves aren't allowed to wear panties." He smiled brightly as though I'd told a terrific joke. "Come along. I, of course, am prepared for the situation."

I followed the demon through the hallway and toward the back bedroom. He stopped suddenly in the middle of the hall.

"Where have you been today?" The demon breathed deeply.

"Home," I replied. The demon stood close and leaned over. He picked up a section of my hair and smelled it. "Stop that."

He was insistent. He pulled my hand into his and brought it to his nose. I allowed the intimacy because this was something I worried about. If demons could smell vampire on me, I was in trouble. That first night at the club, I'd kept my distance from Winter. I wouldn't be able to do that tonight. "I stayed away from Marcus. I took a long shower and then he didn't touch me. He hasn't even fed today. There's no way you can smell him."

The demon ran his nose along my hands and then back to my hair. "It's not the vampire, love. Hush. I want to enjoy this. You spent time with a werewolf."

He could smell Neil Roberts on me? "Damn it. Does that mean I have to shower again? Do you have any idea how long it took to straighten my hair?"

I did not want to go through that again. If they shoved me in a shower for smelling too wolfie, they would have to deal with my waves.

"Dear, I wasn't complaining. You smell delightful. It makes me wish we didn't have to do what we have to do. My brother's scent will overwhelm this sweetness in a heartbeat."

Gray chose that moment to walk out of his den. He was dressed in cutoff sweat pants, track shoes, and nothing else. A fine sheen of sweat covered his utterly perfect body, and I had to stop myself from drooling. He'd obviously just gotten off his treadmill. Usually Gray liked to run outside. I was sure the snow on the ground made it hard. He pulled the earbuds out of his ears and smiled brightly. He looked even hotter than he had months ago. The military cut he'd had then made him look tougher, but there was something about the way his hair curled now that made me sigh.

"You look amazing, Kelsey." My heart skipped a beat at the appreciative tone of his voice. I told myself I hadn't dressed to impress him.

"She's far too elegant." Matthew frowned at his brother. "She has to change."

Gray's eyes were warm as they rolled over me. I didn't like to think about the parts of me that were heating up. How did he do this to me? "Of course. She's dressed all wrong for the mission. But she's lovely and that should be acknowledged, brother."

Matthew inclined his head. It seemed formal to me. I didn't understand demon protocols. "I honor her, brother."

"I thank you." Gray's face flushed when he turned back to me. "Come on, Kelsey. We need to get you ready. We don't have much time before the limo picks us up. Did you drive?"

He reached for my hand. I held back. "I took a cab. And I thought I was ready. Gray, I'm not walking around naked."

His smile was slightly shy and did strange things to my insides. "I bought you a slave collar. Does that count?"

"Asshole." I slapped at his perfectly cut chest.

He laughed. "From you, babe, that's a term of endearment."

I rolled my eyes and pulled away from him. He was too comfortable. I was a bundle of raw nerves and he was laughing. "What's wrong with you, Gray? This is serious."

His lips tugged up in a rueful half smile. His hands cupped my shoulders. "But we're going in together, Kelsey mine. Everything's going to be okay."

He tried to lead me on. I knew where we were going. I remembered where the bedroom was. "Gray, is this some sort of trick? I'm here to back you up. I'm here because this situation is beyond serious. I don't have time to play games."

"No games, Kelsey. You can't go in like that. People would talk."

I noticed the young man from the sex club sitting at Gray's bar. He was quiet. His big blue eyes took in the room with a sort of fatalistic acceptance. There was no curiosity there. He was simply waiting for the next thing to happen to him. I wondered briefly what his childhood had been like. I bet it had been even crappier than mine. All thoughts of Matthew's slave's shitty lot in life fled when I realized he was wearing a perfectly respectable cashmere sweater. Sure the pants were leather, but they covered him up.

"Why does Matt's boy toy get to be all dressed and I don't?"

Matt laughed. He ran a hand possessively through the young man's platinum curls. "Oh, dear, he certainly won't be so clothed when we get to the duke's. How cruel are you? Do you want him to be cold? He would look very silly getting into the limo wearing nothing but leather short shorts and his collar." Matt petted his boy toy. "Don't worry, puppy. I'll take care of you. I won't let the mean girl hurt you."

My eyes rolled. "Yes, I want to hurt the passive victim. Actually, I think I spent time with his twin earlier. It's weird. He looks just like this werewolf…"

I was cut off when Gray pulled me firmly down the hall.

"Let's not talk about that." Gray seemed eager to put some distance between us and the other couple. I heard Matt talking softly to the blond as we walked into Gray's enormous bedroom. "My brother had a relationship with a wolf a couple of years back. They lived together for a long time. Don't bring it up unless you're willing to listen to him moan about his long-lost love."

"Okay, I give, Sloane." He had a goofy grin on his face. It was making me crazy. "Why are you so happy? Don't bullshit me."

"I wouldn't dare." His eyes were that deep purple they got when he was serious. You can tell a lot about a demon by looking in their eyes, at least the half demons you can. "I had a long talk with my brother last night, that's all."

"About what?" I had a suspicion.

"You." And it was confirmed. "I didn't understand the whole Hunter trainer relationship. Now I do." He looked smug, but sadly, smug suited him. "You don't love Vorenus."

"I never said I did." I wanted him so much it felt like love. My life would be infinitely easier if I loved Marcus. Why couldn't what I felt for Marcus be love?

"You need him. You're drawn to him because you need a trainer. But you won't need him forever. You're strong, Kels. So strong. You'll be on your own before we know it."

I backed away from him. It was hard not to look at the big bed that dominated the room, but I was determined to ignore it. It was the first place Gray and I had made love. It was the first place where someone had loved me enough to take care of me. "Hugo Wells married one of his

Hunters."

It was stupid, but I held on to that piece of history like a plate of armor. It could work. Marcus said he loved me. We could have a life. I would grow old and he would stay the same. I would die and he would go on.

I would be a sidenote in his history.

Gray shrugged and took away the option of ignoring the bed. He threw his body on it and grinned up at me. "Hugo Wells isn't your trainer. Vorenus is. Tell me something, Kelsey mine. Has that vampire of yours had any prophetic visions about you lately?"

Gray's power as a demon went beyond his ability to change forms and his strength. He had power that allowed him to see things the rest of us can't. Gray was the culmination of centuries of his father's attempts to breed the power into his line. Gray could touch an object and sometimes he would get a vision. From what I understood, it was sometimes the past, most often the future. Gray had first seen me in a hotel room in Dallas. He'd taken a suite at a hotel and when he lay down on the bed, he was suddenly transported to his wedding night. I played the role of the not-so-blushing bride. According to Gray, our wedding night was hot. Or it was going to be.

"Of course not," I replied. Marcus wasn't a prophet. "Why? Have you had another one?"

Gray wasn't a prophet either. He couldn't truly control his powers. A true prophet was an extremely rare thing.

He shook his head. "No, baby. Just the one. But I believe it, more now than ever."

I felt my eyebrows come together. It wasn't attractive. It gave me a deep crease in my forehead, but I couldn't help it. "I haven't given you any reason to, Sloane. I'm committed to Marcus."

"Two weeks ago, I would have sworn you would never speak to me again. But you did. I would have bet my life that you wouldn't work with me again. But you are. And I definitely knew you would never walk into my bedroom again. Here you are, Kelsey."

"I don't have to stay."

Gray sat up. He chuckled to himself. "It's easy to forget how prickly you can be. I suppose I put you on a pedestal the last few months. It's good to see your stubborn side again."

I wasn't aware I had another side besides the stubborn one. "Sloane, if you spend one more minute on our non-relationship, I'll call Marcus and he'll come get me. He's sitting with his phone in hand praying I'll make that call."

Gray held his hands up in defeat. "Understood. On to business then. So Vorenus doesn't want you anywhere near the duke. Any new reasons?"

"We got attacked last night."

Gray sat up straight. The playful look in his eyes was completely gone, and the Texas Ranger was back in the building. "They attacked at Ether?"

"They attacked in my uncle's home. They were bouncers from the club."

Gray ran a hand through his hair. "That's one of the most secure buildings in the city. Winter has spread the drug a lot farther than I thought. This is bad, Kelsey. Are they dead? Did they manage to hurt anyone?"

"My niece got the scare of a lifetime, but otherwise Quinn and I took care of them. I killed my guy, but Quinn's lived. Henri scanned his brain. It's the same thing as the first victim. The frontal lobe is damaged. We can't give him vamp blood. His own werewolf healing power isn't fixing the problem, so Sharpe wants to try something."

"Demon blood." Gray was sharp as a tack. His eyes glanced down at my arm. "I know it was a different issue, but it worked on you."

"Better than you think, Sloane." I quickly gave him a rundown of my ability to change. He stared at the arm with an odd smile on his face. "Zack thinks it'll go back to normal. I mean, if you consider having a wolf claw pop out of a perfectly human hand normal."

"Can I see it?"

"No," I said crossly. I didn't want to see it again. I certainly didn't want my ex-honey to see my freaky demon arm. "I'm not even sure I can do it again. It took the king's influence to make it go back to normal."

Gray nodded, but his disappointment was an almost tangible thing. "Okay. Tell the king I'll donate for the cause. I might only be a half blood, but I'm royalty. My blood is strong. The doctor is probably on the right track. Brimstone is supposed to weaken wolves and shifters. The duke would have made certain the vamps couldn't use their own blood to save themselves. But he would want an out if things go bad. He's walking a fine line. He can't break the contracts with the vampires."

"Master, I have the clothing you ordered for my mistress." I turned to see Syl standing in the doorway. He carried a small bag that couldn't possibly contain too much clothing. He was roughly a foot shorter than me, and he hadn't bothered with a glamour. His red skin stood out against the pure white of his shirt. He was dressed in a shirt and tie and crisply pressed black slacks. He was every inch the proper butler, if one excused the red skin, small horns, and goat feet poking out of his slacks.

"Hello, Syl." It came out as a low growl. I wasn't trying to be friendly. Syl was the asshole demon who fed me fertility drugs. Syl might call Gray master, but he definitely answered to Gray's dad.

The demon bowed from his waist. His dark eyes seemed ageless in his slightly wrinkled head. "My mistress. It is an honor to behold you once more. You grace the home with your presence."

"I am not..."

Gray stopped me. "Don't bother, Kelsey. He's my familiar. He's connected to me. He's seen the vision. You won't convince him you aren't his mistress. Do you have any idea how many times I've tried to rid myself of him? He always comes back."

The demon got on his knees. "I know I displeased my mistress. I am prepared if she wishes to beat me."

"I'm not going to beat you."

Gray shrugged. "It wouldn't do any good anyway. He likes it."

"Oh, but I promise to cry and wail if my mistress needs it."

I walked over and pulled the bag out of Syl's hands. He cast his eyes down as I stood over him.

"I am here to serve my true mistress." He leaned over and before I knew it, his lips pressed to my feet. I jumped back and nearly fell on my ass. Gray was there to catch me.

"Syl." Matthew's voice was deeper than I had heard it before.

I saw Syl shake slightly. The small demon might be willing to take a beating from me, but I could see he was afraid of Gray's brother.

"My Lord Nem..."

Syl was silenced when Matthew slapped him soundly across the face. "You forget yourself, servant. My brother's mate has what she needs from you. Go and see to my slave's needs. And Syl, if your tongue

225

slips like that again, I shall cut it out."

Syl's body shook as he backed out on his hands and knees. His head was down, but he didn't seem to dare turn his back on Matthew. He didn't get up until he was well out of harm's way. Then he hurried down the hall to do the master's bidding. Matthew's face was perfectly pleasant when he turned back to me. But I'd seen his true nature. Demons are tricky things. They can seem entirely normal, but they are always, always at their core brutal creatures. Gray's brother seemed perfectly human, and he could be quite charming and pleasant when it suited him. It would be a mistake to think that he would act humanely.

"I'm not his mate." I responded out of pure reflex. Why did I care what Gray's brother thought? I found my footing and shook off Gray's hands. They'd gone around my waist when he caught me, and I could feel the heat of his body.

Matt shook his head and clucked sympathetically. "Our mates are stubborn things. I think it's our family curse. First, my mate runs from me after years of bliss, and now yours refuses to accept her fate." He turned his eyes on me and they darkened as though he could press his will outward. "You can play around with the vampire all you like. It changes nothing. In the end, you will marry my brother. You will bear his son, and you will follow him home."

I opened my mouth to protest, but the look in Matthew's eyes stopped me. He wasn't going to listen to me. He really believed. I could see from Gray's face that he believed it, too.

Matthew snagged the bag in my hand. He dumped the contents on the bed. I saw a leather mini skirt, a brilliant red corset, and thigh-high fishnets.

"Am I his lover or his hooker?" I was getting sick of the various costumes this mission required. I longed for the day I would be required to wear sweatpants and a T-shirt.

Matthew shook his head, dismissing the accusation. "My brother would never engage the services of a prostitute. Now, take off your clothes so we can get you properly dressed. Brother, you know what to do."

Gray walked to the bathroom and when he returned, he was running a fluffy towel across his body. It soaked up the sweat from his workout.

"This is your idea of cleaning up, Sloane? Seriously, you smell like a water buffalo." He didn't. He smelled like a hot, sweaty man and it did something for me, but I wasn't about to admit that to him. "Are you telling me we don't have time for you to take a quick shower?"

Gray ran the towel over his head and then under his armpits. "I promise to smell as sweet as a rose, baby. I turned on the shower already. The water is heating up as we speak. This is for you."

He tossed me the towel and gave me a wink.

"Now I'm the maid, too?"

Gray laughed as he walked into the bathroom. He didn't bother to close the door. He kicked off his shoes and shoved his shorts off his hips. I was left with the perfect vision of his muscular backside as he stepped into the shower.

Matthew had a knowing smile on his face. "Do you want a clean towel to wipe off the drool, dear? That one you're holding is for something else. Please get undressed and wipe that all over your body. Pay close attention to sexual erogenous zones. We need you to smell like you spend a lot of time with my brother on top of you. Unless, of course, you would like to do it the old-fashioned way. I assure you, my brother would be more than happy to mark you in any way you like."

"Jerk."

He shrugged. "Get dressed, love. It's almost time to go."

Matthew glided out of the bedroom. He called for Tristan, and I was left with my ex-fiancé's sweat. When this case was over, I promised myself I would stick to cheating spouses and lost dogs. I would take on any case that didn't involve smelling like someone else.

* * * *

Being a duke of Hell pays. I was certain that Winter's place on the Hell plane was probably built on the souls of the damned or something, but here in Dallas, he lived in a gorgeous French country estate complete with a stunning fountain in the circular drive. I stared at it as the driver pulled up. It was completely frozen—as if the weather had flashed it, capturing the perfection of the water. It was a statue now, a tribute to the power of the cold.

Winter was powerful. His mere presence in the city had brought about this crazy freeze.

Gray's hand found mine, his fingers tangling. "It's going to be all right. I'll take care of you."

"What does she think is going to happen?" Matthew asked, his hand on the silent Tristan's knee. "Does she think we're going to allow Winter to kill her in front of us? We're not without power, Kelsey. And all those ridiculous fears you have about the vampire mean nothing since you won't be with him for long."

"Brother." The word was a warning coming out of Gray's mouth.

Matthew put a hand on his forehead as though it pained him. "Well, she's bombarding me with it. I don't understand it. She fears she's unlovable, but you love her. It isn't logical for her to be apart from you. We could take over her training."

"She's afraid of me. I explained that to you. Let her be, and this isn't the place to discuss family issues. There's our host." Gray's jaw had tightened, a sure sign he was anxious.

The door was opened by the driver and Matthew drew Tristan out.

"I'm not afraid of you." I needed to remember Matthew's power. It was easy to think of Matthew as not that powerful. He was in a human body after all. Gray had explained to me that despite Matt's status as a full-blooded demon, he was forced to possess a human body when he wanted to walk the Earth plane. He wasn't physically strong enough to manifest in his demon form here, though he could be called to hand. The singular time Matt could show up in his own form was when a dumbass human managed to work up enough magic to call him. Then he was forced to do the human's bidding. In this way, Gray was much stronger than his brother, but Matt wasn't without power. He was an empath, so he picked up on strong emotions. I was pretty much a big stinking ball of those right now.

Gray glanced down to the place where our hands were joined. "You are and you have every right to be. I pushed you too far, pulled you into a world you weren't ready for. I'm still doing it. I can only promise you that I'll do anything to make sure you're safe. Anything. I'll earn your trust again."

He moved out of the car before I could go over all the ways that would never happen. I had them all on the tip of my tongue, but he gently pulled me along with him, and then there wasn't time to talk or argue. We were being shown through the massive doors of the mansion by a tuxedoed butler who offered to take our coats.

For all that the man loved winter and was likely quite comfortable with the chill, the duke had obviously made concessions for his guests. His home was nice and toasty.

"Welcome." The man himself strode into the foyer. He was dressed in an immaculate suit, his white hair pulled back. Chilly blue eyes stared at us, stopping briefly on me before glancing over Tristan. "I'm glad you all could make it. Please come into the library. I'd like for you to meet my business partner."

Gray walked up to shake his hand. "I've been looking forward to meeting the man. We've all watched Mr. Dellacourt's rise through the business world."

I held back because I'd felt Winter's touch one too many times this week. I wasn't sure I would be able to bring myself too close to the demon.

"Do you own his contract?" Matthew asked, affixing a leash to Tristan's thick collar.

If Gray thought that was happening with me, he was about to get his hand taken off. I didn't give a shit that it would blow my cover. This was my *Dirty Dancing* rule. No one got to put Baby in a corner. Well, no one put a fucking leash around my throat. I could handle the collar. The collar was pretty.

Gray simply reached for my hand and leaned over. "Never in a million years, baby. I like my balls where they are."

He wasn't a stupid man.

"You don't think Mr. Dellacourt got where he is through his own efforts?" Winter's brows had risen, an amused grin quirking his mouth up.

"No," Matthew shot back. "Humans aren't that smart. He had help."

Winter began to lead us down a hallway. My heels clacked against the marble, and I was lucky Gray had such a good hold on me since they nearly slipped out from under me more than once. Again, sneakers wouldn't have done that.

"My partner is a wily one. Apparently, Dante met someone from an alternate plane. The technology on her plane was quite a bit more sophisticated than this Earth's. He stole the tech from her and reverse engineered it."

"Stealing is such a specific word." A lanky man with red hair stood in the middle of the library, a glass of what looked to be Scotch in his hand. "I like to think of it as liberating an important asset. Besides, I'm sure she found another one."

"Other Earth?" I asked the question of Gray, quietly I thought.

Demons have supergreat hearing. The duke was more than happy to answer my question. "Oh, yes, my dear. The planes are infinite. The plane we occupy now is actually quite remote. It's not easily accessible. The old Fae used to cross the veil. There are a few demon species who can move easily from one to another. Usually though, there has to be some form of magic involved. There are some mirrors in this very house that I wouldn't recommend you stare into for long, lest you find yourself in another place, another time."

The red-haired billionaire shook his head. "Which is a shame because I really do like looking at me. I'm pretty attractive. I guess I'll just have to look at you, sweetheart." He walked my way. "What do you say? You up for hanging out with *Time's* Man of the Year?"

"Are you up for getting your balls shoved into your body cavity by my foot?" Gray asked.

I was totally going to ask Dellacourt if he was up to me pulling his balls off his body and treating them like tennis balls. Sometimes Gray and I totally are soul mates.

Dellacourt put his hands up. "Touchy. This one's the full breed, right?"

"Not at all. He's the halfling, but don't think for a second he can't take you apart. Brac, I'll take a Scotch. Why don't you see about getting our guests drinks as well." The duke was good at playing the kindly host. "Dinner will be served shortly. I thought we could spend this time discussing some of the problems we've come up against. Were either of you aware the king has a new *Nex Apparatus*?"

My blood went pretty much cold, but I simply smiled and told the butler I would take a white wine spritzer. I was told I couldn't order a beer under any circumstances, but I would need to look like I was indulging. Apparently beer isn't feminine and it makes me burp. Burping isn't feminine either. So Gray got to order a beer. It was totally cool for him to burp. Sometimes my job reminds me that life can be fucking unfair.

"I had heard rumors," Gray said, seating himself on one of the wine-colored couches.

Matthew sat beside him and Tristan gracefully placed himself on the floor, his head going to Matthew's lap so the demon could pet him.

I nearly crashed on my way down, but Gray caught me, guiding me to the carpet.

When the important men were seated, the duke continued. "I believe we can confirm the rumors are valid. While I haven't been able to place a man close to the king, I do have a few in positions around the club his partner runs. They've heard talk of a *Nex Apparatus*, and I believe he might already be at work."

"What makes you think that?" Gray asked, his hand moving on the nape of my neck. He toyed with the small gold and diamond necklace he'd placed around my throat. My "collar" was nothing like Tristan's.

Winter sat back. "The clinic where I was running trials was breached yesterday. Whoever it was, they were savvy enough to not get caught on camera, but my servant called in prior to being killed. I only heard a few moments of the exchange."

I kept my eyes on the floor and concentrated on keeping up my mental shields. I had no idea what kind of powers the duke could claim outside of the whole freezing my limbs off shit. He could potentially feel my panic. I focused on presenting a calm front.

"I don't suppose anyone mentioned a name?" Matthew asked. "That would have been helpful."

Winter shook his head. "Alas, my man was shot before he could say much, and apparently the call disconnected when he fell. I do believe we have a clue. My servant touched the *Nex Apparatus*. I had imparted a bit of my power to him, so we're looking for someone who's been injured. Likely this man lost whatever limb my servant touched. Ask around. I'd like to meet with him."

Panic gone. There I sat with two whole arms. They were apparently the best camouflage ever. Though I wondered why he thought I was a dude. My voice isn't that low. Is it?

"I'll certainly ask around," Gray murmured.

"And I'll get better security," Dellacourt said with a shake of his head. "There are some programs I've got in the pipe that no hacker can get through. My problem is being able to roll things out without the government cracking down on me. If I look too good, they'll have someone watching me. Believe it or not, those assholes say they want free enterprise, but at the end of the day, they want all the new tech for themselves."

"I'll see what I can do to keep the government off your back," the duke murmured. "The point of this meeting is to talk about a wider distribution of the drug. The brothers here believe they can do a better job than we're doing."

"Getting the drug introduced into Ether is our goal," Dellacourt explained.

The butler returned with an elegant tray. He passed out our drinks and we all settled back in. This was starting to get interesting. I needed to know how and when they planned to move the drugs into Ether. The how would be especially nice. If Gray and his brother got the job, it would be easy to thwart that particular plan, but what I really wanted to know was Winter's endgame.

Was he trying to kill off supes on the human plane? Trying to start that war I'd been worried about since I'd met the man?

I took a sip of wine as Dellacourt began to talk about production. They were planning a large shipment in the near future.

"That's a lot of product." Gray took a long sip of his beer. "I suppose we could find a way to move it. Matthew, do you have any thoughts on the subject?"

"I don't believe we can sell it in the club. Security is far too tight. The key is to get the shifters hooked on it so they come looking for us," Matthew mused. "What we likely need is a way to liquefy the product. Right now, it's the form of a pill, correct?"

Dellacourt nodded. "It's injectable as well. At first, those were the only two ways to get enough of the drug into the user's system. Injecting the drug almost always killed the subjects. Even the demon subjects." He sat forward, his hands on his knees. "Unfortunately, the true subject turned out to be difficult to deal with. We couldn't get him to take a pill and we certainly couldn't inject him without bringing his father's wrath down on our head. So I've spent a good deal of my time refining the drug so it's odorless and tasteless and easy to slip into a drink."

"Demons?" Gray asked. "I thought you said it didn't work on demons."

Winter's smile was the only steady thing in the room. "Brimstone doesn't, but then Brimstone was a smoke screen for my side project. You see, in my line of business, the boss tends to eat you when you don't obey. I have to have something of value to present to Lucifer Morningstar. He doesn't like dissent among the ranks. When I kill Donovan and start a war, I have to have…well, a saving grace, and everyone knows what Lucifer values most in the world."

Gray set down his beer. "I'm not following. What's this side project?"

"Yes, I'm interested in that, too," Matthew stated. "I'm beginning to feel like we've been brought here on false pretenses."

"Not at all," Winter explained with a wave of his hand. "I'm simply trying to explain that the end goal is a bit more involved than I formerly mentioned."

"I get it." Matthew's tone had taken on a distinctly irritated air. "You want to start a war for the Earth plane. You think if you have an army of drugged out werebeasts and shifters, it tilts the balance to our favor."

"That's what I don't get," Dellacourt stated with a shake of his ginger hair. "Demons are like the strongest things I've ever seen. How can a vampire compare?"

"Oh, but we aren't particularly strong on this plane. Vampires belong here. Demons aren't native to this plane with the exception of the halflings, but our culture negates them for the most part," Matthew continued. "So if Winter wants his war, wants to wipe out the vampires who are actually quite an effective guardian for the humans, he'll bring in native creatures he can control."

It all sounded pretty shitty to me. Vampires are the single most powerful creatures in the supernatural world, but again nature had found a balance. Vampires are rare. Wolves and shifters had numbers. If the wolves and shifters became the demon's meat puppets, it could be a very quick and bloody war.

"We're forbidden from breaking our contracts with the vampires," Gray argued. His hand was on my neck. It was odd, but I could feel the heat coming off him.

I glanced up and he was sweating a little. It wasn't hot in the room. Or it hadn't been a moment before. I felt a wave of heat roll over my skin, making me the tiniest bit nauseous.

"He thinks if the wolves kill the vampires, he can argue he wasn't the one who broke the contract," Matthew explained with a sigh of disgust. "He's wrong. That contract is ironclad. Our glorious leader will likely cut off your head for it. I don't see how you get out of this with your brains intact. Everyone knows the only thing Lucifer would give up his precious balance for is…" Matthew stood up suddenly. "Grayson, we're leaving. Right bloody now. They've been after you the whole time."

My vision began to waver, and the glass I'd been holding fell to the floor with a crash.

But I definitely fared better than Matt's boy toy. He sat up, turned a brutal shade of purple, and died right there before my eyes.

We were fucked.

Chapter Eighteen

"Eww, that's what it does to humans? That's awful." I could barely hear Dellacourt over the roaring sound in my ears. "Is the girl going to end up like that? That would be a shame. She's kind of hot."

I glanced down and saw that Tristan's skin was rapidly decaying.

God, I hoped I didn't do that. It was nasty.

"Only if she's actually human. Which it appears she's not. Someone is lying," Winter agreed. "Mr. Sloane, I wouldn't try that if I were you."

Gray had his pistol out and he was trying to aim. The trouble was his arm kept twitching. The gun fell to the ground.

Matthew picked it up. He wasn't having the same trouble Gray did. He stepped over Tristan's rapidly deteriorating body and pointed the gun at Winter like it would actually do something to him. "What did you give him?"

Gray hit his knees. My mind was fuzzy. I reached for him, trying to hold on to something.

Gray's face turned up, his eyes going a dark violet. They widened. "Who the hell are you?"

I hadn't even noticed the new guy. One minute the space was empty and the next there was a young man standing beside me dressed in jeans and a concert T-shirt. He had thick dark hair and even through my haze, I could see his blue eyes. Unlike Winter's, they were warm and seemed infinite.

Winter seemed delighted at the newcomer. He slapped his hands together and stood up before waving a hand Matthew's way. There was a horrible crunching sound and Matt's neck snapped around in a way no neck ever should. He fell to the ground beside Tristan.

It didn't seem to bother Winter at all. He smiled at the newcomer. "Welcome, Jacob. You're here to bear witness and that can only mean that I'm going to be successful."

The young man, who couldn't be more than nineteen if he was human, slowly nodded. "I am. I'm the last of my kind. The final one my father made. There was a reason for that, demon."

I struggled to my feet because Gray had curled in on himself. "What is happening?"

"Sit down, you whore," the duke said. "Actually, I don't care what you are. I don't need you anymore." He raised a hand.

The young man stepped in front of me. "I don't think you want to do that. If you kill her, your new toy will be extremely angry. Better to keep her around and use her as incentive." He looked down at Gray. "If he survives the transition."

"Who is that guy and why isn't the girl dead?" Dellacourt asked. "At that dosage, even a shifter should have died."

"She's far more interesting than a shifter and this man is named Jacob," the duke explained. "He's been walking this plane since before humans. He's a prophet. He felt the birth of his brother."

"I felt a sickening hole open in the universe as we know it. What have you done? He's a demon." Jacob stared down at Gray, and for a second, I was worried something awful was going to happen.

I moved over Gray, protecting his body with my own. The stupid, tiny skirt I'd been given to wear was riding up my hips and the corset wasn't doing me any favors. I didn't bother trying to get the gun. It wouldn't do a damn thing to Winter. I needed to find a way out of here and now.

I glanced at the windows, but they were covered with heavy drapes. Jamie couldn't see in. There was no help coming.

"Calm yourself, youngling," Jacob said, his eyes warming again. He reached out and touched my face, a rush of peace flowing over me. "I see many roads and you are on most of them. You are important and he is stronger than they believe. I rushed to judgment, something I never do. Come and sit with me. Your lover needs a moment to compose himself."

I started to tell the dude that his ass was crazy and I wasn't going to sit and gossip with him while Gray was potentially dying, but that weird peace thing happened again and I found myself on the couch, trying to ignore the dead bodies at our feet.

Jacob shook his head. "Do not worry, child. The young one will be happier in his next life and the other, well, he'll bring you much pain, so don't weep for him. Tell me how Marcus is doing. Does he still curse my name?"

"You were Apollo." Somehow I felt safe with this boy. Though he appeared younger than me, he'd watched humans evolve. "He's pissed about the whole companion prophecy. I think he believes the baby thing is a joke."

Jacob stopped for a moment and then a laugh huffed from his perfectly sculpted lips. "Such a silly mistake to make. Tell Marcus that people who forget history are often doomed to repeat it. He should remember. I know the king does. The king mourns for her every day of his life. Tell Marcus if he wants his death, he must ease the king's heart. That's where he'll find his prize."

"That's very helpful information. You know what's more helpful? A name. Names are great."

Jacob chuckled. "Yes, they are, but I'm bound by certain rules." He glanced over at Winter. "You will tell me what you've done, though it appears it didn't work."

Winter and Dellacourt were both frowning as Gray stood up. He was shaking, but he stood tall.

"I'm fine. My body metabolizes poison quite nicely." Gray reached out for me. "So unless you want to be the one to have killed both my father's sons, I believe I'll take my girl and leave. And don't think my brother isn't in Hell right now telling my father everything."

Winter shook his head and sat back down. "Oh, silly boy. Whose plan do you think this was in the first place? He didn't drink enough. We need to force more down his throat."

The door behind me opened and I watched as a powerfully built man stepped out. He was immaculate in his three-piece suit and shiny loafers. And the resemblance to Gray was uncanny.

"Kelsey, get behind me." Gray's hand shook as he tried to physically move me behind him.

"Hello, Hunter. It's good to meet you," Papa Sloane said. "I've heard so much about you."

It was time to put some distance between us. I tugged on Gray's hand. We needed to get to a place where Jamie could see us. I wasn't sure how much of a cavalry we had waiting for us, but Jamie would call the king and someone would surely come.

"Not so fast." The butler had moved in behind us and he had a nice-sized gun in his hand.

Gray's shoulders slumped. "Brother?"

Apparently Matthew had switched bodies and fast. "I had a chat with Father on the Hell plane. He explained that this is all part of the plan, Gray. Do you understand what's happening?"

"No." Gray pulled me close. I wasn't sure what he thought he could do against two much more powerful demons and a gun, but his arms wound around me as though they could keep death at bay. "Winter tried to poison me."

I looked at the boy on the couch. He hadn't moved, merely sat watching. "Please, Jacob."

"As I said before, youngling, I am bound by more rules than you can imagine." His eyes rolled back in his head and that warm blue was replaced with a milky white. "I see a crossroad. What happens here tonight changes everything. Choose wisely, Grayson Sloane."

"I don't think I have any choices at all," Gray said bitterly. "I've been a fool all along."

"Trying to do good is never foolish," the prophet said. He turned those endless eyes on Winter. "I would like an explanation. My father is the only one who can make a prophet. He has allowed the others to join him. Only I walk this plane now. Only I see the possible futures and only I choose whether or not to alter them."

"Your father?" I wasn't sure I wanted that particular name.

Jacob's lips curled up slightly. "More correctly our father, though you should understand I use the masculine term simply because it's traditional among humans. My father is infinite and wears as many faces and bodies as there are species walking the planes."

Okay, we were talking about the big dude. "Why don't you give him a call? Because we could seriously use some help here."

"Well, he isn't mine," Winter said with a snarl, completely ignoring me. "And you should know that if I had a way to destroy you, prophet, I would take it."

Jacob shrugged off the threat. "Explanations. Mr. Dellacourt, if you don't mind. Your bosses seem to want to avoid the truth. You can give me the explanation I require or I can pull it from your human brain. You won't like my fingers in your brain."

Dellacourt went a nice shade of white. "Okay, that's awful. Uhm, Winter's been working on this for a long time. And the other scary demon guy."

Gray's father had a flask in his hand. He stepped up. "I'll explain. It must be difficult for someone who sees and knows everything to be left in the dark."

"I don't like the sensation, but I couldn't possibly have seen this coming. What you're trying to create is an abomination," Jacob explained.

Gray shook his head. "I have prophecy powers. I'm not a prophet. I don't even have particularly strong powers of prophecy."

"Yes, you do, but you won't use them," his father complained. "You could be as powerful a seer as Jacob given time and proper training."

"There are no dark prophets. None. There have never been any." Jacob's eyes narrowed. "It was not a power the dark ones were meant to have. You've bred it into some of your halflings, but a true prophet is divine."

"Your father, as you call him, is an amazing chemist," Winter said with a smile. "Humans have managed to emulate many of his so-called miracles. Once I figured out the formula, all it took was an accelerant. You are a prophet by your chemistry, Jacob. In the same way that we're demons and vampires are vampires. In the end, it's a simple thing. It's all in the code."

Gray's father held up the flask. "We have to get enough of this inside Gray and his chemistry will change. It's a plan we've had in place for years, but we needed the right subject."

"You needed a royal halfling." Jacob frowned. "With angelic blood. You raped an angel?"

"My mother was a witch," Gray said.

"Your mother was also a companion. One the vampires hadn't found. A strong one." Fangs gleamed from his father's mouth. "I purchased her soul from her father and when she was of age to have a child, I took what was mine. You have enough angelic blood inside you that this will work. Look at my son now, prophet. Look at the roads that stem from my son and tell me what you see."

Jacob seemed to turn inward, his eyes glazing over to that odd white again. The room went silent. "I see war. I see death. Endless death and agony."

Winter's lips curled up. "Then all is right with my world. Force it down his throat."

It was time for me to start kicking a little ass.

Jacob held a hand out. "Forcing it down his throat won't work. That's where you're going to fail. You can't win. Grayson Sloane has to open himself. He has to accept the transition for it to occur. It's what you didn't count on. He can fight it off. He already did once tonight."

I felt a smile cross my face. We were good. There was zero chance of Gray giving in to their evil plans. Gray would fight and they could pour it down his throat all night long because it wouldn't mean a damn thing.

Never get comfortable. If I had to write a book for up-and-coming Hunters, that would be my first piece of advice. You get a shit-eating grin on your face because you think you have the bad guys right where you want them and all their superstinky plans for the apocalypse are going to add up to a big fat zero, and that's when everything falls apart, kiddos. So don't get arrogant. Don't let your guard down and whatever you do, keep your eyes on the dude with the semiautomatic weapon.

Yeah, that was when I noticed Matthew, in his brand spanking new butler body, pointing his gun at my head.

"Brother, I'm afraid I'm going to have to insist. Father, did you bring the chains?" Mathew asked.

Dellacourt was so helpful. "No need. I have brand new handcuffs. They're super high tech. They go on the market in a couple of months. They were originally made for supernatural creatures on another plane. I assume they'll take care of whatever the hell she is."

"Don't," Matthew warned as Gray stared at him. "One move her way and I'll fire. She's strong, but no one survives a bullet to the head. Neither Father nor I wish to kill your promised bride, but we will if we're forced to."

"I'll kill the bitch in a heartbeat." Winter took a step toward me. "I'll freeze her where she stands."

I couldn't help it. I took a step back, despite the fact that brought my head into direct contact with Matthew's gun. I would way rather have the bullet than let that man touch me.

Besides, it was past time to let other people dictate this particular battle. I had to get Gray out of here, and it wasn't like I was some fragile flower. I also played on the fact that Papa Sloane wanted his Hunter grandbaby someday. The dude was seriously into genetics. I brought my head forward and popped it back as quickly as I could. The gun flew out of Matthew's borrowed hands and his surprise gave me enough time to whirl around and shove the bottom of my palm up with great force. I hit his nose and felt the cartilage break. It was an angled hit and it did what I'd meant it to do. The cartilage shattered and I shoved it upward and into his brain.

The butler's eyes widened and then he fell to the ground.

He should have found another job. Matthew would likely be back, but Winter would be looking for more help. I had that gun in my hand before anyone could think to come after me.

"Gray, it's time for us to leave." I stepped in front of my ex, who was still pale from fighting off his last encounter with the drug. "Stay behind me."

Papa Sloane stepped forward, his eyes turning a pissed-off shade of red. "Where do you think you're going, Hunter?"

"You might have mentioned I would be welcoming a Hunter into my home." Winter came to stand next to him. Two incredibly old, powerful demons.

Gray's father waved off the worry. "She's a baby. She's barely a few months into training. She's nothing to worry about, but I would greatly prefer she not be damaged. She's promised to my son. Imagine the child between a dark prophet and a Hunter."

"I am not your son," Gray growled behind me. "And I swear if anyone lays a hand on her, I'll find a way to kill you all. I won't accept this. I won't allow that drug to work on me. Find yourself another prophet."

"Think about this." His father had his hands out as though not having a weapon made him less threatening. "Grayson, the light has always had their prophets. You would be the first Hell prophet. Do you know what power you would have?"

Gray wasn't having it. "I don't want it and I wouldn't use the power for you. You think you can start a war on this plane and placate Lucifer Morningstar by turning my life inside out. I won't accept it. You'll have to kill me first."

I believed him and was damn straight going to make sure it didn't happen. Gray would die before he gave in to his father. The entire time I'd known him he'd been trying to break his ties to Hell, not become their holy prophet.

"Gray, back up. We're going to move out toward the front door." I kept my eyes on the demons.

Jacob stood in the back, watching. Apparently that was what he did. Helping would have been better, but apparently that went against the prophet code. It looked like we were on our own.

I was kind of hoping once we got to the yard, we could make a run for it. In the freezing cold. And the snow.

Yeah, I hadn't thought this one out very carefully, but I was kind of committed at this point. I couldn't let them have Gray. I could tell myself all day long that I didn't want the bad guys to get such a powerful weapon, but it was far more than that. I couldn't let them have Gray. I couldn't let him go.

I might never be able to truly let him go.

"Kelsey, get behind me," Gray ordered in that voice that meant he wasn't taking no for an answer.

He was going to have to this time. He was still a bit pasty, and it was easy to see he was reeling from being betrayed by his family. I personally thought it should have been one of those self-evident things. When your family rules a special section of the Hell plane, you should probably count on uncomfortable family reunions, but Gray was oddly naïve. I think he always hoped his father cared about him for reasons other than his unique and apparently well-engineered DNA.

I had to give us some time. Once more, I turned to my old friend, the bullet. They wouldn't kill the bastards, but a few well-placed ones would buy us a couple of seconds.

The sound roared through the room as I put a slug into both the demon's foreheads. They slammed back, the force of the bullets making them stumble and fall. I would have taken out Dellacourt, but he was a smart human. He was hiding and I didn't have time to play.

I took Gray's hand. Those bad boys would be up and on their feet following us in seconds. "Time to go."

We had to get back to Ether. The king had to know about the plan and we had to get Gray into protective custody and pray he was the only one bred to take on this ability.

Gray followed, keeping up with me. His hand tightened around mine as we made it to the door. No time to figure out where the coatroom was and bundle up. As he opened the door, I swore the next time someone insisted I wear open-toed four-inch heels, I was giving them a smackdown they wouldn't forget.

Cold wind blasted through me. I had to hold on to Gray's hand so I didn't fly back into the house.

"Don't let go," Gray shouted, pulling me out. He put a hand up to ward off the crazy wind. He jogged out into the sudden blizzard.

I could barely see. It wasn't that it was dark. The amount of snow and ice coming at me almost made it too white. The moon was shining down, reflecting off the snow. Where there had been a modest dusting only twenty minutes before, now my feet sank ankle deep into the powder.

So cold. I felt that chill in my bones. This wasn't a mere snowstorm. This was pure killing winter. This was the element undiluted, and this was part of Abbas Hiberna. He was calling the shots now.

Gray pulled me close as we moved past the frozen fountain. "I don't know that I can find the car. I think we should make a run for Jamie. We don't have much time. I don't suppose I can get you to leave me?"

He'd learned much from our previous encounters. "Not on your life. Can you see enough to tell which way to go?"

The wind was picking up and everything appeared white to me. I tried to orient myself. Panic threatened because I couldn't see anything. The minute we moved away from the fountain, it disappeared in a blanket of snow. My feet were starting to go numb, but I forced myself to move. We had to find shelter.

Gray held a hand over his eyes as though he could peer through the pelting snow and ice that contained us. But it wouldn't be eyes that saved us. This was nature at its most primal and nothing so logical as eyesight would win out.

Instinct was the only thing that might save us.

I carry a wolf inside me. The demons had created Gray as the perfect vessel for their sacrilege. They'd spent hundreds of years searching for the perfect bloodlines to pervert.

I was natural, the end product of a lone wolf and his one love. My father's instincts lay in my DNA, and I called on them when I had nothing left.

I stopped and breathed in the air around me. I don't smell like a wolf. They can pick out a single scent from a landfill. I don't have that power. What I have is instinct. I'm not sure why, but I turned to my left and began walking. "Jamie's this way."

"How can you be sure?" Gray asked.

"I just know." Jamie is my brother. We might not share a biological father, but Jamie is in my pack. When I close down the human parts of myself and let the she-wolf have a little sway, I can find my pack.

"Kelsey, your skin." He was staring down at my exposed forearm.

Yep, I was getting used to frostbite. "It'll heal once we get inside."

I'd taken a nice cocktail right before going to Gray's. Donovan had insisted. I will state now and forever that royal blood is a trip, and I was absolutely certain it would heal the damage once I got somewhere I wasn't being bombarded by ice shards.

We tried to run, but the wind picked up. Naturally it was coming in from the very direction we needed to go. Gray pressed on, his demonic strength pushing us through.

I was almost sure we were to the end of the drive when I was pulled back. I screamed out as something infinitely cold wrapped itself around my ankle and pulled. When I looked down, I saw a creature dragging me back.

Snowmen. The bastard had sent crazy, creepy fucking snowmen after us. I was so never telling my niece about this.

"Kelsey!" Gray screamed.

I glanced behind me and could see Gray struggling in the arms of some kind of big-ass white creature. It was at least seven feet tall but it could have been bigger. It blended in with the snow, meshing with it until I almost couldn't tell where it ended and the storm began.

I shot at my snowman.

The bullet went through and he simply kept pulling me back toward the house.

I tried kicking and clawing. Nothing. He was solid ice and nothing worked on him. I wished I'd thought to bring a blowtorch with me.

One crazy fucking snowman became two and then three. They surrounded me, the winds howling when they opened their mouths. One stared down at me. There were hollows where its eyes should be, but it seemed to have no trouble seeing me. When its mouth opened, I saw sharp teeth. Ice as fine as any blade. Those teeth were razors and I wasn't sure what would kill me first—the cold that was making everything seem to slow down or those murderous teeth.

There was a pop and suddenly one part of me wasn't cold anymore. My shiny demon arm seemed to have a built-in heater.

The snowman who had been holding my newly red arm howled, and when I looked at him, I saw those cold hands that had held me were melting like the sun was shining down on them.

"They can't handle demon skin, Gray!" I shouted over the winds as I punched at the snow asshole with all the teeth.

He shattered the instant I touched him.

Snowman number three ran.

I struggled to my feet. There was no chance that I was coaxing my arm back to normal. I didn't care how freaky I looked. I kind of loved the hell out of that arm. I was warmer than before, stronger. My she-wolf and I worked in tandem as another wave of the things came after us. I wasn't afraid of them now. Now they might be strong, but I wasn't helpless against them.

I kicked at one, thrusting him back while I shattered the second with my hand.

Up ahead, I saw Gray in the middle of an army of monsters. His fancy shirt was in tatters and he was trying his hardest, but it was easy to see he was losing.

There were big spots of red on his exposed chest where the blood had frozen on his body as quickly as the wound had opened.

"Gray, you have to change!" I shouted as I shoved my clawed hand into one of the creatures.

It shattered, sending shards of ice exploding through the air. I dropped, covering my abdomen and torso. Anything else I could heal quickly given the king's blood inside me.

It struck me that once again, the king's blood was boosting Gray's. It would be days before Gray's blood was out of my system and until then, a good dose of Donovan would bolster it, making it super strong.

But we were surrounded. No matter how strong I was, I couldn't take them all out myself. A mountain of winter surrounded us as I made my way to Gray.

"You have to change," I insisted, driving back one of the bigger monsters.

"No." Gray's eyes were shining violet, a sure sign that his body knew what it needed to do. I could see the beginnings of his horns blooming through his dark hair, but he was a stubborn man. "I don't want you to see me like that."

And vain. He was quite vain.

A blast of cold punched over me and I turned, taking out another monster with a swipe of my arm.

It wasn't enough. I needed Gray.

"We're going to die if you don't change." While my arm was feeling all toasty and warm, the rest of me was kind of going to shit and fast. My legs had turned a nasty shade of purple. "I'm not going to be able to walk soon, Gray. I have to get somewhere I can heal."

His eyes closed briefly, and I could practically feel his pain. He didn't want this. He didn't want me to see him as a monster.

When he opened them again, his eyes were as dark as obsidians.

He changed quickly, his muscles flowing from human to demon forms with the grace and ease of someone who had done it a thousand times, though I knew damn well Gray hadn't. This easy shift was another gift of his royal DNA, and it made me wonder what Gray had to do to constantly stay in his human form.

He seemed to change in mass, his body growing larger. The snow around him melted as his spine lengthened, shoulders growing broader. His skin shifted to a shiny red, the companion of my right arm, though even here he was more masculine. Where my scales were seemingly delicate, his formed a rough exterior it looked like nothing could tear through.

When he was done, his clothes were in tatters and I almost didn't recognize him. I fell to the grass that was now at my feet. The heat of his transition had given us a few feet where the cold couldn't touch us, and I sighed as I felt the vampire blood in my body begin to heal the frostbite. I hadn't realized I'd been in so much pain. The absence was almost a weird pleasure and so was looking at Gray.

He stood over me, a dark god. His horns were curved, his body sharper than it had been before. This was Gray, the demon, and surprise, surprise—he was fucking hot as hell. Every muscle of his body was perfectly defined, every inch of him a testament to dark beauty.

His clawed hand reached down and touched my head. I could see the possessiveness in his ebony eyes as he rubbed his palm over my hair. "Mine."

I decided it was best to agree with him until we got out of the situation. "Yep. Totally yours. And they're trying to kill me. You should do something about that."

He snarled. Even that was kind of hot. I can be a little perverted at times.

He looked around at the monsters circling us and his fangs lengthened. "Stay."

His demon wasn't big on multisyllabic words. I was cool with that as long as he was big on killing the bad guys.

I felt my arm shift and I was back to normal. Maybe that wasn't the smartest thing in the world, but my subconscious apparently trusted the big guy to take care of us. The wind had picked up again, but the ground beneath me was still warm. Well, warmer than the snow, and it appeared to have formed some sort of no-fly zone for the creatures.

The minute one attempted to come into my circle, they melted. After two lost limbs, the rest backed off.

Gray had to go after them. He left the circle with a roar and then that snow was his killing field.

I watched as he took them all on. Even at his size, he was smaller than the frost giants. He punched out, clawing at his attackers.

I lost track of him, his body covered by more of the creatures than I could count. I struggled with my instinct to go and help him, but right before I would have joined him, he punched his way through, sending snow and ice flying all around.

He was a magnificent killing machine.

All at once, the creatures vanished, disintegrating in the wind.

"Don't you dare change." I shook a finger at the massive demon who had taken down Winter's army. Despite the relative warmth of my circle, the wind was still frigid and my teeth chattered. "You have zero idea when they'll come back, mister, and I don't want to go through that whole transition thing again."

His eyes narrowed on me and he took a step forward, looming over me.

I'm sure to most people he would have been a completely terrifying monster that would haunt their dreams and shit, but I saw Gray behind those demonic eyes and he didn't scare me. "Don't you growl at me. You know I'm right."

He growled anyway.

I growled back. "Pick me up and get me out of here, Gray. You're going to be faster since you're at least a foot taller than normal, and it doesn't look like the weather is bothering you now. And stop the whole self-pity thing. Have you looked at yourself in a mirror lately? You are the hottest demon I've ever seen, and you're all muscly, and I have to admit the fangs do something for me."

I swear that demon preened. He also reached down and picked me up. He brought me high against his chest. Despite the razor-sharp claws, I was cradled as tenderly as he would any baby.

Though I don't recommend handing a baby over to a demon. Many demons find babies quite the tasty treat. That's my point. Even in his full-on demonic form, Gray was still able to care, able to be kind, able to love.

He was so warm in this form. I sighed and cuddled close, feeling his body heat begin to sink into my bones. So warm.

"Love you," he said through his fangs. "Take you back to Marcus now."

And he was able to sacrifice. No one could convince me Grayson Sloane was a true demon. He turned toward the giant gate we'd driven through.

That was when I saw Jamie walking across the yard. My brother. I smiled. He would have loved to watch Gray take out a hundred snow monsters. I was simply happy he wasn't freaking out at the sight of me in a demon's arms.

Gray took a step back.

"Hey, it's all right," I said, trying to soothe him. "It's Jamie. It's fine. We can all get out of here now."

He shook his head and clutched me close. "Not Jamie." He changed, his body flowing from demon to human again. I felt it as I seemed to drop about a foot, and then Gray's human arms were holding me tight. "That's not Jamie, Kelsey."

"Oh, but it is, brother." Jamie's body moved toward me, but it wasn't his voice. A British accent flowed from my brother's mouth. "It is very much his body. How about that, Hunter? Did I find one you won't kill?"

Matthew. Gray's brother had possessed my brother's body. Jamie was still inside there. Somewhere deep inside his own body, Jamie was likely screaming and trying to get out.

"Please," I said.

Gray held me close. "I'll get us out of this. I won't let him kill Jamie. I promise."

I shook my head but before I could protest, Gray looked to his brother.

"You know what I want," Matthew said.

Gray went still. "I want a contract."

And just like that Gray decided to become their prophet.

Chapter Nineteen

I couldn't help but watch my brother. Matthew. It was still hard to think of him as Matthew. Jamie was sitting right there. He was dressed like a refugee from the nineties in a flannel shirt and faded jeans. I wanted to reach out and touch him, to assure myself that my brother was alive.

Then he would turn the right way and the light would catch his eyes. They would flash a nasty red and I would remember.

I couldn't lose Jamie. Not like this.

Gray studied the contract, his head shaking. He'd been provided with a pair of slacks and a new dress shirt since he'd ripped up his clothes during his change. He hadn't utterly destroyed them, but he'd definitely had a Hulky vibe with the rips and tears. Now he was back to looking sleek and in control. Yeah, appearances can be deceiving. "Simpler. I told you. I'm not signing anything that has duties or rules concerning my life here on the Earth plane."

His father stared down at us. "You'll sign whatever I want you to sign or the boy dies."

Jamie…Jamie's body stood up. "No, he won't, Father. Gray has agreed to take the drug and try to transition. He won't agree to anything beyond that and he doesn't have to."

"Do you forget who is in charge here?" Winter asked.

Matthew shook Jamie's head. "Not at all, Your Grace, but I still have to watch out for my brother's interests. I agreed to do this because it puts him in a position of power. You seek to take not only his power away, but his life here on the Earth plane. Have you thought about that, Father? If Gray spends all his time in Hell, how will he give you the grandson you require?"

Sloane's eyes pinned me for a second before looking back at his elder son with a sigh. "It's a nice word I call rape, son. Ms. Owens's consent isn't needed. Despite what certain politicians will have the idiotic public believing, a woman's uterus doesn't give a fuck if she welcomed the sperm or not. She can come with us willingly or not."

"Then kill Jamie now. Kill me now. Kill Kelsey now," Gray said, his voice bleak. "I won't rape her. I won't force her to go to Hell."

"Then we're at a standstill, son." Gray's father was completely unmoving.

Gray's head dropped. "If I consent to go with you, Kelsey and her family must be left alone."

"No." I couldn't let them change Gray and then haul him back to Hell for me.

Before we could argue, Jacob chuckled. "How little you people know. You're all fools. Has no one asked why I've walked this plane for millennia? I must. My powers draw from this plane. You could force the dark prophet to go to Hell, but good luck with getting any sort of reliable prophecy out of him once he's there."

"Why are you still here?" Winter snarled.

Jacob's eyes turned grim. "To bear witness, as I always do to the world's great events. Tonight is a turning point. The trouble with a prophet is you can't control him. You can set him loose and hope for the best, but he will do as he wishes. Lucifer is insane if he thinks simply creating a thing means he controls it. After all, he rather started that trend."

"He's my son and I can control him," Sloane shot back.

"Really? It doesn't seem like you can control the other one. Perhaps if I kill his host, we can clear things up," Winter said.

Sloane's eyes narrowed. "Don't you touch him. My son is right. We'll only kill the boy if an arrangement can't be made. Grayson, I agree to your terms. Kelsey and her family are off limits if you sign this agreement and accept your place. You'll still have the years left to you. I can't promise you anything after that. Prophet or no prophet."

My mind was running through the possibilities. If Gray couldn't work this mojo they wanted in Hell, it would be hard for them to enforce his contract. This could work in our favor.

His favor. Not mine. But I had been trying to find a way to get him out of that stupid contract. It wasn't something Gray had signed. It had basically been written into his DNA. His mother had signed over his soul before he'd even been born. Talk about shitty parents.

I looked over at Jamie's body. "Can he hear me?"

Matthew frowned. "Yes."

"Jamie, I'll call Mom as soon as I get us out of this. And Nate. I love you and I forgive Mom and Nate." It was totally easy in the face of Gray's family sins. I wasn't sure I would talk to Jamie again. I wasn't sure he would be here with us. He could die or be rendered insane from Matthew's use of his body, and I needed him to know that I'd been foolish. "I forgive them all. I love you."

I forgave my father. Not the shitty one. Not the one who'd tried to kill me. He could burn in Hell for all I cared.

But I forgave my dad. Lee Owens. I hadn't realized how angry I'd been until this moment. It was irrational. My mother had been the one to walk away. She'd left him, but there was a part of me that thought he should have followed through. He should have come after her or made certain there hadn't been a me to take care of.

I'd been told that he would have loved me, but for the first time I accepted it. My father would have loved me. He would have protected and taken care of me.

It was enough.

"He understands," Matthew said. "Though he isn't entirely certain you mean it. He wonders if you haven't found a new family now. He misses you. Misses Gray. Misses everyone because he's all alone. He'll die alone. He'll die without a wife or children because that's his destiny, the path his father set him on long ago."

"Stop it," Gray said, his voice a low growl. "Leave him alone. You have no right to drag his emotions into this. I'll sign a deal to accept the drugs. I'll do my absolute best to become what you want, but I want Kelsey and Jamie safe. That is nonnegotiable."

"And he wants his time." He wouldn't ask for it himself. "He wants his original contract in play. You can't force him back to Hell before his time."

Sloane's lips curled up into a satisfied smirk. "Perhaps he won't have to resort to rape. It sounds like she cares for you."

"Do you accept?" I ignored the rest. I wasn't getting into bed with Gray anytime soon, but I also wasn't about to willingly let him go to Hell. He'd proven a valuable ally.

Yeah, I actually told myself that.

Winter and Sloane stared at each other, and for a moment I had to wonder if they couldn't communicate on a level I didn't understand. An evil, telepathic level, but one I couldn't hear.

"Lucifer will be thrilled that we created one," Papa Sloane stated. "He'll forgive the transgression because we're the only ones who can give him this gift. It doesn't matter that Grayson might prove uncooperative. I've always found ways to make him help in the past. I'll do it in the future. Sign the deal."

"I will be signing away your best bet at making him cooperate. He loves the girl." Winter stared at me as though he was thinking about all the fun stuff he could do to make Gray cooperate right that moment.

"He is unreasonable about the girl," Matthew argued. "He won't ever help you if he thinks it will hurt her. Your best bet is to give him the one thing he wants. My brother is far too attuned to the humanity in his DNA. Or I suppose it's that bit of angelic DNA you managed to pump into his background. He'll honor his contract. He'll honor his word. Sign the deal and let us be done."

I wasn't exactly grateful for Matthew in that moment. I still wanted to strangle the bastard, but I was happy when that contract went in front of Gray and it seemed like we would leave this mansion with both our heads intact.

Gray gave it another pass. I'd argued he deserved a lawyer. They'd argued that was simply my excuse to bring a vampire into the discussion since I'd explained the only one I would accept was Hugo Wells. It was totally true, so I lost that argument. It was precisely why Gray insisted on simple language. The original contract had been twenty pages long. Gray had gotten them down to a few lines no one could misinterpret.

I hoped.

He seemed satisfied and signed his name quickly, as though he had to do it in that particular moment or he wouldn't have done it at all.

I stood up and faced Matthew. "It's done. Get out."

I wanted my brother back. Every minute that asshole stayed in his body was a minute too long. What was Jamie feeling? Was he afraid? He was likely pissed as hell, and it would take a lot to keep him from immediately trying to hunt down Gray's brother.

That was my job.

Matthew sighed. "I can't until he transitions. I promised Father. I didn't want this, Kelsey. I know you won't believe me, but I'm doing this for him. And I'm not even doing anything to torture your brother. He's angry, but he'll come out of this as whole as he was when I took over. I vow it."

There was absolutely nothing that demon could say that would make me believe him.

Gray stood beside me, his eyes blank as he looked to his father. "Let's get this over with. What do I have to take?"

Winter snapped his fingers and Dellacourt produced a goblet. It was easy to see this evening hadn't gone the way the billionaire thought it would. His hands were shaking as he stepped back. He moved close to the curtains as though he could hide himself in their voluminous fabric.

He could try that all he liked. I would remember his face. I didn't particularly care that he was one of the richest men on the planet. Or that he was human. He'd helped to do this to Gray. He would pay.

Jacob watched with patient eyes as Gray took the goblet in his hand. "Grayson, are you ready for this?"

Gray shook his head. "No."

"It can be quite painful. While your physical form won't change, parts of your mind will, shall we say, open in a way they haven't before. You have to remember that much of the pain you will feel comes from various futures. Ones that will be, could be, are only the vaguest of possibilities. You will see them all."

"Everyone's future?" I asked, unable to truly comprehend.

Jacob shook a finger. "It's more complex. So much more. He will see everyone in the world and all of their potential futures. It can be a bit much at times, and he won't have a way to stop the flow if this goes the way they hope."

"Are you trying to talk him out of it?" Winter complained. "I thought you were only able to watch."

"I'm explaining what is about to happen because I've read all the signs and I believe this will happen. The other paths have faded. This is Grayson's path now. He will transition, but how he comes out on the other side is up to her." Jacob stared my way.

"What does that mean?" I wasn't sure I wanted to be in the middle of Gray's destiny. I still hadn't even figured my own out yet. The one thing I knew was that destiny kind of sucked.

"Leave her out of this," Gray warned.

Jacob stepped up to me, taking my hand in his. He flipped my wrist over and one finger traced the blue veins he found there. "The drugs will change the chemistry of his brain, but also his blood. If you take a portion of the drug, you can take some of the chaos for him. I can help. It's your future he'll try to hold on to. You're the one his mind will instinctively reach for, and that is what will cause him the most pain. It's better for him to let it flow. I'll stay in the room with the two of you and direct a single path into your mind. Is there one thing he'll look for?"

"No," Gray said, his jaw tightening.

"Our wedding night." There was no question about it. If Gray could find that single flash, he would hold on to it as tightly as he could. He'd been trying to get back to that one blast of the future he'd seen years ago. That one single path would hold him back. "He thinks he saw our wedding night and he'll look for it."

"Stay out of this, Kelsey."

"Not on your life." If I could spare him some pain, I would do it. He was taking one for the team.

I couldn't let him go through it alone. Not if I had the choice.

Jacob glanced over to where Winter and Sloane stood. "I see the path. If she aids him, takes some of the pain, it will work. If not, the odds are great that he will be damaged."

"Why would you help?" Winter asked, his eyes narrowed in suspicion.

Jacob sent him a serene smile. "I seek only to manage his pain. I remember well how it felt, even after millennia. And I was an angel at the time. His transition will be more difficult. If you would rather he faced it alone, of course, do as you will. I am not here to change destiny. I am a simple watcher."

"My contract stated she wouldn't be harmed," Gray ground out.

Sloane stood before his son, his tone as smooth as any con man's.

"And she won't be. Besides, your contract was only that Winter and I and our minions can't bring her to harm. This is a choice she will make herself. Mr. Dellacourt, I believe the lovely *Nex Apparatus* requires a serving."

Winter's eyes laser focused on me. "You bitch."

"Way to blow a girl's cover," I groused. "Now might be a good time to reiterate all those nice contractual words like 'no harm comes to Kelsey.'"

Sloane's lips curled up in a satisfied smile as he looked me over. "There's only one reason my son's blood would be coursing through your veins. You're the one who got her arm frozen off. I can actually see the line. It's fascinating. And I keep a closer eye on Donovan than anyone. He thinks he has the upper hand, but we intend to show him tonight exactly how little power he has."

"What does that mean?" I didn't like the sound of that. Especially the time line. Tonight was right freaking now. If something was going on, I needed to be wherever it was happening.

Dellacourt passed me a wine glass. It was filled with a rich amber fluid that probably didn't taste anything like wine.

I glanced back at Matthew. "When are you going to give my brother back to me?"

I was beginning to believe we should have had Matthew sign that contract, too.

"When my own brother is alive and this can be done," Matthew explained. "He must transition or his usefulness to our father is at an end. He's been stubborn and rebellious, and I can't stand the thought of him crushed under the boot of some minor Hell lord, but that's what will happen if he has no value. I love my brother. I'm willing to risk a lot to save him. How about you, Hunter?"

"Kelsey, don't." Gray's hand came out to stop me.

I swallowed the drink as quickly as I could. Truly, I've learned nothing of white magic tastes good. In my days, I've had to take more than my share of a witch's tonic and brews to heal and help. There's always an earthiness to it that makes one think of dirt or other things one doesn't particularly want in one's gut.

Oh, but dark magic tastes like the finest of liquors. It touched my tongue and was easy to swallow. I wanted more the minute I finished because it was sheer perfection. It soothes and eases down your throat right before your body catches fire.

I gasped and pitched forward, right into Gray's arms. He caught me, cursed, and then he too was drinking the potion down.

I held on to him as all the fates of the world swamped my senses.

"Ease her down on the bed."

I was moving. Someone held me. I wasn't sure. My mind couldn't keep up with the flashes, the warnings, the moments that might be. They flashed through my head, tendrils I couldn't quite catch.

"Kelsey, I need you to follow the sound of my voice."

I could make out the words but they seemed so far away. The low moan that came from my mouth was much closer. I moaned because my body ached. Age. I could feel it. So much age and death. Those were certain fates, and those lines seemed to crawl across my flesh like ants, biting and stinging their way. Anger. There was so much anger in the world. It was fuel for fate. So many different outcomes could be traced back to a single act of fury.

"If you don't follow my voice, none of this will work, youngling."

Jacob. He was the way out of this terrible place. I caught on his voice and tried to follow.

"That's right. Grab on and ride with it. Come to me."

The flashes of fate changed suddenly to vines. The world around me was filled with a million plants and trees. The leaves and branches were infinite possibilities. I strode through the jungle I found myself in, pulling away when the vines would try to wrap around and haul me back in. If I got lost, I would be here forever. I would be adrift in the never-ending potential. As one fate became reality, another formed to take its place. As one event occurred, another tree or bush sprouted.

"Hello." Jacob was suddenly in front of me. He turned, taking in the space we found ourselves in. "Everyone views this place differently. It says something about you that the worst possible fates are dandelions. An interesting choice."

Anyone who's ever had a yard knows how awful the fuckers are. One small breeze and one weed becomes a hundred. "How do I stop this? I don't even understand any of it."

"You don't need to, though I should note you're handling it beautifully. The fact that you formed a world for yourself to walk through is testament to your strength. Most would simply sit and scream. Your mind found a way to take some control. You're taking a great deal of pain from him. The physical transformation is…unpleasant."

"Will he live?" I glanced around. Things were making more sense now. The vines still tried to cling to me, but I was able to brush them off. It was all about acceptance. Sometimes the worst pain is made better by simply accepting it, riding it, and knowing it has some purpose.

The answer was here. All answers were here.

My eye caught on a massive tree in the distance. An oak. It was thick and strong, and it was coated in numerous flowering vines that looked as though they might choke the tree. Gorgeous blossoms covered the trunk with a possessive clasp.

"That's us. That's me and Gray." I stepped closer and noticed a second vine. The flowers were stunning, opening for me even as I watched. As though they knew I stared and they wanted me to see, to see that two vines coveted that great oak.

Someone else loved Gray.

"Silly girl. Why on earth would he be the oak?" Jacob's hand was in mine. "Your choice now. You can stay here and seek answers or you can do what you came to do. Already your lover has lost himself. You were correct. He's trying to hold on to that one moment, but it's changing, morphing, and he can't handle it."

I glanced back at that tree, trying to see it, but we'd somehow moved away. That tree represented all of the potentials of my life. Was I the oak? Or one of the vines competing? I studied the tree more closely and saw what I hadn't before. The vines had been as wrapped around each other as they had the tree. The vines had somehow learned to need each other. They had to in order to hold up the tree. The tree felt so heavy at times, the branches weighing it down, but the vines lifted, gave it strength, brought great beauty.

"Kelsey? It's your choice," Jacob reminded me.

My choice. Save Gray or see the possibilities of my own life.

A whole bunch of those possibilities wilted and died if Gray didn't pull this off. I turned firmly away from the tree. "What do I do?"

He stared at me for a moment. "It's going to be fun to be around you, Kelsey. I miss my last friend. I find so few. He left me for a woman in Bali. Married with a baby. He'll have a good life, but I miss his spirit. I think you and your group shall enliven my existence again. I do so love to watch the important events play out. Take my hand."

He reached out and the rest of my jungle seemed to quiet. He was the master of whatever wild plane we found ourselves on. We couldn't possibly still be on Earth. I hesitated for a moment, but took it. The minute he touched me, my mind felt calmer, more centered.

"Will I retain any of this ability?" I asked, not sure which answer I wanted.

"Perhaps, but unlike Grayson, your gift will likely come in the form of dreams that have to be interpreted, and they'll be sporadic at best. Even what Gray sees will be highly open to interpretation. It's the sad fact of our existence. If we could simply tell a person which path to take, the world would be so much simpler. Such is life." He turned, gently moving me with him, and I saw a door in front of us.

"Does that mean Gray's blood won't ever leave my system?"

Jacob began walking toward that very elegant door in the middle of the jungle. A low light came from around it, giving the entire door a halo. "Ah, if it had only been Gray's blood, then yes. It would leave. But there was another component, wasn't there? The king's blood is an interesting thing. It has long-term effects, especially when used the way you did. Almost always his blood is ingested when he heals his loved ones. Only once before did it go directly into one's bloodstream at a precious, changeable time. Yes, I'm certainly waiting to see how that plays out. The next several years are going to be fun. But enough of that. What you'll see behind that door is a single future moment. I'll be with you while you experience this particular possibility. Don't be surprised if it changes in odd ways, though the setting will remain the same. It's merely the circumstances of the moment affecting the potential outcome. I'll be gone when you wake, but make sure Gray knows I'll come for him soon. I'll teach him our ways."

"You said he would be an abomination."

Jacob smiled, a truly brilliant thing. "I said I couldn't actively affect the outcome. Of course, I never said a prophet can't lie. I lie quite well, thank you."

"Nice." It was good to know the prophet had some human flaws.

His hand squeezed mine, giving me strength. "I might lie on occasion, but never to myself. That's what people like Winter and Gray's father get wrong. What they don't understand is they choose. The demons believe they are one way, that they were born to do evil. In fact, they were not. They choose. They choose their culture, choose what those around them deem as acceptable. It takes true courage to see the rottenness of what is familiar and choose to change. Gray is brave. Tell him that though a prophet might be dark, though his power might have come from evil, how he uses it is the true gift our father gives us all. We choose who we are every single day. That is what all of this is about. So choose wisely, Kelsey Owens. So much rests on who you are."

The door opened and I walked through.

Chapter Twenty

He is my husband. It's hard to believe. After everything we went through, we made it to this day. I stare at the man on the bed. Naturally he insisted upon this hotel and this room. It was where he first saw me, first understood the potential of me.

I saw him for the first time standing in my hallway all those years ago. I'd been coming out of the bathroom, trying to pull myself together after going on a bender.

I look nicer tonight. Tonight I wear a white silk gown that clings to my every curve. It plunges to show off the slope of my breasts. The color makes my skin appear luminescent. Or maybe that's the fact that I love him with all my heart.

"Kelsey mine." He gives me that slow smile that makes everything female inside of me respond.

Gray hasn't taken off his tuxedo pants and white dress shirt, though he ditched the tie and jacket long ago. He got rid of them during our first dance. I can still hear the song. It's from a few years back. *All of Me.*

Our wedding was perfect. My family surrounded me. I suppose it was odd that one of the bride's former lovers gave her away, but Marcus and I have found a comfortable friendship since we parted. I even love his new companion like a sister.

My mind fights the image. It's wrong. Pain flashes through my system, an alarm bell telling me to wake the fuck up.

Let it happen. See all the possibilities. *Jacob's voice whispers to me, reminding me that I'm still me. This is all one long "what if" scenario playing in my head. I relax. I won't fight this. The moment I accept what's happening, I'm right back in the moment.*

He sits up and I can see a flash of perfect skin peeking from behind the buttons of his shirt. I love his chest. Smooth and warm, I love to lay my head on it and hear the sound of his heart beating. When I need peace, I'll lay for hours wrapped around him. He holds out his hand and I walk to him.

"Have I told you how beautiful you are?" Gray's eyes skim my body. He tells me all the time. He's told me so many times, I've started to believe him.

"Have I told you I think about you all the time?" Years of training with Marcus and the academics have made me comfortable with talking about how I feel. I'm a different person. A better person.

He pulls me close and drags the pretty gown off my shoulders and exposes my breasts. I stay still. He likes to look at me, treating my body like a private work of art. Slowly his hand comes up, fingers brushing from my neck along my collarbone.

"You're all I think about, Kelsey mine." His hand cups my breast as the other curls around my neck, dragging me close for a kiss. His lips meet mine, soft velvet rubbing my lips, seeking entry.

I give it to him. I give him everything I have.

I only miss Marcus at odd times. It's been so long and I know he's happy, but there are moments I wish I hadn't walked through that painting. She'd been waiting there. Not for me, but for him. For them all.

The room shifts slightly. It's such a small thing. The light flickers and I feel a hand on my back.

"I would like some of that, *bella*," a deep voice says.

Gray's lips curl up against mine. "Give him what he wants or he'll pout."

I turn and Marcus is there, his night-black hair falling over his forehead. His eyes heat as he looks down at the breasts Gray has revealed.

He smiles at me, a sexy hint of fangs peeking between his generous lips. "I don't pout, *bella*. Please tell our partner this. I'm far too old and proper to ever pout."

The very thought makes me grin. I reach out and begin to unbutton his dress shirt. He and Gray were in gorgeous, matching tuxedoes. My men. "I don't know how proper you are, baby. You participated in a wholly illegal marriage ceremony."

"I was promised that ceremony was entirely legal in Fae society," he replies.

He kisses me while I undress him.

"And if you ever try to leave us, we'll take you right to a *sithein*," Gray promises.

Gray slides in behind me. I can feel the heat of his breath on the nape of my neck. It makes me shiver, but I'm certainly not cold. I'm trapped between their bodies, and it's where I love to be. It's my favorite place in the world.

Four hands on my body. It's certainly not the first time they've made love to me together, and it won't be the last. This is my future. This is my home.

Slowly, I find myself naked, but it's all right because I am with them.

Fangs scrape over my neck and I shiver.

"You like that, don't you?" Gray whispers in my ear. He's watching Marcus as he drags those fangs, barely breaking the skin before my vampire runs his tongue back over the line of blood before I heal.

I am breathless. I can do nothing but nod.

"He's not the only one who loves the taste of you. I'm going to spread your legs, Kelsey mine. I'm going to lick you and suck you and taste you. My favorite treat."

"I believe I'll like watching that, *bella*," Marcus promises. "But I want to touch, too."

His hands find my breasts, cupping them, and I lean back against Gray, offering myself to Marcus. He falls to his knees in front of me and before I can take my next breath, he's leaning forward to lick my left nipple. The sensation pours over my skin. I start to squirm as he sucks the nipple inside his mouth, but Gray is there. His strong arms form a cage around me, holding me still for his partner.

They're truly partners now. How slowly that happened. One day rivals and then slowly, so incrementally, friends and partners in my pleasure. It's hard for me to believe that Marcus walked away from her. He's waited for her all his long life, but he chose me.

He'll live long after me because of that choice. He'll never have the one woman he could love enough to follow into death.

I am holding him back from what he needs.

The world flashes and it's Gray at my breast now. Marcus is gone and we're alone, our wedding a quiet affair. No family. No friends. Just him and me. After everything that happened, there's no one left who would celebrate with us.

"I love you," Gray says, pressing me back against the bed. "I don't need anyone but you."

We're on the run. It's probably dangerous for us to be here, but we couldn't resist. No one knows of our wedding anyway. I was forced to make a choice between my job, my loyalty to the royal family, and my love.

I'll miss them all, but I will always choose him.

My legs hit the back of the bed and I let gravity do its work. I fall, the soft comforter covering my skin.

Gray spreads my legs. I am submissive to his desires. It's easy since his desires mirror my own. We play at this. Dominance and submission are games for our bedroom. I'm his partner in life and accept nothing less than to stand beside him. I have friends who choose to submit on other levels, but this is all I can give and it works for us. He's softened and I've relaxed. We've grown together.

"I found a place for us to hide for a while." His mouth hovers over my pussy.

I am a ball of anticipation. So much stress today and all I've longed for is his touch. "It better be good. I don't think the king is going to stop searching for us."

Us. The two of us on the run. There's something romantic about it. Until I remember what's waiting for him at the end of his contract. One day his father will come for him. Gray has promised to leave me behind. He will not allow me to follow him into Hell.

One day it will be me. Only me.

I shake off the thought. We have years ahead of us. Years to seek a way out. I should have done this the first time. I should have taken his hand and run.

Then I wouldn't miss Marcus the way I do now.

"I'll take care of you," he promises. His mouth covers me and I stop thinking about anything but the feel of his tongue on me.

I breathe in and there's music playing on the radio. When did I turn it on? Gray is still between my legs. So good. It feels so good. My hands fist in the sheets. How many times have we made love and it still feels like the first? I still gasp in wonder.

He spears me with his tongue, diving deep inside me while he works my clitoris with the pad of his thumb.

A hand on my head makes me open my eyes, and warm brown eyes stare down at me. "I love watching you come."

My wolf. I can't help but smile at him. He's so big, so flipping gorgeous. It's hard to believe once I considered him an enemy and then an annoyance.

He was our salvation. Mine and Gray's. We wouldn't be alive without Trent.

"That's good, babe," I say with a breathless laugh. "Because I really like to come."

He's let his hair grow out from that rigid military cut he'd first worn. I loved how it curled a bit now, how he smiled so much more. We live in the apartments I once shared with my trainer, but he's a fond memory. Marcus is happy in Italy with his wife. His final wife. I'm in love with my men. The king gave me away at our wedding.

We will fight when the time comes. We will fight in this terrible war that is coming. I pray I don't lose them. Please don't let me lose them.

Gray moves up, ceding his place to Trent, who moves his muscled body with the grace of the predator living inside him.

"My turn," Trent says, putting his mouth on me and beginning the process all over again.

"Do you know how good you taste?" Gray kisses me and I can taste my own desire.

The hands on me change.

God, I don't know how much more I can handle. It moves so quickly now. I never leave the room, but I can feel fate shifting, changing.

I am with Gray but we do not speak, the hostility between us a palpable thing.

I am with Marcus and he looks down at the ring he's recently placed on my finger, and I remember the way she cried as we left the ceremony.

Jacob's voice intrudes. Hold on. Not much more. He's almost there.

I flash through a hundred wedding nights, some changes so minute I wouldn't recognize that they were different if I wasn't in this place.

Gray tears down the door, attacking Marcus, and I am helpless as they fight. They will kill each other and I will be alone.

Shift.

Trent holds me while I cry, mourning my lost husband. *Shift.*

My whole body is flush with desire as I look down at my brand new husband. Trent smiles up at me, my Boston boy.

"I love you. Take me you crazy she-wolf. He's not going to wait forever." Trent's massive hands tug on my hips, and I can feel his big cock begin to enter. So good. I've waited so long for this night.

A perfect sense of happiness settles on me. There is nothing here but joy between the three of us. We need each other. There is no one else waiting, no other destiny. We're the right people at the right time.

I need them. My demon and my wolf. The war we averted could come back to haunt us, but I know we'll be stronger then.

We'll have children to protect. I'm already carrying him.

"Relax, Kelsey mine." Gray gently pushes me down.

I know what he's planning. My men love to get me in between them. I'm convinced they like the feel of their cocks sliding against one another, though they're far too manly to ever admit it. They claim we're a perfectly straight ménage, but I have hopes.

I'm having lunch with the queen tomorrow and I intend to ask her how to get my men to play.

My body is pressed against Trent's. Chest to chest. I look into his eyes, a hint of his wolf there, claiming his mate. Claiming me. His cock fills me, but I can't be completely full. Not without Gray.

I feel him. The broad head of his cock begins to press inside. So much pressure, but it doesn't matter. I know the pleasure it will bring. He is relentless.

The scene shifts and it is Marcus beneath me as Gray thrusts his way inside.

"That feels so good, *bella*. You're so tight this way."

I kiss him as Gray begins to thrust in earnest. Marcus presses up and my men go to town. I'm lost in between them. Lost in the pleasure they bring me. Lost in their overwhelming love.

Pleasure crashes over me and I scream out their names.

The scene shifts and I scream as they drag Gray from my arms. So many demons. I don't know how they fit into the room. I try to hold on to him, but they're too strong. They can't take him from me. Not now. Not when we've just started our lives together. I watch his eyes as he fulfills his contract and he's lost to me.

Another shift and I'm weeping in Trent's arms. I've lost them both.

"It's all right, Kelsey. I'll take care of you."

The scene shifts and it seems as though the whole world stops. The room is the same, but I feel a change. Time has shifted as surely as the fates do. I am older. There's a child bouncing on the bed. A boy with dark hair and my eyes. I yell at him to stop jumping on the bed. It's a nice hotel. I don't mention that's probably the bed he was conceived on.

His sister joins him. Little she-wolf and my demon child. They jump and laugh and I can't help but give in and join them. When their fathers walk in, they laugh at us, too.

A bright light flashes and I try to hold on. I don't want to leave this scene. This potential is everything I desire. God, I didn't even know I wanted it until this moment, until I can feel the love I have for them. My husbands. My children. In this scene, I am complete and happy and everyone I love is whole and alive.

But the scene slips away and I continue on.

* * * *

I woke on the hard floor, a chill shaking me to reality. My head pounded like someone was taking a hammer to it.

"Are you all right?"

I hated that voice. So very upper-crust and British, and so wrong coming from my brother's mouth. Placing my palms on the stone floor beneath me, I lifted my head and saw Jamie sitting there, leaning back against the wall of the prison we found ourselves in. "Get out of my brother."

My brother's normally brown eyes shone a nasty red. "When my brother is safe and not a moment before. Now be polite and tell me if you're all right."

I flipped him off. All right was definitely not a phrase I would use at that moment. My stomach wasn't resting easy, but I didn't think I was going to puke.

So many choices. I'd seen so many possibilities, and I had zero idea how to make any of them come true. I'd seen a piece of the tapestry but not the threads that came before or after it.

Even as I sat up, the images were fleeing my brain. I couldn't hold on to them. They were too fast, too many of them, so I chose one.

Those children jumping on the bed. Little monkeys. I loved them so much.

One memory of something that might or might not be. Not a memory at all really. Just a hope. I'd been happy there. I'd been complete.

"Whatever happened in that place, it's changed you," Matthew said quietly. "I can feel something from you I've never felt before. It's as if you finally found what you want."

For that second, I'd understood what it meant to be more than me. I was part of something, integral but not alone. That was my family.

"Why does it make you sad?"

Because no matter how hard I tried, now I couldn't see their small faces, couldn't remember who had walked into the room behind me. Had it been Gray? I could only remember that brief burst of joy.

I was sure Gray had been there. And Marcus. I think there was someone else, but he eludes me. A wolf, perhaps. Yes. A werewolf. Why can't I see his face? I loved him and now I can't see his face.

Now I knew why Gray had tried to get the vision back. I knew why he wanted to be in that room. That hotel room was somehow tied to us—to me. It was where I would start or end my life.

"Where's Gray?" My mouth felt dry.

"He's behind you. He hasn't woken yet. I wondered if he will, but I think so. Otherwise, why would our father have left? He's begun the night's chaos. I don't even know the full extent of what he's planning. Where did the prophet go?"

I glanced around our cell. It was nice to know Winter had put a dungeon in while he was redecorating. Gray was on the only bed in the cell. I moved toward him, needing to see that he was breathing and alive. Jacob was nowhere to be found.

"He said he wouldn't be here when I woke up. I think he had another appointment." I sat down on the cot, putting a hand on Gray. His body was still, but he was breathing. I smoothed back his hair, his forehead hot under my hand. "He's got a fever."

"I believe it's part of the transition."

"Why won't you leave Jamie's body?" I decided to ask the question I didn't want an answer to. "Are you going to kill Jamie if Gray doesn't survive?"

The idea that I could lose them both ate at me.

"No. I simply don't have another body to jump into. Do you understand that they would have killed both you and Gray had I not forced him into this? My brother is too stubborn to live. I did this for him, but no, I'm not going to be petty and kill this human. I don't need to. The way he's going, he'll almost certainly kill himself soon."

"What is that supposed to mean? And why didn't you take that idiot Dellacourt? You know there's a guy I wouldn't mind killing."

Jamie's lips curled up. "Dellacourt is a smart chap. He has a specific symbol tattooed on his body that keeps demons like me out. As for this vessel, he smiles but he's full of self-hatred. He hates himself for everything. He hates that he didn't protect you and Nathan. Hates that his father is still breathing. Hates that he's weak and has to watch while you go off and save the world. He definitely hates what happened that night." Matthew winced. "Fine. Apparently I'm not supposed to talk about that. You're not ever supposed to know. He thinks he's weak but he's quite strong when he wants to be. That hurt."

Yeah, Jamie and I would be having a talk. I wanted to know what kind of chances he was taking and what night Matthew was talking about. He would also be getting one of those tattoos. "What do you know about what your father is planning for tonight?"

"Not much. I know he and Winter think taking out the king will lead to civil war among the vampires. If the king's Council disintegrates, there will be a huge power vacuum. The supernatural world will be in chaos, and there's always money and power to be had in the midst of chaos."

"Why not simply wait until the contracts run out in a few years?" I asked as Gray was starting to stir. He moved closer until his body curled around mine. "Once the king allows the contracts to run out, y'all can war against the vamps all you like."

That was a thing I didn't like to think about. War. It would devastate both sides. I knew Donovan was basically leading us into war because a demon had killed my father, but I was worried the cost would be too great. What did vengeance serve if we were all dead?

"It's not that simple. If Father were to wait, he wouldn't be the first in line. It's why he's working with Abbas Hiberna. If they wait, they have to honor the hierarchical system, and we don't fare as well as we do if we lead the charge. Secondly, this is the vampires' natural plane. They're stronger here than we are, and I don't suspect they'll all come down to the Hell plane for a battle. It's best if they use other supernatural creatures to take out the strongest vampires before the war ever starts. We fracture them. We weaken them. None of this violates our contracts since we're not the ones doing the actual damage. We're poor demons trying to make our way in the world. It's not against our contracts to manufacture drugs that don't even have an effect on vampires."

Demons really knew how to make a contract work for them. "I don't suppose you would care to tell me what's happening tonight?"

"I actually would. You see, I have a loved one who could get harmed in this battle. My beloved mate. He's out there and he's unprotected. Yes, I would tell you and I would help you stop it. I don't want a war. He won't sit it out and he'll get killed. I can't let that happen. Not when I've worked so hard to get us back together. Which is precisely why they told me nothing. They know I'll betray them."

So we had nothing and I was stuck in this cell with my possessed brother, a deeply tired prophet, and no weapons of any kind.

"Kelsey?" Gray tried to lift his head.

I urged him back down. "Rest, babe. I'm tired and I only saw one piece of the tapestry. I can't imagine what you saw."

"I still see it. It's running through my head. You have to get out of here. You have to get to Ether."

"What's happening?"

He shook his head. "I can't…it's too much. It's all here and I can't pick what I want to see."

"Don't." I remembered what Jacob had said. There was too much information, and fighting it would only make things worse. Until Gray got control, he wouldn't be very helpful. "Let it go. Can you try to focus on the here and now?"

His eyes had gone completely white. He reached for my hand.

"Keep talking to me."

"Okay." I was willing to try anything. I needed Gray if we were going to get out of here. "We need to figure out how to bust out of this cell and get to Ether. I think your hot demon ass is going to have to make another appearance tonight."

"You liked his demonic form?" Matthew chuckled. "Well, I knew you were the right woman for him."

"She's a little perverted, but she's not ready for me." Gray took a long, shuddering breath. "I saw bits and pieces of us. We can make so many mistakes, Kelsey. We can cause each other so much pain. It's best you go with Marcus for now. We're not ready."

We weren't. We might never be. I leaned over and kissed him, a soft brushing of lips that had nothing to do with sex and everything to do with the fact that I still loved this man. I couldn't stop loving him. At every turn he made the right decision based on what was best for me.

"We'll be okay, Gray. Someday, we'll be okay." I had to believe it because I wanted those children. I wanted them with all my being. I'd never wanted to be a mom before. God, I would have told anyone who asked that it wasn't for me. I didn't want some nameless, faceless thing taking over my life. I still didn't.

I wanted them. My boy and my girl. I would fight for the right to bring them into the world.

"One day." This time, he breathed deeply but with steady intent. His eyes were slowly going back to normal.

"We can't use his strength to get us out of here," Matthew said, getting to Jamie's feet. He put his hands on the bars. "They're reinforced, made specifically to stop demons. And there are plenty of wards to keep someone from using magic to locate us or get us out. I'll find another vessel and try to find a way."

So having a non-corporeal demon could be a plus. "You could go to the king. You could find him or Marcus and they'll come and get us out."

Matthew grimaced. "Not really possible."

"Why?" The king didn't like demons, but Marcus dealt with them when he had to. This was kind of a worst-case scenario thing.

"Or I could use this key and let you out," a new voice offered. Dante Dellacourt stood at the cell door, key dangling from his hand. "But I'm going to need a few promises from you first."

"I promise to kill you quickly." I could be magnanimous. It really was a good deal since my original plan had been to slowly eviscerate him and force him to watch as I fed his entrails to a cat.

"You see, that's what I was afraid of." Dellacourt stayed outside of my reach. "Do you think I want all this chaos crap? Do you know what it's going to do to my stock?"

I couldn't help but roll my eyes. "I don't give a crap about your stock. You knew what you were getting into."

He grimaced. "Sort of. Look, all the demons I'd met before had next to no interest in this plane. They wanted to be left alone to do their thing. I built this company. You all think I signed a contract, but I haven't. I've managed to make myself valuable enough that I haven't been forced to sell my soul, and I'm not going to."

"You won't have to. You'll be dead as soon as Winter and my father figure out what's happening," Matthew pointed out.

"Not if we kill them all." Gray groaned as he rolled off the cot. "I think I have this under control for the time being. I have to concentrate, but I can stay in the now. I wish Jacob had hung around though."

"He said he would come back for you. I would bet anything he's wherever this thing is going down." Apparently we were in the middle of something important, and watching was what Jacob liked to do.

"We can't kill Father," Matthew argued. "I agree that we need to slaughter Abbas Hiberna, but without Father, both Gray and I are vulnerable. Especially now."

Without his father, Gray didn't have to go to Hell, so I was kind of all for killing Papa Sloane. "I think we'll worry about that later. I'm going to take out anyone who tries to disrupt the balance on this plane."

"You don't understand. All Father was trying to do was create his prophet. He wanted to give his son power and Abbas Hiberna was the only one who could help him. He's already left this plane. You won't be able to find him again. Abbas Hiberna, on the other hand, will be wherever the chaos is," Matthew insisted.

"You give our dear old dad way too much credit," Gray said, touching his forehead as though it pained him. "This was never about giving me power. It was about taking it for himself. He doesn't care about us. He never has."

"You are so cynical," Matthew replied with a little snarl. "Family is all we have and you'll see it one of these days. I'm going to do what I should have done hours ago. I'm going to protect the love of my life. Whether he likes it or not."

His eyes went blank and he fell.

I shot over to try to catch him, but Gray got there before I did. Jamie opened his eyes and shuddered as Gray moved him to the cot.

"Dude, your brother's an asshole," Jamie said with a frown. "And I'm so getting inked."

"Are you all right?" I knelt beside my brother, looking into his eyes because I wasn't completely certain Matthew wouldn't try to trick us.

"I'm never watching *The Exorcist* again. That was horrible. I could feel his...he was evil, Kelsey. So evil and he doesn't even know it. I think he thinks he's normal." Jamie looked over at Gray. "You are not your brother. You are nothing like him."

Gray sent him a sad smile. "Many would disagree with you. A demon's a demon."

The things Jacob had said to me made perfect sense. "Even a demon has choices. We choose who we become." I looked back at Dellacourt. "I promise no retribution if you let us out of this cage and tell us what Winter is planning."

"And you'll kill him? You'll kill Julius Winter?" The key dangled from his hand.

"You better believe it, buddy." That was one choice I had no problem making.

Chapter Twenty-One

"So he's found a way to get the drug into Ether?" I tried to wrap my head around everything Dellacourt was telling me as he drove his outrageously outfitted Audi through the snowy streets toward downtown.

Outside the snow kept falling, but we'd made it out of Winter's compound with no struggle. No giant snowmen had been waiting this time, likely because Winter was concentrating his efforts elsewhere.

"Well, this is really the part where you should remember that you promised not to do that whole playing with my entrails thing," Dellacourt reminded me.

"I didn't promise anything." Jamie was kind of itching to hurt someone.

"James," I warned before turning back to Dellacourt. He was driving with Jamie in the seat beside him while Gray and I sat in the back, our hands tangled together. Maybe it was wrong, but after what we'd been through, I needed to have his flesh against mine in some way. I needed to have him close. "Your entrails are safe, Dellacourt. Tell me what's happening."

"My labs might have tweaked the drug and now it sends shifters and werewolves into fits of rage. Some alphas might be able to control themselves, but no one else will be able to. The drug is in a shipment of beer scheduled to be on sale tonight. It's Ether's on tap brew of the night. Winter has a man on the inside who's making sure everyone gets a taste."

"It's going to be a bloodbath. Thank god they can't get into the residential parts of the building." Gray's hand squeezed mine.

"I might have found a way to override the security systems. Not the individual ones, but they can make it to the residential portion," Dellacourt admitted.

And cell phone service was out due to the storm. Winter had covered the place with a blizzard and knocked out cell service for the building. I'd been trying and trying and couldn't get hold of anyone.

Panic threatened to overwhelm me, and I didn't hold it back. Marcus needed to know there was a reason to panic if he didn't already.

"The doors won't keep out werewolves if they want to get in," Jamie pointed out. "But how many are we talking about? The king truly is a death machine. He can handle a lot of werewolves. Not everyone drinks beer."

Dellacourt got off the freeway and made the turn to get on to Pearl. "The drug will take roughly an hour to truly set in. By my count, we should be getting there just as things get interesting. And it's a lot of wolves. And shifters. If the king slays them all, he's going to have to deal with the ramifications of killing so many of his allies."

"Beyond that he'll have to deal with rumors and conjecture from an already unstable alliance," Gray added. "No one understands what's going on, and they won't believe the truth from the king's *Nex Apparatus*. There will be many conspiracy theories, including the one where the vampires are trying to thin the were populations."

"That's ridiculous." Donovan had no reason to do that. He needed them on his side.

"It doesn't matter," Jamie agreed. "The rumors will be out there."

"We have another problem." Dellacourt made the turn that would take us to Ether. The winds were whipping up, getting stronger the closer we got. "I've done a lot of research on Winter, and there's something you all should know. He can't be killed by anyone but demonkind."

Gray's eyes closed. "That's a rumor. Fucker probably started it himself."

"What do you mean? I can't kill him? I have no shot at this?" I didn't like going into something all pessimistic, but it was better to know.

"There are four elemental demons," Gray explained. "They have the powers of the seasons. Fall can touch you and cause you to age. Winter can obviously freeze. Summer can start fires with his gaze. You don't want to know what spring can do. The rumor is they can only be killed by flesh of their flesh. Demonkind. Kelsey, you were right. My demon will be making another appearance."

He was far too weak. "No. We have to hope that's a rumor. If I have to I'll find another way. Gray, you don't know when your new powers will take over and how they'll affect you. I think you should sit this one out. Apparently your brother will be in there somewhere. Maybe I can get him to try to kill Winter. I don't suppose you can tell me who his lost love is?"

"I've never met him," Gray admitted. "When they were together, they lived on the Hell plane. For obvious reasons, I don't go there. He called his lover his sweet puppy. I know he's a werewolf."

I had a couple of people I could ask—if they weren't currently fighting for their lives.

Up ahead, I could see the building that housed Ether. It housed all of us really. So many of us lived in that building, but I was happy for Quinn's complete psycho paranoia about keeping business and pleasure apart. It wasn't easy to get from Ether into the residences. Even if a few got in, it would take time to get through those reinforced doors.

I breathed a sigh of relief as Dellacourt stopped inside the parking garage.

"This is where I leave you. I'm going underground for a while."

He was going to try to wait it out and see who wanted to kill him at the end of our venture. I couldn't blame the idiot for that.

Gray, Jamie, and I hightailed it for the elevator. I had the code memorized, and we all stood waiting as the elevator started the trek down. We were all wondering the same thing. What would we be walking into? My heart was pounding in my chest at the idea of those elevator doors opening and facing a bloodbath. How many of our people had already died?

And where would Abbas Hiberna be? How the hell was I going to take down a demon who could only be killed by another demon?

"Jamie, I think you should take Kelsey and run," Gray said quietly.

Jamie's head turned and one brow arched over his eye. "I don't think she wants to run. Have you tried making her do something she doesn't want to do?"

Gray was being Gray, and arguing wasn't going to help anything. The doors opened and we were assaulted by the sounds of...

Industrial music? I stepped off the elevator. The entrance to Ether was packed, as it was every night. The red carpet and red velvet rope that marked the line to get into the nightclub were the only red I could see. Thumping music could be heard coming from the club, and the line was almost back to the elevators.

"Could Dellacourt have been wrong?" I asked.

"Maybe," Gray allowed as we skipped the line and started for the bouncers. "But my brother wouldn't lie. Not about this."

"I actually agree. I had the fucker in my head for hours. He was worried about the wolf. He's really in love. Well, it's a perverted, crazy-creepy-stalker kind of love, but it's what he considers love. I got a vision of the guy. It was hard to see because mostly I was screaming because being trapped in your own body sucks, but he looked familiar. I think he's a wolf who works with the king."

My mind immediately went to Trent and I laughed it off because that big wolf wouldn't ever look at another man. He liked pussy too much... A vision of Trent Wilcox naked flooded my head, assaulting my senses. He had the sweetest smile on his face as he leaned over to cover my lips with his.

Oh, god. I'd seen a potential future where he was my lover. That had to be one of those offshoot weird worlds that wouldn't ever, ever really happen.

I couldn't remember much, but I remembered he'd been amazingly good in bed. The man liked to use his tongue. And his cock. Oh, I needed to stop thinking about it.

"Kels? You okay?" Jamie asked because I'd stopped in the middle of the lobby.

"Kelsey?" Gray was staring at me like he could see what I was thinking.

I didn't need anyone to ever know I'd seen that. Ever. For the rest of all time. It was embarrassing. And had me a little bit hot. Which was also embarrassing. I broke into a jog. "I'm good. Let's find Marcus and the king and talk this out."

Up ahead, who should I see but the object of my complete and utter denial. Trent stood at the front of the line talking to three of the bouncers from the club. He was altogether too masculine in his T-shirt and jeans and close-cropped hair. He was all muscly and wolfy, and it absolutely, one hundred percent didn't do anything for me. When he turned and saw me and his face lit up with a kind of crazy, sexy smile, I did not care. My heart rate stayed the exact same, and any deviations were from the run.

Totally.

"Kelsey, hey. You're back. We didn't expect you back for another couple of hours. Not that I was…" He stopped. "I was actually. I was kind of counting the time. I was worried about you. I'm glad to see you're all whole and shit."

This was the time I would give the big were a mouthy comeback. I would show him my sarcastic side. Instead, I kind of stared because flashes of what I'd seen were coming back to me, and I couldn't help but think about how good he looked naked.

What the fuck?

"I believe what she's trying to say is where is the king?" Gray's tone was rough and he was looking at me with terrifically judgey eyes.

What had he seen before I took that moment away from him?

"Or maybe Marcus?" Gray continued. "She probably wants to see her boyfriend."

Yeah, he'd seen something, too.

Trent's eyes went from Gray back to me as though he felt the weird tension between us and wasn't sure what was going on, but then he hadn't been treated to the "all possibilities in the world" sex show this evening. "They're up in the penthouse."

"Have you seen Winter?" Thank god Jamie was focused on the mission and not his potential sex life. "We need to know exactly where he is."

Trent shook his head. "No idea, man. I thought he was with you guys. You had a meeting tonight. Kelsey, maybe you need to fill me in."

"Yeah, I bet you'd like that," Gray said under his breath.

Trent ignored him. "Let's go and grab a beer and talk."

Beer bad. Beer was the vehicle for Winter's coup d'état. "No. Absolutely not. We have to shut down the bar right fucking now. As a matter of fact, shut down the whole club. Everyone needs to go home. Now."

If I could get them out of the building, we might have a chance.

I expected a fight. I expected Trent to look at me like I was fuck-all insane and start to laugh. Instead, he picked up a walkie-talkie. "Security, I need a full shutdown and evacuation procedures. Right now. I'll inform Dev."

"Just like that?" I hadn't had to talk him into it. No explanations at all and he was shutting down the club.

Trent gave me a half smile. "Just like that. You're the *Nex Apparatus*, Kelsey. Now that you've passed all the tests, you tell me to shut down the club and I shut it down. I take my orders from you and the royal family."

No one had explained that to me. I could give orders? Maybe this gig wasn't as bad as I thought it was. "Winter is somewhere in the building and he's got a mega shit ton of rabid weres and shifters ready to take out anyone in their way."

"Are they targeting the king?" Trent asked. His shoulders had straightened back, his whole body going into a military stance.

"I suspect the whole royal family." I couldn't forget that Winter had said he would take out Evangeline. He would kill them all if it brought him closer to his goal.

Trent got back on the phone, calling up to the penthouse and getting it locked down.

The bouncers were already hard at work, trying to get the line of people waiting to get into Ether moved back.

"Come on," Trent said as he started for the club entrance. "We have to find Dev and get him to safety. Everyone else is in the penthouse. They should be relatively safe, but Dev is in the open."

I jogged to keep up with him. We did have a couple of issues to deal with. "Please tell me you haven't had a beer tonight."

"Sure," he replied as we came to the doors. "Dev brought in a new craft beer. Naturally it required tasting. You know that's what we wolves are for."

He grinned at me as he opened the door and I heard a long scream.

"Kelsey, get back here," Gray said.

Trent stepped inside and then his hand was reaching for his gun. I ignored Gray because I couldn't spend the evening cowering behind him. I'd let him take care of all those creepy snow creatures, but this was one hundred percent my job.

"What the hell is going on, Owens?" Trent surveyed the dance floor with a critical eye. "I gave specific instructions for the club to be shut down. Why aren't they moving? They should have turned on the lights."

"Who did you give the instructions to? One of your drinking buddies?" Fear flashed through me on several levels. Trent was a powerful alpha wolf. If he went crazy, he would take out a bunch of us with him.

He'd taken the drug. The last couple of people who'd taken the drug had died, their brains destroyed. Despite our issues, I really didn't want that to happen to Trent.

Out on the dance floor, people were still moving around, though I could see a portion starting to move back. A man was on his knees in the middle of the dance floor. I watched as he changed, becoming a sleek mountain lion. The cat roared and immediately attacked a woman to his right.

"Shit." Trent took aim and fired.

The cat's head exploded and that got people moving.

"What the hell is going on?" Trent didn't look my way. He kept his gun up, looking for more threats.

"Winter put the drug in the beer. You've all been exposed to it," I explained.

"You need to get every wolf and shifter who drank that beer somewhere safe. When Winter begins to use his influence, none of you will be able to resist." Gray held his hand out. "I'm going to need a weapon. This is going to get nasty and fast. I'm the only one who can take out Winter."

"I feel fine," Trent insisted, but handed Gray his backup. "And my men are fine. Look, they're taking care of the problem on the dance floor."

Sure enough, three of the bouncers were moving in, helping the woman who'd almost been bitten get to her feet. She was nodding, looking infinitely grateful to the man who'd helped her up.

That was when he shot her in the head.

"What the fuck?" Trent shouted.

Jamie put a hand on the big wolf's arm. "It's going to get worse."

Trent didn't hesitate. He lifted his gun and shot the wolf between the eyes. He was a hell of a shot.

"I don't feel anything." Trent had to shout because the whole club had erupted into chaos. He kept his weapon up, his eyes scanning for more trouble.

I moved in close so he could hear me. "How much did you drink?"

"Half a beer, maybe. I got called away," he explained. "Fuck, I just killed a man who's been my friend for ten years."

"Unless you get them somewhere they can't hurt anyone, you're going to have to kill a whole lot more," I said.

"I think we're past that now." Jamie watched the dance floor.

Trent looked down at me, his eyes beginning to turn. "Kelsey, you should run."

Gray's hand was on my arm, hauling me back when Trent howled. The sound shook the damn roof, but before he could change, something slammed into him from behind. He fell to his knees, gun clanging to the floor right before his head hit.

Dev Quinn came out of the smoke, one rifle in his hands and several more slung over his shoulder. "Tranquilizer dart. Extra extra druggy. Even Trent will sleep for at least an hour."

We all stared at the faery.

He shrugged and started passing out the rifles. "My contingency plans have plans. Did I ever dream a day would come that our allies could be turned against us? Every damn night and twice during the day. James, how good a shot are you?"

"Excellent," my brother replied.

"Good, then come with me. There's a perfect sniper position up in the lighting unit. I've already called Daniel. He'll be here as soon as he can," Dev explained. He was perfectly calm even as the club collapsed into chaos. "So I figured out that Winter must have drugged my beer shipment when two of my best bodyguards attempted to behead me. They're sleeping it off in a cell. Do we have a way to bring them back?"

"My blood amplified by the king's." Gray's voice sounded even deeper than normal and I heard Quinn gasp.

When I turned, Gray's eyes had gone white. He stared ahead, though it seemed like he was seeing something.

"What the hell?" Jamie asked.

Gray's eyes returned to normal. "Sorry. That happened quickly and honestly, it was more about common sense than prophecy. But I do know it's the right way to go. I feel it deep inside. The most efficient path is the same we took healing Kelsey's arm. The drugs are booby-trapped in a way. Any use of normal vampire blood will amplify the damage. Demon blood accelerated with the king's own is the only way to heal the wolves."

"I've only seen those eyes once before," Quinn said, his voice unsteady. "On a prophet."

"Yeah, Gray picked up some cool new powers at the mansion tonight," I explained. "But we're not going to be able to use that information if we stand here talking. I need to find Winter. He's got to be here somewhere."

I had to move. There was a massive crowd coming our way, likely trying to get away from the now crazed wolves and shifters.

Quinn and Jamie started shooting anything that looked vaguely psychotic. I took one of Quinn's tranq guns and so did Gray. Luckily it wasn't a full moon or the wolves would be at peak strength.

The crowd shifted and started running the other way, back away from the exit.

That was when the outliers showed up. Our wolves were simply crazed, but the group from Brimstone had been introduced to the drug slowly.

They strode in like they owned the place, a massive alpha at the head. I'd seen him before. I was fairly certain he was a werelion. He was also a drug addict. He stopped and took a long breath.

"Take them all boys. Winter's promised us all the Brimstone we can handle and a million dollars to whoever brings him the king's head."

The werelion stared down at his chest where a very large dart was now stuck.

Sometimes I love my job. The leader went down but the rest of them scattered.

"Dev, you and Jamie pick off as many as you can," I ordered. "Gray and I are going to find Winter and put a stop to this. Where did you say the king is?"

"He was upstairs with our family. He'll be down here once he's sure they're safe." Dev stood next to Jamie, ready to do his job.

I would never call the man paranoid again. He was prepared and it was a beautiful thing. "Tell him to stay upstairs. They're looking for him. There are too many of them. He would have to kill them and he won't like that option."

"I'll do it." Quinn and Jamie headed for their spots.

"Where would Winter be?" Ahead of me, the dance floor was empty. As far as I could tell, everyone was hiding or trying to. I was fairly certain I'd seen a bunch of non-shifters hightailing it for the bathrooms. Hopefully they could hole up there or in the kitchen. I didn't want to have to worry about civilians.

The vampires were fighting. I saw my assistant holding off a brown werewolf. The wolf snapped at him, drawing blood, but he wouldn't fight back. He merely tried to keep the wolf off of him.

One neat shot and the wolf went down.

Justin immediately dropped to his knees, pulling the wolf into his arms.

His girlfriend. He was weeping over her, trying to get her to respond.

"She'll be out for about an hour," I explained.

"She's not dead?" Tears streaked down the kid's face. He loved the wolf.

I had to give him something to do. "Not dead. It was a tranquilizer. I need you to take her and lock her up somewhere. I don't know if they'll still be in the same state when they wake up. We have to be prepared. When you've found a place to stash the sleeping wolves, go back to the bar and grab Trent for me, please. I had to leave him there."

Someone grabbed me from behind, jerking me off my feet. I lost the rifle as Gray and I were separated. I heard Gray call out my name, but I was suddenly in a crowd of outliers.

"Hey, look what we have here," one of the women said. "Looks like a human decided to sneak in."

A big shifter walked right up to me and sniffed my hair. "She smells good. Almost good enough to eat."

Someone needed to learn some manners. I brought my elbow back and up, crunching his nose while I kicked out and shoved the female down.

"Kelsey Jean, heads-up," Gray shouted.

I put a hand up and the rifle was perfectly placed for me to catch and start firing. Gray and I were a good team when we weren't fighting.

"Shit." I saw Scott up ahead. He was standing at the bathroom doors, his hands claws against the metal.

Not only did it make a horrible annoying sound, it proved how far gone he was. He didn't seem to be making progress at getting the door open, and I had so few darts left. I could see that Jamie and Quinn had made a dent in the army Winter had sent, but there were still so many of them.

A calm wave washed over me, and I turned toward the office door in time to see Marcus and the king at the top of the steps.

I expected the king to jump straight into the fray. I was actually kind of looking forward to it. Donovan, it seemed, had gotten lazy in his old age. He let me take on all the fights now that he was a father of three, but I'd heard stories about what the man could do when he decided to take someone out. If Donovan wanted to, he could probably take on all these guys. The only trouble was he would have to kill them, and that wouldn't look good on his royal resume.

Instead of leaping into the fight, Donovan searched the floor. I wasn't sure who he was looking for until Marcus pointed my direction.

"I think they want us over there." I gestured to the office so Gray could get a lay of the land. He hadn't been in Ether more than a few times. Most of the times he'd been in the club, he'd been raiding it or getting himself tossed out on his ass.

"Why isn't Donovan fighting?" Gray asked as he took my six.

We had to fight our way through the crowd. The weres and shifters now seemed to be fighting amongst themselves. They hadn't caught Donovan's scent yet or they would have been all over him. I was going to shove the king right back in Quinn's neat as a pin and probably hyper-secure office.

I looked up at Marcus, happy to see his face. "Things didn't go the way we'd hoped."

Marcus nodded. "They never do, *bella*."

"We need Donovan to get up to his condo. They're after him," Gray shouted.

"I can't," Donovan shouted back. "I can't do a damn thing until I find my son."

A chill went up my back as the place suddenly went quiet. I was staring at Donovan, the words not quite processing in my mind.

Donovan went pale, and I didn't want to turn around. Gray closed his eyes and when he opened them again, there was a horrible resignation there. As though he'd seen the available futures and he hadn't liked the outcome.

"Lee," Donovan said, his face tight with emotion.

I turned and Lee Donovan-Quinn had slipped his bed again. Unfortunately, this time he was in the hands of a demon. Julius Winter stood in the middle of the dance floor, one hand around Lee's neck.

Chapter Twenty-Two

The door behind us opened and I heard the queen cry out.

"Zoey, get back upstairs," Donovan growled, his hands tightening on the railing.

"He has my son." The queen's face was streaked with tears, but there was more than fear. She was pissed.

I was, too.

"Don't you think it's time we talked, Your Highness? You seemed to have effectively taken my shifters away, but I promise you more will come. These will wake up and there won't be anything you can do to stop them." Winter stared up at us.

We were standing on the landing right outside the safety of Quinn's office. If I thought a tranq dart would take the fucker out, I would have had a spectacular shot. As it was, I could jump on the asshole. I wasn't sure what I would do then, but I could provide a hell of a diversion.

"Don't, Kelsey," Donovan said, a plea in his voice. I'd never heard the man sound so desperate. "If Winter turns on his power, Lee dies."

"That's right, Your Highness. Your boy here is very curious. I found him sneaking about in the kitchen. Apparently he was looking for something sweet. I can give him something cold," Winter promised.

"We have contracts," Marcus insisted. He shook his head as he glared down on the demon. "They state plainly that demonkind cannot interfere with Vampire or anyone belonging to Vampire."

Winter hissed and used his free hand to pull a dart out of his arm. "Tell your snipers the next one to fire on me can bury this little fucker."

"Dev, come down," Donovan commanded. "No one fires another shot."

"And those contracts are only for vampires and their companions," Winter said with an elegant shrug. "This one is human. I would never attempt to harm a hair on the head of the queen, but this is a human child. He cannot belong to Vampire."

"He's my son," Donovan protested. "Let him go and maybe, just maybe I'll be kind when I kill you."

"Such anger, Your Highness. One would think a man in your position would know not to get too attached to anyone. Humans are so very fragile." Winter's fingers seemed to snake around Lee's neck as if to prove his point. The demon could snap it or hold it until Lee couldn't take a breath, or he could simply freeze him where he stood and all of Lee's potential futures would be lost to us.

"Be calm, *bella*." Marcus's hand slid over mine, his mouth tightening. "There is nothing you can do."

"I have to do something." I couldn't leave Lee standing out there. He was wearing pajamas with some Disney character all over them. I couldn't watch him turn to ice. I'd had that happen to me. It wasn't happening to a kid.

Not a kid. I was distancing. It's what I did. Lee. Sweet Lee. He was my friend and I felt a connection to him, and I wasn't letting him die so some old as fuck demon could prove a point of law.

"Kelsey, if you go down there, you will die and so will the boy. Allow the king to handle this," Marcus counseled. "You had a chance to gather information. It didn't work out. Now it is for the king to deal with."

"What do you want, Winter?" Donovan asked.

Lee's eyes grew wide. "Papa?"

He'd seen Quinn making his way toward the stairs. The faery had his hands up and his eyes were on his son. "Stay calm, Lee. We're going to get you out of this. You're going to be all right. Do you understand?"

There were tears on Lee's cheeks as he nodded. His mouth firmed and his shoulders straightened as though he was determined to be brave.

I was determined to kick a little ass. My she-wolf was twitching inside.

"Kelsey, calm down. You can't kill Abbas Hiberna. He can only be killed by demonkind. If we had time, I could find a way around it, but we don't and I won't send you down there when there's nothing you can do." Marcus had a hand on my arm.

Quinn made his way up the stairs. "Daniel, don't do anything crazy."

Donovan put a hand on his partner's head, drawing him close. "I'll save our son, Devinshea, and you know what to do after that." He turned my way, his face so grim, so devoid of hope. "Kelsey, I have no right to ask this of you, but will you see my family safely to Faery?"

"Sure, but I don't think this is a time for a vacay, boss."

"He isn't talking about a vacation, *bella*," Marcus said. "His family will be in danger after this. There will be a power vacuum in the Council. There will likely be civil war."

"What are you talking about?" I looked to the king. "He can't touch you."

"Ah, the king is an intelligent man," Winter proclaimed. "I cannot touch him myself. That would break our contracts, but we demons go very much by the letter and not the intent of the law."

They do that because their intent is pretty much always evil. "And what is that going to get you, Winter?"

"It means he can't harm me unless I ask him to. Unless I sign a contract. Lee's life for mine," Donovan explained with grim determination. "Do we have to go through the motions? Or is a verbal contract all right?"

Winter's satisfaction was a palpable thing. He smiled his chilly smile and the world seemed infinitely colder. "I agree to this contract. In exchange for the human I have caught, I will accept the sacrifice of the king's head."

"Danny, no!" the queen shouted.

Quinn moved in and pulled the queen away. She fought him and I watched as the king gave her one long look.

"I love you, Z. You tell the kids how much I love them. Devinshea..." He stopped, staring at his partners, and I could feel his love.

Damn but I wanted someone to look at me like that. Those three were connected, committed, passionate.

They were also drama queens. I turned my attention to Gray. He kind of had an in now. As Donovan began his long, stirring march down the stairs, I leaned over to Gray. "How does this end?"

His brows nearly knitted together. "I don't know."

"You're all prophety," I complained. After what we'd been through, I wanted some answers. His brain could tap into the big life computer and run those numbers for us. "Give me a clue at least."

"Dev, stop him," the queen begged.

Quinn had lost his arrogant look. He held the queen in his arms. "I can't. We have to save Lee."

"I'll save Lee," I promised. I seemed to have gotten Quinn's arrogance.

The queen's eyes lit with hope. "You have a plan?"

"Not really. But I'm pretty good at winging it."

Marcus turned his dark eyes my way. "I told you there is nothing to be done. I won't have you sacrifice your life and the boy's. Zoey, Abbas Hiberna has us in a Catch-22. As long as he has hands on your son, he can kill him. Unless Mr. Sloane has strength we don't know about, we are at a loss because none but demonkind can kill an elemental. Do you truly wish for my charge to waste her life when there is no hope?"

The queen choked back a sob and wrapped her arms around her husband.

I wasn't as ready to give up as Marcus was.

I'm here to tell you that I have seen some bad shit. Seriously bad shit. I've seen things that would make your toes curl, your stomach churn, your brain want to fry. And there is one and only one truth to every situation.

As long as you are alive, there is hope. Full stop. No arguments or questions. Sometimes hope is all we have but until the deed is done, it's a gift given to each one of us.

"He must have taken down our wards," Dev said, cradling his wife. "I had wards against violence placed here long ago."

"Abbas Hiberna would leave nothing to chance," Marcus stated grimly. "I would assume several of your security team were likely turned weeks ago. They infiltrated the club, and our own people are the ones we must fear."

Donovan made it to the dance floor. It seemed wrong. It was a cheery thing with lights going off in crazy patterns. It was a place to party, but now it was the agreed on stage of an execution.

Winter and Donovan were saying something to one another. I couldn't hear them. I turned back to Gray, who really needed to get his prophet on. I was a bit surprised to see Jacob standing beside him, watching the proceedings.

Hey, two prophets are better than one.

Marcus was consoling Quinn and the queen, but I wasn't giving up yet. There was that crazy hope thing.

I turned to the prophet with the most experience. "Jacob, I need to know what to do."

He sighed, a smile on his face. "Be yourself, Kelsey."

I was ready to smack him. "Dude, it's not a date. The King of all Vampire is about to lose his head and I'm the only one left conscious. We had to freaking tranquilize everyone else, so look through all those cool potential outcomes and get me a good one."

"I'm not a slot machine, Kelsey," Jacob complained.

"I can't focus." Gray's fists were at his side, a sure sign of his frustration. "I'm trying, baby, but it's too much."

"You have to be calm." Jacob stepped up to the railing. "Trust that things will play out as they should. You can't have any control of the lines of fate if you're too emotional. Take a deep breath and you'll see what I've seen."

Marcus took my hand. "Kelsey, I believe we need to prepare for the worst. Once the king is gone, you'll have to get Lee and we'll run. The nearest entrance to a *sithein* is outside of Austin."

"We're not going to a *sithein*." I was sick of Debbie Downer. I loved Marcus. I really did, but all that negativity was getting to me.

"Prophet, it is so good of you to make an appearance," Winter proclaimed.

When I looked down, there was a crowd of demons. They'd come from Hell to witness the death of the king. They were in all various forms. Some were red skinned, with scales showing and horns aplenty. Some were in their human forms, including one well-known politician, and didn't that explain a whole lot. I counted two satans, with their cherubic cheeks and ever-present notebooks. Satans are the law clerks of the demonic world. They would ensure the king's death was completely legal by the standards of all contracts.

Jacob nodded. "You know I bear witness to history's interesting events."

Donovan was looking at his son. He said nothing to the demons, simply spoke quietly to the boy in Winter's hold. I had to wonder how he felt. He was the single most powerful man in the world and because of Winter's hands, he was utterly helpless. Had Winter laid those hands on the king himself, Donovan would have frozen and then broken free and come out twice as pissed as he'd been before.

Lee was human. Lee would simply die.

It occurred to me that family was a true weakness. Unfortunately, it was also the only thing that made life worthwhile. These people we love, they can destroy us. But without them there is no person to destroy. I am the sum of the people who love me, who I love. The alpha and omega of my soul rests with who and how I've loved. Yes, it is weakness, but there is no strength that isn't balanced by weakness.

I loved Gray and Marcus. I'd seen myself love someone else. I'd seen myself lose. I'd seen myself laid out and aching on the floor because I'd lost the men I loved.

So I would fight harder to keep them. I was done being a coward.

If Donovan was willing to risk his life for his kid, I was willing to put mine on the line to save him.

"Your Highness, I myself obviously can't wield the sword, so I brought in an ally." Winter nodded toward the crowd, and a man I'd never seen before stepped forward.

"I'll want my reward."

I might not have seen the body he was occupying, but I knew the voice. Matthew.

"Brother, don't!" Gray called out.

Donovan snarled Matthew's way, but stopped when Lee cried out.

"Not so quickly, Your Highness. I don't think I would like you killing my chosen executioner. I think that might make my hands slip," Winter promised.

"I'll want my payment," Matthew said.

"You can have the wolf. He's being held right now for you." Winter had both hands on Lee now as he watched Matthew take the silver sword one of the others handed him. His hand was gloved or it would have smoked at the faintest touch.

They'd come prepared. Winter had outsmarted all of us. He would get his civil war and Lucifer couldn't really complain because he'd followed the letter of the demon/vampire contracts. If he did, Winter would serve up Gray as his get out of jail free card.

All because no one but demonkind could kill him.

"No." The queen clutched the railing, having pulled away from her husband. "He can't take Neil again. Oh, god. It's happening all over again."

Neil. Matthew's lost love was Neil Roberts? Neil Roberts was married. He was happy.

The demon who had taken Neil Roberts was the same one who had betrayed the king and caused the death of my father.

"He killed my father." The words came out of my mouth in a dull, almost dumb tone, as though I needed to say them for it to be real. "Matthew killed my father."

"I believe I warned the queen about it at the time," Jacob offered.

Gray shook his head. "No. He wouldn't do that."

"If your brother is Nemcox, then I assure you his betrayal led to the death of Lee Owens," Dev swore. "He took Neil against his will and raped him on the Hell plane for years."

"It is true." Jacob put a hand on Gray's shoulder.

The queen turned to Gray. She wasn't a woman who was too proud to beg for a friend. "Please, Mr. Sloane. Please, if you have any power at all with him, don't let him kill my husband. Please don't let him take Neil again. He almost didn't survive the first time."

"But he's my brother." Gray had a blank look in his eyes.

He'd lost everyone. Again. His father had sent him in as a sacrificial lamb and now he'd learned the truth about the one person who seemed to put him first.

"Gray, you are not defined by your family." I know I should have railed at him. His brother was the reason my father no longer walked the Earth plane, but Gray wasn't Matthew or Nemcox or whoever he called himself. Choices. Jacob had told me we got to choose who we are. We choose every day, and I needed Gray to choose to be strong. I looked him straight in the eyes. "If your brother killed my father, I still care about you."

I couldn't tell him I loved him. Not with Marcus here. It was so fucked up and jumbled in my head, but I needed him to know his brother's crimes weren't a stain on his soul.

His hands squeezed mine and he turned sad eyes to the queen. "My brother won't listen to me. I'm so sorry."

Down below, Nemcox was holding the sword in his hand and Winter was talking about the coming demon swarm. He went on and on about some kind of new fucking demon day, and I wouldn't have been surprised if the asshole broke into song.

I was concentrating on something else while the demon monologued.

"Please tell me what to do," I begged Gray.

The king was on his knees, waiting for the swing of a sword that would end his life and save his son's.

Gray's eyes rolled and became pure white orbs.

Jacob watched in obvious wonder. "The prophet is truly born. Do you know how long it's been since I had kindred, child? It is a good day."

"Celebrate by helping him figure out what I should do." It was bitchy, but I was on a time line. Winter, it seemed, was finishing up his "I'm the shit" speech and they were going to get down to some serious king killing.

And only demonkind could kill an elemental.

Gray's head rolled forward. "One changed can be change. Blood of the demon runs through the veins of the righteous. The war is on her. Instinct shall lead the Hunter and she alone will decide the battle."

His eyes cleared and I stared at him.

Yeah, this was probably a really meaningful moment for him. His first true prophecy. He'd stared into the storm and come back with the answer. And he sounded like a flipping apocalyptic poet. "What the fuck is that supposed to mean?"

He frowned. "I told you what to do."

Jacob's grin was about a mile wide. "It made perfect sense to him. It's part of our nature. When it's truly important, the answer comes to him in this fashion. Nothing comes easy, child. He told you what to do in the way of a prophet." Jacob nodded Gray's way. "I see many ways this could go, but only one stands out."

"Because she will always choose to be brave," Gray said.

I turned. It was on me. One changed can be change. I'd been changed. Only demonkind could kill an elemental.

Maybe not demonkind, but at least I had a hand. I would decide the battle.

Oh, I knew what my decision was.

"Dev, I can't watch it. Please. Please." The queen pleaded with her husband or whoever could help her.

I was betting when she'd woken up this morning, she hadn't thought that she would be bargaining with God for her husband and her son.

"Your Highness, it's going to be all right." I was surprised at how calm I was now that I had some amount of certainty that I would control the outcome. Live or die, I kind of wanted the control.

It would be all right. Gray had seen it. All I had to do was be brave. Make the right choice. Not the safe one.

I was born to hunt demons, and Fate or our father or God or whatever you want to call that benevolent power in the universe that watched over us had sent me on that turn that ended with me not getting the wolf hand I'd been promised.

It ending with me having the tools I needed to save one little boy and his father.

The queen looked at me, her eyes pleading for a moment, and then she calmed. She nodded and took a long breath. "Do what you need to do."

Marcus reached for my hand. "She needs to prepare herself."

Yeah, I did need to do that. I let the wolf in. She and I worked together now, and the good news was we both hated assholes who used children as shields.

The queen's lips turned up. "Yes, those are your father's eyes, Kelsey."

"Shit, that's actually kind of scary," Quinn said.

They could talk all they liked. I moved away from Marcus because he would try to stop me. I placed my foot on the second rung on the railing and let the adrenaline take over. I would get one shot and only one. I had two people to save because Lee really required two fathers.

Three for good measure. He was hard to handle and I wasn't going to let the kid down.

It flashed over me, the warmth that came when my arm changed. It sizzled along me and some people might call it pain. I liked the sensation. The burn meant I was stronger than I'd been before. More capable. A little more unhinged.

I was going to need that.

Matthew glanced up at his brother with almost sad eyes.

I no longer gave a shit. He could love his brother all he liked, but he was an evil son of a bitch and if he'd really killed my father, then I would have another demon to hunt.

"Long live the king," I yelled to get Donovan's attention. I held up one hand. The right hand. The one I was going to use to murder his enemy.

Donovan's eyes flared briefly and I knew he'd gotten my message.

"Do it!" Winter yelled.

The minute the blade started to move, I did, too. I pushed myself off to the third rung and leapt, never taking my eyes off the demon.

He did exactly what I thought he would. He let go of Lee as the blade swung for Donovan's neck. The contract worked both ways. It ensured there would be no betrayal from Winter. He wouldn't wait until Donovan was down a head and then freeze Lee. Demons take contracts seriously, so I had an in. He relaxed, sure of the outcome. All eyes were on the king, who leaned back at precisely the right moment to avoid his head being cut from his body.

I had eyed my target perfectly. I landed right on top of Winter, who roared my way, but it didn't matter because my demon hand knew where it wanted to go. I shoved it into his chest cavity as Lee screamed and scrambled back. I didn't think twice about him. His dad would move heaven and earth to keep him safe.

Winter's eyes widened when he fell back, my weight on top of him.

I made a fist and pulled my hand out with my prize. His withered and wintery heart.

Abbas Hiberna was no more.

Donovan stood, his son in his arms, and the minute he turned toward Matthew, the body he was occupying fell to the ground and the demons around us fled.

Ether was quiet.

"Dad? Did you see that? Kelsey pulled out that dude's heart. It was so cool," Lee was saying. "Can I see it?"

I dropped the heart. I've found whenever I'm forced to pull someone's heart out that I'm almost overwhelmed by the instinct to lift it over my head in victory, but it feels weird when children are watching.

Donovan set his son down on his bare feet, his head drooping. I was pretty sure if he hadn't had all that keep-him-young vampire DNA, he would have gone gray right then and there. "Lee, we're going to have a serious talk about you and bedtime."

The queen and Quinn were running down the stairs.

Lee stared up at his father, eyes wide. "I don't suppose we could celebrate the fact that I'm alive, huh, Dad?"

"You are the most grounded child in the history of all time." Donovan said before pulling his child close. There were tears in his eyes when he looked back at me. *Thank you*, he mouthed.

I didn't need thanks. I needed the knowledge that they were alive.

I glanced up at the landing above me and Gray was staring down. He stared at the body of the human his brother had been occupying. He seemed so hollow, his eyes blank. He hadn't known the truth. He hadn't known his brother had been the one to lead my father to his death.

"You are getting a raise." The queen fell to her knees beside her husband, but her eyes were on me. "Whatever the hell you want, you get."

I kind of didn't need the money, but a little goodwill might help me out. I'd been a bitch when I first got here, and now I kind of liked it and wanted to stay. "Actually, my assistant could use fifteen percent more. I'm afraid I made him think I'd killed his girlfriend, and he's going to need some serious therapy."

"Done," Quinn said as he too surrounded their boy.

Marcus ran down the stairs and threw his arms around me, not minding the fact that I was covered in the blood of our enemy. "*Bella*, that was the single bravest thing I've ever seen. I can't believe you did that."

His peace, his happiness with me flowed over my soul and I was eased. No matter what the prophet had shown me, I needed Marcus now. I held on to him even as Gray moved down the stairs.

I saw Jamie running in, smiling my way.

Marcus held me tight. "Forgive me, *bella*. I've been too cynical, too afraid of losing you."

I let myself sigh and sink into his warmth. His joy seeped into me.

I needed Marcus for now.

And yet, I stared over his shoulder, watching Gray the entire time.

Chapter Twenty-Three

I knocked on the door to the hotel room, knowing damn well who the current resident was.

It took him a moment. A few really. I stood out in the hallway like an idiot before knocking again.

"Gray, I know you're in there."

Three days had passed since Abbas Hiberna had attempted his coup. The wolves had been spared thanks to Gray and a couple of halflings who donated blood Henri had mixed with the king's. They were all healed, though Trent had claimed he'd never been in any actual danger and Quinn had fired too soon. Like I was buying that.

Ether was getting back to normal, but the kids were in lockdown and Donovan was currently reevaluating most of his political decisions concerning the demons.

With the exception of one.

He wouldn't be moved on the demon he called Stewart or Nemcox.

I was going to have to kill Gray's brother.

Gray had disappeared shortly after his blood donation, and Jacob had shown up on my doorstep this morning asking me to find him. I was fairly certain the prophet knew where he was and had an agenda sending me out, but I already missed Gray, so I went to the one place I knew he would be.

Gray opened the door. He was wearing a pair of pajama bottoms and nothing else. His dragon tat glowed, and I could have sworn it winked my way. "What do you want, Kelsey?"

So he was in a good mood. I didn't let it get me down. I smiled at the dragon and resisted the urge to reach out and touch it. So tempting. I've come to believe that tat is the pure demon portion of Gray and it's not evil. Like Jacob said—we make the choice. The dragon is neither good nor evil, but animated by the choices Gray makes every single day. So it wouldn't be wrong to lean over and kiss the damn thing.

"Jacob's been looking for you." It was better than saying I'd missed him.

Gray opened the door wider and allowed me in. "Then Jacob should have come for me himself."

I entered the room that was so all-fired important to the rest of my life. It was a nice suite, done in earthy tones and with very elegant furnishings. It bespoke of a wealth I would never have, though Quinn had mentioned riches for saving his boy.

I'd turned him down. I did that stuff for fun.

And love. I was kind of learning that saving the people I loved was the ultimate rush.

"So this is the famous room." I stopped in the middle and took it in. It was the way I'd seen it, though I'll admit the recollections weren't exactly perfectly clear. It felt like the right room. This was the room where my life would truly be decided.

"I can't see it anymore." Gray sat down on the couch. "I can see everything but my own future. During the transition, I got threads of it, but now it's all unclear."

"Jacob told me it would be hard to see your own future. It would hurt."

"It gives me a migraine that hurts like a motherfucker and still I try. I was happy here."

Longing filled me. I couldn't see their faces now, but I knew my children existed on some potential plane. "I was, too."

"Not always." Gray's head dropped forward. "Kelsey, I've done you a grave disservice."

"We're all alive. I think we're good. Though you should know I plan on spanking that Dellacourt bastard." The billionaire with the extra-planar tech had gone underground. Like he wouldn't pop up again—and when he did, I would give him something he wouldn't forget. On any plane.

I didn't mention the fact that I meant to kill Gray's brother.

Gray's head came up. "I saw enough during my transition to know how things could go for you. Kelsey, please believe me. I never meant to hurt you."

I sat down beside him. When I'd left today, I'd told Marcus I was looking for Gray. I didn't want to lie to my lover. I'd spent more than forty-eight hours with Marcus beside me or inside me and holding me. He'd driven all my stress out, but it was coming back because of this discussion with Gray. "I know that. Gray, I told you I don't blame you. You're not your family. No one believes that more than I do. I was raised by a man who hated me. I came here to ask you to come back to Ether with me. The king wants to open talks."

"The king sent you?"

"Actually, everyone sent me. The king asked me to bring you back. Jacob wanted me to find you. Quinn and the queen would like to thank you. I know your biological family turned out to be crappy, but that's not the only family we get. We can choose. Jamie would really like it if you came home."

"Jamie would?"

He was pressing me and I caved. "I want you to come home, Gray."

"I don't think I have a home."

Had he listened to a word I said? "All you have to do is choose."

He shook his head and turned to me, violet eyes darkening. "I always choose you, Kelsey. You're my home, but I don't think that's what's best for you anymore."

"It's not our time, but I'm starting to believe that there will be a time for us. Gray, I still love you. I never stopped. I love Marcus, too. I don't know how or why or if any of it lasts, but I'm going to take all the honest love I can get in this world." I might have to choose one day. Between my love for Marcus and his needs. She was out there. That woman Marcus would die for existed and she wasn't the queen's toddler. I'd felt her. Would I love him enough to let him go?

We sat on the couch for a long moment, space between us. Our shared history was there, a massive wall that kept me from reaching out to him.

"I'm going to go with Jacob, Kelsey."

Tears sparked in my eyes, but I held them back. I'd expected he would need some time to deal with the whole prophet thing. "Will you call me when you come back?"

"I don't know if I will come back." He sighed and the afternoon sunlight made his skin glow. He was beautiful and so far from me. "I remember thinking most roads led to you here alone. I saw it over and over again. You crying on the floor, desperate and alone because I'm going to Hell."

"That was one possible future, Gray."

"No, many choices lead to that future. It's most probable. I won't put you through that. Marcus can make you happy." His jaw tightened. "Apparently that wolf can make you happy."

Jealousy looked cute on him. "What we saw were possibilities. The game's not over. Not until the minute they drag you to Hell, and even then it's not done. We don't know what comes after that moment. You said I'll always choose to be brave. Well, if you get dragged to Hell, you should know I'll be mounting a damn rescue party after I finish my well-deserved cry."

He reached out and his fingertips brushed my face. "And that's why I have to stay away from you."

"You say you're going to stay away, but you're here. You came back to this place. You'll always come back to this place, and I think I will, too."

"I'm going to try to stay away. I can't stand the thought of being the reason you don't find happiness, the reason you die. If I have to spend an eternity serving on the Hell plane, at least I'll know you're somewhere happy." He stood up, a clear signal he was done. "Tell Jacob he can come for me at any time. I'm ready to go. I've spoken with both my father and brother and explained that if either of them attempt to contact me again, I'll offer my services to Lucifer on one condition."

I could guess what that was. "Their heads."

"Oh, yes. The word is Lucifer wasn't happy with Winter's plans. He's a patient man, though. He hasn't punished my father yet. I can tip that scale if I want to."

I stood up and moved to face him. "Don't do anything foolish, Gray. And I'm sorry about your brother."

"Another reason for me to leave. I don't want to watch you kill him.

I know what you have to do. I didn't know about your father. Or Roberts. I was naïve. I thought Nemcox's mate was happy with him. Yet another idiotic play I've made."

"He was your brother. We want to believe the best in the people we love." Maybe it was a good thing for Gray to travel for a while, but I couldn't let him leave like this. He had no hope. It was like his spark was gone. "Can I touch him before I go?"

Gray looked down at the tat that had started to glow, and I wondered if he could feel it vibrating. He took a moment and I thought he would tell me no. Finally, he nodded.

I couldn't reach the man. The man was stubborn, but the demon knew what he wanted. The demon wanted to fight for our future. I ran a hand over the dragon, sighing at the connection I felt.

Gray's whole body shuddered.

I stared up at him, my hand still petting the dragon. "Do you know what I saw in this room, Gray Sloane? I saw our children. I saw them laughing and happy and whole, and I will fight to make that possibility come true. So run all you like, but we will be right back here someday."

I turned to go and he caught me, dragging me back into his arms. His warmth encased me.

"Don't talk. Just let me hold you for a minute. Just let us be." He wrapped me up, holding on to me like he would never let go.

We stood that way, not speaking, simply holding on until the sun finally went down.

* * * *

Marcus turned to me as he stopped the car in front of the small house that was my destination. It had only been a few days since I'd done in old Father Winter, but the streets were snow free and I hadn't seen a single snow monster. I could go the rest of my life without seeing another one of those. The weather was back to being perfectly Texan, and by that I meant predictably unpredictable. Today had been a nice toasty sixty-five, with light winds and not a single snowflake. I'd spent the day with Liv, who was mourning Scott.

Oh, he wasn't dead. He'd survived, but the whole experience had made Liv realize she needed something more. Apparently Liv's version of mourning included Mexican food, margaritas, and a whole lot of tears.

I was already mourning Gray, though I hadn't cried. It was easier to concentrate on Liv.

"Are you sure you're all right, *bella*?"

"I'm going to miss him. Maybe I shouldn't tell you that, but it's the truth." I fiddled with the bag in my hand. It contained all the necessaries for the evening. Snacks, beer, gaming dice. I was getting back to my geek roots tonight.

Marcus leaned over and kissed me. "I know you will. I have a feeling he's going to be coming back, and then we will have to make some decisions of our own."

We would have to decide how to proceed because I loved two men. I tried not to think about Trent. I'd been avoiding him the last several days because every time I saw him, all I could think about was how good he'd looked naked.

And the fact that one of those children I'd seen had been a little she-wolf.

I tangled my fingers with Marcus's. "I love you."

He squeezed my hand. "And I you, *bella*. I'm going to take this time to reconsider some of my long-held beliefs."

"What does that mean?"

"It means that I never thought I could share my lover, but if I don't, I could lose you. I'm not ready to lose you." He brought my hand to his lips. "We have time. Your training is simply moving along a bit faster than expected."

He was afraid I wouldn't need him soon. I was afraid I might always need him. I hadn't told him about the woman in the prophecies. I couldn't quite see her face now, but I knew the one Marcus had waited for was out there. She was a woman, and his fate would be on us sooner than I expected.

For now, I kissed him. We had this time. For however long it lasted, I wanted to love this man. "I'll catch a ride back with Dan."

Marcus chuckled. "It's Dan now? Are we no longer cursing the king's name?"

The king and I were cool. I'd actually read a couple of those histories Marcus had tried to hide from me. Hunters could go dark. I mean seriously kill whole towns and lay waste to the land kind of dark, if they weren't properly trained. Dan was used to being the bad guy. He made the hard decisions, but once I'd proven I wasn't going to burn down a large portion of Dallas, we'd found a good place.

We'd been friends once. Before I'd known he was a king, he'd been my online gaming buddy. "Dungeons and Dragons is a bonding experience."

So was saving the supernatural world. I kissed my boyfriend and thanked him for the ride before stepping up to the house. Justin and Angelina lived here. From the smells coming out of the place, I was betting Angelina had cooked. Nice.

Marcus drove off. Tomorrow we were going to have dinner with my mom and Jamie, but tonight there was another family member I needed to see. I knocked on the door.

There was some male laughter and then the door opened.

Nathan. My brother stood there for a moment, his eyes wide. "Kelsey?"

I'd been so wrong to not talk to him. "Hey. Dan invited me. I brought your favorite beer."

A smile crossed his face. "I told them I wasn't coming. I haven't played a lot lately. I've been concentrating on school and work. Blake hijacked me and said there was a surprise for me. I was about to leave."

He'd been concentrating on his guilt, and I needed to do something about that. "Please stay. Can you forgive me for being a bitch?"

"Can you forgive me for lying to you? Kelsey, I'm so sorry."

But I understood now. He had read those histories. He knew there was a darkness inside me and if he'd told me, I very likely at that point would have run. "I love you, Nate."

He sighed and opened his arms. I walked into them and hugged the brother who had gotten me through all the hard times when we'd been younger. Forgiveness, I was discovering, was a gift that gave the giver as much as it did the person she was forgiving.

"Yo, Owens, get your ass in here. We've got a campaign to run," the king yelled.

"Sorry, he gets bossy when he's the DM," Nate explained.

"I think he's bossy all the time. Keep your panties on, Dan. I'm having a moment with my brother here." He wasn't the king now. He was just one of the guys and so was I.

"Angelina made us nachos," Nate said as he drew me inside. "I like it when she-wolves host. They know how to cook. When we go to Blake's, he puts out a bowl of chips and thinks that's a buffet."

"Oh, we're going to have to work on that if I'm playing regularly." This girl needed fuel to roll her dice.

I walked in, took a seat, and flipped open a beer.

Yeah, I was starting to feel at home.

Kelsey, Gray, Marcus, and the entire Thieves family will return in *Sleeper*, now available.

Author's Note

I'm often asked by generous readers how they can help get the word out about a book they enjoyed. There are so many ways to help an author you like. Leave a review. If your e-reader allows you to lend a book to a friend, please share it. Go to Goodreads and connect with others. Recommend the books you love because stories are meant to be shared. Thank you so much for reading this book and for supporting all the authors you love!

Sign up for Lexi Blake's newsletter
and be entered to win a $25 gift certificate
to the bookseller of your choice.

Join us for news, fun and exclusive content
including free Thieves short stories.

There's a new contest every month!

Go to www.LexiBlake.net to subscribe.

Sleeper
Hunter: A Thieves Novel, Book 3
By Lexi Blake
Now available!

When Neil's past catches up to him, Kelsey must choose between her new family and an old love…

With tensions rising between the Council and demonkind, Kelsey finds herself investigating a series of murders that threaten the fragile truce between them. If she can't stop these killings soon, they could ignite a fire sure to burn the supernatural world down.

Unfortunately for her, Kelsey's problems don't stop with a pile of dead halflings. Her connection with Marcus is frayed at best, and Gray hasn't been heard from in months. Her only semblance of peace comes from a new man in her life. When Gray storms back into the picture, her love life goes from incredibly complicated to apocalyptic.

Just as Kelsey begins to unravel the mystery, the forces of Heaven decide to take an interest in her actions. Outclassed with these powers in play, Kelsey knows that one misstep could leave the human and supernatural worlds in ashes.

* * * *

"Your Highness, please back away. In fact, it would be best if you left the room altogether." Felix put himself between me and Roberts. "Kelsey, I need you to push her down. Push her back down for a few moments. Marcus will be back soon and he's going to take care of you. Being around those angels unsettled you. I don't know if you noticed, but at the end of the meeting, your ward fell off. You didn't have it on when Oliver shook your hand. He's unbalanced and now you are, too. It's like a contagion for someone like you. Oliver's illness has called up your inner wolf and she's angry."

"Perhaps if I touch her," Henri began. "I'm an academic. I don't have the same connection she has with Marcus, but I might be able to help."

"I'm not unbalanced." It didn't matter that my hands were shaking and they had been ever since I'd left the angels behind. "I'm going to talk to the wolf whether you like it or not. He's been handling silver. It's the only reason his hands wouldn't have healed. Even then, a couple of hours would have done it. Unless the freaking silver he held came straight from Heaven. What about it, Roberts? How did you spend last night?"

The wolf was shaking his head. "I don't know."

That wasn't an answer I was willing to accept. I was about to explain that to everyone when Chad stepped up and got in my face.

"I'm taking him out of here now," Chad explained. "You'll let me or we're going to have trouble."

I was ready for trouble. I was fairly sure I grinned, the idea of fighting a vamp lifting my spirits high. For the first time in what felt like hours, I went still. "You're not going anywhere."

Chad turned, his shoulders squaring, and I felt the world begin to bend around me. Chad belongs to one of the rarest classes of vampire—the magicians. As far as I knew, he was the only one walking the night at this time. He could form illusions so real you could taste food, feel imaginary rain on your skin, utterly believe whatever he wanted you to believe. I'd come up against him before. I might be one of the only people in the world who could see through him.

"It won't work," I said calmly as reality seemed to go dark and I heard the hissing of snakes all around me. "Do you not remember what happened the last time you pulled this shit on me? It took three tranqs to take me down. I don't think you have those on you today."

"I won't need them." Chad lifted his hand and the world shifted.

"Holy shit," Casey said, climbing up on his desk. "What the fuck is happening?"

Snakes were happening. They were crawling from the woodwork, twitching and hissing my way. The fibers of the carpet beneath my feet lengthened and formed more snakes until they were a menacing mass, threatening everyone in the room.

Well, except for Chad, who had lifted his husband into his arms and prepared to take him away.

I let my wolf loose a bit. She knew this was all an illusion. That primitive part of my brain that Chad was accessing, the lizard brain that merely wanted to survive, was taken over by the wolf inside me. The alpha wolf didn't want mere survival. She wanted to dominate, and that meant seeing past fear, trusting her instincts over what her eyes perceived.

The minute I opened the door, I felt her surge through me.

"I'm not letting you go. I can't. I'm conducting a murder investigation, and I believe your boy here just became my prime suspect." My hands twitched, eager for a fight, and I realized how long it had been since Marcus and I had thrown down.

Too long. Remember that whole thing about needing sex or violence to feed my inner wolf? Well, she was hungry and there was a whole lot of violence in Chad's eyes.

I welcomed it. I could feel the need rise like a wave threatening to engulf me. This was why I had a trainer in the first place.

I gritted my teeth because Chad turned on his power. I could feel those fucking snakes climbing my legs and sinking their fangs into me. I refused to pay any attention to them despite the fact that I ached to rip the fuckers off me and toss them aside. To do that would have given the magician more power. If I bought into it, if I took my eyes off the only thing in the room that was real, I would end up like Casey, who was screaming like a girl.

"Let me pass, Hunter," Chad said.

I stood my ground like the good Gandalf I was. Except I kind of wanted to shove my nonexistent staff right up old Chad's ass, and then we would see if he sent snakes my way again.

The anger rose, rapid and quick, a flash fire coursing through me. I didn't even realize when I had reached for the fireplace poker. All I knew was it was suddenly in my hands and I was going to use it. I could see myself shoving that piece of wrought iron right through his heart. It wouldn't kill him. I would need wood for that, but then again, I didn't want the fight over so quickly.

I raised the poker, ready to start.

"Stop it, both of you." Donovan stepped in between us, but I didn't care at that moment. I hadn't felt this way in forever, not since Marcus had taken me in. I hadn't been so out of control that I didn't care who I hurt as long as I got to hurt someone. I would fuck up Donovan, too. All that mattered was seeing blood, feeling bones crush.

"You see, I told you she's far gone and I can't fix her anymore. I've called Gray and he has an idea of what to do," Marcus was saying.

I wasn't listening.

I started to bring the poker down Donovan's way, but I was stopped in mid swing. A hand held my wrist, an arm going around my middle and hauling me back against muscled flesh.

"Stop it," Trent growled in my ear. "You stand down right this second."

Master No
Masters and Mercenaries, Book 9
By Lexi Blake
Now Available!

Disavowed by those he swore to protect…

Tennessee Smith is a wanted man. Betrayed by his government and hunted by his former employer, he's been stripped of everything he holds dear. If the CIA finds him, they're sure to take his life as well. His only shot at getting it all back is taking down the man who burned him. He knows just how to get to Senator Hank McDonald and that's through his daughter, Faith. In order to seduce her, he must become something he never thought he'd be—a Dom.

Overcome by isolation and duty…

All her life, Dr. Faith "Mac" McDonald has felt alone, even among her family. Dedicating herself to helping others and making a difference in the world has brought her some peace, but a year spent fighting the Ebola virus in West Africa has taken a toll. She's come home for two months of relaxation before she goes back into the field. After holding so many lives in her hands, nothing restores her like the act of submission. Returning to her favorite club, Mac is drawn to the mysterious new Dom all the subs are talking about, Master No. In the safety of his arms, she finds herself falling head over heels in love.

Forced to choose between love and revenge…

On an exclusive Caribbean island, Ten and Mac explore their mutual attraction, but her father's plots run deeper than Ten could possibly have imagined. With McKay-Taggart by his side, Ten searches for a way to stop the senator, even as his feelings for Mac become too strong to deny. In the end, he must choose between love and revenge—a choice that will change his life forever.

Scandal Never Sleeps
The Perfect Gentlemen, Book 1
By Shayla Black and Lexi Blake
Now Available!

They are the Perfect Gentlemen of Creighton Academy: privileged, wealthy, powerful friends with a wild side. But a deadly scandal is about to tear down their seemingly ideal lives...

Maddox Crawford's sudden death sends Gabriel Bond reeling. Not only is he burying his best friend, he's cleaning up Mad's messes, including his troubled company. Grieving and restless, Gabe escapes his worries in the arms of a beautiful stranger. But his mind-blowing one-night stand is about to come back to haunt him . . .

Mad groomed Everly Parker to be a rising star in the executive world. Now that he's gone, she's sure her job will be the next thing she mourns, especially after she ends up accidentally sleeping with her new boss. If only their night together hadn't been so incendiary—or Gabe like a fantasy come true...

As Gabe and Everly struggle to control the heated tension between them, they discover evidence that Mad's death was no accident. Now they must bank their smoldering passions to hunt down a murderer—because Mad had secrets that someone was willing to kill for, and Gabe or Everly could be the next target...

About Lexi Blake

New York Times bestselling author Lexi Blake lives in North Texas with her husband and three kids. Since starting her publishing journey in 2010, she's sold over three million copies of her books. She began writing at a young age, concentrating on plays and journalism. It wasn't until she started writing romance that she found success. She likes to find humor in the strangest places and believes in happy endings.

Connect with Lexi online:

Facebook: Lexi Blake
Twitter: authorlexiblake
Website: www.LexiBlake.net
Instagram: www.instagram.com

Printed in Great Britain
by Amazon